LOOKING AFTER YOUR OWN

Paisley 1941: Chloe is the eldest daughter of Julia and Frank McCosh and her evenings are dominated by the dance band her parents run. It is not the music that interests Chloe, but young trumpeter Dennis Morgan. Dennis, however, has other things on his mind. He's busy working for the fire brigade and keeping an eye on his wayward brother Ralph. There is also Dennis's close friendship with the mysterious Lena Fulton which is starting to get the neighbours talking. Then an unexpected guest arrives on Julia McCosh's doorstep – a face from her past she'd hoped she would never see again...

LOOKING AFTER YOUR OWN

LOOKING AFTER YOUR OWN

by

Evelyn Hood

Magna Large Print Books
Long Preston, North Yorkshire,
BD23 4ND, England.

British Library Cataloguing in Publication Data.

Hood, Evelyn
Looking after your own.

A catalogue record of this book is available from the British Library

ISBN 0-7505-1951-7

First published in Great Britain in 2002 by Little, Brown

Published in Large Print 2002 by arrangement with Time, Warner Books UK

Magna Large Print is an imprint of Library Magna Books Ltd.

Printed and bound in Great Britain by
T.J. (International) Ltd., Cornwall, PL28 8RW

All characters in this publication are fictitious and any resemblance to real persons, living or dead, is purely coincidental.

To Alastair and Simon

Acknowledgements

My thanks go to Jessie McMaster and other former 'clippies' who took time to tell me about their lives as bus and tram conductresses; to Bill Peacock, who patiently explained the intricacies of playing the trumpet to one who has never been able to get a sound out of these elegant instruments, and to Assistant Divisional Officer Iain Glover, of Strathclyde Fire Brigade, for his advice on some aspects of fire-fighting.

1

The rich, warm smell enveloping the entire building, rising effortlessly through floorboards and swirling up the communal stairway, evoked memories of happier pre-war days, family gatherings, generous meals and full stomachs instead of making do with ration books and warm fires on cold winter nights.

Customers in the two shops on the ground floor sniffed the air as the aroma drifted down the flight of steps leading to the close, vying with the tang of paraffin, firelighters and soap in Binnie's the drysalter's, and even with the sweeter, fruitier aromas in Clark's sweetie shop.

'Is that dumplin'?' An elderly woman rested her basket on Mr Binnie's counter and sniffed noisily, distinguishing the smells of currants and raisins, sugar and spice and cinnamon. 'Who's got the makin's of dumplin' these days, with a war on?'

'It happens sometimes, in this building,' Mr Binnie said with a shrug, while his stomach, remembering the joy of homemade dumplings, gave a low rumble.

In the flat directly above the drysalter's, Julia McCosh, her face flushed with the heat from the big pot that had been simmering on the stove for the past two hours, wrapped a cloth about her hand to protect it against the steam and gripped a wooden ladle by the rounded spoon.

'Are you ready now?'

'I'm ready! Mum, it's nearly time I was back at the shop and I've not even had my dinner yet,' her daughter Chloe fretted.

'I know, pet, and I'll not be a minute. You're holding the plate tight?'

'Any tighter and it'll break. My hands are getting sore from gripping it and if you don't hurry up they'll go all weak and then I'll drop it.'

'Here goes, then.' As Julia took the lid from the pot she and her daughter leaned back to avoid the great gout of steam that rushed towards the kitchen ceiling. 'Now...' Julia poked the handle of the ladle into the steam, blinking to clear her vision, and wiggled it until she managed to spear the knot fastening the cloth that gave the clootie dumpling its name. 'Got it. Ready...'

'Mum! I'm ready!' Chloe snapped, tightening her white-knuckled hold on the plate as Julia braced herself and then began to ease the heavy bundle up from the boiling water, over the edge of the pot, and on to the plate.

'Down now ... put it down.' Julia held tightly to the ladle, trying to take some of the strain as the plate dipped dangerously beneath the weight of the huge dumpling.

'I've got it,' Chloe said through set teeth, and then gave a great sigh of relief as both plate and dumpling were settled safely on the shelf by the stove.

Duncan and Leslie arrived as though drawn by a magnet, leaving their toy soldiers to battle it out on the hearthrug. 'Can we try a bit now, Mum?' Duncan asked eagerly. He was thirteen, and his voice broke endearingly on 'now'. His mother eased the kink in her back and then ruffled his short brown hair.

'Later, pet, when it's cooled down and your dad's home.'

'And then we'll only get a wee scliff each,' mourned seven-year-old Leslie, the youngest of the three McCosh children, adding, reproach in the green eyes he had inherited from his mother, "'cos you'll be giving it all away to the neighbours again!'

'That's to keep them from minding the noise of the band practice. Anyway, it was Mrs Borland who gave me the ingred– is that the time?' Julia asked in alarm as the door-knocker thumped hard against the flat's outer door. She darted to the mirror, dragging at the ties of her wrap-around overall with one hand while the other dabbed at her auburn hair, her strong, flexible musician's fingers tucking errant strands deftly back into the neat roll about her head. 'Chloe pet, can you get yourself something to eat? There's bread, and some dripping in the pan from your daddy's sausage this morning. You could do a slice for the boys too. Keep an eye on that dumpling, will you, and don't let them lay a finger on it.'

'It's not fair,' Leslie groused as his mother whisked out of the kitchen. Chloe's heart went out to him. She had been only two years old when Duncan was born, too young and immersed in the pleasure and wonder of her own existence to bother much with him; but when Leslie arrived six years later, red-haired and green-eyed and with a smile fit, as Mrs Megson from upstairs said, to warm the heart of a water pump, eight-year-old Chloe had loved him at first sight. Now, she ruffled his hair in imitation of her mother.

'Nothing's fair, son, because there's a war on. If you're good,' she promised, 'you might get a bit of my slice too.'

'Just because he's wee!' Duncan stormed at once. 'You never gave me anything when I was wee!'

'I did so, but you were too little to remember it. Oh, all right, you can have a bit of my slice too.' At this rate, Chloe thought resentfully as she lit the gas cooker under the frying pan, she'd be lucky if there was a decent mouthful left for her. Sometimes being the oldest could be hard. She took the drab grey National loaf from the breadbin by the sink, listening to her mother's voice in the hall, and then the underlying murmur of the newly arrived music pupil.

'Quiet now, while Mum's teaching.' Keenly aware of the two pairs of eyes fixed on the bread she was slicing and the two snub noses sniffing in the aroma of the heating fat, she shooed her brothers back to their game of toy soldiers and pushed the cooling dumpling to the back of the shelf, out of the reach of prying fingers. Then, with one eye on the clock, she began to rub slices of bread over the frying pan to mop up the dripping.

The tea had already been made and left to stew over a low heat before she and her mother had taken the dumpling from the pot. After putting the boys' food on the table Chloe poured three cups of tea, dark and strong, then treated each of them to half a spoonful of condensed milk.

Washing down her own bread and dripping with generous mouthfuls of tea, she leaned against the sink, surrounded by a wooden frame and known among Scottish tenement dwellers as 'the jaw-box', and stared down into the backcourt. Once, it had been a pretty place, cared for by a tenant who had been a former gardener with Paisley Council, but old Mr Brown had died almost three years ago, just before Prime Minister Chamberlain's promises of peace went wrong and war was declared. And now his precious flowerbeds had been dug up to make way for vegetable beds, mainly tended by Chloe's father, Frank, and Dennis Megson, who lived with his mother, brother and sisters on the top floor.

She took another bite of bread, another mouthful of tea. When Mr Brown was alive she had still been a child; now, in February 1941, she was months off her sixteenth birthday, almost two years out of the South School and earning a weekly wage in Cochran's emporium opposite Paisley Abbey. Now quiet, shy Mrs Fulton lived in Mr Brown's flat, and everything had changed because of the war. Nothing, especially the future, was certain any more.

The halting strains of 'To a Rose', played by small, uncertain fingers, trickled through the wall from the front room as Chloe drained her cup and began to wash it and her plate.

She stared unseeingly at the sink, visualising the piano keys and her own fingers moving across them.

When she had first heard the old saying about the cobbler's children never getting their shoes mended she had been at a loss to understand it, but now she knew only too well what it meant. She herself would have loved to learn to play the piano but her mother and father, both talented musicians, never had the time to teach her. Instead, her mother taught other people's children, while Chloe was left to learn as best she could by watching and listening and picking out tunes on the rare occasions she found herself alone in the flat with nobody to hear her and laugh at her.

'If you want me to wash your cups you'd better hurry up,' she told her brothers, who were squabbling over possession of a comic. Then she sighed over what might have been, filling her nose and lungs in the process with the powerful scent of the cooling dumpling. Nobody could make dumpling like her mum, and this one, she could tell, was going to be one of the best. It was a pity that she had promised most of her slice to the boys. Still, the less she ate the slimmer she would be, and if she got really slim, then perhaps Dennis Megson might notice her. Her thoughts changed from imagining herself as a successful and talented pianist to Dennis, handsome in his Fire Brigade uniform, coming into the backcourt when she was helping her father to dig the carrot patch ... no, wait, coming into the shop where she worked, though goodness knows what Dennis might want in the kitchen department ... walking in, then all at once looking up to see Chloe standing at the counter, smiling at him, slender and smart and asking if she could help.

And then – Chloe's imagination had always been ripe – he would suddenly find himself looking at her as a woman instead of the way he thought of her now ... wee Chloe McCosh who used to take his younger sister Amy out in the battered old pushchair.

It would be just like it was in the pictures. Imagining the look in his eyes – wonder at first, mebbe, then dawning recognition followed by admiration and then adoration – Chloe sighed again, while across the hall, her mother's pupil switched to scales, making them sound like an old, moth-eaten teddy bear being dragged, bump-bump-bump, up a flight of steep, badly lit stairs.

Dennis, gazing at her in awe and wonder across the pots and pans and wooden ladles, suddenly vanished and Chloe opened her eyes and found herself staring at the clock, which was trying to tell her that she had five minutes to get up the road. As she slammed the last of the cups on to the draining board and scrambled into her coat, she ordered, 'Don't touch that dumpling, mind. If you do, Mum and me'll kill you!'

Fergus Goudie, varnishing one of the two kitchen chairs in his top floor flat, inhaled deeply and asked in wonder, 'Do I smell dumpling?'

Cecelia, sitting on the other chair and polishing the buttons on Fergus's khaki tunic, lifted her head and sniffed the air. 'Surely not ... but mebbe...' She looked at him, puzzled. 'Who would have the ingredients for dumpling these days? D'you think we're dreaming?'

'Not me, definitely, because when I dream, I smell you.' Her husband of two weeks put down the brush and came round the table to bury his face in her hair. 'But that's because you smell like flowers.'

'I'll be smelling of peeled onions and boiled cabbage when you get back for your next leave. Have you noticed that this entire tenement smells of onions and cabbage?'

'It's an old building. It's absorbed generations of living,' Fergus said in the lovely Highland lilt that still melted her heart each time she heard it. He kissed the end of her nose then went back to his work. After a while he straightened, easing his back with one hand.

'Done. What d'you think?'

Cecelia glanced up briefly and then returned to the task of polishing the buttons, so intently now that her soft fair hair broke free of the restraining hairpins and flopped down over her forehead. 'It looks great.'

'I wonder if I could manage the other one before I go?'

'No, leave it. You're off tomorrow morning ... we've only got tonight left and I don't want you to be working all the time. Anyway, we'd have nowhere to sit. It takes hours for that stuff to dry.'

'I'll do it on my next leave, then.'

'I can do it while you're gone.'

'But it's a man's job.'

'Lots of women are doing men's work now, or hadn't you noticed? I'll have to find myself a job when you're – when I'm on my own.'

'You could go back to the work you did before, in Glasgow.'

'I should probably be doing something more useful than working in an insurance office.' She was rubbing so hard at the buttons that her voice jerked involuntarily. 'A munitions factory, mebbe.'

'But that's heavy work!' he protested, and then jumped as she rose from her chair like a Jack-in-the-box.

'For goodness' sake, Fergus, there's a war on! Someone's got to do the bloody work, and all the men are busy figh–' her voice broke and she spun away from him, dashing the tears angrily from her eyes.

'Cecelia?'

She felt his hands on her arms and pulled away, but he insisted, turning her about to face him.

'Don't, darling, I can't bear to see you like this!'

'Blast and ... and damn this damned war!' she wailed, clinging to him, her head buried in his chest. 'I don't want you to go away and leave me!'

'I don't want it either, but I'll be court-martialled if I don't. Shot at dawn or something.'

'Don't joke about a thing like that!'

'Sorry. Look, mebbe you should go back to Glasgow,' he said. 'I'm sure your father would like to see you back home.'

'The return of the dutiful daughter, you mean?' She stopped weeping at once, pulling herself back slightly so that she could glare up at him. 'Looking after him and his house, doing as I'm told and making sure that I'm home by ten o'clock every night?'

'It would only be for a little while.'

'Fergus, that's what people said when this war started, and it's gone on longer than anyone thought it would. And what would we do when you came home on leave? We couldn't ... I couldn't...'

'Couldn't what?' he asked, and she punched him in the chest.

'You know very well what. And you know very well that we couldn't; not under my father's roof.'

'But we're married. Husband and wife.'

'Exactly.' Cecelia had forgotten her tears. 'And if I go home I'll stop being a wife and go back to being a daughter. I won't have that!'

'It might be for the best, sweetheart. I'm not happy, leaving you in a town where you don't know anyone.'

'I'll manage fine. I'll not give Father the satisfaction of thinking that I can't cope with being a married woman. Anyway, he's got that lady friend of his now, that Mrs McFadden. I'm sure they won't want me around to spoil things for them. So...' she said, letting go of him and returning to her work, 'we'll hear no more about that idea.'

'You're in danger of rubbing those buttons away to nothing.'

'I want you to have the brightest buttons in the regiment.'

'I'm sure the captain will appreciate it. I tell you what, let's go for a walk.'

'It's freezing outside!'

'We can wrap up well, and it'll give us a chance to cuddle without folk staring. Nothing wrong with trying to keep warm. We could go and have a look at those Fountain Gardens across the street. We've scarcely set foot outside the door since we arrived here. That's what happens when a man marries a demanding woman.'

'Fergus!' She put her hands to her face, glancing nervously at the walls as though afraid the neighbours might hear. 'You've been just as demanding as me.'

'I know, isn't it great? I'm so grateful to you for agreeing to marry me now instead of waiting until after the war like your father wanted,' he said, suddenly serious.

'I couldn't have waited a moment longer.'

'I noticed.' He grinned, pulling her up from the unvarnished chair. 'Come on, Mrs Goudie, let's catch a breath of fresh air before it gets too dark.'

When Chloe got home from work that evening her mother was cutting the cooled dumpling into slices.

'Busy day, pet?'

'Busy enough.' Chloe put her coat and hat away.

'D'you think you could give me a hand with this lot?'

The supervisor in Chloe's department insisted on all her staff standing at their counters even when there were few customers, and, young as she was, Chloe's feet and legs were aching. She shifted her weight from one foot to the other as she helped her mother to wrap most of the slices in greaseproof paper.

'There's not much left for us, is there? It doesn't seem fair, since you made it,' she mused wistfully.

'Better a wee bit than none at all, and we wouldn't have any if Mrs Borland hadn't got the ingredients for me.' Julia stacked the little parcels on to a battered tin tray.

'Mum, how can Mrs Borland manage to get things like that? Does she not have the same ration books as the rest of us?'

'She's thrifty, and after raising a big family on not much money she knows how to make things stretch.'

'Even so–'

'I'll get the tea ready if you'll take the dumpling round,' Julia interrupted briskly. 'We'll eat early tonight because I've a lot to do before the others arrive for the practice. Your dad can have his dinner when he gets home from work.'

'Can Duncan not take the tray round tonight?' Chloe rubbed the calf of one leg with her other foot, and tried to keep the self-pitying whine from her voice.

'With his appetite? Are you daft? He'd have the lot eaten before it reached the first door. Go on now, there's a good lassie. Sooner started, sooner ended.'

With the stairs and landings only dimly lit because of the blackout a stranger would have found it hard to find his way around the tenement, but Chloe had lived there all her life and her feet knew the hollows of every single step. She hesitated outside her own door, working out a plan of action. It was only commonsensical, she thought, to cross the landing first and, balancing one edge of the tray on a raised knee, knock on the door that had once belonged to old Mr Brown, the gardener, and now belonged to Mr and Mrs Fulton. Then the next floor ... the Borlands and old Mrs Bell; and finally, on the top floor, the new people and the Megsons, who would be saved till the last.

Even as a small child Chloe had made a point of saving the best to the last ... opening the least interesting parcels first on Christmas morning, eating up all her boiled potatoes and turnip before starting on the fried sausage at dinner time. Now that she was grown, leaving the Megsons to the last on her dumpling round gave her the same pleasure.

After knocking on Mrs Fulton's door she waited for a reasonable length of time before knocking again. This time, her hand had scarcely left the door when it opened and Mrs Fulton, her face almost ghostly against the darkness of the hall at her back, peered out.

'Yes? Oh, it's you, Chloe.' She frowned slightly and glanced back into the hallway.

'Sorry to bother you, Mrs Fulton.'

'It's all right; it's just that Mr Fulton's having a wee nap. He's going back to his regiment tomorrow morning.'

'Oh. Sorry.' Chloe lowered her voice to a whisper. 'My mother thought you might like a wee bit of dumpling.'

'Is there going to be a band practice tonight, then?'

'Uh-huh, but they'll try to keep the noise down.'

Mrs Fulton gave a wan smile. 'That's all right. I quite like the music they play, and George'll be up by then anyway.' Her fair hair was loose today; normally it was pulled back into a bundle on the nape of her neck, but Chloe had noticed that when Mr Fulton was on leave from the Army Mrs Fulton tended to wear her hair loose so that its natural curls framed her small neat-featured face. It made her look very young, not much older than Chloe's own fifteen years.

'It's not a very big bit because there's the whole tenement to go round, but I'm sure there's enough for Mr Fulton as well,' she volunteered.

'I'm sure there will be, dear. Thank your mother for me, Mrs Fulton said, and closed the door very quietly.

2

'Lena!'

Lena Fulton, tiptoeing back along the hall, the small, greaseproof paper parcel warm in her hand, stopped in her tracks. Her shoulders drooped as she opened the door of the front room just a crack. 'Did you call, George?'

'Who the blazes was that at the door?'

'Only a neighbour handing something in. I'm sorry you were wakened. Go back to sleep.'

The bedsprings creaked as her husband surged

up into a sitting position like a sea creature bursting through the surface from the depths below. 'I'm wakened now. Come over here.'

'I can't, I've left the kettle on and it'll boil dry.'

'Well, if it's on anyway you can make us a cup of tea. I'll be through in a minute.'

Back in the kitchen Lena hurriedly filled the kettle, keeping the flow from the tap low so that he wouldn't hear it and catch her out in the lie, then she lit the gas ring. She had taken advantage of George's afternoon sleep to do some work for a woman further along Glen Street who wanted a pair of curtains converted into a summer coat, and her old sewing machine was opened out on the big kitchen table.

Putting aside the small and fragrant parcel, Lena wiped her hands on a towel before gathering up the material. Once it and the machine had been put aside she began to unwrap the dumpling. The mingled smell of spices and fruit reminded her of happy hours spent during her childhood, helping her own mother to make a clootie dumpling. She could still recall the effort it took for her small hands to force the wooden spoon round in the rich mixture, and still hear her young brother Alfie clamouring impatiently for his turn, his little nose barely reaching the top of the kitchen table, even though he stood on tiptoe. It had been a red letter day for Alfie when he first saw over the table without having to strain every muscle. She remembered the threepenny bits wrapped carefully in greaseproof paper and stirred into the dumpling for special occasions such as Christmases and birthdays.

Tuberculosis had taken her father just before Lena left school, and her mother had died of the same disease fifteen months later. Alfie had been killed in the first months of the war and now there was only Lena left ... though George didn't like it when she said that she had no family. She had him, didn't she?

'I'm yours,' he was fond of saying. 'And you're all mine, for always.'

He came into the kitchen just then, his hair still tousled from the pillow and his eyes heavy with sleep, snuffling loudly at the air as he entered.

'Dumplin', eh? You folks on Civvy Street know how tae look after yerselves.' He had pulled his trousers on and now, as he came to the other side of the table, he looped his thumbs below the braces to flip them over his shoulders.

'It's from Mrs McCosh across the hall. She'll have got the ingredients from Mrs Borland.'

'Borland? Oh aye, the black market woman up the stair.' He pulled his thumbs free and the braces thudded into place against his broad chest. Lena flinched at the stinging 'thwang' they made.

'George, she's not a–'

'Don't be so stupid, woman, of course she is. How else does she get the nice wee cuts of meat and all the other bits and pieces she doles out tae the rest of youse? It's not by sellin' her body, that's for sure.'

'She knows a lot of folk, and she's well respected throughout the neighbourhood. I'd not take anything from her if I thought it was got illegally.'

'Yes you would, and that's an order, my girl.' He broke off a piece of dumpling and tasted it. 'It's good,' he commented, and picked off another piece between thumb and forefinger. 'Now you listen tae me, Lena, you'll take anything that's offered. You've got tae keep yer strength up ... ye're lookin' after my son now, don't forget that.'

Her hand flew to her flat belly. 'George, it might be a girl, we'll not know for sure till after the summer.'

'It'll be a laddie.' George's voice took on the hectoring tone that said he was right ... and that if he was proved wrong, there could be trouble. 'And you mind and look after him while I'm away.' He broke off a lump of dumpling and pushed it at her mouth. 'Eat up, it's good.'

'I thought we could have it for our tea. I could fry it with what's left of the boiled potatoes.'

'Ach, there's not enough tae feed a sparrow here.' His fingers pushed painfully against her lips. 'Go on, eat it.'

'I'll have mine la–' she began, and then choked as the dumpling was forced between her teeth.

'There now; it's good, isn't it?'

Once, visiting Paisley Swimming Baths in Storie Street with her school pals, Lena had almost drowned. Ever since then she had had a mortal fear of choking, a fear that came back as the wad of spicy dumpling almost went down the wrong way. She doubled up, coughing vigorously.

'For any favour!' In two strides George was round the table, thumping her hard on the back. 'What's the matter with ye? Can ye never do anythin' right?'

'S-sorry.' She sucked in a long breath and recovered, wiping the tears from her eyes.

'So ye should be. Eat it properly now. Good, isn't it?'

It was good. Lena chewed, swallowed, and smiled up at him. 'It's lovely.'

'Aye.' He picked up the last of the slice and popped it into his own mouth, then said, 'So what's the occasion, then? Someone's birthday, is it?'

'The dumpling? No, it's just that Mr and Mrs McCosh are having a band practice tonight. D'you not remember Mrs McCosh making a cake or some scones as a wee thank you to the neighbours for not complaining about the noise?'

'God, they're no' still at that, are they?'

'You used to like it.'

'Aye, but that was before the war, when I lived here all the time. I'm only able tae get home on leave now and again, and I'm off tae God knows where tomorrow,' he protested. 'I don't want that lot wastin' my last night at home.'

'They won't waste it. Their music's quite good.'

He scowled. 'If I'd known what the dumpling was for I'd have taken it back across and rammed it down their throats!'

'Don't make a fuss,' Lena begged. 'We could go to see Aunt Cathy if you want.'

'I suppose so,' he said slowly. Then, brightening, 'We could have our tea there. Use her rations instead of our own.'

'That wouldn't be fair, George...'

'Nothin's fair durin' a war, has nob'dy told ye

that yet? It's not as if we can go to my parents, is it?'

Lena bit her lip and concentrated on folding the square of greaseproof paper neatly, so that it could be returned to Mrs McCosh. George always spoke as though it was her fault that his parents disapproved of his choice of wife.

'You could go and see them on your own. I'd not mind.'

'But I would.' He went on, emphasising every word as though speaking to an idiot for the umpteenth time, 'It's my last night, isn't it? And I'm damned if we're goin' tae spend it apart.'

'But you've only been to see your parents once during this leave.'

'That's their fault, not mine. Anyway, this nonsense of theirs won't last for much longer, will it?' A grin broke through. 'The old man's fair desperate for a grandson and it's lucky for us that our Neil and that wife of his have only been able to produce three lassies between them. I tell you, Lena, once our boy's here my old man'll be fallin' over himself tae welcome us ... all three of us. He'll never be away from this door once the bairn comes, you wait and see!'

'Will he not?' Lena asked faintly. Her overbearing in-laws terrified her, and she had been secretly relieved when they told George that if he insisted on marrying beneath his station in life they would refuse to have anything to do with his wife.

'Oh aye, I know the way his mind works. I'll be the one callin' the shots once the wee one arrives.' Her husband's big hand clamped on to her belly, his fingers digging painfully into her hips. 'The bairn you're carryin' in there'll give me the upper hand all right. You wait and see!'

'Aye, whit is it?' Mrs Bell's voice screeched from behind her door as soon as Chloe rattled the knocker. 'Who's there?'

'It's just me, Mrs Bell ... Chloe McCosh.'

'Who?'

Chloe sighed, and then put her mouth close to the door panel. 'Chloe McCosh!'

'Ye're on the wrong landin'. Mrs McCosh bides doon the stair.'

'I know, Mrs Bell. This is *Chloe!*'

'Who?'

'I've brought a wee bit o' dumpling for you, Mrs Bell.'

'Dumplin', ye say?' It was amazing how much the old woman could hear when she wanted to.

'Aye. My mother made it.'

The letterbox suddenly shot open against Chloe's hip. 'Doon here!' the old woman ordered, and Chloe obediently crouched down to peer into the open slit. Eyes glittered back at her.

'Oh, it's you. Wait a minute.'

There came the sound of a large key turning in a reluctant lock, and then the door creaked open just wide enough to reveal Mrs Bell, small and stooped, dressed as usual in a skirt and jersey beneath a wrap-over apron. All the garments were just a bit too large for her; according to Mrs Borland, Mrs Bell had been a big woman before age shrank her bones and wasted her muscles, and most of the clothes she wore had been bought in earlier, taller days.

'Aye, it is you right enough,' she said now.

'I said it was me, Mrs Bell.'

'Ye never know. Ye might have been one of thae German parashooters.'

'They're not coming, Mrs Bell. My father's in the Home Guard and he'll not let them come.'

'They're like cockroaches,' the old woman shot back at her. 'Gettin' in everywhere when ye least expect them.' Her eyes fastened on the tray. 'Dumplin', ye said?'

'Here.' Chloe balanced the tray on one raised knee so that she could lift a parcel. Mrs Bell's hand, made clawlike by arthritis, shot out to claim her packet.

'I'm partial tae a bit of dumplin',' she said, and began to close the door.

'My mum and dad are having a band practice tonight,' Chloe gabbled to the narrowing gap. 'They'll try not to be a nuisance...'

'If they are, I'll soon let them know about it,' Mrs Bell said tartly, and slammed the door.

Chloe, trying to rid her mind of the sudden image of the old woman scurrying back to her kitchen like a spider scuttling along its web to devour its latest catch, crossed the landing and knocked on the Borland's door.

'Ellen!' a man's voice bawled from within. 'Someone's knockin'!' Then came the heavy tramp of feet before the door opened to reveal Mrs Borland, her head still bound in the scarf she wore for her work in the Anchor Thread Mill.

'It's you, Chloe hen.' Her voice was like the rest of her, big and confident. A mouth-watering smell of broth and liver and bacon and onions wafted out from behind her, and Chloe had to swallow a sudden flood of saliva back before she could speak.

'My mother sent you some dumpling, Mrs Borland.'

'Aw, did she? Is that not kind of her!' Mrs Borland always made it sound as if the dumpling was a surprise gift, when the whole tenement knew that she was the one who supplied most of the ingredients. With rationing biting as tightly as it did, nobody could afford to make a big dumpling without a lot of help.

'Ye'll come in for a minute, pet?' the woman asked as Chloe handed over the largest packet.

'I have to help my mother to get ready for tonight. They're having a band practice...' Chloe launched into her usual spiel and Mrs Borland nodded.

'That's nice, hen, me and my Donnie both like a wee bit of music. And our Chrissie's coming for her tea, with a friend. They'll be able tae enjoy it too.'

'Ellen...' Mr Borland's deep voice yelled from the kitchen. 'The soup's boilin' over, hen!'

Most women, including Chloe's own mother, would have shouted back, 'Well, turn the gas down then!' But Mrs Borland merely called, in the special soft voice she used for her husband, 'I'm just comin', Donnie pet.' Then, her eyes skimming over the remaining packages on the tray, 'Did ye bring some dumplin' for Mrs Bell?'

'She's got hers.'

'That's good.' Ellen Borland gave a brisk,

satisfied nod. 'She needs all the nourishin' food she can get, the old soul. Just a rickle o' skin and bone, she is. I mind her as a big handsome woman when she was my mistress in the mills, hen, and now look at her.' She sighed gustily. 'Old age doesnae come itsel', pet. It brings all sorts of sorrows with it.'

'Yes, Mrs Borland,' Chloe agreed sympathetically, but she knew, as Mrs Borland went off to see to the boiling soup and she herself began to climb the stairs, that Mrs Bell would be getting a plateful of soup and whatever was cooking in the Borlands' kitchen. 'We all need tae look after our own,' was one of Mrs Borland's favourite sayings, and there was no disputing that she lived by it. Those she considered to be her own included the tenants at 42 Glen Street, especially Mrs Bell, who was so well looked after that Chloe couldn't understand why there was so little of her.

There was no reply when she knocked at the new tenants' door, and her heart began to flutter as she crossed the landing and prepared to make her final, very special call.

The Megsons' door looked just like the others, but as far as Chloe was concerned it was entirely different, because *he* lived here. She knocked upon its panels almost reverently, hoping that Dennis himself might answer, but the door opened to reveal Bessie Megson, with her younger sister Amy peering round her arm.

'Is it dumplin'?' Bessie asked eagerly. 'We could smell it when we came up the stair a wee while back.'

'Aye. We're having another band practice. Is your mum in?'

'She's still in her bed because she's been working at the hospital all last night. We're making the tea,' nine-year-old Amy said importantly.

'Is Dennis not at home, then?' Just saying his name made Chloe's heart skip a beat.

'Not yet. We're making scrambled eggs with fried potatoes. And dumpling to follow.' Bessie seized the package, held it to her nose, inhaled deeply with her eyes closed, and then pushed it against her sister's face. 'Smell, but don't touch,' she ordered. 'We don't want it all mashed before we get it on to the table. And you'd best put it away in the press where our Ralph can't see it, else he'll have it down his throat before the rest of us get a taste...'

The door closed on the final sentence. Rejected now that the dumpling had been delivered, Chloe turned back to the stairs then hesitated when she heard footsteps coming up towards her. There were voices too, a man's and a woman's, and a lot of laughter. Then the couple who had just moved into the flat next door to the Megsons' rounded the bend at the landing, and began to come up the final set of stairs.

Cecelia and Fergus had walked all around the Fountain Gardens, ending up in front of the huge, handsome fountain with its three carved and decorated upper basins from which, in peacetime, water cascaded down and down and down to splash, finally, into a large shallow pool occupied by four life-sized sea lions. A statue close by depicted the world-famed Ayrshire poet Rabbie Burns, dressed in the good sturdy clothing of a well-to-do farmer, a broad-brimmed hat on his head, and with one hand resting lightly on a ploughshare.

'One of the best Burns statues I've ever seen,' Fergus remarked, studying the figure. 'And by God, nobody's ever been able to put words together the way that man could.'

'Shakespeare?' Cecelia ventured, but he shook his head.

'Shakespeare never penned anything like "Ae Fond Kiss".'

When they left the gardens they wandered hand in hand about the town, walking first to the Cross, where they strolled past the war memorial then leaned on the stone balustrade by the handsome Town Hall to gaze down into the river hurrying through the town on its way to join the Clyde and eventually spill into the Irish Sea. After that they walked to the west end of the town and then back again. By the time they returned to Glen Street it was dark and Fergus was getting hungry.

'Hello,' he said as they climbed the stairs and caught sight of the auburn-haired girl hovering uncertainly by their door. 'We've got a visitor, Cecelia.' Then, his eyes on the battered tin tray, 'Selling something, are you?'

The girl's dark eyes met his shyly and then darted beyond his shoulder to Cecelia. 'It's some dumpling. It's for you.'

'Ahh!' Fergus bounded up the last few steps.

'So you're the angel that makes it, are you?'

She flushed. 'It's my mum, not me. You're Mr and Mrs Goudie, aren't you?'

'Fergus and Cecelia.' He stuck out his hand, then laughed as he realised that she was holding the tray with both hands. 'Sorry. Here, give it to me.' He took it with his left hand and waited until she had gained the courage to put her own right hand in his. 'How do you do, Miss...?'

'Chloe McCosh from downstairs. The first floor, above the shops.' Blushing furiously, she retrieved her fingers and snatched the tray back. 'My mum wondered if you'd like a wee bit dumpling for your tea.'

'Like it? You've saved our lives, Chloe McCosh from downstairs. That smell's been driving me crazy, hasn't it, Cecelia? I was getting desperate for a good slice of dumpling, and now here you are, sent from heaven like an angel, bearing gifts.'

Fergus was so good with people, Cecelia thought enviously as the girl giggled. He, who had been born and raised on a Highland croft, could talk to strangers as if he had known them for years, while she, a Glaswegian, hovered in the background trying to think of something to say. It was all topsy-turvy.

'The thing is,' Chloe was hurrying on, 'there's a band practice tonight, in our flat, and mum says that she hopes the noise doesn't bother you.'

'Band practice?' Fergus's eyebrows shot up.

'They've got a dance band ... my mum and dad ... and they play at dances and things, so they have to practice. They're quite good,' Chloe added anxiously. 'And they always try to keep the noise down.'

'I don't believe it.' Fergus's voice was suddenly hushed. 'I've found heaven on earth – this lovely new wife...' he drew Cecelia close to his side, 'a neighbour who hands out home-made dumpling to all and sundry, and a dance band.'

With his free hand he took the final wrapped bundle from the proffered tray, closing his eyes, just as Bessie and Amy Megson had done, to savour the aroma. 'And to think that I have to rejoin my regiment tomorrow and leave it all behind!'

'You don't mind the music, then?'

'Absolutely not. Are we allowed to dance?'

Chloe giggled again. 'If you want.'

'We want, don't we, darling?' He beamed at Chloe, digging into his pocket for his door key. 'Where did I ... ah, here it is. Chloe, delightful bearer of delicious treats, can we offer you a cup of tea?'

'I have to get back to help Mum.'

'Well, thank her most kindly from us, and tell her that we're looking forward to the music.' Fergus fitted the key in the lock and the door swung open. 'Although I have to go and help to fight the war, you'll no doubt be seeing a lot of Cecelia.'

'Oh yes. If there's anything you need, or if you get lonely,' Chloe said, 'we're just above Binnie's the drysalter's. This is a nice tenement, very friendly.'

'I'm happy to know that I'm leaving my wife in good hands.' Fergus grinned at her, then ushered

Cecelia into the hall and closed the door.

Looking at its panels, Chloe heaved a deep sigh. It was all so romantic ... such a nice young couple, newlyweds, cruelly separated because he had to go and fight for his king and country. Just like something you might see at the pictures. She couldn't wait to tell her pal Marion about the new folk in the tenement.

Then all thought of the new residents fled from her mind as she heard more footsteps on the stairs ... only one set this time, a man's boots taking two steps at a time. The fading blush bloomed again as she hurried to look over the railings, and the empty tray almost slipped from her fingers as she saw Dennis Megson breenging up towards her.

3

Dennis stopped short on the half-landing, leaning against the door of the water closet that served the residents on the upper floor. 'Hello, have you been up to play with the lassies?' The question was asked in all innocence, but if she had been closer it might have cost him a bang on the head with the empty tray.

Chloe drew herself up to her full height. 'No I have not!' Did he not realise that she was fifteen, and a working woman now? Did he not know that she was far too old to play with children like Bessie and Amy? 'I've just been taking some

dumpling round to everyone,' she said haughtily.
'Oh aye.' His square, fair-skinned face broke into a grin. 'It's band practice tonight. What time does your dad want me there?'
'About the usual time, I suppose. Half-past seven.'
'Great!' He began to mount the final flight and as he came towards her she tried frantically to think of something to say ... anything that would keep him there for even a moment longer.
Unfortunately, all she could come up with was, 'How was work today?'
'Fine. How was school?'
'For goodness' sake, Dennis Megson, I don't go to school now! I'm fifteen and I work in Cochran's, as you very well know.'
'Oh, sorry, I forgot.'
'Did you have to put out any fires?'
'Not today. Fires don't happen every day.' Dennis had followed his late father into the Fire Brigade.
'I'm glad.'
'So am I. We don't want folk to be hurt, you know, and there's always plenty to do at the station. Fighting fires is just part of the job.'
'Do they scare you? Fires, I mean,' she added as he looked perplexed.
'Oh. I'd not be much of a fire-fighter if I was scared of fighting fires, would I?'
'But they're dangerous.'
'So's crossing the road. See you tonight, then,' he said.
Angry tears filled Chloe's eyes as he vanished into his flat. Why couldn't he realise that she had

grown up, that she was no longer a little girl, but a woman? And how was she ever going to have a fairytale life like Mrs Goudie's if the one person she yearned to share it with kept lumping her together with his wee sisters?

Anyway, she had never played with the Megson girls. She had taken Amy out in her pram and she had taught Bessie to play skipping rope, and peevers on chalked beds on the pavement outside the close, but she had always been far too old to play with them!

Dennis Megson's heart was singing as he went into the flat. Dumpling, and then band practice! It was a grand day!

He found both his sisters in the kitchen, the heart of the flat. Bessie was swathed in her mother's wrap-around overall, and being small for her age she had to gather up the hem whenever she moved about the small room to avoid tripping on it. Amy, only an inch smaller than her sister although she was two years younger, had pinned a dishtowel about her own waist for use as an apron.

'Mammy's still sleeping,' she told her brother in a loud whisper.

'Is Ralph not in yet?' Thirteen-year-old Ralph contributed to the meagre family income by working as a message boy for the Co-op branch at Number 4 after school and on Saturdays.

Bessie, carefully slicing cold boiled potatoes while her sister stirred the contents of a jug, pushed a wisp of reddish fair hair back from her forehead then clamped her fists on to her hipbones. 'Can you see him?' she asked irritably. 'If you can't, it means that he's not back.'

'He should be, by now.'

'I'm not bothered, we've got enough to do,' Bessie snapped, tottering against the table as the overall tangled itself round her legs. 'He'll be in when he's hungry.'

Dennis went into the small room he shared with his younger brother, where he knelt down and groped under one of the two narrow beds that took up almost all the floor space. Drawing out a battered case he opened it to reveal the trumpet within, and all thought of Ralph vanished as the instrument seemed to glide from the case and into his hands. Dennis had never had a girlfriend ... between his music and being the man of the house, he had little time for lassies ... but the silky coolness of the trumpet against his fingers, the soft yet firm touch of it on his lips, were surely better than any girl.

Mindful of his mother asleep in the room across the tiny hallway, he didn't breathe sound into the instrument; he didn't need to, for it was enough to hold it, closing his eyes and fingering the valves, and imagining the notes pouring into air. Mebbe Mr McCosh would let him play a solo tonight, but then again, mebbe not. He was young yet and there was a lot of learning to do, and plenty of time ahead for solos. For the time being it was enough just to be part of the band.

As he laid the instrument back in its case he heard the front door open. Leaving the case on the bed he hurried to the door then jumped back as it flew open, narrowly missing his face, and his younger brother breezed in.

Ralph gave a yelp of surprise as Dennis's hand clamped on to the lapel of his jacket. 'Here, what d'ye think ye're doin'?'

'It's not me, it's you.' Dennis tossed his brother on to his bed and closed the door quietly, mindful of his mother and the girls. 'Right, you, what have you been up to?'

'None of your business! You're not my dad.'

'No, but I'm the nearest you've got to one. D'you not think that that's just what he would be asking you if he was here right now? So what have you been up to?'

'Playin',' Ralph said sulkily, starting to get up from the bed, then as Dennis pushed him back down, holding him with one hand while the other foraged in his pockets, 'You've no right ... you stop that!'

'Mum's sleeping, so keep your voice down or I'll shove that pillow in your mouth. What's this?' Dennis withdrew his fingers from his brother's pocket and held up the shilling he had found there.

'It's mine! I earned it!' Ralph made a grab for the silver coin, but Dennis stepped back, holding it out of reach.

'How did you earn it?'

'Some old lady gave it to me when I delivered her messages.'

'A whole shillin'? What did you do ... put them all away for her and cook her dinner intae the bargain? And why are you home so late?'

'I told you ... I was out playin'. I met some pals.'

'You've been runnin' for that Mrs Borland again, haven't you? Collectin' payments for her? She's the old woman that gave you this.'

'I have not!' Ralph blustered. 'She did not!'

'You'd better be tellin' me the truth, because if you're lyin' I'll find out. And after I've sorted you out I'll be havin' a word with Mrs Borland.'

'You'd not dare! Give me that...' Ralph struggled to his feet and tried to grab the money. Dennis closed his fist about it.

'Would I not? And this is for Mum.'

'It's mine! I earned it!'

'Mebbe the police would like tae know how. It's against the law tae have school bairns collectin' debts.' Dennis wasn't sure of his facts, but he knew how to subdue his cocky younger brother. 'Will I give it to her, or can you be trusted to do it yourself?'

'I'll do it,' Ralph mumbled, sticking his lower lip out.

'I'll be watching,' Dennis said as he relinquished the coin, 'so make sure you do. And no more workin' for that Borland woman, I've already told you.'

It was hard, he thought as he herded his brother out of the bedroom, to be the man of the house. He worried about Ralph, who was more interested in earning money than in being honest. His father wouldn't have tolerated the boy's behaviour, and his mother, if she had any idea that Ralph was working for their upstairs neighbour, would have fretted.

Nan Megson came into the kitchen, still heavy-eyed with sleep, her long fair hair loose about her shoulders. 'Oh, that's lovely,' she said when she saw the table set and the evening meal in progress. 'You're such clever lassies and I've been a lazy mum, lolling in bed and making you do all the work.'

Both girls beamed at the compliment, and Bessie said smugly, 'We can manage fine. It's almost ready and there's dumpling from Mrs McCosh for afters.'

'A band practice? I wish I could be here to listen to it.' Nan began to brush her hair out before the wall mirror. 'You'll be playing, Dennis?'

'If Mr McCosh lets me.'

'I'm sure he will. You're a grand musician.' Laying the hairbrush aside, Nan took an old stocking from her pocket and fastened it about her head like a coronet. Dennis watched, fascinated, as she began to twist thick strands of hair around it. In no time at all the stocking was completely hidden by a neat, continuous roll of hair and Nan had reverted to her usual prim everyday self.

He could still remember how, as a little boy, he had loved to sink his fingers into his mother's thick, clean-smelling hair, and had been fascinated by the way it framed her face like shining curtains. She had always been full of laughter in those days; it was still there in the warmth of her smile, but since his father's death and the coming of the war there was more sadness than joy.

His mother, he realised with a shock of surprise, was getting older. Then he comforted himself with the thought that he, at least, had known the good days, the early days when his father was alive and life was good. Not like the others ... Ralph had been eight years old and Bessie six when their father died. At least they remembered him; Amy, who had just reached her fourth birthday, scarcely recalled him at all, though she pretended that she did.

Dennis had been the lucky one, and it was up to him to carry on the responsibility that his father had laid down the day the walls of a blazing factory had collapsed on top of him as he followed his fellow fire-fighters to safety.

By the time Frank McCosh arrived home from work his family had already started on their evening meal. Julia got up at once to fetch his plate from the oven, where it was keeping hot.

'We'd have waited for you, but we've not got much time before the others arrive.'

'Quite right, love ... and leave it,' he said firmly, putting an arm about her and easing her back to her seat. 'I'll see to it myself.'

'But–'

'Do as you're told, woman, and stop behaving as if I'm your lord and master,' he ordered, cupping her shoulder in his big hand for a moment, smiling over her head at his daughter. 'She's a fusspot, your mother.'

'I'll see to Dad's dinner in a minute, I'm nearly finished here,' Chloe told her mother. From what she had heard from the other girls at school, their parents weren't as lovey-dovey as hers, she thought, and then, scraping up the last of the food from her plate, she corrected herself. Lovey-dovey wasn't the right phrase; they weren't always kissing and cuddling like the men and women she saw at the pictures, but they were both given to brief moments of contact and she had never known them to quarrel ... which was very unlike what she had heard from the girls at school. Seeing them so happy together made Chloe happy. One day she and some lad ... perhaps even she and Dennis ... might be like that together, she thought as her father eased the canvas bag containing his gas mask and dinner tin from his shoulder and then began to unbutton his coat.

'I got held up ... something that had to be finished before I left.'

'Frank, it's band night. Could someone else not have done it for you just this once?'

'It didn't take long.' He went into the hall to hang his coat in the cupboard that held his Home Guard uniform and rifle, while Chloe wrapped a dishcloth about her hands and drew two plates, one upended over the other to keep the contents as moist as possible, from the oven. She set them on the table and removed the cover, blinking as a waft of heat swept up and around her head.

'It's a cold night out and I'm a lucky man, with a nice warm home to come back to. Eh, lads?' Frank came back into the kitchen to stand between the boys, clapping a hand to the nape of each neck. They squealed and wriggled away from him.

'Your hands are freezing!' Duncan accused.

'And you're nice and warm. By Jove, Julia, that looks good!' Frank enthused, rubbing his hands together. 'Sausage and onion, eh?'

'I've put some hot water from the kettle into the wee basin, Daddy. You can wash your hands in that.'

'Thanks, pet.'

Julia peered at the plate. 'It's begun to dry up.'

'I don't mind, I quite like it when it gets like that.'

'There's dumpling for after,' Leslie piped up.

'Dumpling too? It's at times like this I'm fair heartbroken for that poor wee Hitler man,' Frank McCosh said over his shoulder as he washed his hands at the sink. 'He's on the wrong side altogether, is he not?'

'Aye, well, if he came to us he'd get no dumpling, that's for sure,' his wife said tartly. 'Now then, boys, you can get washed as soon as you've eaten. You can stay up for some of the practice as long as you go to your beds when you're told, without any arguments. It's school tomorrow.'

'Did you manage to do the band parts?' Frank asked as he picked up his knife and fork.

'Aye, they're all through in the room.'

'Good lass.' The band consisted of Frank on the saxophone, Julia on the piano, Bert, an older man who ran a small hardware shop in the town and was also in the Home Guard, on the drums and Dennis Megson with his trumpet. A considerable pile of sheet music had been amassed over the years, but now, with it being wartime, printed music was hard to find, so Julia had taken on the arduous task of writing out the different parts for each member of the band.

'Is your dinner all right?' she asked anxiously as

she watched her husband eat. She had had to augment the sausage and a half with a lot of vegetables.

'It's better than all right. I don't know how you manage on the rations we get. And I have a feeling,' Frank said, grinning at her, 'that it's going to be good band practice too.'

At Fergus's insistence he and Cecelia went out for a breath of fresh air after they had eaten. As they left the flat a young man already heading towards the stairs glanced up at them and grinned. 'Evening,' he said, then, 'Sorry, in a hurry. I'm late...' and he continued his headlong rush, taking the steps two at a time, what little light there was glinting on the rounded curves of the trumpet he clutched in one hand. As the Goudies began to descend the stairs the youth gained the landing below, catching the banister at the bottom of the flight with his free hand and swinging round it so that he gained momentum.

'He must be in this dance band we've heard about,' Cecelia said, low-voiced, as they crossed the small landing and prepared to follow him down.

'Must be.' They heard knuckles giving a smart double rap on a door below. It opened and closed, and then another door opened. As they left the next floor and turned at the half-landing with its blacked-out stained-glass window, they saw that the only people below were a small, fair-haired woman and a burly young man. The man was glaring at one of the doors, and muttering under his breath.

'Good evening to you,' Fergus said cheerfully. The woman glanced up at them and then looked swiftly at her companion, as though unsure about what to do.

'You're the new people, I suppose,' the man said.

'Fergus and Cecelia Goudie.' Fergus stuck out a hand as he reached the bottom step. The man gave him a long hard stare before offering his own large fist.

'George Fulton.' He twitched his head in his companion's direction. 'This is the wife. You're gettin' out before the ruckus starts too, are you?'

'The band practice, you mean? We're quite looking forward to it,' Fergus told him breezily. 'Just getting a breath of air first.'

George Fulton snorted. 'Lookin' forward tae it? You're welcome, pal. We're stayin' right out of this place until it's over. It's a fine thing when a man cannae spend a peaceful evenin' in his own home. Come on, Lena,' he added impatiently, and hustled his wife down the stairs ahead of the Goudies.

Following, Cecelia noticed that the girl walked with a slight limp, but even so, her husband hurried her along and by the time Cecelia and Fergus had reached the close opening the other two had disappeared into the night.

'Now that's what I call a friendly neighbour,' Fergus murmured, drawing Cecelia's arm through his. 'A bundle of laughs.'

'She looked quite nice.'

'She probably is, when he gives her the chance

to speak for herself. Which way would you like to go?'

'Are you sure you want to go out at all?' She hesitated, gazing into the chill dark night. 'I can't see a thing, and it's awful cold.'

'Your eyes will get used to the darkness,' Fergus slid an arm about her, 'And the blackout's great for kissing in closes.'

'We don't need to kiss in closes now that we're married.'

'We've only been married two weeks, though. Old habits die hard, and anyway, I like to kiss you in closes. It's romantic.'

They took only a short walk, along to Caledonia Street and then along to Greenock Road, which in turn led to the Paisley Racecourse, but it took quite a while because they had to feel about for the kerb each time they crossed a side street, and take care to avoid walking into the baffle walls that had been built in front of most closes to protect them from bomb blast. They were also slowed by Fergus's insistence on stopping frequently for a kiss. Despite her protestations, Cecelia didn't really mind because she was storing up memories to hold on to once he had gone back to his unit and she was alone. And there was truth in what he said about the romance of kissing in a dark close, she thought, tingling to the strength of his mouth on hers and the cool touch of his hands on the warmth of her skin.

'I wish the moon was out,' she said as they passed the Fountain Gardens on the way back home. Walking through such darkness was like wading across a river, with the ankle-turning kerbs like crocodiles lying in wait for the unwary.

'Don't wish that, for we'd be more likely to get enemy planes overhead if there was a moon to guide them. Listen to that,' Fergus added suddenly as the strains of 'Sweet Lorraine' wafted through the darkness. 'It must be the band started on their practice. That means that we're nearly home.' Then, as they reached the close, 'And they're not bad at all.'

Forty-two Glen Street, like its neighbouring tenements, was blacked out with not a chink of light to be seen, but the heavy, dark curtains couldn't muffle the sound of music. It grew louder as they turned in at the close entrance, and as they climbed to the first floor they could almost feel the throb of the drum and the haunting wail of the saxophone.

There was another noise ... the shuffle and stamp of feet from above, and an occasional feminine giggle underlined by a man's laughter. Gaining the second landing, they saw, in the dim lighting restricted by war regulations, that a couple were dancing there.

Just as Fergus and Cecelia reached the top step the music halted suddenly in mid-flow, and the dancers came to a stop.

'That's the only thing about a practice,' the girl said. 'They keep stoppin'. Oh, hullo, you must be the new folk.'

'The Goudies from upstairs. Fergus and Cecelia.'

'I'm Chrissie and this is Marty. My mam lives in that flat.' The girl, a curvy blonde, nodded towards the well-polished door, letting her eyes flicker to Cecelia for a brief second before they returned to Fergus. 'D'ye like dancin', then?'

'I've got two left feet, but luckily for me Cecelia doesn't mind. Bye,' he added as the music started up again and Chrissie and Marty rushed back into each other's arms. 'Enjoy your dance.' Then, as he and Cecelia reached their own floor, 'That's you met two of the neighbours now. Mebbe you and Chrissie could be friends.'

'I think she'd prefer to be your friend, not mine.'

'Don't be daft.' Fergus unlocked the door and drew her into the small hallway, and into his arms. 'You know that you're the only one I've got time for,' he murmured against her face. She clung to him.

'I don't want you to go away tomorrow!'

'And I don't want to go either, sweetheart, but it won't be long now,' he comforted her. 'I'll soon be home for good.'

'Th ... that's what they said when it all started, and it's been two years, almost. Two years!' Cecelia wailed. 'And who knows how much longer it might be? I can't bear it!'

'You can, we both can, because we must. Come on...' He eased himself from her grip and began to unbutton her coat. 'Let's go dancing.'

'I don't want to go back down where those other people are.'

He hung up her coat and took his own off. 'You don't need to, we've got our own dance floor,' he said, and led her back on to the dim landing as the musicians, who had halted once again, began to play 'Goodnight Sweetheart'.

They danced silently in the half-dark, holding each other close, quite unaware of Bessie and Amy Megson, who had fled from the stairs outside their own door at the sound of the Goudies' approach and were now in their own hall, peering at the new tenants from behind the part-opened door.

As she moved about the dark landing in Fergus's arms Cecelia wished that they could stay there, alone and safe, for the rest of their lives.

Two floors below, Frank McCosh nodded to Dennis Megson and lowered his saxophone as the lad, flushed with excitement, took a deep breath and moved forward to take over the next chorus.

'Remember, son,' he had said earlier, 'no pressure on the mouthpiece. Gentle, like a kiss, no more than that.'

Duncan and Leslie began to snort suppressed laughter at the word 'kiss', and paid the penalty when their father, reminded of their presence and of the time, immediately halted the rehearsal and ordered them both to their minute bedroom.

Chloe, squeezed into a corner, hugging her knees, felt a pleasant little shiver as Dennis put the instrument to his lips. She drank in every golden note from the trumpet, and, like Cecelia Goudie on the landing above, wished that the evening could go on forever.

4

'Tell you what,' Fergus said, 'once this is over and the ration books have been burned, let's have dumpling every day. You know how to make it, don't you?'

'You're not still on about that dumpling, are you?' Cecelia drew her coat a little closer about her body in an effort to avoid the draught sweeping down the open platform. They were waiting at Gilmour Street Station, not far from Glen Street, for the train that would take Fergus away from her.

'I'm collecting and keeping every single memory of the past two weeks that I can, and last night's band practice is part of it, dumpling and all.'

'You'd get tired of it if we had it every day.'

'Right now I love the thought of getting tired of dumpling. What are you going to do today?' he asked. The words 'when I'm gone' hung in the air, unspoken, between them.

'I'll have to see about getting a job. We can't have able-bodied young women lounging about during wartime.'

'Desk work in a military establishment, mebbe. There's the Fleet Air Arm place out at Abbotsinch.'

'You think I could aspire to something as grand as that?'

'It's the sort of thing you did before.'

'I was a clerkess in an insurance office before. Fergus, isn't that the couple we saw in the tenement last night? There, further along the platform.' She craned to see through and around the crowd, and caught another glimpse of the burly man, in army uniform today, and the slight, fair woman.

'Who cares? Listen, Cecelia, you have office skills and I don't want you to be pushed into munitions, or into the services. If that happened they could send you anywhere, and then we'd find it difficult to get together during my leaves. Get yourself a job before the authorities do it for–' He stopped, then asked, 'What's the matter?'

'Nothing.'

'Yes there is.' He bent to study her averted face. 'Oh, my darling, I thought you'd done all your crying last night.'

'I can't help it.'

'Perhaps we should have listened to my parents and your father, and waited until after the war was finished and done with before we got married.'

'No!' she snuffled, knuckling back the tears. 'We wanted to be together!' Then, passionately, 'Together, Fergus, not you away fighting and me alone here, worrying about you!'

'Look, mebbe it would be best for you to go back to your father's until I–'

'No! He's got his own life now, and anyway, I'm a grown married woman and I shouldn't be behaving like this. I'm Mrs Fergus Goudie, and proud of it.'

'Not half as proud as I am.'

'Want to bet?'

'Oh, Cecelia,' he said, kissing her wet face.

'Fergus, there's other people on the platform!'

'To hell with them,' he said, and kissed her again. She clung to him, digging her fingers into the roughness of his khaki greatcoat, and then pulled herself away as the clatter of the signals told of the train's approach.

'You've got your sandwiches?' She had spread the meat paste as thickly as she could, in an attempt to make the dreary sandwiches a little more interesting.

'Yes, ma'am.'

'I hope there's enough of them.'

'They'll be fine, and so will I. There's nothing to worry about, honest. I'll be back before you know it,' he reassured her as the train, already filled with men and women in uniform, roared into the station.

In no time at all Fergus was on board, his final kiss still tingling on her mouth, his last tight hug still warming her. Up and down the platform people were leaning out of the train exchanging goodbyes with those about to be left behind, and then all too soon the guard's whistle shrilled, the green flag fluttered, and the train began to move.

As the back of the guard's van slid past the end of the platform Cecelia felt the fixed smile begin to slip from her face. The warmth of that last embrace vanished and she was suddenly aware of the wind rustling discarded scraps of paper against her feet. She waited until the train had disappeared from sight, then dug her hands deep into her pockets and turned to find that she was the last to leave the platform.

Going down the stairs to street level she saw her fair-haired young neighbour ahead, holding on to the banister and descending carefully, step by step. Cecelia caught up with her easily.

'Hello, I thought I saw you on the platform just now. We met last night,' she added as the girl turned and gave her a blank blue-eyed stare, 'at forty-two Glen Street. We've just recently moved into a flat on the floor above you.'

'Oh ... yes,' the girl said, and went back to concentrating on the stairs. When they reached street level and walked out into County Square, Cecelia saw that she did indeed have a limp.

'Were you seeing your husband off?'

'Yes.' Cecelia was of average height, but this girl only came up to her shoulder. She was remarkably pretty, with a neat little face and hair like silk.

'Me too. It's a rotten business, isn't it? I'm Cecelia Goudie, by the way.' She thrust out her hand and after a moment a small, work-reddened hand clasped it briefly before being withdrawn.

'Lena Fulton.' Her voice was low and soft.

'Are you going back home? We could walk together.' And have a cup of tea together, and get to know each other, Cecelia thought, her spirits rising slightly. She had never felt so alone in her entire life and she longed to find someone she could call a friend. Lena seemed to be as shy as she herself, and was probably just as lonely now that her man, too, had gone back to the war. But to her great disappointment the other girl shook her head.

'I'm ... I've got things to do,' she said, and turned away.

Cecelia bit her lip as she watched her only chance of companionship move slowly across the cobbled square and away from her. She wanted to offer to keep the girl company, but it was painfully clear that Lena Fulton wanted to be alone.

She sighed and turned towards Glen Street. She had intended to go straight to the employment office from the station, but instead she decided to wait until later, or perhaps the next day. At that particular moment, she could not face the thought of searching for work.

Trailing into the close, she realised that she was scuffing her feet just as she had done as a child on her way to school. In those days she had wanted to stay home; now, she hated the thought of returning to the empty flat. If only, she thought as she began to mount the stairs, her mother was there to nag at her for ruining her shoes. But her mother had been dead for years and her father besotted by a woman he had met only months before. Adult though she was, Cecelia had mixed feelings about this because it meant that for the first time in her life, her father no longer belonged only to her. In a way it felt as though he was rejecting not only his dead wife but the child they had created together.

'Get out of here!'

Startled, Cecelia stopped halfway up the stairs and then jerked back against the wall as she saw a witchlike face, old and deeply lined, peering over the banister at her. A hooked nose jutted from the crumpled skin, and above it, two black eyes spat venom. At first it seemed as though the face had no mouth, for the nose and the sharp chin almost met; then they separated and a pink toothless crack appeared amid the mass of wrinkles as the old woman hissed, 'Get out of here, I'm sayin'. I'll no' have your sort comin' intae my hoose. I'll see tae ye!'

'But I live here. I'm–'

'Get oot, I'm tellin' ye!' The woman's voice rose to a screech on the last few words, and an arm as thin as a twig was thrust through the banisters towards Cecilia, who saw to her horror that the knotted fist at the end of the arm was clenched about the handle of a carving knife.

She retreated step by step, too terrified to argue, but clearly she was not moving fast enough, for the old woman began to descend the stairs towards her, the knife sawing viciously through the air.

'Go on with ye! Get oot of here!'

Cecelia almost fell down the last few steps, and had to slap a hand against the wall in order to keep her balance. A wail escaped as she suddenly pictured herself falling and the woman, who looked just like the witch in one of her old story-books, rushing down the stairs to plunge the knife into her body again and again as she lay helpless on the ground. 'Fergus,' her mind screamed as she ran through the close. Why did he have to go away? Why wasn't he here, to look after her and protect her from witches?

As she erupted from the close entrance, panic-stricken, she ran into something large and soft on its way in. 'Here, here! What's the rush?' a voice boomed at her as she rebounded. 'Is the place on fire or somethin'?'

'It's...' Cecelia drew a swift, shaky breath and said to the woman standing before her, 'there's someone on the stairs ... with a knife. She was going to kill me!'

'What? I'll have none of that in my close! Here, hold these.'

Two message bags were thrust at Cecelia. She took them, sagging at the knees as the weight of them jerked her arms down. As she managed to hoist them up and turned to peer into the close, her rescuer clumped along it and then set foot on the first step.

'What's goin' on up there? Is it you, Jessie?' Her voice floated back to Cecelia. 'Hold on, hen, I'm comin'.'

She disappeared up the stairs, and Cecelia, waiting anxiously on the pavement, heard the faint mutter of voices. After several minutes had passed she rested the bags on the step to rest her aching arms, and wondered what to do. Was her rescuer now in need of help herself? Should she fetch a policeman? She had been brought up to avoid making a scene in public, her mother's greatest fear. Calling for help or, even worse, for the police, was something she had never done before and never wanted to do.

She looked up and down the street, and was just beginning to wonder if she should go into one of the shops on the ground floor in search of assistance when she heard footsteps clumping back downstairs.

'See's my bags, then.' The woman took them from Cecelia then asked, looming over her from the single step that led up from the pavement to the close, 'And who are you?'

'Cec ... Mrs Goudie. I live on the second floor.'

'Oh, ye're the new tenant, are ye? Why didn't ye say? Come on in, lassie, it's too cold tae be standin' on the step and I need tae sit down. I've been workin' all night.'

Cecelia hesitated. 'What about…'

'Ach, don't fret about her. That's only Jessie Bell ... Mrs Bell tae you. A harmless wee soul.'

'But she had a knife!'

'Ye didnae think she'd use it on ye, surely? Jessie wouldnae harm a fly. She thought ye were from the council, come tae take her intae the workhouse.'

'The workhouse?' Cecelia began to wonder if she had stumbled into some mad Alice-in-Wonderland fantasy.

'Aye, that's what I said.' The voice was suddenly sharp. 'In Jessie's younger days all the old folks with nob'dy tae look out for them were put intae the workhouse. Not that I'd ever let that happen tae her, as well she knows, but even so, strangers about the tenement make her nervous, poor old soul. For goodness' sake, will ye come on in afore the two of us turn tae ice right here on the step. I'm Mrs Borland, by the way,' she added over her shoulder as Cecelia followed her along the close. 'Mrs Ellen Borland that lives on the middle floor.'

'Cecelia Goudie.'

'That's a right fancy name.' Mrs Borland began to mount the stairs. 'Dae they cry ye Cissie for short?'

'My mother wouldn't let anyone call me that.'

'Would she no'? Well then, Cecelia, tae let ye understand, when I started work in the Anchor Mills I was just a wee skelf of a lassie scared tae say boo tae a goose. In these days Jessie was my mistress.'

'Mistress?' Cecelia asked the huge swaying backside going up the stairs before her.

'In the mills the women supervisors are cried mistresses. Anyway, Jessie was awful good tae me, so now that she's on her own I do the same for her. Ye have tae look after yer own, hen, 'specially in wartime.'

The old woman was waiting for them on the second floor.

'Is this her?' The malevolence had left her voice; now it was merely frail and creaky.

'Aye, this is the new tenant, Jessie. Mrs Cecelia Goudie from up the stair. Mrs Jessie Bell,' Ellen Borland introduced them primly, as though they were in a drawing room.

'Ye should have said who ye was,' the woman accused.

'Aye well, I'm sayin' now, for her.'

'How do you do?' Cecelia held out her hand, then drew it back as Mrs Bell, about half her height and bundled up in woollen jerseys and skirts, topped by a faded wrap-over apron, stared up at her and repeated, 'Ye should have said. How am I supposed tae know who bides here and who doesnae when they don't say?'

'Ye'll know her the next time, eh, Jessie? Come on, hen,' Ellen Borland said as Cecelia prepared to go on up to her own flat, 'come in and have a cup of tea.'

'I'd not want to take up your time...'

'I've got all the time in the world, hen. We'll get tae know each other, and ye can meet my Donnie. Come on,' Mrs Borland insisted, unlocking her door and sweeping inside with Mrs Bell scuttling in her wake like a dinghy bobbing behind a yacht in full sail. There was something in her voice that made Cecelia obey without further objection.

Her mouth dropped open as she entered the kitchen. She had expected the Borlands' home to be an ordinary tenement flat like her own, but instead she found herself in the most comfortable and richly furnished room she had ever seen. The chairs and sofa were deep and luxurious, and instead of being covered by the chenille cloth used in most houses, the highly polished table had a lacy runner pinned down by a beautiful china vase filled with artificial flowers. The rugs, soft underfoot, looked and felt expensive, and the shelves of the large and handsome dresser against one wall were crammed with decorative plates and ornaments. More ornaments filled a beautiful little corner display cabinet and stood cheek by jowl with a cluster of photographs in elaborate frames along the mantelshelf.

A canary chirruped a welcome from an elaborate cage on its own stand, and Mrs Borland made kissing sounds at it as she laid down her bags.

'Hello there, wee Tommy,' she crooned and then, turning to the man who was sprawled out on the sofa, 'Donnie, pet, this is Mrs Goudie, the new lassie from up the stair. She's come in for a cup of tea. This,' she added proudly, her voice suddenly softening and her eyes taking on the glow of a young girl in love, 'is my man, Donnie.'

'I could fair do with a cup myself, hen. I've been right parched, waitin' for ye tae come home.' Donnie Borland nodded at Cecelia. 'Hello, pet, sit yerself down.'

'Aye, sit down while I get my coat off. Jessie, mebbe you could put the kettle on for us.' Mrs Borland disappeared into the hall, reappearing for a moment to add, 'the nice china, Jessie, since we've got a visitor.'

'Not there,' Mrs Bell rapped as Cecelia made a tentative move towards an armchair. 'That's where I sit ... and that's hers,' she added swiftly as Cecelia glanced at the other armchair. Meekly, she turned one of the upright chairs by the table and perched on its edge as her hostess returned, her coat off to reveal that she, like Mrs Bell, was wearing one of the all-covering aprons beloved of most working women. Her headscarf remained in place.

While the old woman, moving about with the ease of one who knew the flat well, filled the kettle, set it on the gas stove to boil, and began to set out fluted china cups and saucers, Mrs Borland lowered herself into one of the armchairs and removed her shoes, sticking her varicosed legs out in front of her and wriggling her toes.

'That's better. See standing at those machines all night? My feet were killin' me by the time I got off this mornin'.' She bent forward to give her feet a good rub. 'And then there was the shoppin' tae see tae before I could get home. There's chocolate biscuits in my bag there, Jessie, just put them out and all. I wouldnae mind a wee taste of chocolate,' she went on, fumbling beneath the chair and producing a pair of slippers, which she slipped on before relaxing back in the chair with a huge sigh of relief. 'Oh, that's better!'

'Ye're late, pet. I was beginnin' tae wonder where ye'd got tae.'

'Did ye miss me then, Donnie?' Ellen Borland asked archly. It was amazing, Cecelia thought as she watched the woman lean over to touch her husband's hand, how she seemed to revert back to her love-struck youth every time she looked at him or spoke to him. She wondered if she would still be like that with Fergus when their middle years arrived. If this beastly war allowed them to grow older together, she suddenly remembered, a lump coming into her throat.

'Of course I missed ye,' Donnie Borland was saying. 'And I missed the wee *Express* tae. Did ye mind tae get it for me?'

'Of course I did, same as I do every day. And your cigarettes an' all. Here...' His wife eased herself forward in her chair so that she could reach into one of the shopping bags. 'That Jocky Beaton wanted away smart this mornin',' she said as she handed over the paper and the cigarettes, 'so I stayed behind tae finish off the job for him.'

'You're too good tae those men.'

'Ach, I don't mind. And it's worth it,' she added, then, to Cecelia, 'Donnie's got a bad back. He got hurtit at the shipyard and he's no' been able tae work since, the poor soul. No' even a decent bit of compensation, so we've just had tae struggle on as best we could.'

'You've managed to get the place very nice.' Cecelia waved a hand at the luxury all around them.

'Ellen's a great wee housewife,' Donnie Borland said proudly. 'And a great worker. She's always stayin' behind at the mill tae finish the men's work so's they can get off havin' tae work late.'

'Aye well, when ye have tae start wi' nothin' ye learn the hard way,' his wife chimed in. 'And ye learn tae work for what ye get, tae. Thanks, hen,' she added as Mrs Bell, clearly very much at home in this flat, brought her a cup of tea, then handed one to Donnie. 'Has Donnie's tea got two sugars in it?'

'Aye, and it's been stirred.'

'I'll have a couple of thae biscuits,' Mr Borland said, and they were brought to him on a plate.

Donnie Borland had once been a very handsome man; and as often happens with men, he still retained most of his good looks although his thick hair was now mostly grey, his square-jawed face slackening into lines and folds, and a paunch pushing the waistband of his trousers down almost to his hips. He was unshaven, and wearing an open-necked, collarless shirt, grey trousers and warm carpet slippers.

Cecelia got her tea last, and then the plate of chocolate biscuits went past so quickly that she only just managed to claim one. Mrs Bell glared at her as she put the plate back on the table and went to 'her' armchair.

5

'Now then, hen, you'll want tae know all about the tenement,' Mrs Borland began. 'On this floor it's me and Donnie and Jessie. Our bairns have all grown up and married now. We've got seven wee grandweans tae.' She pointed proudly at a large photograph on the mantelshelf. It showed a small girl in a white dress, with a white lace veil drifting about her head. 'That's our Anne-Marie at her confirmation. She's the oldest grandwean.'

Cecelia looked at the picture. 'She looks lovely,' she said dutifully and then, to the old woman, 'Do you have grandchildren, Mrs Bell?'

The old woman had been licking the chocolate from her biscuit as though it was a lollipop. Now she stared and said, 'Grandweans? Me?' and then she and Ellen Borland looked at each other and broke into cackles of amusement. 'Me?' the old woman said again. 'Cheeky bizzum!'

'Jessie was never married, hen,' Ellen Borland explained. 'In the mills, the mistresses were all called missus as a mark of respect.'

'Oh, I see. I'm sorry.'

'I'm no', hen.' Jessie Bell wiped tears of mirth from her eyes. 'I'd plenty offers, mind, but I never found a man worth havin',' she said, and went back to licking the biscuit.

Embarrassed, Cecelia returned her attention to the photographs, her eye lighting on a wedding photograph. The bride looked vaguely familiar. 'Is that your daughter?'

'Aye, that's Chrissie, the youngest.'

'We met her last night, dancing on the landing with her husband during the band rehearsal.'

'Her man's in the Navy, hen, that was just a friend she brought here for his tea. Chrissie's in munitions, workin' for Beardmore's, and in her spare time she works at a canteen for the poor young lads far away from their own folk because of this war. She's awful good tae them. Have ye met yer neighbours yet ... the Megsons?'

'I've seen a young man on the stairs, and two wee girls, but I've not met their parents.'

'You'll no' meet him because he was killed in the line of duty years ago. He was a fireman. Now Mrs Megson's a widow, poor soul. She nurses at the Alexandra Infirmary, and her oldest lad's followed his father intae the Fire Service. There's another lad, Ralph, and two wee lassies, all still at the school. Nice, well-brought up family they are. On the first floor, above the shops, there's the McCosh family. He's not been called up because he does war work for the India Tyre Company. He's in the Home Guard and him and his wife's awful musical. The two of them run a wee dance band.'

'I heard them practising last night.'

'They've got two laddies still at school and a lassie workin' in Cochran's across from the Paisley Abbey. Mrs Fulton lives on the same landing as them. She's a quiet wee soul but very good with a needle if you need anythin' done. That's how she earns her keep while her man's in the army. I put some work her way because it's only right tae help yer own neighbours, d'ye not think so?'

'Yes, indeed.'

'You can use the drying green on Wednesdays, that's Mrs Fulton's day but with her being on her own she hasnae much washin' tae hang out. The same'll go for you, and there's enough line for the two of you. And Friday's the day for beatin' the carpets, so nob'dy puts out a washin' on a Friday. You're no' from Paisley yersel', hen...?'

Jessie Bell's long grey tongue took a final lick at the biscuit and then, examining it closely and deciding that there was no chocolate left, she dipped it into her tea before sucking noisily at it. Cecelia was so mesmerised by the procedure that before she knew it she had furnished Mrs Borland with almost every detail about herself and Fergus.

The woman gave a satisfied nod. 'You'll fit in all right. Now, what are you goin' tae do with yersel', hen?'

'I'll need to start looking for work tomorrow.'

'There's plenty tae be had but ye'd be best tae find the right thing for yersel'. If ye don't, they'll decide for ye.' Mrs Borland considered Cecelia with her head on one side and her eyes narrowed. 'What did ye work at before?'

'Office work.'

'Ten a penny, hen, and anyway, it doesnae count. They mostly use lassies straight from the school in offices these days, and older women that won't be called up. Munitions wouldnae suit you; too hard. And the same goes for the mills. Can ye do sums?'

'I worked with money in my last job.'

'If I gave ye a shillin' tae pay for some things that cost a sixpence halfpenny and a threepenny bit, what would you give me back?'

'Twopence halfpenny.'

'Ye're probably right, hen. Ye should go on the buses.'

'Go where on the buses?' Cecelia asked, confused.

'Tae the terminus and back again, where else? Bein' a clippie counts as war work.'

'Oh, I don't think I could...' The very idea of working with the public and being at their beck and call terrified Cecelia.

'Of course ye could. Ye can handle the money side of it and ye look presentable. Donnie, where's yesterday's paper?'

With some difficulty Mr Borland heaved his body about so that he could scrabble down the side of the sofa. Eventually, after a lot of huffing and puffing, he hauled out a crumpled newspaper. 'Here,' he said and his wife ferreted busily through the pages.

'There, I thought so. Glasgow Corporation's lookin' for clippies. What age are ye, hen?'

'Twenty-one ... and four months.'

'That's all right then, ye have tae be twenty-one tae work for them. Go on now,' Mrs Borland said above Cecelia's protests, 'you take the paper and write in tae them.'

There was something about Mrs Borland that made argument difficult, perhaps even unwise, Cecelia thought as she left the flat, the newspaper in one hand and the other clutching a small bag containing two pork link sausages.

'For yer tea,' Mrs Borland had said as she handed them over.

'But I can't take your rations!'

'Ach, we've got plenty. Go on now, they'll cheer ye up, after yer man goin' back tae the fightin'. And ye'll need tae keep yer strength up if ye're goin' tae be a clippie,' Mrs Borland had added before closing the door on her visitor.

The sausages were delicious, but even as she ate them, savouring every mouthful, Cecelia was determined that whatever her forceful neighbour said, she was going to find work for herself. She was not going to become a bus conductress just to please a woman she scarcely knew.

The bottle-green uniform issued to its bus and tram staff by Glasgow Corporation Transport was surprisingly smart, and fitted surprisingly well. Cecelia was amazed at how right it felt when she donned it.

She had sailed through the interview in the offices at Bath Street in Glasgow, then through the medical inspection. Even the test, strongly reminiscent of school exams, was quite easy, at least as far as the arithmetic section went. The worst question on the paper before her had been, 'What do you think are the four most important duties of a conductress?'

Panic mounted as she chewed at the end of her

pen. Honesty? Sobriety? A love of travel?

A shadow fell across the paper on the desk before her and a voice whispered, so faintly that she wondered if she had imagined it, 'Efficiency.' Startled, she looked up at the overseer, who was slowly pacing along between the rows of desks. Their eyes met briefly, and he gave an imperceptible nod before moving on.

'Efficiency,' she wrote, and noticed that at each desk, as he passed, a head was raised sharply and then lowered as the applicant began to scribble busily.

On his next round he breathed out the word, 'Safety,' and next came 'Caution and courtesy.'

The four most important duties were further impressed on them the next day, when those chosen, including Cecelia, were required to attend a practice in a hall. Rows of seats had been laid out and the trainees spent half the day learning how to deal with passengers, how to give the right change and how to fill in their reports, known as waybills, at the end of the day, giving details of the different prices of tickets issued. They also learned how to cash in at the end of a shift and about the importance of memorising the different stages throughout a journey, and the need to alter the fare at each stage. They were also issued with a book of rules, which they were expected to know by heart.

Then, finally, the uniforms were issued, and suddenly Cecelia began to feel that being a clippie might, after all, be the right job for her; though her first run on a real bus was nerve-wracking. She was given into the care of an elderly woman called Anna, who inspected her from head to toe, said grudgingly, 'Aye, you'll do,' and showed her how to put on her money bag.

'There's three compartments, see? One for coppers, one for silver, one for notes. Not that ye'll get many of them, unless it's from the servicemen and women. They get a good pay. Ye'll see yer tickets all fixed intae that bar at the front of the bag ... they're very important, the tickets. They're in the right order, from the halfpenny ones up, and ye mustn't get them mixed up because at the end of the shift ye'll be expected tae account for every one of them. And if ye're short with the money ye'll have tae make it up out of yer wages. You know how tae stamp the tickets?'

'Yes.'

'And mind tae give them out tae everyone. There's some that would slip off the bus without payin' if they got the chance, and ye never know when an inspector's goin' tae come aboard tae make sure ye're doing the job right. Come on then, time we were off.'

Cecelia watched, her mouth dry with nerves, while Anna took up her position directly behind their bus and guided the driver out of the depot. Then they both climbed on board and Anna pressed the bell.

'One bell means stop, two bells mean go,' she said briskly as the bus moved out on to the street. 'Three means the bus is full so yer driver cannae stop tae take on any more folk, and four bells means there's an emergency and the driver has tae stop quick tae help ye. Ye have tae remember that the driver cannae see what's goin' on behind his back, so he depends on the conductress and the bells tae let him know what tae dae.'

'Do you get many emergencies?'

'It's been known,' Anna said enigmatically. 'And ye don't sit down while ye're on duty, it's not allowed.' Then, plumping herself down on the seat by the door, 'Right then, here's the first stop comin' up, and there's folk waitin' tae get on. So ye'd better bell the driver. And get goin' with the tickets right away,' she added as a handful of people clambered aboard and chose their seats, 'or ye'll fall behind and get intae trouble if an inspector comes aboard.'

'I thought I was going to watch you first,' Cecelia faltered.

'Doin's a better way of learnin' than watchin',' Anna informed her. 'You leave the watchin' tae me. And it might be an idea tae give Harry two bells tae let him get started, otherwise we'll be sittin' at this stop all day.'

It was a baptism of fire, especially as the bus began to fill up, keeping Cecelia busy on the lower deck as well as running up and down the stairs to the upper deck. Anna sat where she was, like a Buddha in uniform, saying nothing but giving the occasional grudging nod of approval, or, sometimes, curling her lip in a sneer when Cecelia did something wrong.

'How's it goin', hen?' the driver asked when they reached their terminus and had twenty minutes to themselves before starting back on the return run.

'All right, I think,' Cecelia ventured, and he gave her an encouraging smile.

'Ach, ye'll be fine. At least ye've got the best driver on the force, and the best teacher. Eh, Anna?'

'Stop yer nonsense, Harry Dobbs,' she said sourly, and he winked at Cecelia. He was middle-aged, as were most of the drivers now that the younger men were being called up, and his calm friendliness cheered Cecelia. The worst was over; she had done her first run and nothing drastic had happened. Perhaps her new job was going to work out after all.

She started the next run with more confidence. The passengers, swiftly realising that she was new to the job, tended to be kind, waiting patiently while she found and stamped the right tickets and then sorted out their change. On the final run of the shift the bus was very busy; Cecelia, having taken all the fares on the upper deck while keeping an anxious eye on the mirror that showed when passengers on the lower deck wanted to dismount, scurried downstairs to pick up the few fares that had just got on.

A heftily built man who had been taking up the best part of a double seat at the furthest end from the door got up while she was stamping a ticket halfway down the bus and he stood behind her, waiting patiently for the chance to get past. It took her some time to sort out the change, and she could feel his impatience mounting until finally he said, 'Gonnae let us by, hen? My stop's just comin' up.'

Cecelia belled the driver to stop and then

turned, pressing herself back against the seats in order to give the man as much space as possible, but he was so large that he really needed the entire passageway and more. Cecelia squeezed herself back even further, until she was almost sitting on the knee of the woman who had just paid her fare.

'Excuse me,' she said breathlessly.

'It's all right, pet,' came the reply, just as the man, squeezing by like a reluctant cork coming out of a bottle, got tangled with the leather money bag as he went. Cecelia felt the strap bite into her back and shoulder as the bag was dragged across her stomach in his wake, and then disaster struck as the bar holding the tickets unclipped and fell, showering small pieces of pasteboard in all directions.

'Oh no!' Cecelia wailed. 'Oh, my tickets! Look at them!'

'Awful sorry, hen,' she heard the man say above her head as she dropped to her knees on the floor, 'I'd give ye a hand, but I have tae get off here.'

'My tickets!' She snatched them up from beneath the seats as the bus halted at the stop. It was fortunate that nobody got on at that stop, because almost at once, most of the passengers on the lower deck were crawling about the passageway or standing up to peer under seats.

'There's one there, hen ... hey, missus, there's one below your seat there, no, over a bit, aye, that's it.' Meanwhile, the driver, belled by Anna, continued on his way.

'Ye'll have tae sort them all out before ye can

hand yer bag in,' the woman said sourly when Cecelia finally joined her on the platform, stuffing handfuls of tickets into her pockets. 'And look at yer skirt, the hem's comin' down.'

'Oh...!' Cecelia looked down at the dip in the line of her neat uniform skirt. 'Someone stepped on it just when I was trying to get up.'

'Lucky yer stockin's werenae torn and all. It's not easy gettin' new stockin's these days. Aw, come on, sit down,' Anna said gruffly, realising that her trainee was close to tears. 'I'll take the bus while you sort out yer tickets. And cheer up, there's worse things happen on a wet Saturday!'

The hem, Cecelia discovered when she finally got home, required quite a bit of sewing. She stared at it, chewing her lower lip. Needlework had never been her best subject at school, and she couldn't afford to make a mess of this job because the uniform belonged to Glasgow Corporation.

'Mrs Fulton's a quiet wee soul,' Mrs Borland had said, 'but very good with a needle if you need anythin' done.'

Lena Fulton's door opened just wide enough to let one blue eye peer through the crack. When Cecelia explained her business, the door opened further and Lena stepped back. 'You'd better come in.' Then, as Cecelia went past her into the hall, 'Go on into the kitchen.'

The kitchen table was covered with material, and a middle-aged woman was stitching busily. 'My auntie,' Lena said from behind Cecelia. 'Mrs Blacklock. Auntie Cathy, this is the new neighbour, Mrs...'

'Goudie. Cecelia.'

The woman nodded. 'How d'ye do?' she said briskly and then, putting the work down and getting to her feet, 'I'll be on my way then, Lena.'

'Please don't leave on my account. I just wondered if Mrs Fulton could put up this hem for me.'

'I was going anyway. I was just giving her a bit of a hand and a bit of company, but now you're here...' Mrs Blacklock peered at the skirt in Cecelia's hand. 'A uniform, eh?'

'I've just started work as a bus conductress,' Cecelia confessed with a mixture of shyness and pride.

'Now there's a job you could have done, Lena, if it hadn't been for your limp. Infantile paralysis,' Lena's aunt told the visitor as she buttoned her coat. 'When she was seven years old. We thought we were going to lose her, but devoted nursing pulled her through. Left her with a bad leg, though, so she can't do much. It's fortunate she's so good with a needle.' She picked up a message bag. 'I'll look in next week, Lena ... and mind you eat well, you owe it to George to look after that bairn of his.'

When Lena came back after showing her aunt out there was an awkward silence between the two young women for a moment; then Cecelia thrust the skirt forward.

'I dropped my tickets on the bus and while I was kneeling down to get them someone stepped on the hem of my skirt. The stitching's come out and I think there's a wee bit of a tear.'

'Let me see.' Lena took the skirt and examined

it closely, one hand reaching up to push back a lock of fair curly hair that had come loose and fallen over her face. She really was very pretty, Cecelia thought enviously. Her own fair hair was straight, and her eyes were an uninteresting grey. If Lena Fulton had more confidence in herself, she would be quite stunning.

She glanced about the kitchen, which was as plain and serviceable as her own. A wartime kitchen, she thought, then eyed the large wedding portrait in the very middle of the mantelshelf. Lena, in a plain dress and a small hat with a veil, clutched a posy of flowers. Her smile was hesitant, as though she was not sure that she had done the right thing, and one hand was looped through the arm of the tall, broad man Cecelia had seen on the night before Fergus returned to his regiment. George Fulton stared smugly into the camera lens with such an air of satisfaction that for an instant Cecelia felt as though Lena should have been on the ground with his foot planted on her back and a hunter's rifle in his other hand.

'I can sew this up, and mend the tear,' Lena said just then. 'D'you want to come back for it in an hour?'

'That would be grand. How much?'

'Oh ... ninepence.'

'Are you sure that's enough?' Cecelia asked doubtfully, then, as the other girl ducked her head in a swift nod, 'Mrs Borland said that you did sewing for folk. It looks as if you're busy.'

'It's other folk that are busy these days, so they're pleased to find someone willing to take on some sewing for them.'

'That's pretty.' Cecelia fingered the patterned material on the table.

'It's for Mrs Borland's daughter.'

'She's lucky, finding such nice material when there's a war on.'

'Mrs Borland knows where to find things.'

Cecelia hesitated, then said, 'Your aunt said you're having a baby?'

'Not for months yet.'

'That's nice. You must be excited about it.'

'Yes,' Lena said flatly, moving to the door. 'You'll be back in an hour, then?'

When Cecelia Goudie had gone, Lena returned to the kitchen and pushed the pretty flowered material aside, then laid the green skirt on the table and began to hunt through her sewing box for thread of the right colour. Thread was as hard to get now as nice material, but Mrs Borland kept her supplied, in return for the sewing jobs she did for her and her family.

As she threaded a needle and settled down to repair the skirt she recalled the fleeting envy in the other girl's face as she said, 'You must be excited...'

Lena paused and looked down at her stomach, still not rounded enough to be noticeable. 'You mind and look after that laddie of mine, ye hear me?' George had said, just before the end of his leave, his big hand clamped on her belly and his thick fingers biting into her flesh. 'You're in charge till I'm able tae come back and see tae him myself.'

She put her own hand on her stomach at the memory, but gently, not in the possessive way George had done it. During their courtship and marriage he had talked a lot about his parents and had painted a picture of his father as an obstinate, stubborn bully who dominated his entire family. She had seen at first hand the results of such an upbringing, and knew with a sick certainty that her child, if it were a boy, would almost certainly be forced into the same mould.

She hoped that it might be a girl ... then began to wonder what George's reaction might be if he was deprived of the son he longed for. He might ignore a daughter, or he might insist on disciplining her as he would have disciplined a boy. Or, even worse, he might punish her for being born a girl.

It would have been better, Lena thought miserably as her deft fingers repaired the hem of the green skirt, if the child nestling comfortably and confidently in her womb had never been conceived.

6

Chloe begged, pleaded, promised willing slavery for the rest of her life, sulked, and finally managed to coax her parents into agreeing that she could go to the dance they were playing at, in the Templar Halls.

'It means that I'll have to find someone else to stay with the boys,' her mother pointed out reproachfully.

'Mrs Norris in the next close said she would come in,' Chloe said at once.

'You've asked her already? Chloe...' Julia began, and then stopped as Frank laid a hand on hers.

'Since Chloe's asked and Mrs Norris has agreed, we'll leave it at that. But just for this once,' he added. 'You're not to do that again without your mother's permission, Chloe. You hear me?'

'Yes, Daddy, I promise. So I can tell Marion that I'll be able to go with her to the dance?'

'You can.' Frank avoided Julia's accusing gaze as Chloe threw her arms about his neck and kissed him.

'You spoil that girl,' Julia said that night when Chloe and the boys had gone to bed. 'She had no right to make arrangements with Betty Norris behind my back.'

'Ach, it's just this once. I'll not let her get away with it a second time. She's a good lassie, Chloe; she never complains about seeing to the boys when we're out playing anywhere.'

'And why should she?' Julia, who was drying the dishes, put the last cup into the cupboard by the sink, and shook out the dishcloth. 'Older children are always expected to look after the wee ones.'

'But she's not much more than a child herself.'

'She's earning a wage, and where are your eyes, Frank McCosh?' Julia turned to face him, resting her hands on the edge of the sink. 'Do you not see why she's so desperate to go to that dance? It's not to hear you, or me; it's so as she can be near young Dennis Megson. The lassie's daft about him.'

'Our Chloe?' He was stunned. 'But ... what makes you think that?' he asked, suddenly gripped with the jealousy that most fathers feel when they discover that their daughters, so dear to them, have set their sights on another man.

'For goodness' sake, Frank!' Her lovely green eyes widened in mock despair. 'When we play, I'm at the piano with my back to the room, and you're standing right there facing her, and you've not noticed the way she never takes her eyes off him? The way she tingles every time he moves, let alone plays that trumpet of his? The way she feels about him is so strong that I can feel it in the air, even when I'm not looking at her.'

'Ach, you're havering, woman!' Frank returned to reading his newspaper, rustling it loudly.

'Maybe I am and maybe I'm not. Time will tell.'

'She's too young!'

'She'll be sixteen on her next birthday, old enough to get married if she wants to. So mebbe it's time to let her go to a dance. We can't hold on to her childhood, Frank, it wouldn't be fair.'

'D'you think young Dennis feels the same way about her?' Frank asked after a thoughtful pause.

'Him? He's too caught up in his music and being a fireman and trying to take his poor father's place as the man of the house. He scarcely notices our Chloe at all.'

'And her the prettiest lassie in the whole street? He's got a cheek...' Frank said hotly, and she started to laugh, a warm, genuine laugh that seemed to come from the tips of her toes and travel the length of her tall, almost boyish figure. He loved it when she laughed like that ... it stripped the years from her, and reminded him of the day he had first set eyes on her.

'For any favour, man,' she said on the last breath of the laugh, 'will you stop your nonsense? Whether Dennis Megson notices our Chloe or not, it's none of our business. That's something they'll have to sort out for themselves, if they ever get that far. It's the way of the world. Though mind you, he's a nice lad and she could do a lot worse for herself.'

'Mebbe so, but ... well, I suppose Chloe's special to me.'

'You shouldn't have favourites. Just because she's the only girl...'

'It's not that at all. It's because she brought us together, Julia, and I'll always have a special love for her because she happened.'

'Now don't put that sort of responsibility on her, Frank. Bairns don't ask to be born.'

'I'm glad this one was, though. Awful glad,' Frank said huskily. The newspaper he was reading fell from his hands, and he got up and went to stand behind Julia, who was mopping the draining board.

'Frank McCosh!' she protested as he slid his arms about her waist. 'What d'you think you're doing?'

'Holding the only woman I ever wanted to hold,' he said into the soft skin just below her ear. 'Come to bed.'

'I've got things to do yet.'

'They can wait.' He turned her about and kissed her, a long hard kiss.

'Remember that we're the parents of three growing bairns,' Julia protested faintly when he finally let her catch her breath.

'I do remember, and if they grow up to be half as happy as I am with you, lass, they'll do fine. Now,' he said firmly, 'stop your arguing, woman, and come to bed!'

Because most of the younger men had been called up, many of the couples stepping round the Temperance Halls dance floor to the tune of 'I've Got The World on a String,' were women, dancing with each other.

'We could do that, just to start with,' Marion said eagerly, her feet and shoulders twitching to the beat of the music.

'I'm not dancing with you!' Chloe cast a glance at the stage. What if Dennis was to look down and see her dancing with her pal? He'd think she couldn't get a lad of her own!

'Just to start with,' Marion begged. 'Come on, Chloe, what's the sense of coming to a dance if we just sit like a couple of wallflowers?'

'No. Well, all right, then.' Chloe changed her mind as she spotted two lads, clearly still school age and both of them a good head smaller than she was, edging through the crowd towards them. Better to dance with a girl than with someone the same size as her wee brother.

It took a few moments to sort out who was leading, then they were off, caught up in the crowd that circled round and round the hall. As they passed the stage Chloe kept her head down, hoping that Dennis wouldn't notice her. Looking back once they were clear, she saw that she needn't have worried, for the musicians were all too busy to look at the dancers. Her father stood at the front, eyes half closed as always when he was playing, and Dennis, to one side, watched him like a hawk, his trumpet halfway to his mouth in readiness. At the back of the stage Bert crouched over his drums, head nodding to the beat, while her mother, beaming and mouthing the words of the songs, vigorously thumped the piano. Julia McCosh seemed to her daughter to take on a new lease of life as soon as her hands came in contact with the ivory keys, and Frank joked more than once that she had taken him on only because his solid, square-shouldered figure and the strong white teeth revealed whenever he smiled reminded her of her beloved piano.

'We're not bad, are we?' Marion said into Chloe's ear.

'You've not stepped on my foot yet, if that's what you mean.' The two of them practised assiduously whenever they got the chance, usually in the McCosh's front room, following the steps as laid out on diagrams they had found in newspapers, and taking turns to lead as they danced to records played on the wind-up gramophone.

As the music took hold of their thoughts they both relaxed, letting it and the throng of people carry them along. Then suddenly they had reached the stage again, and without thinking

Chloe glanced up and found herself looking straight into Dennis's eyes. He grinned and winked; she gaped and then, mortally embarrassed, tried to hurry Marion deeper into the crowd.

'Ow, my foot! It's all right,' Marion said, her voice heavy with irony, 'don't worry about my crushed toes, luckily I've got a spare foot at the end of my other leg.'

'Stop fussing,' Chloe snapped, heat flooding into her face. 'Come on, let's sit down.' She struggled through the dancers, Marion limping along behind her, and found two empty chairs. 'Your foot's all right, isn't it?'

'I'll live. What happened? We were doing so well.'

'I went over on my ankle,' Chloe lied.

'You've gone bright red.'

'It's hot in here.' She fanned herself with one hand. The music ended to a smattering of applause, then as it started again, she said, 'We'll sit this one out, eh?'

'I'm sure there's a lot of foreigners here.' Marion stared around the hall. 'Paisley's full of them. I wish one of them would come over and ask us to dance. It would be romantic, dancing with someone from another country. Look over there, Chloe, is that not Mrs Borland's daughter?'

'Where?'

'She's just coming past us now.'

Chrissie Harper's pretty face was heavily made up and her blond hair well styled. The best-dressed woman in the hall, she was laughing up into the face of the man who held her close.

'That's her, right enough.'

'She's beautiful,' Marion said wistfully. 'D'you think we'll ever look like that?'

'I don't know that I'd want to. Look at the colour of her hair, it's not natural.'

'You're just jealous. I wonder where she got that pretty frock, and that lovely man. Is it her husband, do you think?'

'He's away in the navy. Every time I see her she's with a different man. Mrs Borland says that she helps to keep the men from abroad from getting too homesick.'

Marion's elbow dug painfully into Chloe's side. 'Doing her bit for Britain, eh?' she said, and giggled so hard that she let out an unladylike snort. Clapping a hand to her mouth, she suddenly tensed and muttered from behind her fingers, 'Oh look, no don't look, there's two fellows coming over!'

Chloe glanced up. The youths bearing down on them were both around her own age, and both reasonably tall. 'They'll be on their way to someone the other side of us,' she said flatly, and then to her astonishment they stopped, and the red-headed one grinned at Marion.

'You dancing?'

'You asking?' she returned pertly.

'Aye.'

'I'm dancing, then.' The formalities over, she rose and scurried after him on to the dance floor, while the other boy smiled at Chloe.

'It looks like me and you, then ... if you want to dance.'

'I don't mind.'

To her surprise, he held out his hand to draw her to her feet instead of simply strolling away and expecting her to follow, as most boys did. 'I'm glad of that,' he said as they walked the few steps to the floor. 'Because this is my favourite piece of music.'

'"Stardust"? It's nice, isn't it?'

''Specially with a band that knows how to play it,' he said, drawing her into his arms. 'And this one knows.'

It was lovely to be dancing with a boy instead of with Marion. They moved well together, Chloe thought as they circled the floor in silence.

Dennis got a chorus to himself, and the trumpet took over from the saxophone, its golden voice soaring through the melody. Chloe's heart sang in tune; this was turning out to be a perfect evening, though it would have been even better than perfect if Dennis could somehow have partnered her as well as being the trumpet player. Perhaps, she daydreamed, he could have leapt down from the stage between his solo pieces to dance with her...

The music ended, bringing her back to reality. 'Let's stay on the floor,' her partner was suggesting, and then adding at once, 'if you don't mind, that is.'

'That would be nice.' She smiled up at him shyly. He was a head taller than she was, slim built, with bright blue eyes and a tumble of straight black hair that flopped over his forehead. His mouth was wide and his chin strong. An interesting face, she thought.

'I'm Charles ... Charlie Hepburn.'
'Chloe McCosh.'
'Are you enjoying the evening?'
'It's all right,' she said, then the music began again and they lapsed back into silence.
'They're all right, aren't they?' Marion said to Chloe as Charlie and his friend went off to fetch them some tea at the interval.
'I suppose so.'
'Don't be so picky, you! Mine's called Robert, what's yours?'
'Charlie.'
'Robert says they were at school together, and they work together too. D'you think they'll want to walk us home?'
'They can't, my mum promised yours that they'd see that you got home safely.' Marion lived in Caledonia Street, one of the streets overlooking the Fountain Gardens.
'Oh, bother,' Marion said. 'When are they going to realise that you and me are women now, not wee lassies?'
Secretly, Chloe was pleased when Charlie stayed with her for the rest of the evening. They danced well together and each time they passed by the stage she hoped that Dennis would notice what a perfect couple they made, and that he would begin to feel quite jealous.
'They're good,' Charlie said again as the band swung into 'Goodnight, Sweetheart' for the final dance. 'Have you heard them before?'
'All the time. They practise in our front room; that's my dad playing the saxophone, and my mum's at the piano.'

'Really?' Charlie stopped dancing so suddenly that the couple close behind bumped into them. When apologies had been made and they were moving around the floor again, he said, 'It must be wonderful, having parents that run a dance band. Do you play?'

'The piano, just a bit. My mother teaches piano.'

'I play the accordion. I'd love to be in a band.' Charlie's eyes were shining. As the dance finished and Chloe's father acknowledged the applause with a stiff little bow before stepping aside to indicate the other musicians with a sweep of his hand, Charlie Hepburn asked shyly, 'Can I ... would it be all right if I walked you home?'

'Marion and I have to go home with my mum and dad.'

'Oh yes, of course. Well then ... could we mebbe go for a walk on Sunday afternoon?' His face had turned quite pink and she suspected that hers had, too. Clearly, courtship was new to him, too.

'If you like.'

'Two o'clock at the war memorial?'

'Make it half-past.' She would have to help her mother to clear up after they had had their Sunday dinner.

It was only when she was in bed and half asleep that she realised that he had suggested walking her home after, not before he discovered that her parents ran the dance band. Her eyes flew open. Would he have asked her out if he hadn't known that?

'Going out with Marion?' her mother asked on

Sunday as Chloe, the household chores done, pulled on her coat.

She had known that the question would be asked, and had been dreading it. 'No, not today.' She tried to keep her voice casual. 'I said I'd go for a wee walk with that lad I was dancing with the other night.'

'What?' Her father, in his Home Guard uniform, came into the room just in time to catch the last words. 'What lad's this?'

'Just someone I met at the dancing.'

'Where's he taking you?' Frank looked entirely different in khaki; taller and broader, and more stern, too. Chloe swallowed hard.

'Daddy, we're only going for a wee walk.' If he put his foot down and refused to let her go out, she would die!

'She's our daughter, not our prisoner. She is entitled to go out when she feels like it, Frank,' her mother said calmly.

'But we don't know this lad. She should bring him here first, so that we can have a look at him.'

'Daddy! Mum...' Chloe, horrified, appealed to her mother.

'It's broad daylight and I'm sure Chloe won't come to any harm. In any case, she's a sensible lassie ... she was brought up to be sensible. If she likes this bo ... this young man enough to meet him again,' Julia said, 'then I'm sure he's decent enough. You'll be back by five, won't you, pet?'

'Yes,' Chloe promised, and gave an inward sigh of relief when her father gave a reluctant nod.

'All right, then, but mind and look out for yourself,' he warned as he began to gather up his gas mask, cap, rifle, tin hat, and the box containing the sandwiches Julia had made for him. He would not be back until late that night, and then only if the air raid sirens stayed quiet.

'I'm not a child,' Chloe grumbled when he had gone.

'I know, but you're his only lassie and fathers worry about their daughters.'

'Did your father behave like that?' Chloe had never known her maternal grandparents; they had died before she was born. Frank's parents had both died before Chloe's twelfth birthday, but she remembered them clearly, and with affection.

'He did indeed.'

'But surely he must have realised that Daddy was a decent man.'

'I was his daughter, his wee girl, and men seem to want their daughters to be their wee girls for ever,' Julia said, a shadow crossing her face. Chloe suddenly wished that she had never brought up the subject.

'I'll have to go. Are you all right?'

'Of course I am.' Her mother smiled at her, the shadow gone as quickly as it had arrived. 'I'm looking forward to a nice peaceful afternoon, just me and the boys. Go on now, and enjoy yourself.'

Scampering out of the close, Chloe ran into Dennis Megson on his way in.

'Slow down or you'll meet yourself coming back,' he advised as they bounced off each other. Then, looking at her more closely, 'There's something different about you today.'

'D'you think so?' She had given her auburn hair an extra one hundred strokes of the brush, and lightly applied a touch of her mother's precious lipstick; she had done it for Charlie's benefit, but she would forego a hundred Charlie Hepburns in return for a compliment from Dennis.

'I know what it is ... you've washed your face, haven't you?'

The glow within her withered and died under his broad grin. 'Very funny. If you must know, I'm going out for a walk with a lad I met at the dancing the other night.'

If she had hoped to arouse envy, or even interest, it did not work. 'Good for you,' Dennis said cheerfully. 'Have a nice time, then.' And he brushed past her and disappeared up the close, leaving her fuming.

7

Charlie was already at the memorial, pacing back and forth. His long, expressive face lit up as he spotted her.

'I'm not late, am I?'

'No, I got here a bit early. You look nice.'

'Do I?'

'Yes. Where d'you want to go?'

She shrugged, suddenly shy. 'I don't care.'

'Up towards the West End?'

'All right.' She matched his long, easy stride as

they headed along the High Street, half relieved that he had not taken her hand or her arm, but at the same time half annoyed.

As they gained the west end of the town and began to walk down Maxwellton Street, Charlie, nodding at a tenement building they were passing, said, 'My mum used to live there. We live in St James Street now.'

'St James Street? I live in Glen Street.'

'You don't! That means we're almost neighbours.'

'Nearly back to back.'

He laughed. 'Imagine us both walking up to the war memorial to meet when I only needed to go round the corner to fetch you! Where do you work?'

'Cochran's.'

'Where all the rich folk do their shopping,' he teased.

'What about you?'

'Craig's Engineering, in the drawing office.'

They crossed the junction with George Street, where a horseshoe set in the cobbles marked the spot where the Paisley witches had been burned at the end of the eighteenth century, then walked on past the swing park and round by West Station, where Charlie hesitated. 'Which way now?'

Before them, as they stood outside the railway station, lay the Ferguslie Mills cricket ground, dividing the road into two. The road on the right passed the great Ferguslie threadmill complex while the road to the left held large houses, and headed towards the Glennifer Braes. To their immediate left was a smaller road, Craw Road.

'D'you want to go up the braes?' Charlie suggested, but Chloe shook her head.

'Let's go up Craw Road to Brodie Park. It would be dark by the time we got to the braes.'

'You're right. We can go there later on in the year, when the lighter nights come in,' Charlie said, linking her arm in his as they started to walk again. The gesture, and his words were warming. Then, as they passed the small wooden gate that led to the big houses at Castlehead, he added, 'that's if I'm still here when the nights are longer. I turned eighteen last month, so I'll probably be called up in the summer.'

'How do you feel about that?'

'All right, but my dad isn't too happy. He was in the last lot and he doesn't believe in war.'

'Neither do I,' Chloe said drily.

He laughed. 'Nor me. What I meant was, he's against ordinary men fighting with ordinary men to please the power-hungry dictators that stay safe behind their desks when they should fight their own battles.'

Chloe gave it some thought, then said, 'I suppose he's right. What does your mother say?'

'She doesn't want me to go, but she says it's better than having me thrown into prison if I refuse. She says that she's had enough of visiting my dad in the jail without having to visit me there too.'

Chloe felt as though her stomach had just fallen through a hole in the pavement. What was her father going to say about this? In his eyes it was bad enough that she was walking out with a lad he didn't know, but the son of a jailbird...!

'Your father's in ... in prison?' Her voice had gone squeaky and she had to cough in mid-sentence before it got back to normal.

'Not just now. Not for about ten years. He isn't a criminal,' Charlie assured her hastily. 'He used to be put in prison because he took part in marches and made speeches and caused riots ... according to the police. But he's more respectable now.'

'What does he do? My dad works at the India Tyre Company, so he's in a reserved occupation. He's in the Home Guard too.'

'You wouldn't catch mine in any sort of uniform. In any case, he's not at home much these days. He works for the trades unions and he's always away at meetings and making speeches and that sort of thing.'

'And are you going to do ... that sort of thing too?'

'I'm not all that interested,' Charlie confessed. 'I think he's disappointed about it, but you have to care a lot about something before you're prepared to be slung into jail for it, or beaten up.'

'He's been beaten?'

'Oh yes. But not for a good while,' Charlie added hurriedly as they reached the great green expanse of Brodie Park.

As they wandered around the park, which was quite well populated on this dry February afternoon, they talked about schooldays, likes and dislikes, families. Like Chloe, Charlie was the oldest of his family, with a young brother and two sisters. He asked a lot of questions about the band, and when they reached St James Street some two hours later, he suggested, 'Why don't you come up and meet my family?'

'Is your father at home?' she asked nervously, and he grinned down at her.

'No, he's not, he's in Leeds or somewhere like that. And when you do meet him you'll probably like him. Come on.'

'They've got a very nice flat, and Mrs Hepburn's such a nice lady,' Chloe reported to her mother when she arrived home. 'They've got two Belgian refugees living with them, and Charlie says that half their furniture's gone because his mother's given it away to folk that were bombed out of their own houses. We had tea and lovely little biscuits that her brother and his wife sent from America. The Americans call them cookies. She sent you this, it came from America too.'

'Chicken?' Julia almost snatched at the tin, turning it round to admire it from all directions. Then, putting it down, 'But it's too much. You'll have to take it back, Chloe, we can't accept it.'

'I said you'd say that.' Just looking at the picture of a plump roasted chicken that decorated the tin made Chloe's mouth water, and she knew that it had had the same effect on her mother. 'But Mrs Hepburn said nonsense, we've to enjoy it. They get food parcels quite often, and Charlie says that she always shares them with folk.'

'But it's like taking charity!'

'Mrs Borland gives us things and you don't call that charity.'

Julia flushed slightly. 'But I know Mrs Borland ... and don't you ever tell anyone about the things she gives folk.'

'You know Mrs Hepburn too, she says that you're in the Women's Voluntary Service together.'

'Hepburn...' Julia stared at her daughter, realisation dawning. 'Mirren Hepburn? Of course I know her, we were sorting out silver paper together last week. I didn't know she had a son your age.'

'Two years older than me,' Chloe confessed, then rushed on before her mother could object to the yawning age gap, 'and when I said that you taught piano lessons she wondered if you'd take on her wee girl, Daisy. She's coming round some time to talk to you about it. So we can keep the chicken then?' she finished hopefully.

'I suppose it would be rude to return it.' Julia put it into the cupboard. 'We'll keep it for a special occasion. And since Mirren Hepburn has entertained you, we'll have to invite your Charlie round here some time.'

'He's not my Charlie!'

'You like him, though, don't you?'

'He's all right. You can invite him if you want, I suppose. Mum,' Chloe ventured after a pause, 'he said that his dad had been in prison.'

'I seem to remember hearing about that, but it was before he became a town councillor.'

'Charlie's father was on the Council?'

'He was a Bailie for a few years, just before the war started. I mind there was quite a row about that, with him having a record himself. Bailies sit in court and try cases, but just for small things like fighting and being drunk and disorderly,'

Julia explained, 'and some folk felt that it wouldn't be right for Mr Hepburn to try folk when he'd been had up in court himself. But he was so well thought of by most of the Paisley people that they let him be a Bailie. And a good thing too because he's done a lot for this town.'

'If he's such a good man, why was he put into prison?'

'Because he believed that ordinary folk have rights, and I suppose he still believes it. A lot of men who fought in the last war were thrown out of work in the thirties. Joe Hepburn used to speak at their rallies, and go on marches for workers' rights. Only, the authorities declared most of these meetings to be illegal, so he kept being arrested and put into prison for giving speeches. They saw it as inciting the workers.'

'So he's not really done anything wrong.'

'It depends,' Julia said wryly, 'which side you're on, pet.'

'Cecelia, here a minute!'

Cecelia Goudie, on her way out to her bus to start her shift, spun round and stared at the inspector beckoning her from the office doorway.

'Aye aye, been up tae mischief, have ye?' one of the other conductresses teased.

'No. At least, I don't think so.' She looked at her driver, panic-stricken. 'Have I done something wrong, Harry?'

'Of course not, hen, ye're a fine wee clippie. Come on, we'd best both go tae see what the man wants, since I cannae take the bus out without ye.'

Following Harry Dobbs's broad back across the yard, Cecelia suddenly wondered if the inspector had received bad news about Fergus. Her mouth went dry with fear, then she realised that the dreaded telegram would have been delivered to Glen Street and not to her work. Unless, her panicking mind clamoured, it had arrived at the flat and one of the neighbours, knowing where she worked, had brought it here...

'No need tae look as though ye were walkin' tae yer execution, pet.' Harry had turned to wait for her. She summoned up a smile, and a nod of the head.

A month had passed since she had first donned the uniform of a Glasgow Corporation 'clippie', and she had come to enjoy every minute of the job. She liked the passengers, many of whom travelled her route regularly, she got on well with Harry, her regular driver, and she loved being in control of her own bus. She still missed Fergus dreadfully, but work kept her so busy that she had little time to think of anything else while on the bus. But today her comfortable, safe routine had been broken, and the timid, self-doubting Cecelia she still was when out of uniform, was quick to take advantage of the fact and start worrying about the reason.

The inspector had gone ahead of them and was waiting in his office, together with another crew.

'Cecelia, I'm going to have to put you on to a different run for today. You're changing places with Nancy here.'

'Why?' Harry wanted to know.

'Because I'm not workin' with him, that's why!'

Nancy, who had been standing glowering out of the window, jerked a thumb at Les, her usual driver.

'What's wrong with him?' Harry persisted.

'Nothin' wrong with me, pal, it's her. She's a thrawn wee b–' Les began, and Nancy, a pretty girl who had somehow managed to make her regulation uniform look as though it had been tailored especially for her, swung round on him, one red-tipped finger stabbing in the direction of his face.

'You use that word tae me, Les Nisbet, and I'll have yer eyes out!'

'Here here, I'll not have this in my office!' The inspector stepped between them, while Cecelia wondered where Nancy managed to get hold of nail polish. It was in very short supply, but her nails were always painted.

'Aye, well, tell him tae mind his tongue,' Nancy said sulkily.

'You'd better both mind your tongues or you'll be out of a job,' the inspector snapped, and the two of them subsided, glaring at each other.

'Ye've had a row, is that it?' Harry asked. The whole terminus knew that for more than a year Les and Nancy had been having an affair that was both intense and stormy. They also knew that Les had a wife at home.

Cecelia had heard the girl telling the other conductresses that she intended, by hook or by crook, to marry Les. But today it looked as though the romance was off.

'More than a row,' Nancy sniffed, while Cecelia went cold as the inspector's request sunk home.

'You want me to switch places with Nancy?'

'Just for today. This'll have blown over by tomorrow.'

'I'd not count on it,' Nancy said icily.

'Oh yes, milady, I would, because if you and him...' It was the inspector's turn to wag a finger, 'don't get yourselves sorted out by tonight you'll both be lookin' for another job. Now get your buses out and give me some peace.'

Les's bus went out first. Cecelia stood behind it, signalling him out, then as she jumped on to the platform and reached for the bell, Nancy came running across the yard and leapt on board.

'Watch it, you,' she said, her dark eyes flashing. 'Just behave yourself today, d'ye hear?'

'What else do you think I'd do?'

'I'm just warnin' you. He's mine,' Nancy's red mouth spat (where did she get the makeup? wondered Cecelia, who was hoarding her one and only lipstick for when Fergus came home) and then she reached past Cecelia, gave the double-bell that told the driver to start, and jumped off as the bus moved out of the depot.

It was a difficult shift. Cecelia, new to the run and its fare stages, had difficulty in keeping up. She didn't know the passengers and she soon got heartily sick of seeing faces falling as passengers waiting to board, mainly men, saw her on the platform, and asked, 'Where's Nancy, then?'

When they reached their turning point and had a ten-minute wait before setting off again, Les ignored her, and to cap it all, she discovered that she was on the special run that took Ferguslie

Mill workers home for their midday break. They were waiting at the mill gate, a seething mass of mostly women, with their headscarves and coats covered in caddis, the flecks of cotton from the machines. They surged on to the bus in a steady stream, showering flakes of cotton on all sides, filling the bus almost at once and leaving angry faces behind with each stop Len drove past. There was another bus at their backs, but all the workers had only a short break and every second was vital to them.

When Cecelia went to collect the fares a hundred hands were thrust at her. 'Come on, hen,' one of the women said impatiently as she stamped tickets until she felt that she was wearing out the machine. 'I've got three weans and my mother tae feed, and the wean tae put tae the breast too. I'll never get it all done and get back for the next shift if you and your driver don't hurry up.'

Even though she worked faster than she had ever done before, at least a third of her passengers left the bus without paying their fares.

'How can one person collect all these fares and give out all these tickets in one short journey?' she asked Les, almost in tears, when they reached the end of the run.

He shrugged. 'Nancy manages.'

'Well, she's welcome to it!' And she was welcome to Les as well. He was one of the younger drivers, exempt from the Forces for some medical reason. He was undeniably good looking in a flashy sort of way ... when she had time to think of it later, Cecelia realised that Les probably resembled Donnie Borland in his younger days. But even if Nancy had not warned her off, and even if Fergus's wedding ring had not been on the third finger of Cecelia's left hand, she would not have found him attractive.

As she belled him for the start of the next run it suddenly occurred to her that the quarrel might be more than a lovers' tiff. What if Nancy refused to work with Les again, and asked for a transfer? Most of the bus crews got on well enough, and if a driver and conductress found it impossible to work together they could get an exchange with another crew only if all four signed a form saying they agreed to it. What if Nancy continued to refuse to work with Les, and Harry agreed to keep her on his bus? Cecelia would have no option but to go along with the scheme. She didn't think that she could bear to continue as Les's clippie.

It was a great relief to her when the bus finally turned in at the depot. It had been a long hard day and she was glad to have reached the end of it. She never wanted another like it ... but perhaps, she thought, the panic returning, she would have little choice.

Harry's bus was already in, and Nancy prowled around the yard. As their bus arrived she stood and watched it, fists rammed on to her slim hips, then she stalked forward to the driver's door.

'C'mere, you,' she ordered as Les climbed down. Running her arm through his she led him away, turning just once to glare back at Cecelia as though blaming her for the situation.

'How did it go, hen?'

'Oh, Harry!' She could have kissed his dear familiar face. 'I'm so glad to see you. I had a terrible day!'

'You only had Les,' he told her. 'I had Nancy, and Nancy in a rage is even worse. I'm the one that had the terrible day.'

'I thought she might want to stay with you and then I'd have to stay with Les.'

'Don't be daft,' he said kindly as they crossed the yard behind the tempestuous lovers. 'She just wanted tae teach him a lesson, that's all. And even if she'd gone down on her knees and begged, I'd as soon throw the job in as work with that yin every day. No, no, hen, you and me's a good crew and that's the way it's goin' tae stay.'

It was the highest praise that Cecelia had ever received, and as they went into the office she glowed with pleasure.

8

'As you can see, we have a piano.' Mirren Hepburn gestured to the small upright piano against the living-room wall. 'Joe bought it from a man who'd been threatened with bailiffs if he didn't pay his bills. He bought half the man's furniture too ... the half that he and his family could manage without,' she went on as Julia McCosh examined the piano, which had open fretwork panels over red silk, and candle holders. 'We'd precious little money ourselves, but a wee thing like that didn't matter to my husband. I found good homes for most of the furniture, but Joe insisted on keeping the piano because his mother had always liked music though she never had a piano of her own. He'll be pleased to hear when he comes home that it's going to come in useful at last.'

Julia ran her hands over the keys. The tone was mellow, and it could do with some tuning, but it was a good piano. 'Your husband's away from home just now?'

'In Liverpool for a trades union conference.' Mirren poured tea for them both then called, 'Tea, Magritte.'

The only answer was the whirring of a treadle sewing machine from elsewhere in the flat. As Chloe had already told her, the Hepburns had taken in two Belgian refugees; the mother, Magritte, a shy, gentle woman, had excused herself almost as soon as she and Julia were introduced, and gone off to do some sewing. Her daughter Anna, Mirren explained, was working in munitions at Beardmore's factory nearby.

'She can't hear me. I'll take some through to her,' she said now, and filled the third cup.

Left alone while her hostess delivered the tea, Julia sneaked quick glances about the living-room. The Hepburns' flat in St James Street was larger than her own home in Glen Street. It held a well-used but comfortable three-piece suite, several other chairs of assorted design, the piano, a large dresser with deep solid drawers and more bookcases than Julia had ever seen outside a public library. The walls were lined with them, some low, most tall. They were crammed with books; when the shelves had been filled to capacity, more volumes were fitted into the gaps between them and the base of the next shelf, and books were also stacked on top of the bookcases and in piles on the floor. She strained to see the titles on the nearest bookcase; they all seemed to be about politics and economics.

'I'd not be surprised if the tea goes stone cold before she thinks to stop and drink it,' Mirren bustled back into the room. 'She's busy repairing some of the clothing handed in to the WVS. I've never met a worker like her; if it wasn't for her being here to look after this place for me I'd not be able to do so much war work. Have another biscuit. Magritte made them.'

'To think that we've been working together in the WVS and I didn't even realise you were married to Bailie Hepburn,' Julia marvelled.

'To think that I'd no idea that you and your husband had a band, come to that. To tell you the truth, it's nice to be with someone who doesn't know about Joe. Those that do seem to think that I'm as passionate about politics as he is.'

'But you're not?'

Mirren leaned back in her chair with a sigh of contentment. 'This is nice, just sitting here together after being on our feet all day, sorting out that stuff for refugees. I do care, of course I do, but not as strongly as Joe does, and not as much as he would like, either. When he first met me I was working in the Ferguslie Mills and he was all for me getting the women formed into unions to fight for their rights, and going to rallies and on marches, and even making speeches.' She laughed. 'Can you imagine me, standing on a platform, making a speech?'

'I think you could do it as well as anyone if you wanted to.'

'But I never wanted to, for that's not me at all. My job's to look after Joe and the flat and the children. He could live in a cave and eat wild berries and not give a jot about it, but that doesn't put food on the table.'

She took a sip of tea. 'We make a good team, though, between us. He looks after the working-class folk and I make sure that there's always a home for him to come back to. Not that he's here as often as I'd like, 'specially since the war started.'

Watching the soft smile that lingered round her mouth when she spoke about him, Julia realised that this woman was still in love with her man, just as she herself was still deeply in love with Frank. They were both fortunate.

Aloud, she said, 'You must be proud of him, though. He's done a lot for this area.'

'Yes, he has,' Mirren agreed. 'And I can't complain, for I knew what he was like before I wed him.' The smile deepened into a mischievous grin. 'And because of that, it took a lot of persuading before I said yes.'

'How did you meet each other?'

'My brother Robbie was one of his followers, so Joe was around our house quite a lot. I spent so much time patching the two of them up after they'd been to meetings that ended in fights that I could have been a nurse instead of a mill lassie.

Or a prison visitor... I've had my share of that too.'

'That must have been a terrible worry to you.'

'There was no sense in worrying. Joe was so strong in his beliefs that being locked up was just a part of the man he was. Not that he's been in prison for...' She squinted at the piano, thinking, then said, 'My goodness, it's almost ten years now. Port Glasgow, that's where it was. Joe and a deputation of the unemployed shipbuilders there wanted to talk to the Public Assistance folk about the inhumanity of means testing, only they were denied a meeting, so they protested by marching through the town.'

'I don't blame them, if they were out of work and with families to feed.'

'Good for you,' Mirren approved. 'The thing is, someone broke a window while they were passing by one of the town's banks, then their band played the "The Red Flag" outside the Provost's house. That was enough to bring in the police with their batons, and off Joe went to the jail again. I've said to him that I've had more trouble with him fighting than with both my sons.'

'And you were a mill girl?'

'A twiner at Ferguslie, and proud of it. I ended up in the welfare department, and I still do some work for them when I'm needed. Now then,' Mirren set down her empty cup. 'The girls will be back from school any minute now so I'd best tell you about our Daisy. She's six years old and she's been on at me to let her learn to play the piano.'

'I'd be happy to take her on if you want. She might well decide that she doesn't want to learn after all, once she realises that it means practising regularly.'

'I doubt that. Once Daisy puts her mind to something she doesn't let go. I have to warn you, Julia, that she's a stubborn wee creature. Out of the four of them she's the one most like her father; I'd not be at all surprised to see her marching and demonstrating along with him in another ten years or mebbe less. And in a way I'd be quite pleased, for I think he's a wee bit disappointed that none of the others is of the same mind as him. Grace is a quiet lassie, and Bobby's never got his nose out of a book ... that's the one thing he's inherited from his father, I suppose ... and Charlie's looking forward to going into the Air Force if he can. He'll be old enough for call-up in June,' Mirren said quietly, the light leaving her face. She stared down at her hands. 'He can't wait, but I'm praying that the time will drag by.'

'Oh, Mirren...' Julia leaned forward and laid a hand on her friend's arm. 'Mebbe the war'll be ended by then,' she said, although she knew that there was little hope of that.

'Aye, mebbe,' Mirren Hepburn said, then drew a deep breath before looking up again, a smile pinned to her face. 'I like your Chloe, and so does Charlie.'

'I should warn you, I have a suspicion that she's got her heart set on a lad that lives upstairs, only he never seems to notice her.'

'Poor Chloe, and poor Charlie too, if he really fancies her. We'll just have to wait and see,' Mirren said as the outer door opened and feet came scampering along the hall. The living-room door burst open and a small girl erupted into the room.

'We did sums in our sand trays,' she announced, and then skidded to a halt as she saw Julia.

'Where's your manners, miss? Say how d'you do to Mrs McCosh. She's the lady who's going to teach you to play the piano.'

Daisy stuck out a hand. 'How d'you do, Mrs McCosh, I want to learn to play "The Blue Danube",' she said, all in one breath.

'You wee heathen,' her mother admonished. '"The Blue Danube" is a German piece.'

'It's music,' Daisy corrected her sharply, then, to Julia, 'Can you play it?'

'Yes, I can.'

'Will you teach me to play it?'

'You'll have quite a lot of learning to do before you get to that stage.'

'I don't mind. Can I please have a biscuit?'

'Just one.'

Daisy palmed the biscuit with the practised skill of a gambler and asked, 'Where's Magritte?'

'Through in the kitchen.'

'When can I learn to play the piano?'

'You can start next Tuesday after school, if your mother agrees.'

Daisy's head swivelled round towards her mother, who nodded.

'That's that settled then.' She took a bite out of her biscuit. 'I'm going to see Magritte now,' she said, spraying crumbs.

'Er ... have you not got something to say to Mrs McCosh first? She's just agreed to give up valuable time to teach you how to play the piano.'

'Oh yes. Thank you, Mrs McCosh,' Daisy rattled out, and disappeared as swiftly as she had arrived.

'You're still willing to take her on? I'm beginning to think that if you can get her to sit still on a piano stool for more than thirty seconds it'll be a miracle.'

Julia laughed. 'I'm still willing.'

'Bless you. It might be Magritte that brings Daisy round for her lessons, or whoever's free at the time.' Mirren glanced at the door and called, 'Grace, come and meet my friend Mrs McCosh. This,' she went on as an older girl in school uniform came into the room, 'is my older and more respectable daughter.'

Daisy was dark-haired and dark-eyed and quite wiry, but Grace, Julia saw at once, probably looked just as her mother had done at her age. Tall and slender, she had long fair hair, striking features and her mother's air of serenity. Mirren Hepburn's body, like Julia's, had been thickened by childbearing and years of hard work, and the light from the window glittered on threads of silver in the soft, fair hair drawn back into a loose coil at the nape of her neck, but the serenity was still there. Mother and daughter had the same quick smile and the same clear eyes.

'I must go,' Julia said a few minutes later. 'My own boys will be home from school at any minute.'

'Fetch Mrs McCosh's coat, will you, Grace? It's in the hall press. I won't be a minute,' Mirren said, and disappeared. When she came back a few moments later, she said, 'Put these in your bag, Julia. My sister-in-law Ella sent a food parcel and there's always more than we can eat.'

'I couldn't take all that!' Julia stared at the large tin of meat and the generous slab of cake that Mirren had wrapped in greaseproof paper.

'Och, away with you, woman, of course you could. Robbie and Ella send these parcels from America regularly and I like to share them out. That's what war's all about, isn't it?' Mirren said. 'Sharing the good as well as the bad.'

Chloe dreaded Charlie's visit to her home.

'I don't see why,' Marion said when she confessed. 'My parents liked Robert, and so did my gran and my auntie.'

'What did you invite the poor lad to ... a family party?'

'No, but you know my Auntie Belle, she likes to stick her neb in when anything's happening. And when Gran heard that my auntie was going to drop in, she decided to drop in too. But Robert was neither up nor down about it, and we all had a great time. I don't know why you haven't asked Charlie over before this.'

'Why should I?' asked Chloe, who had resisted her mother's suggestions that Charlie be invited for tea for as long as she could. 'It's not as if we're walking out together.'

'But you are. You go for a walk with him at least once a week. I couldn't wait to get Robert to our flat. My sister's as jealous as anything!'

'Charlie Hepburn's just a friend, and I don't want my mum and dad to think that he's any more than that.'

'You know your trouble, Chloe McCosh?'

Marion said. 'You're too choosy. You'll end up as an old maid on the shelf if you're not careful.'

Chloe had no idea that her father was even more reluctant to bring Charlie into the bosom of the family than she was.

'I thought you'd want to have a good look at the young man our Chloe's been walking out with,' Julia said when her husband asked if they really needed to invite Charlie for his tea. 'It'll give you the chance to decide whether he's worthy of her or not.'

'D'you mean that she's getting serious about this lad?' he asked, alarmed.

'He's not exactly a lad, Frank, he turned eighteen recently and he'll be called up soon.'

'Eighteen? She's too young to be courting a man of that age!'

'Frank!' She put her hand over his lips to silence him. 'Will you listen to me, man? I said they were walking out, and that's all they are doing. They enjoy each other's company, and where's the harm in that, while they're free to do as they want?' She gave a sudden shiver, then added almost grimly, 'Young folk have to take their pleasure where they can these days ... they daren't look to the future.'

He freed himself, but kept her hand in his. 'And that's exactly why some of them try to grab life while they can. Who's to say that this lad Charlie isn't one of them?'

'I know his mother and I've been in their flat. He's as well raised as our bairns, and if you ask me, it's time you met him. You've built up a picture of some irresponsible lunatic in your mind and I want you to see how wrong you are.'

'Aye, I suppose you're right.' Frank gave her a rueful smile, and then kissed the tips of her fingers before letting go of her hand. 'I'm an over-possessive idiot.'

'You're a good, caring man, and I'll not let anyone say different. Chloe can bring him here, then?'

'Aye, she can,' he agreed, then just as Julia thought that the discussion was over, he added, a steely note coming in to his deep voice, 'I suppose it works two ways. I'll get the measure of him, and he'll get the measure of me. He'll see for himself that I'm not the man to let anyone treat my daughter lightly.'

It was difficult to decide, Julia thought with amusement when the two men met, which of them was the more nervous. Charlie looked quite pale when Chloe, who had been waiting for him at the close entrance, brought him in to the front room, but at sight of Frank he strode forward, his chin up and his hand stuck out.

'Mr McCosh sir, I like your music very much and it's an honour to make your acquaintance.'

For a moment Frank was nonplussed, then he shook the lad's hand. 'I've been interested in meeting you as well, son.' His steady brown eyes met and held Charlie's blue gaze for a long moment.

'You've got the look of your father.'

'You know him, sir?'

'You don't have to call me sir; you're not in the services yet, son. Plain Mr McCosh'll do. No, I can't say that we've ever moved in the same circles, Joe Hepburn and me, but I've seen him going about his civic duties. He's served Paisley Town Council well, though there's been times when he was over-zealous in expressing his views.'

Charlie laughed. 'That's what my mother always says, Mr McCosh. I know I have his looks, but I can't say that I have his political beliefs.'

'You could do worse, though it's understandable that you don't feel as strongly as he does about things. You're young, for one thing, and for another, you've had life easier than your da did, from what I've heard.'

'Until now, Mr McCosh.'

Watching, Julia saw a shadow come over her husband's face. 'Aye, son,' he agreed quietly. 'Until now.' Then, the shadow lifting, 'My daughter tells me that you play the accordion?'

'I do. I like music, 'specially the sort of music your band plays.'

Throughout the meal Julia and Chloe had prepared Charlie listened, spellbound, to the story of how the band was set up, and answered all Frank's careful questions openly, talking about his work, his hopes of ending up as an engineer and his intention, one day, to visit his relatives in America.

'I was supposed to go over there for a wee while when I left the school, but by then the war had started. But I still mean to go once it's all over.'

'Would you be thinking of settling there?'

'My uncle and aunt like it very well, and so do my mother's cousins, but I don't see me moving away from Scotland,' Charlie said. 'I'm mebbe not like my dad in ways that he would like, but I'm with him in wanting to stay in my own country. He's put a lot into Scotland, and I'd like to do the same, but in a different direction from him.'

When the meal was over Charlie, to the boys' disgust, offered to wash the dishes.

'I can be trusted not to break anything,' he assured Julia earnestly. 'My brother and I often wash the dishes at home. My dad had to look after himself for years and he says that a man should be able to turn his hand to anything.'

'Very sensible of him,' Julia approved. 'But another time, perhaps. Chloe can help me just now while the lads finish off their homework. Why don't you let Charlie have a look at some of the music we play, Frank?'

If her dad hadn't had his Home Guard duties to go to, Chloe thought when she found the two men later in the front room, talking animatedly and with their heads together over a bundle of song sheets, she might not have seen Charlie at all that evening.

'Mum says do you realise the time, Daddy?'

'Eh?' Frank glanced up, his face absorbed and then startled as he glanced at the clock on the mantelshelf. 'Good G ... rief, I'm going to be late!'

'He's great,' Charlie enthused as his host rushed through to the kitchen, where Julia had spread his uniform out before the fire to take the worst of the chill off it. 'He knows so much about music.'

‘I know,’ Chloe said with smug modesty, as though she was solely responsible for her father’s talent. She began to collect the sheets of music that had spilled over the floor and Charlie knelt by her side, helping.

‘So ... now do you feel better about me being here?’

‘Feel better?’

‘You didn’t want me to meet your parents, did you? I could tell that as soon as you met me at the close entrance. You looked as if you’d been sent for by the headmaster.’

‘I did not!’

‘Aye you did. What was it ... did you think I’d spill my dinner on the tablecloth, or scratch my backside?’

‘Charlie!’

‘Or say something rude, like I’ve just said, in front of them?’

‘No, it was just ... you’re the first lad that’s come for his tea. And your parents aren’t anything like mine. Mine are just ordinary.’

‘Ordinary? You think that musicians who have their own band are ordinary? They’re great, Chloe, and so are Duncan and Leslie. You’ve got a great family.’

Chloe gathered up the last of the music sheets and tapped their lower edges on the floor to tidy them. ‘I know,’ she said, from the bottom of her heart as the door opened to admit Frank, in uniform.

‘Very nice to meet you, son.’ He held out his hand to Charlie.

‘And you, sir. Thank you for your hospitality.’

'Any time, lad. The boys are getting ready for bed now,' Frank added to his daughter, 'so your mother says you and Charlie should just stay here. The kitchen's been turned upside down, the same as it is every night at their bedtime.'

'Let me hear you play the piano,' Charlie suggested to Chloe when her father had gone.

'I'm not good enough for that. We can play some records, though,' she offered before he could argue. They leafed through the great pile of records her parents had amassed, and when Charlie found 'Stardust' – 'My favourite piece of music!' – he wound up the gramophone and put the record on.

'It's grand, isn't it?' he asked as the first strains of music began. Then, holding out his arms, 'May I have this dance, madam?'

He was just the right height, and it was lovely, Chloe thought as they circled around her mother's good front-room carpet, to be dancing with him instead of with Marion.

She closed her eyes, and gave herself up to the music, and to the thrill of being held in a man's arms.

9

It had been a long, hard day, and as Cecelia dragged her tired feet along the street she promised herself that she was going to have a nice long bath when she got home, with as good a soak as anyone could have in the permitted five inches of water. Then she was going to eat a whole square of milk chocolate after her supper ... perhaps instead of her supper, since she had not been able to find the time to join the queues at any of the food shops.

After getting her clothes ready for the next day, she was going to bed early, with a library book. And then would come the best part ... dreaming about Fergus. As though on cue, as she reached Number 42, the strains of 'Stardust' came drifting through the cold night air from behind the McCosh's front-room window.

She climbed the first flight of stairs, almost having to feel her way in the weak light. Past the permanently blacked-out stained-glass window and the privy door, with its notices, 'Please keep clean' and 'Please bring your own paper', and up to the first landing, where she almost fell over a body, sprawled at the bottom of the next flight.

The fair curly hair identified the unconscious woman as Lena Fulton, her eyes closed and her face so white that it seemed to float in the dim light. When Cecelia put the back of her hand against the other girl's mouth she found that although the lips were cool she could feel the faint stirring of a breath against her own skin.

'Mrs Fulton? Lena?' There was no reply, no movement, but just then she heard someone coming into the close below, whistling cheerfully as they began to mount the stairs towards her.

'Hello?' Cecelia, still on her knees, pivoted round to clutch at the railings with both hands, pressing her face to the gap. 'Hello? Someone's been hurt! Can you help me, please?'

The whistling stopped at once. The man coming up the stairs craned his neck to look up at her, and then came up the rest of the stairs two at a time, hauling off his cap. 'What's happened?'

'I don't know, I was just coming home and I found Lena ... Mrs Fulton lying here. I can't get her to waken up.'

The man knelt beside her, pushing Lena's soft hair back and laying two fingers gently against her neck. His own hair was fair, and when he looked up again Cecelia recognised him as a member of the Megson family. As yet, between shyness and work, she had not had time to get to know anyone other than the Borlands and Lena.

'She's still breathing, at any rate. Best not to move her.'

'Should I go and telephone for an ambulance, do you think?'

'My mother's a nurse; you stay here while I fetch her down. She'll know what to do.' He got to his feet and hauled off his jacket, then stooped to put it over Lena. 'Back in a minute.'

'It's all right, there's a nurse coming to see to you. You'll be fine,' Cecelia reassured Lena Fulton as she waited. Almost certainly the girl couldn't hear her, but it helped Cecelia to talk.

The young man returned almost at once. 'My mother's coming directly, she says we've to leave her as she is.'

'I feel so helpless! Thank goodness you came when you did. I don't know anything about first aid.'

'I know a bit, from the Boys' Brigade and the fire station. I work there,' he added in explanation, then, 'You're Mrs Goudie, aren't you? We live on the same landing. I'm Dennis Megson ... and here's my mother coming now.'

'What happened to her?' Mrs Megson had brought a few towels; she laid them aside as she knelt down by Lena.

'I just found her like this. I don't know if she fainted, or tripped,' Cecelia said helplessly, watching as the woman ran her hands swiftly over Lena's limbs.

'No bones broken at any rate, and no head wound that I can see. Mrs Fulton?' She tapped her fingers gently against Lena's cheek. 'Can you hear me, dear?' Then as she was answered by a faint moan and a slight movement, 'It might just be a faint. Best to get her into her own place. I'll have to go through her pockets for the key.'

'No need, it's still in the door,' Dennis had stayed on his feet, out of the way. Now he pushed the door and it swung open. 'And it hadn't been turned, so she didn't mean to go far. I can carry her in if you think it's safe, Mum.'

'Best to do that.' His mother began to ease Lena over on to her back, and then stopped suddenly and nodded to the towels she had brought with her. 'Just give me one of these, will you? The big one on the top.' She took it from Cecelia and wrapped it tightly round Lena's still body. 'There now, be careful with her, Dennis. Mebbe you'd go on ahead and make sure the blackout's in place before you switch on the light,' she added to Cecelia. 'We don't want him blundering into furniture and dropping the poor lassie.'

The flat was exactly like Cecelia's and she tried to remember, from her one brief visit, what the kitchen had looked like. She edged round the big table, tripping on a chair that had been pulled out from beneath it, and fumbled her way to the sink to find that a blackout curtain already covered the single window above it. Feeling her way back to the kitchen door she called, 'It's all right, I can put the light on once you're in.'

'Follow me, Dennis,' she heard Mrs Megson say in her calm, firm voice. 'Once we get inside I'll close the door and then we can get a light on.'

A moment later they were blinking at each other in the sudden burst of light.

'Is there a bed in the kitchen?' Mrs Megson wanted to know, and Cecelia darted back in to look.

'She's got a big cupboard in the recess.'

'Can you wait for just a minute longer, Dennis,' his mother asked, 'while I make sure that it's safe to put on the bedroom light?'

'I could wait all night, for there's nothing to her. She's as light as a wee bird,' the boy said in awe, looking down at the fair head against his shoulder.

'Good lad.' His mother threw the words over her shoulder as she went into the dark bedroom. There was a pause, then a muffled thud followed by an exclamation.

'Mum?'

'It's nothing, I just walked into the corner of the bed.' The light went on. 'You can bring her in now.'

Cecelia followed Dennis into the room as his mother pulled back the bedclothes, and she watched as the boy laid his burden down carefully. Then, straightening, he said sharply, 'There's blood on the towel, Mum! She's hurt!'

'She'll be all right, son, just you leave her to me and ... er...'

'Cecelia Goudie.'

'Me and Cecelia. You don't mind staying, do you, dear?'

'No, if I can be of help.'

'Good.' Nan Megson eased her son's jacket free and returned it to him. 'You go on upstairs, Dennis, and see to the others. I don't want them coming down here to find out what's happening.'

When Dennis had gone Cecelia moved closer to the bed, a shiver running through her as she saw the red stain blossoming on the towel that had been wrapped about Lena Fulton.

'Did you know she's expecting?' she asked Mrs Megson.

'I thought she might be. Mebbe not any more, though, poor lassie. Would you boil some water for me, dear, and find some clean towels or pillow cases?' Mrs Megson rolled up her sleeves and bent over her patient as Cecelia hurried to obey.

'She's lost her bairn,' the older woman said when Cecelia brought in a basin of hot water and a face cloth and towels. 'But at least she'll be all right.'

'Should I try to find a doctor?'

'There's no need. She just needs to take things quietly for a week or so.'

'D'you think it started to come away, and she

ran out to get help and fainted?'

'I doubt it. Look at that bruise, and this one...' She had undressed the unconscious girl and now, as she washed her, she pointed to the bruising. 'And she's going to have a black eye to add to her troubles. It's my guess that she fell down a flight of stairs. It's all right, pet, you just had a wee bit of a tumble,' she soothed as Lena's eyelids fluttered and then opened.

At first the young woman tried to fight off the hands that were tending her, and then, as she recovered her wits, she lay back and let the two women get on with their work. When Mrs Megson said, 'We'll need to get a nightdress for you,' she was able to tell them where one could be found.

'My bairn?' she asked faintly as they raised her up to slip the gown over her head and she saw the towelling swathed, tucked and pinned about the lower part of her body.

'I'm sorry, love, it's gone,' the older woman said gently, and Lena let out a long, tired sigh.

She took some bread and milk and sipped a little tea, then fell into a deep sleep.

'She'll be fine,' Nan Megson said. 'It's just a matter of getting her strength back now.' Then, giving Cecelia a tired smile, 'I'm on night duty in an hour and I wouldn't mind some hot tea before I go upstairs to get ready.'

'Mrs Megson...' Cecelia ventured when they were drinking their tea in the kitchen.

'Call me Nan. My mother-in-law's been gone these four years now but even so, whenever folk say "Mrs Megson" I still think it's her they're speaking to and not me. You're our new neighbour, aren't you?' Then, when Cecelia nodded, 'I should have looked in to make you welcome, but I've had that much to do.'

'So have I. I'm working on the buses now.'

'D'ye like it?'

'More than I thought I would. It was Mrs Borland who suggested it to me.'

'Aye, that sounds like Ellen all right.' Nan Megson gave her tired smile again. She was fair, like her son, with the same steady gaze, but the similarity ended there, for Dennis was broad-shouldered, and his face strong and square, while his mother was thin, probably too thin, with permanent worry-lines between her eyebrows.

'About Lena,' Cecelia pressed on. 'You say that she must have tripped and fallen downstairs, but we found her on her own landing. Mebbe she fell down the stairs on her way out then managed to crawl back up again. But why would she go out and leave her door unlocked?'

'Well now, dear, that's not really important, is it? All that matters,' Nan went on as Cecelia opened her mouth to speak again, 'is that the poor girl's lost her bairn and she needs our support in her time of–'

Sirens began to wail, the sound climbing towards the night sky. Hob-nailed boots hastened by in the street below and far away, someone shouted something. Nan clattered her cup on to the table.

'A raid. I'd best get the girls downstairs before I go off to the hospital. And Dennis'll be wanting to get to the fire station.' She hesitated at the door, biting her lip. 'I don't think Lena should be moved out of her bed tonight.'

'I'll stay with her.'

'Are you sure?'

Cecelia nodded. 'What about your younger children?'

'Julia McCosh takes them downstairs with her children if me and Dennis are away during a raid. I'll get her to tell the rest of them that Lena's not well and you're staying with her. Good luck,' Nan said, and went.

In the distance, Cecelia could hear the rumble of enemy planes approaching, and from much nearer came the thud of feet, the banging of doors and the sound of voices as the tenement's occupants hurried down to the storeroom behind the drysalter's shop, where a space had been cleared and some bits and pieces of furniture set up to create a makeshift shelter.

Very quickly, the human noises were drowned out by the drone of wave after wave of planes passing over, and by the thud of anti-aircraft guns. Cecelia glanced at the ceiling nervously, only too aware that the night sky overhead must be filled with enemy aircraft. She looked in on Lena, who was still sound asleep, and then returned to the kitchen to pour out the last of the tea.

The building was silent now; she thought of her neighbours all huddled together in the ground floor storeroom, and of the other flats, all empty. Picking up her cup, she took it to the bedroom, where she pulled a low chair close to the bed, and the only companion she had.

The raid seemed to go on for hours. Cecelia, remembering that she had a late shift the next day, managed to doze, her head on the bed. Once, she was startled awake by the muffled thump of an explosion, but after a while sleep overtook her again, and she heard nothing more until someone knocked on the door.

Jumping up to answer it, she ran into a dresser just where she had expected to find the door. Befuddled, she stared around at the unfamiliar room, and then as Lena stirred in the bed and murmured something in her sleep, the previous evening's events came rushing back to her. The knocking sounded again, louder this time, and she fumbled her way to the door, opening it to find grey daylight flooding the landing.

Dennis Megson stood before her, in his uniform and with his face anxious beneath smears of dirt. 'Are you both all right?'

'We're fine.' She blinked at him. 'What time is it?'

'Just after eight o'clock.'

'In the morning?'

'Aye. I'm just back from the station and I thought I'd look in to see if there was anything I could do to help.' His hazel eyes flickered past her to scan the hall. 'How's Mrs Fulton?'

'Still asleep.'

'That's good. She didnae get disturbed when the bomb fell, then?'

'Bomb?' Cecelia was fully awake now. 'We were bombed?'

'A tenement in Seedhill Road got it. Two dead.

It's been a busy night.'

Cecelia suddenly remembered waking during the night with the echoes of some noise in her head. But she had heard nothing else, and fallen asleep again. 'Is Seedhill Road near here?' she asked nervously. It could have been their tenement, and if it had been... Suddenly the war seemed to be much closer than before, and much more threatening.

'It's by the Anchor Mills, on the other side of the river. Near enough. I could mebbe clear out the kitchen grate and light the fire for you,' he offered eagerly. 'She'll need to be kept warm till she's better.'

She was suddenly aware of her untidy hair and rumpled clothes. 'What about your own family?'

'Ralph can see tae himself, and Mrs McCosh took the girls into her flat after the All Clear. She says she'll get them off to the school.'

'Well, if you're sure you've got the time. Thanks.' She stepped back to let him in, then went to the bedroom, where Lena was trying to sit up.

'Just lie back for the moment. Remember me?' Cecelia asked as the other girl stared at her warily. 'Cecelia Goudie from upstairs. You mended my uniform skirt for me the other week when I got it torn.'

'What's happened?' Nan Megson had been right, Lena did have a black eye, and one side of her face was badly bruised. Cecelia winced at the livid rainbow of colours marring the girl's white skin.

'You took a tumble down the stairs in the dark

last night. Mrs Megson got you to bed and I stayed with you during the night.'

'Oh.' Lena fell back against the pillow, the bedclothes tangled about her waist, and asked in a voice so faint that it was a mere whisper. 'I lost my bairn, didn't I?'

Cecelia wished that Nan Megson were there to take charge. 'Yes,' she admitted awkwardly. 'Yes, my dear, you did.'

Tears came swiftly to Lena's blue eyes and she reached down to lay one hand lightly on her stomach.

'Poor wee thing,' she whispered. 'God rest its wee soul.'

Cecelia laid a hand on Lena's, and felt it flutter beneath her touch like a terrified moth trying to escape. 'You're young yet; there'll be other wee ones for you and your man.'

'No.' Lena said the word with finality, as though she knew it to be true. She pulled her hand free and turned her head away. Cecelia straightened up, feeling helpless.

'I'll make some tea, and fetch some warm water. You'll feel better when you've been washed and had something to eat.'

Lena said nothing, but when a sound came from the kitchen her head whipped round. 'Who's that?' Her voice was suddenly strong and her undamaged eye opened wide with alarm. 'Is it George? Did someone send for him?'

'It's Dennis Megson from upstairs, making up the fire for you.'

'Oh.' Lena fell back as though exhausted, and her eyes closed. When Cecelia returned to the bedroom, balancing a large tray that held tea and toast and a small bowl of hot water, she was almost asleep again.

10

'Best thing for her,' Nan Megson said when she arrived later that morning, still wearing her uniform. 'Rest's what she needs ... and nourishment. You managed to get her to eat something?'

'Yes, and I've made some soup for later. I washed her, though I didn't know what to do about the...' Cecelia flushed, one hand gesturing about her own hips.

'I'll see to that. It was good of you to stay up here with her. I'll just go and have a word.'

Cecelia took advantage of the other woman's presence to run upstairs to her own flat, where she changed hurriedly before returning to find Nan in the kitchen, stirring the soup.

'I've made some tea and taken a cup to Lena. Pour some out for yourself.'

'I'll have to go in an hour or two, to start my shift.'

'You've done more than enough as it is, and she's on the mend. She can manage on her own, though she's very weak. We'll all have to keep an eye on her for a wee while.'

'Your Dennis came in this morning to take down the blackout and light the kitchen fire, and Mrs Borland handed these in.' Cecelia indicated the jar of calves' foot jelly and the bottle of tonic wine on the kitchen table. 'She said to let her know if Lena needed anything else.'

'I thought they must have come from her.' Nan's voice was a touch dry.

'Where did she get them?' Cecelia marvelled. 'I'm hard pressed to find a stomach powder these days.'

'Oh, Ellen Borland can get anything you need ... and she will, if you care to ask, for she's a great believer in looking after all the folk that live in her tenement.' Nan smiled wryly as she emphasised the word 'her'. 'She works in the mill dyeworks. It's a hard, dirty job, but she's more than fit for it, and if any of the men she works beside wants to avoid doing overtime Ellen'll always do it for him ... for a price.'

'What sort of price?'

'A few coupons here, a shilling or two there, or mebbe a favour to be called in.'

'Is that why her flat's like a palace?'

'That's why.'

'But that's black-marketeering, surely!'

'Lassie, I'm normally as law-abiding as the best of them, but the thing that's really wrong these days is that we're all fighting for our lives in a war we never wanted. If the likes of Ellen is willing to make it a bit more comfortable for herself and her family and the folk about her, I'll not criticise that. Would you prefer it if that lassie lying in the bedroom didn't get these to help her recover?' Nan indicated the tonic wine and calves' foot jelly.

'No, of course not, but...'

'Then best just keep your own counsel, for Ellen Borland's not a woman who takes well to being critici – now who's that?' Nan asked as a determined hand plied the doorknocker.

'I'll go,' Cecelia volunteered.

As soon as she opened the door the elderly woman on the landing outside slapped the flat of her hand against it and pushed. She barged in, past Cecelia, and then stopped in the hall, staring. 'Who are you?'

'Cecelia Goudie from the top landing. And you're Lena's aunt. We met the other week when I came in to see if she would mend a skirt for me.'

'Aye, I mind. So what are you doing here now, and where's my niece?'

Cecelia, never good with strangers, began to panic. 'Come on through and we'll explain.' She shepherded the woman into the kitchen, where Nan was rinsing the cups.

'This is Mrs Megson from the next landing; she's a nurse, and–'

'Another neighbour?' the woman interrupted. 'Is the whole tenement making free with George Fulton's home while he's away? And where's my niece? What have you done with her?'

'I'm Nan Megson, Mrs...?' Nan said easily.

'Blacklock. Cathy Blacklock. Where's Lena? What's happened to her? Oh my God...' Mrs Blacklock dropped her shopping bag on the floor and fumbled for a chair, pressing her free hand against her chest. 'It's that bomb, isn't it? The one in Seedhill Road. What was she doin' there at that time of the night?'

'Lena's fine, Mrs Blacklock, and it's nothing to

do with the bomb. She's not very well, that's all. Cecelia, pour out some tea for Mrs Blacklock. No, wait,' Nan said, taking up the bottle of tonic wine. 'Just give me a cup.'

As she poured out a half-cupful of wine she told the distraught woman about Lena's miscarriage, finishing with, 'but she's fine, I've just changed the dressings and all she needs now is rest and building up.'

'Poor George!' Mrs Blacklock took a deep drink of wine. 'He was fair delighted about that bairn, and now it's all come to nothin'. He's been so good to her ... she was lucky to find a man like that, and her crippled the way she is.' She took another drink, then asked with sudden suspicion, 'Is that what made her lose the bairn? Bein' a cripple?'

'Lena's not a cripple, Mrs Blacklock, she's just been left with a weak leg after having infantile paralysis, and it had nothing to do with her losing the baby. It certainly won't stop her having children in the future. It seems that she tripped and fell in the blackout, and that brought it on. Nobody's fault,' Nan said firmly, pouring some wine into another cup. 'Now then, I have to go and see to my own place, and Cecelia here has her work to go to, but if you can stay with Lena today I'm sure she would be pleased to have your company.'

'Of course I'll stay, I'm her auntie! I'm the only blood kin she's got. It's my duty to stay with her,' the woman said self-righteously, then added, 'but I can't be here all the time though; I've got a job cleaning for some very nice professional families and I'm just a widow woman so I need the money...'

'Of course you do, and you can be sure that we'll be keeping an eye on your niece until she's better, won't we, Cecelia? So no need to worry about that,' Nan soothed as she put on her coat. 'Cecelia, mebbe you'd go through with Mrs Blacklock and let Lena know that someone'll be in during the evening to make sure she's all right. Seeing you will do her a lot of good,' she added to the woman.

Cecelia wasn't so sure that seeing her aunt did Lena Fulton good. As soon as she saw her niece's black eye and bruised face the woman skirled, 'Dear God in heaven, lassie, what have ye done tae yerself?'

'I ... nothing ... I didn't do anything,' Lena whimpered, for all the world, Cecelia thought, like a naughty child. One hand flew up in an attempt to cover the bruising. 'I...'

'Like we said in the kitchen, Lena lost her footing last night and fell down the stairs,' Cecelia broke in. 'It's happening all over the town, folk getting hurt in the blackout.'

'Ye should have been more careful, when you knew ye were expectin',' Mrs Blacklock lamented. 'And there's poor George far away an' fightin' for his country, with only the thought of that bairn tae keep him goin'. I've never seen a man so pleased about becomin' a father,' she added to Cecelia, and then, turning back to her niece, 'and now you're goin' tae have tae write and tell him that the wee soul's gone afore it got the chance tae take in a lungful of air…'

'No!' Lena reared up in the bed, her voice frantic. 'I don't want George told!'

'What d'ye mean, ye don't want him told? He's goin' tae notice somethin's amiss when he comes home on his next leave, isn't he?'

'I mean, let me tell him in my own way, Aunt Cathy. Like you said, he's away fighting for his country, and I don't want him to start fretting about what's happening here. He's got enough to think of,' the girl pleaded.

'Aye well, right enough. I'll leave it tae you tae do what ye think best,' her aunt conceded. 'Now then, drink yer tonic wine and I'll stay here for today. We'll not be needin' you now, Mrs … er…' she added firmly to Cecelia.

Cecelia wondered on her way to work if Lena Fulton was afraid of her husband. The girl had gone into a real panic when her aunt mentioned George Fulton's reaction to the news of her miscarriage. Then she realised that she herself had no right to question or criticise Lena, for she had not yet told Fergus that she was working as a clippie on the buses.

Fergus's family were crofters, and he himself would have become a crofter if the 1930s depression hadn't driven him, and many other young men like him, south to the industrial towns and cities in search of work.

He had found a job as a tenter in the Paisley thread mills, and when he and Cecelia first met, he had been so impressed to discover that she worked in a Glasgow insurance office that he became convinced that he was not good enough for her. It had taken some time before she managed to get him to change his mind, and even then he had felt guilty when she gave up her job in order to marry him and move to Paisley.

He had assumed that his wife would find an office job just as important, or perhaps more so, in Paisley, and when she was taken on by Glasgow Corporation, Cecelia had found it difficult to tell him the whole truth. Better, she told herself cravenly, to wait until his next leave, when she could explain things face to face. In the meantime, telling herself that she had not really lied, but had merely blurred the truth a little, she had given him to understand that she was working in the transport department's offices.

In a way, she thought ruefully, she and Lena were sisters under the skin.

Dennis Megson, on his way to work, hesitated when he reached the first landing, glancing over at Lena Fulton's door. He hadn't seen her since that night he and Cecelia Goudie had found her lying in a crumpled heap at the bottom of the stairs; his mother said that she had made a full recovery, but Dennis would have liked to have seen her for himself, just to make sure. Each time he passed her door he hoped against hope that it might open, and she might come out, but today, as always, it remained stubbornly closed.

Dennis sighed, and continued on down the stairs to the close, remembering the softness of her limp body in his arms, the tumble of fair curls against his shoulder, the curve of her cheek pale against the dark material of his jacket.

He was still thinking of her when he stepped down on to the pavement and turned to see his younger brother coming along the pavement towards him. The boy was scowling, and he was being escorted by a police constable.

'Ralph?'

'You know him, son?' the policeman asked.

'He's my brother Ralph. I'm Dennis Megson.' Dennis's mouth had gone dry.

'Is yer faither in?'

'He's ... he's dead.'

'Sorry tae hear that, son. Yer mammy then?'

'She's at work,' Dennis lied. 'I'm in charge. What's he done?'

'He's been runnin' for one of the street bookies. You know that's illegal. What age is he?' the man asked, speaking across Ralph.

'Thirteen.'

'Is he, now? Telt me he was fifteen, didn't ye, son? Mind you, he could get away with it, for he's big for thirteen.'

'What's...' Dennis's mouth was dry with fear. If Ralph had to go to court, what would it do to their mother? 'What's going to happen to him?'

'A lot of bad things if he doesnae learn a lesson from this,' the constable said. 'But for now, seein' as he's never been in trouble afore, I'm inclined tae let him off with a warnin' ... providin' you make sure he behaves himself in future.'

'I will, I can promise you that!'

'Aye, right, then. Ye hear yer brother?' the man asked Ralph, who was staring sullenly at the ground. 'You behave yersel', laddie, and we'll say no more about it. But I know yer face now, and I'll be watchin' out for it. Take one step out of line, and I'll have ye. And I'll not be so lenient the next time. Are ye listenin' tae me?'

'Aye.' Ralph spat the word out, screwing up his face around it as though it tasted bitter.

'Fine, then. I hope I don't have tae meet up with ye again.' The man's voice was grim, but at the same time the wink he gave Dennis said 'Laddies will be laddies.' Then he wheeled round and strode off up the street.

'Come here, you!' Dennis grabbed his brother's arm and threw a swift glance about the street before hustling the younger boy into the close. There were no loiterers around, no women out sweeping their own stretch of pavement or down on their knees whitening the edges of the close steps. No sign of anyone watching, but goodness knows how many sharp eyes might have been spying on them from behind curtains and through the tape that criss-crossed every window.

'Mum's at home,' he said, pulling Ralph back when he began to mount the stairs. 'She mustn't know about this. Through here.'

They went out into the backcourt, then into the small washhouse, where Dennis closed the door and leaned his back against it, while Ralph took up a stance by the big double sink and growled, 'Get it over with, then.'

'Is that all you have to say? Ralph, you were lucky that it was that policeman that caught you. Another one might have had you in the cells and then up before the sheriff officer.'

'I'm too young tae be treated like a criminal.

They cannae touch me.'

'Who told you that?' Dennis asked sharply, then as his brother shrugged and stared at the opposite wall, saying nothing, 'Whoever it was, they're wrong. You couldnae be sent tae the jail, but there's always the Kibble School for bad boys in the Greenock Road, and that would be just as hard for ye. And what d'ye think it would do to Mam if you were locked away? Did ye never think of that? What if I hadnae been comin' out of the close just now, and she'd seen you brought home by a policeman when you should be in the school?'

'She didn't see me, so there's no harm done.'

'Mebbe she didn't, but who's to know which of the neighbours were watching from behind their curtains? Mam could still hear about it from them. Where's the money?' Dennis wanted to know.

'What money?'

'The policeman said you'd been runnin' for a bookie.'

'He took all the money I had on me. And some of it was mine!' Ralph said, aggrieved.

'It serves you right. Who were you running for?'

'Mind your own business.'

'You are my business, Ralph, though I wish you weren't. Look, I've got my work to go to,' Dennis said, suddenly aware of the time. 'Come on, I'm going to walk you to the school and see you inside before I go to the fire station.'

'What? I'm not going in late, I'll get into trouble!' Ralph began, then yelped as his brother shot across the small space and grabbed him by the arm so roughly that he was swung round to land with a painful thud against the big mangle.

'You're already in trouble! And you'll only make it worse if you don't get to that school!' Dennis snarled, almost beside himself with worry.

'You hurted me,' Ralph snivelled, rubbing at his shoulder.

'That's nothing to the hurt you'll get if you don't behave yourself from now on. Now get moving!' Dennis roared, and opened the door.

He was sick with worry as he stood at the North School gate watching Ralph stamp across the playground towards the entrance. The collapsing wall that had killed his father had also sent Dennis's future crashing down about his ears. Alex and Nan Megson had decided, when their firstborn showed promise in his schoolwork, to encourage him to stay on at school and then, if the money could be found, go to university. But when Alex died, Nan had had no option but to return to work at Paisley Alexandra Infirmary, and Dennis had immediately rebelled against the idea of university.

'But you can't miss out on the chance to get to the university, son,' his mother had protested on the day he told her that he was leaving school to get a job. 'Not many boys from tenement families manage it; that's why your father wanted it for you.'

'But I never said that it was what I wanted,' Dennis protested in a voice that, at that time of his life, was still uncontrolled and given to soaring from top to bottom of the scale during one short sentence. 'And I'm the one that would have to go through it. I just want to work.'

'Doing what?'

'Doing what my dad did. I want to be a fireman.'

The last sentence came out in a defensive mumble, and Dennis, unable to meet his mother's eyes, stared at the fading pattern on the well-scrubbed linoleum. There was a pause, then, 'No!' Nan almost shouted the word at his bent head.

'But, Mum, when I went to the evening classes the station held for the Boys' Brigade I learned a lot about–'

'I said no and that's an end of it!'

Two days later, Tom MacIntosh, her late husband's colleague and close friend, called to see her. 'Dennis has asked you to come and talk me round, hasn't he?' she said when she saw him standing on the doormat.

'I'll not lie to you, Nan, he did.'

'Then you've had a wasted journey.' She began to close the door, but the man put a big hand, calloused from years of hard work, on the panels.

'At least give me a hearing, lass.'

She bit her lip, staring up at him. He had been Alex's best friend for years; it was Tom who had come to tell her that her man would not be coming home at the end of his shift, or ever again. She knew that it had not been an easy task, but he had insisted on doing it because he knew that if things had gone the other way, Alex would have done it for him.

'Come on in then,' she said at last, turning and going into the kitchen, leaving him to close the door and follow her. When he did, she faced him squarely and went straight into the attack.

'Who do you think you are, Tom MacIntosh, coming here to ask me to throw my boy's life away the way his father's went? If you need recruits, why don't you go to some woman who's not suffered already?'

'Nan...' He twisted his cap between his hands. 'The lad wants to join the service.'

'He wants to go to the university!'

'And I want tae be King of Britain but it's not goin' tae happen. You cannae afford tae pay for him tae go tae the university, hen.'

'There's scholarships and...'

'I know that, but he'd not get enough money tae cover everything, and even if ye could afford tae help him out, he'd not let ye. He sees himself as the man of the family now, and ye've got tae let him be just that. D'ye want tae destroy his pride, when it might be all he has tae keep him goin' in the sort of future we've just pushed our bairns intae? We won the last war, but who knows what's goin' tae happen in this one?'

'You could be jailed for defeatist talk,' she said wryly.

'Aye, mebbe so, but it's the truth I'm sayin' and you know it.'

'Even if I do agree to Dennis going to work instead of the university, I'd never agree to the Fire Service. You've got a right cheek on you, Tom, asking me to even consider it.'

He grinned fleetingly. 'You know me well enough to know that cheek's just about all I've got goin' for me,' he said, and then became serious again. 'But let's be practical about this, Nan. In two years' time, if the war's still on, your Dennis is goin' tae be called up and sent tae God knows where. But if he comes intae the Service now and we start trainin' him up, he'll be in a reserved occupation.'

'I don't want to see him making the Fire Service his life, not after it was his father's death,' she said bitterly.

'I'm not talkin' about the rest of his life, Nan, I'm talkin' about now ... and that's as far as we should be lookin' these days. He could work as a messenger to start with, and a general a'things. There's always somethin' needs doin' at the station and he's a clever lad, he'd learn fast.'

'Too clever to be picking up and cleaning up after a bunch of firemen!'

'We're trainin' up auxiliaries now, because of the war,' Tom said patiently. 'Why not let him apply for that, and see how it goes? He needs tae start earnin', Nan.'

'Are you saying that I can't provide for my children?' she flared at him. 'They're as well fed and well clothed as they ever were!'

'Wheesht, woman, you don't have to bite the face off me every time I try tae explain somethin'.' He held out his hands towards her, palms up as if to ward off her anger. 'I was never good with words but I'm doin' my best, and I'm sayin' that your Dennis needs tae to know that he's bringin' in a wage now. He needs tae feel that he's a man, and no' a wee laddie dependent on his mother. He's worried about you and he wants tae help.'

'There's no need to worry about me, I'm managing fine.'

'He's worried anyway,' Tom said, his eyes on her pale, tired face. 'He sees you workin' hard at the infirmary and then comin' back here and bein' mother and father tae him and the wee ones, and it's breakin' him in two, Nan. He's desperate tae help.'

'He does help. He looks after the others when I'm working.'

'But he needs tae do more than that. He wants tae be the man of the house, because he thinks that that's what his father would expect of him. And before ye say anythin' more, Nan,' Tom added swiftly as she opened her mouth to argue, 'he knows fine that Alex was out workin' when he was twelve years old tae support his own family after his father was hurt and had tae leave the pits. Times have mebbe changed, but not that much. And folk don't change as fast as the times.'

'I don't know, Tom...' Her shoulders slumped.

'Give him a bit of rope, Nan. Show that ye trust him enough tae let him make his own decisions. I'd look after him, I promise you. For your sake, and for Alex's, I'd lose my own life before I'd let your laddie get hurt, as God's my witness!'

'You're taking on a lot, making promises like that.'

'They're not made lightly, and I'll keep them, ye've no fear of that. I've always felt as though he was my son as well as Alex's, what with him talkin' about his bairns so much, and me not havin' any lads of my own,' said Tom, father of three girls.

He had won her round, and Dennis had no regrets about his decision, for he loved the work and was hungry for more and more experience.

And now, he realised as Ralph, with a final backward glance to see if he was still under observation, disappeared into the school building, he was going to be late. He took to his heels and ran all the way to the fire station in Gordon Street, where he had to endure a tongue-lashing from the officer in charge.

11

True to his promise, Tom McIntosh had taken Dennis under his wing when the boy started work at the fire station in Gordon Street. Every man in the brigade had a trade apart from his fire-fighting skills, and under Tom's guidance Dennis had started attending night classes at the Paisley Technical College as the first step to becoming an engineer. His mother may not have liked the situation, but she learned to tolerate it, which was all that Dennis asked of her.

Today, he was put on to helping Tom with some maintenance work. 'It's not like you to be late, son,' the man said after a while. 'Everything all right at home? Is your mother well?'

'Everything's fine. I was doing some reading for tonight's class and I forgot the time,' Dennis said brusquely.

'Classes goin' all right, are they?'

'Aye, they're fine.' Now that the subject had changed Dennis relaxed. 'I'm enjoying the course. We've got a good teacher.'

'You're certainly comin' on. Yer father would be proud of ye,' the older man said, then added carefully, as Dennis glowed at the compliment, 'You know that if you ever need a bit of advice, or a bit of help, ye can come tae me, don't ye?'

'I know. You've told me often enough.'

Tom nodded, wiping his oily hands with a rag. 'Mebbe more than ye care tae hear, eh? But your faither and me were good friends, and I think well of your mother. You and her are doin' a grand job between ye, raising the younger ones; but you're still young yersel', Dennis, and there's times when ye might feel that need tae speak tae someone like me. Anytime, lad, that's all I wanted tae say.'

'Thanks, Tom.' Dennis swallowed back a sudden rush of emotion as the man put a paternal hand on his shoulder. Tom had helped to some extent to fill the hungry black hole that had been left in his life after his father died, and that, together with the knowledge that he was bringing a wage into the house, gave Dennis the strength and confidence he had badly needed.

He would have dearly loved to tell Tom MacIntosh about Ralph, and to ask his advice; but at the same time he could not bear to tell anyone about his younger brother's behaviour. Ralph's love of money and, perhaps, the loss of his father's authority in the house had led him to the edge of a precipice; if things went on as they were, he could well start the long slide down towards a life of shame, carrying his family with him.

By the time Dennis got home from work that night Ralph was in bed and, apparently, asleep. The next morning the younger boy bolted down his breakfast and left the flat without a word for anyone.

'What's the matter with him?' Nan fretted.

'Nothing, he's just in a thrawn mood. Best leave him tae work himself out of it,' Dennis advised. Nothing had been said about the previous day's escapade, which meant, with any luck, that nobody had seen the policeman and tattled to Nan.

'If you ask me,' Ellen Borland pronounced, 'thon lassie didnae lose her bairn out of misfortune. She flung hersel' down thae stairs on purpose.'

It was Saturday afternoon and she was sitting at one side of the table, dusting the photographs from the mantelshelf and some of the ornaments from the corner cupboard, while Jessie Bell, sitting opposite, rubbed up the silver tea set that was kept on the bottom shelf of the kitchen cupboard, out of sight. Saturday afternoons were always put aside for cleaning.

'For one thing...' Ellen waved the duster at Jessie for emphasis, 'she was found on her own landin' and that means that she must have fallen down from the flight above. Now what was she doin' up there?'

'Mebbe she was visiting,' Chrissie suggested from one of the armchairs where she sat with one heel propped on the knee of her other leg so that she could paint her toenails. She wore slacks and a blouse, and curlers peeped from beneath her headscarf. She was going dancing that night with a young serviceman she had met at the La Scala Picture House a few evenings before.

'Or mebbe she was borrowin' a screw o' tea or somethin',' her father put in from his own chair.

'Lena Fulton doesnae visit and she doesnae borrow. She went up these stairs just tae throw herself down them again. And it worked.'

'Why would she want tae lose her bairn, but?' Donnie persisted, deciding that this conversation was more interesting than the newspaper in his hands. He spent most of his time alone when his wife was out working, and he enjoyed a wee bit of a crack at the weekends, even if it was only woman talk.

'That's what I'd like to know,' Ellen said. 'She's got a ring on her finger, and a decent enough man. He did this place up lovely.' She looked around at the expensive paper on the walls and the glossy varnish on the doors and skirting boards, and then added, lowering her voice, 'Unless, of course, it's not his.'

Chrissie had been concentrating so hard on painting a little toe that her eyes were squinting and her tongue sticking out from between her teeth. Now she stopped, and looked up at her mother. 'That quiet wee limpy lassie ... seein' another man? Who'd look at her twice?'

'Her husband, for one,' her mother pointed out, and Chrissie nodded.

'Aye, right enough, he's a fine good-looking fellow. I don't know what men like him see in the likes of her. She's too timid to say boo to a goose.'

'And there's better ways of getting rid of an unwanted bairn. She could have hurtit hersel', goin' down the stairs like that,' Jessie Bell contributed in her wavery, raspy voice. 'There's knittin' needles, for one, and a good bottle of gin and a hot bath for another. I've seen them both used more than once in my time as a mistress in the mills.'

'I know you have, Jessie, and the church is right, it's a terrible sin!' Ellen's eyes flashed. 'That's one thing I agree with!'

Raised in the Catholic faith, Ellen had made the mistake of falling in love with Donnie, a Protestant. When both families opposed their marriage the couple had retaliated by renouncing families and religions. 'And never regretted it once,' Ellen had said frequently during the years between, gazing fondly at her husband. She still loved him passionately, and ever since the accident that had damaged his back she had been happy to work every hour of the day to keep him in comfort. Sometimes people wondered if his injury had really been as permanent as he claimed, but none ever dared to voice their doubts to Ellen.

Now, when Donnie, losing interest in female gossip and turning to the racing pages, said, 'See's over that pencil, hen,' she was more than ready to abandon her work and fetch the pencil, which had fallen from the arm of his chair and rolled just out of his reach.

'There you are, pet.' She returned it to his hand before going back to her seat. The pieces before her included some statues of saints, because even though she had not set foot inside the chapel since her marriage Ellen had not been able to make a complete break.

Now, she had no sooner started work again than the doorbell rang.

'Chrissie...'

'My nails are still wet.' Chrissie waggled her foot about in the air to dry the varnish, adding when her mother had trudged out into the hall. 'It'll be for her anyway.'

Sure enough, they heard the front-room door open and then close almost immediately. Ellen Borland had a finger in many pies and when the doorbell rang, which happened quite often, it was always for her.

The three left in the kitchen lapsed into silence and after a while the room door opened and closed again, then the front door closed and Ellen came back, remarking as she sat down at the table again, 'It's all go, so it is. Helpin' folk tae get through this war's wearin' me away tae a shadow.'

Chrissie, still brooding over the interrupted conversation, cast a glance at her mother's ample form and said, 'I don't ever want to have weans.'

'Of course you'll have them ... eventually, when the war's over and Stanley comes home.'

'I don't know, Mam. I don't fancy losin' my figure and drippin' milk and havin' tae stay in at nights tae look after them.'

'I'd help you,' Ellen coaxed. 'You'll come round to the idea once Stanley's home for good. It's not natural not tae have bairns, is it, Donnie?'

'Eh? Aye, I suppose so. Ye'll find that they just keep on comin', pet,' Donnie Borland explained to his daughter. 'And there's not much ye can do about it.'

'There is,' Jessie muttered, rubbing hard at the elaborate teapot in her hand. 'There's knittin' needles and gin and–'

'You'll make a lovely wee mother when the time comes, Chrissie,' Ellen broke in. 'And ye'd not begrudge me and your daddy some grandweans, would ye?'

'You've got plenty, Mam!'

Ellen and Donnie had raised five children, all married now and out in the world doing quite well for themselves. 'Only seven,' Ellen said now, 'and only one of them a wee lassie.' She picked up the elaborately framed photograph of a little girl in a snowy white Confirmation dress and veil and began to polish it lovingly. 'Isn't she a wee angel?'

The split with her church had meant that Ellen had missed out on the joy of watching her three daughters take Confirmation. It had broken her heart, and she had been secretly delighted when her eldest daughter married a Catholic, became one herself, and had her own daughter confirmed. Chrissie, too, had married into her mother's faith.

'Mebbe she looks like a wee angel there, Mam, but ye know well enough that she's a right wee bugger the rest of the time.' Chrissie said now, starting on her other foot. 'I'd drink all the gin in the world if it spared me from havin' a wean like that one.'

'You'll change your tune, lady, when Stanley comes home and the priest calls round to find out what's wrong between you that ye've no bairns.'

'Stan'll do what he's told and the priest'll get a flea in his ear if he tries tae tell me what tae do.'

'That's no way to speak of the church!'

'I've heard you say worse.'

'Donnie, tell her!'

'Put the kettle on, Chrissie,' Donnie said without looking up from his newspaper, 'and make some tea.'

'But, Daddy, my nails aren't properly dried yet!'

'I'll do it,' said Ellen, putting down her work and hauling herself out of her chair again.

Being the youngest and newest recruit at the Gordon Street fire station, Dennis Megson came in for a lot of teasing from the older men. 'Not got yerself a girlfriend yet?' they would ask. 'You want tae get a move on, son, afore all thae servicemen going about the town in their smart uniforms drain the place dry. Paisley lassies for Paisley men, eh, Dennis?'

He had learned to grin and to hold his tongue. No sense in telling them that he had quite enough to do looking after the women already in his life ... his mother and two little sisters. And right now he didn't have any time to spare for courting and walking out with girls. As well as work and studying for his night-school class, there was the backcourt vegetable garden, too.

Dennis enjoyed the manual labour on the

vegetable beds, finding that it freed his mind to think over his text books and all the things he had to memorise at work. He was turning over a section that had recently been cleared of winter turnips when he heard the clash of a metal bucket being set down on flagstones. Glancing up, he saw Lena Fulton making her way towards him, carrying a cup and a plate.

'I saw you from my window,' she said shyly, 'and I thought you might like some tea and something to eat.' Then, as he stared at her, her voice began to falter. 'Or mebbe you don't want it.'

'No! I mean, yes, I do.' He found his tongue at last, just as she was about to retreat to the tenement. 'It's very kind of you.'

Her pale face went pink as she thrust the cup and plate at him. 'It's just a wee thank you for what you did the other week, when I fell and hurt myself. I've never seen you to thank you since then.'

Dennis rammed the spade into the earth and dusted his hands together before he accepted the proffered cup and plate. 'Och, that was nothing.' He took a big swallow of tea to cover his embarrassment.

'It was more than that,' she insisted, and then, as he glanced from the cup to the plate, trying to work out how he could lift the jam sandwich without dropping the cup, 'Here, let me.' She took the plate, leaving him free to lift the food from it. 'I should have brought a tray.'

'No, it's fine,' he assured her through a mouthful of bread and jam, recalling the moment when, gently laying her on her bed, so as not to add to her hurt, he had seen the blood, red and wet, staining the towel his mother had tucked around the young woman. He had thought that she was dying, but his mother had explained later, embarrassed and unable to look him in the eye, that Mrs Fulton had lost the child she was carrying.

'You were all very kind,' she said now. 'Mrs Goudie too, and your mother.'

'That's what neighbours are for. It's as well that my mother was at home, and not at the hospital when you fell. She's a good nurse.'

'Yes, she is. And a kind woman too.' She looked around at the vegetable beds. 'Do you like digging?'

'I don't mind it. The vegetables are worth it.' Frank McCosh had a colleague with an allotment, and he was fortunate enough to get seeds and even seedlings now and again. The whole tenement, following Ellen Borland's edict that in wartime folk should look after their own, shared in the produce, whether they worked in the garden or not.

'I miss the flowers,' Lena said. 'They were nice to look out on.'

'Aye, they were. I sometimes think,' he confessed, 'that it's a good thing old Mr Brown went when he did, for it would have broken his heart to see what's happened to this place.'

'That's what I think too, only I've never liked to say it because we're all supposed to put food first now.'

'I've never said it to anyone either.' Dennis beamed down at her, delighted to discover that they shared a secret. He broke off a corner of his sandwich and tossed it to a bird that had been hopping about close by ever since he started turning the earth over. 'It's not really waste when it's eaten and enjoyed,' he said apologetically, watching the bird snatch at the offering. 'Birds need food too, and he's been working hard.' Then he rammed the last of the sandwich in his mouth, washed it down with tea, and held out the empty cup. 'Thanks.'

She nodded and turned back towards the tenement. Instead of going in she put the cup and plate down on the ground and picked up a bucket she had brought downstairs.

'Are you fetching some coal?' Dennis called over, leaving the spade where it was and hurrying across to her. 'I'll see to it for you.'

'You're busy. I can manage.'

'Ach, I'm dirty already, I might as well do it for you.' He held out his hand and after a moment's hesitation she relinquished the bucket. 'Half full will do me.'

There wasn't much in her bin, Dennis noticed as the lumps clattered into the bucket. He straightened, shaking his head when she reached out for the handle. 'I'll take it upstairs for you. It won't take a minute, and I can finish the digging when I come back down.

'Well...' she glanced around as if to see if anyone was listening, then said, 'If you're sure it isn't a bother...'

'It's not!' Dennis said fervently. 'My mother would want me to.' A stupid remark worthy of a kick in the backside, he thought at once, his face reddening as he followed Lena Fulton into the close and up the stairs.

There was something missing in the Fultons' flat and at first Dennis couldn't think what it was. True, there was little furniture other than the basic requirements, but that was common enough in these tenements. He glanced around the kitchen as he put down the coal bucket, and realised that not only was the room cold to the point of being chilly; it also gave off a bleak air of something he couldn't quite understand. Then it came to him ... the flat felt lonely.

'Thank you for your help,' Lena was saying. Her voice had become animated when she'd talked about old Mr Brown and the way he had filled the backcourt with flowers; now it was flat, as though she, too, was affected by the atmosphere in her own home.

He glanced at the small grate, neatly laid with twists of paper and a few sticks. 'Will I light the fire for you before I go?'

'It's too early. I always wait until it gets dark outside. It's comforting to have a fire then.' Lena wore a shawl over her jersey and skirt, and now she drew it closer about her shoulders. For some reason the gesture reminded him of that moment on the dark landing, when he had gathered her into his arms and carried her to her flat. He recalled it vividly; it was as though she had left a physical imprint of herself on him.

'You surely need a bit of warmth, though, for your sewing.' He indicated the material spread over the table, and the open sewing machine standing to one side.

'I manage fine. I have a pair of mitts, and this jersey's warm.'

'You know, this room feels colder than it should.' He lifted his head, testing the chill air against his face, then glanced over at the window. 'It's the window.' He went over to it, reaching across the small chipped sink to run the tips of his fingers round the edge of the pane. Gentle though his touch was, a chip of dried putty came free to rustle down into the sink. 'The glass is loose in the frame, and letting in a draught. All it needs is some fresh putty.'

'Does it?' Her voice was anxious, and when he glanced back at her he saw worry in her blue eyes ... the same deep colour, he saw now, as the bluebells under the trees in Donald's Wood, where he sometimes went walking. 'Does that mean that the window could fall out?'

All that held the glass in place was the criss-cross pattern of sticky paper which covered everyone's windows these days, to protect people from shards of glass should the pane be shattered by a bomb explosion, but Dennis, unwilling to frighten her, said reassuringly, 'No, but there's quite a draught getting in round the edge of the glass. I could fix it for you if you like.'

'You know about windows?'

'My dad could turn his hand to anything,' he boasted. 'I used to watch him working about the flat and then I helped him when I got older. One of the men at the fire station served his trade as a builder; he'd be able to tell me what to do.'

'I wouldn't want you to go to any trouble...'

'It wouldn't be a bother,' Dennis assured her. 'And it wouldn't cost you either, because he'd probably be able to give me the putty too.'

'If you're sure...'

'I'm sure,' he said firmly.

12

Cecelia jumped off the bus that had brought her back to Paisley from the Ibrox depot, gave the driver a wave as she passed his cab, and started the walk home from Paisley Cross. It was the end of her shift and she was tired, but even so she stepped out briskly because that was what the uniform demanded. Every time she put it on she felt herself turning into a different person. The old Cecelia was quiet, diffident, a little unsure of herself, but Cecelia the bus conductress was confident and able to take on the world.

Glancing down at the green jacket and skirt, wondering if wearing different clothes could really make a person different inside as well as outside, she reached the end of Moss Street and crossed the junction, heading towards Love Street.

'Hello.'

A young woman, also turning into Love Street, had paused to wait for her. As Cecelia blinked at her, the girl's smile faltered a little.

'Mrs Goudie, isn't it? I'm Chloe ... Chloe Mc-Cosh.'

'The clootie dumpling!' Cecelia suddenly remembered. Then, as the girl started to laugh, 'I don't mean you, I mean...'

'I know what you mean. I thought it was you coming along the street.'

'With my mind far away,' Cecelia admitted as they fell into step together. 'I've been up since just after four this morning. We have to be early to catch the service bus that takes us to the depot so that we can run the workers' buses. Hello.' She smiled at the little girl clutching Chloe's hand. 'Is this your wee sister?'

'No,' the child said firmly. 'I'm Daisy and I'm Grace's wee sister.' She tugged Chloe onward. 'Come on, I'll be late!'

'Daisy lives in St James Street,' Chloe explained as they hurried along. 'My mother's giving her piano lessons and I said I'd fetch her today. It's my half-day; I work in Cochran's.' Her voice, as she mentioned the big emporium, was filled with pride.

'Magritte usually brings me, but she's got toothache,' Daisy piped up, 'and my mummy won't believe that I can come through the streets perfectly well on my own. She's taking Magritte to the dentist to have the tooth pulled out but Magritte doesn't want to because the dentist will leave a big hole in her mouth and it'll bleed and it'll hurt and hurt and–'

'Yes, all right,' Chloe interrupted. 'We don't want to hear any more about poor Magritte. She's a right wee talker,' she confided in a lower tone to Cecelia. 'The only time she shuts her mouth is when she's playing the piano. She's not worked out yet how to do both at the same time, but I'm sure she will. Are you settling in all right at Number forty-two?'

'I like it fine, though I've not had much time to meet my neighbours. Well, there's you, and I've been to the Borlands' flat, and I've met old Mrs Bell and Mrs Fulton, and Mrs Megson and her son...' Cecelia's voice tailed away as she realised that one way and another she had met almost everyone without realising it.

'That'll probably be Dennis.' There was a certain ring to the girl's voice as she said the name. 'There's Ralph Megson, but he's still at school. It'll be Dennis you met.'

'That's right. A nice boy, very kind.'

'Oh, he is! And he's a great musician too, he plays the trumpet in my father's band.' This time there was no mistaking the hero worship in Chloe's voice, or the glow in her eyes as she beamed at Cecelia. The girl was head over heels in love.

'We enjoyed hearing the band practising. Are there any more evenings planned?'

'Next Friday, for a dance on Saturday night. There'll be dumpling,' Chloe said, the dimple in her left cheek deepening.

'I'll still be on the early shift, so I can look forward to the music. And to the dumpling,' Cecelia said as they turned in at their close. Once inside, Daisy shook off Chloe's restraining hand and raced ahead of them and up the stairs.

As they began to climb the first flight they heard her small hands slapping impatiently at the door panels, and by the time they gained the first landing the door of the McCosh's flat was ajar and Daisy's shrill voice could be heard chattering away in the depths of the flat.

'I'd invite you in, but with Mum having a piano lesson…'

'I'm too tired to be a proper visitor anyway,' Cecelia assured the girl, and began to climb the next flight, wishing, as she often did when returning home after a long and busy shift, that she lived on the lowest floor.

Chloe was a nice lassie, she thought as she climbed, and pretty, too. She hoped that Dennis Megson liked her as much as she clearly liked him.

Ellen Borland was standing at her own door, talking to a youth. Their heads were close together, and Ellen seemed to be giving him low-voiced instructions. As soon as they became aware of Cecelia, Ellen said something to the boy, who immediately bolted across to the stairs leading up to the top floor. As he went, he stuffed something into his jacket pocket.

'It's you, Cecelia hen,' Ellen Borland said easily. 'Just gettin' home from work, eh? How's the job goin', then?'

'Very well. I like it more than I thought I would.'

'I thought it might be your cup of tea. Here, talking of tea, I've got a nice wee bit of cold ham that would just do you a treat. Come on in.'

'If you don't mind, Mrs Borland, my feet are aching and I'd like to get these shoes off…'

'Wait here a minute, then,' the woman said, and hurried into her hallway, to reappear almost at once.

'There you are.' She proffered a small grease-proof parcel.

'I can't take it, Mrs Borland!'

'Ach away, you need the nourishment and thae rations books scarce give ye enough tae feed a cat. I'm just lucky, havin' friends that can help me out.' Ellen thrust the parcel into Cecelia's hands. 'And I believe in passin' luck around. That way, it comes back tenfold.'

'There's not much I can do in return, though.'

'Ach, you can always let me off my fare if I get on to your bus some time,' the woman said cheerfully. 'Don't worry about it, pet, those that can help me do help me, and I'm grateful. Young Ralph Megson, that you just saw me talkin' tae ... he goes messages for me now and again. A nice lad, well brought up. I like tae see young ones with good manners.' Ellen was in the process of settling her shoulder comfortably against the doorframe for a good chat when a voice called from within the flat.

'Ellen hen, what about that tea ye were supposed tae be makin'? My throat's parched!'

'Better go and see tae Donnie,' Mrs Borland said. 'Enjoy the ham, pet.'

It was a day or two before Dennis got the chance to return to Lena Fulton's flat. When he tapped on the door he had to wait for so long that he was beginning to think she had gone out. Then, hearing soft movement from the other side of the panels, he knocked again.

'Who is it?' a voice asked timidly,

He squatted down and opened the letterbox.

‘It’s me, Dennis Megson.’

‘What d’you want?’

‘I’m here to mend that window of yours. I’ve got everything I need for it.’

There was another pause, then he straightened as he heard the snib being lifted.

‘Come in,’ Lena said as the door was opened wide enough to admit him. Then, as he stepped into the dark hallway, ‘Go on into the kitchen.’

Glancing back as he obeyed, he saw the woman peering out on to the landing as though making sure that it was empty.

‘We’re neighbours, Mrs Fulton,’ he said when she followed him into the kitchen. ‘There’s no harm in me coming to do a wee bit of work for you. I’d do the same for Mrs Goudie if she needed help, and for old Mrs Bell ... only she sent me off with a flea in my ear the one time I tried to offer to do something for her. Anyway, Mrs Borland looks out for her.’

Lena leaned against the doorframe, huddling the shawl about her thin shoulders as usual, and chewing at her bottom lip. ‘I’d not want anyone thinking that I’m takin’ advantage of your kindness,’ she said at last.

‘It’s not kindness, it’s...’ he fumbled for a word, and could come up with nothing better than, ‘neighbourliness. I’m always happy to fetch some messages for you, or bring up coal, or...’ he indicated the canvas bag in his hand, ‘do a bit of repair work.’

‘George doesn’t like us to be obligated to folk.’

‘I know that Mr Fulton would see to your window himself if he was here, but he’s away just now and so it makes sense for me to help out. I'd never want you to feel that you owed me anything for my help.' Dennis wished that he could get her to understand. 'He'd surely be pleased to know that your neighbours were there for you when you needed them.' Then, as she said nothing, but just stared at him, worrying, 'I'll just get on with mending that window, eh?'

After a while, she went back to her own work. Dennis found the whirring of the sewing machine pleasant to listen to.

'There now,' he said as he stepped back, 'that didn't take any time at all, and I'm sure you'll feel this place much warmer now.'

The whirring stopped and he felt Lena's shoulder brush his as she came to look at the window. 'It looks grand.' The admiration in her voice made his chest swell with pride.

'Ach, it wasn't any bother at all.'

'Are you sure I can't pay you something for your time?' she offered hesitantly, and he grinned down at her.

'My charges are a wee bit steep; I usually ask for a cup of tea, but if you can't manage that you can always owe me till another day.'

The first part of the sentence had made her frown anxiously and catch her lower lip between her teeth once more; when he mentioned the tea, she blinked at him for a second or two, then laughed before she could stop herself. He had never heard her laugh before ... come to think of it, until recently he had not even heard her speak.

'I think I can manage that.'

'Good. I'll just wash my hands first.'

'There's some hot water in the kettle.' She poured it into a basin sitting within the old, chipped sink, then refilled the kettle, and stepped out of his way. He spread his hands out before him, eyeing them and then the small piece of yellow washing soap by the edge of the sink doubtfully.

'D'you have anything I can use to get the worst of this stuff off first? Turpentine, mebbe?'

'There might be some in the big cupboard in the lobby.' Lena was lighting the gas stove. 'George ... my husband ... keeps some of his things there.'

'Right you are.'

In the small hallway, lit only by the fanlight, Dennis had to drop to his knees and rummage about amongst the clutter on the floor of the cupboard. He pulled out a small tool bag first, then some tins of paint and varnish.

When he returned to the kitchen he was holding a bottle. 'I found this Ligroin. It's a white spirit that painters use to thin down paint and varnish.'

She nodded. 'It'll be for George's work.'

'Did you know that it's inflammable?'

'Is that bad?'

'It's best to keep it away from naked flame.'

'It's quite safe in that cupboard, surely. Nobody's going to strike a match in there.'

'I know, but...' he hesitated, reluctant to frighten her by talking about the possibility of fire during an air raid, then said, 'It's just that this sort of stuff's best kept outside. I could take it all down to the shed for you, if you want. It would be safe there.'

'But it's George's,' she said again. 'He'd not like his things to be touched.'

'He surely wouldn't want anything to happen to you.'

'It won't, will it? Not if I leave it alone.'

Dennis went to the sink, where he carefully tipped a little of the liquid into the palm of one hand. 'I'll screw the top on tight and put it right at the back, out of the way,' he said as he cleaned his hands, 'but you should mebbe ask him in your next letter to let you store it outside, just to be on the safe side.'

He returned the Ligroin to the cupboard, checking the other tins and bottles to make sure that they were well sealed, then went back to the sink, where he picked up the sliver of yellow soap.

'Mr McCosh is working in the garden,' he said, glancing through the window. 'I'll go down and give him a hand.'

'After you've had your tea. Here.' Lena handed him a small towel as he shook the water from his hands. 'Have you not done enough for today?'

'It's all right. I get peace tae think when I'm digging. There's not much chance of that in our place, with five of us.'

'When I was a wee girl my father had an allotment. He gave me a corner to myself and I planted flowers in it.' A slight smile warmed her pale mouth at the memory.

'Have you never thought of working down there yourself?'

Her eyes widened and then narrowed as she frowned, thinking the proposal over. Finally she said, 'I'd just get in the way. I don't know much about planting and pruning.'

'You don't need to, there's weeding, and earthing up the potatoes and that sort of thing. And you'd not be in the way, the more folk helping the better. Mr McCosh does most of it and I try to help him as much as I can. Mrs McCosh does a bit now and again but she's busy with housework and piano lessons and her WVS work, and my mother works hard enough at the infirmary as it is.'

'She's a good woman,' Lena said. 'You're right, she does enough. Mebbe I should take my turn at working in the garden.' Then, shyly, 'Could I work alongside you? I don't know Mr McCosh very well. You can show me what to do.'

'I'll knock on your door the next time I'm going down there and if you've got the time, you can come with me.'

Leaning back against the sink as he dried his hands, he watched her gather up the cloth strewn over the table, shaking it out then folding it again and again until it was small enough to put aside, on the top of the dresser in the recess that had once held a bed. Then she covered the treadle sewing machine, gathered pins and spools of thread, and put them into an old box. The kettle boiled, and she turned her attention to making tea in a battered metal pot, still with the same swift, deft movements.

'I can feel a difference,' he said, and when she looked at him, puzzled, he jerked his head in the direction of the window at his back. 'No draught.'

'Oh. You're right, it makes a real difference. You're a good neighbour,' she said, and he felt his face redden.

He was further embarrassed, when he sat down at the table, to find that she had made up a cheese sandwich for him.

'But that's your ration. You mustn't go giving it away to folk!'

'You deserve something to eat after the work you've done.' She indicated the window. 'I'm going to be warmer now, thanks to you. Anyway, I don't eat much.'

That, Dennis thought, studying her thin arms and wan face, was obvious. A bit of gardening in the fresh air, or as fresh as the air was allowed to get in Glen Street, would do her good. Aloud, he said, 'Can we not share? Then I won't feel so greedy.'

She laughed, ducking her head shyly and glancing up at him from beneath her lashes, 'If you insist.'

'I do.' He took the knife she offered, and cut the sandwich in two, offering her half.

For a moment they ate in silence, then she asked, 'Have you lived here long?'

'I was born here. My parents moved in when they got married. I like Glen Street, it's a great place to live.'

'Are you still at the school?'

He felt his face redden. 'Not for a long time. I'm training to be a fireman.'

'Oh! I forgot...' A soft pink flush came over her pale face. 'How stupid of me.'

'It's all right. I said just the same thing to Chloe

McCosh a few weeks back. Now I know why she glared at me. Not that I'm glaring at you,' Dennis added hurriedly, and almost choked on a mouthful of bread and cheese. He took a swallow of tea to wash it down.

'A fireman?' She looked impressed.

'My father was a fireman,' he told her proudly. 'I'm following in his footsteps.'

'George ... my husband ... followed in his father's footsteps too. His father has his own painting and decorating business in Well Street.'

'Fulton's ... I've heard of them. I didn't realise that it was your man's da that owned it. It must be useful to have a painter...' His voice died away as he looked round the shabby room.

'You know what they say about a cobbler's children never having any shoes. The business keeps George and his father and brother busy, so he never found the time to do this place. He's always promising, but ... well, he did start varnishing the woodwork in this room when we first moved into the place, but then he was called up before he got round to finishing it. I thought he might manage to finish that the last time he was home on leave, but he couldn't be bothered.'

'I'll do it for you if you want.'

'It's good of you to offer, but George wouldn't like it.' She drew the shawl closer as though protecting herself against something. 'Anyway, you've got enough to do. You play the trumpet in that band, don't you?'

'Mr McCosh's band? Yes, I do.'

'I saw you taking it into their flat a while back, when they were having a practice.'

'Aye, I remember.' She and her husband had been coming up the stairs at the time, and in his haste, Dennis had almost bumped into George Fulton. He could still remember the scowl the man had given him.

'D'you like playing?'

'It's grand!'

'Where did you learn?'

'In the Boys' Brigade. Trumpet and cornet,' he told her proudly. 'I played the cornet mostly while I was in the BB, because it's best for marching music. The trumpet's best for a dance band.'

'It must be very difficult.'

'Not once you realise that you don't want to put pressure on the instrument. Most folk,' he explained, 'push the mouthpiece against their lips and blow into it, but that only makes their muscles ache. The way to do it is to just rest your lips against the instrument and use them to shape the notes.'

'How do you make the music go up and down?'

'Tonguing ... using your tongue to shape the notes. And there are three valves as well. I use my fingers to operate them.' Then, as she frowned and pursed her lips in her attempt to follow the explanation, he added, 'I could bring the trumpet down some time, if you like, and show you what I mean.'

'Would you?' Her face lit up, and then suddenly she was solemn again. 'I'd not want you to go to the trouble...'

'It wouldn't be any trouble at all. I'd like to,' Dennis said. 'It's not often that anyone's interested in hearing about music.'

13

'I'd not want Charlie to think that there's anything special between us,' Chloe told Marion. 'He's a nice enough lad, but I'm too young to get serious about that sort of thing.'

'You speak for yourself.' They were in the McCosh kitchen, ripping down an old jersey of Julia's. It was evening, and Chloe was in charge of her brothers because her parents were both out, her mother on WVS work and her father on Home Guard duty. 'I really like Robert,' Marion went on dreamily. 'I'd not mind getting serious about him.'

'Don't be daft, he'll be getting called up soon and there's no knowing what might happen then.'

'That's right, tell me that he's going to get himself killed. That's a nice thing to say!'

'That's not what I meant. I'm just saying that folk change a lot when they go away from home. He might be a different person when he comes back, or he might have met someone else. Or you could meet someone else,' Chloe tried to explain. Although they were both working women, it seemed to her that she and Marion were still poised on the verge of adulthood, not quite ready to plunge in, because once they did there would be no turning back, ever.

'Robert says we were meant for each other.'

'Are you sure he's not just telling you that because he…'

'He what?'

'You know,' Chloe hinted, then as her friend continued to stare blankly, 'him going away to fight and all; he isn't trying to get you to do anything you shouldn't, is he?'

Marion's uncomprehending stare lasted for a few more seconds, then realisation set in, swiftly followed by shock. 'Chloe McCosh, how could you even think of such a thing? What d'you take me for? What d'you take Robert for?' Her voice rose to a screech, and Leslie, who had been playing in the front room with his train set, put his head round the door.

'Is everything all right?'

'No it is not!' Marion snapped, while Chloe smiled at her brother and said, 'Everything's fine. We were just singing.'

'Oh. Can I have a biscuit?'

'No, you know you're not supposed to.'

'I'm hungry!'

'You've not long had your dinner. Go and play.'

'I'm tired of playing on my own. I'm going out the back to play with Duncan.'

'It's getting dark, and it's nearly time for bed.' Chloe cast a glance at the kitchen clock. 'I'll be calling him in any minute now.'

'But I want to go out…' His voice took on a nasal whine, and Marion shot an irritated glance at him.

'Mebbe just the one biscuit,' Chloe capitulated, laying down the half-unravelled jersey sleeve and going to fetch the biscuit barrel. 'And only if you go back to your train set.'

'There's times,' Marion remarked pointedly as the door closed behind Leslie, 'when I'm glad that I'm the youngest of my family.'

'Mebbe now you know what your big sisters have had to put up with.'

'So what's wrong with Charlie Hepburn, then, that you won't get serious about him?' Marion wanted to know as they got on with their work.

'Nothing's wrong with him. He's a pleasant, decent lad and I like him, but I don't think I like him as much as he likes me. He's got his mother to ask me round for my tea on Saturday. His father's going to be home and Charlie wants me to meet him.'

'Oh, that sounds serious,' Marion mocked.

'I wish he hadn't, with his father being the way he is. An important man,' Chloe explained as Marion raised her eyebrows. 'Travelling round the country and making speeches the way he does.'

'What are you going to wear?'

'I thought my navy dress with the puff sleeves and the wee flowers all over it.'

'It might be cold for short sleeves.'

'I can wear my good pale blue cardigan over it.'

'Mmm.' Marion considered for a moment. 'I think that would be all right,' she agreed; then, holding up the ball of wool she had just created from one sleeve of the jersey, 'D'you think that this would knit up into a decent hat?'

'You'd suit the colour. And you could use this sleeve to make mitts, or mebbe a wee scarf.'

'You're not thinking of making a hat from it

too, are you? We couldn't both wear the same colour.'

'I was wondering about a sort of waistcoat. You could borrow it, if you want, when you wear the hat.'

'And you could borrow the hat when you wear the waistcoat,' Marion said, and the quarrel between them was over.

When the jersey had been converted to four balls of crinkled wool Chloe dragged herself back to her duties as babysitter, instructing Leslie to tidy away his train set and then going downstairs to fetch Duncan in.

He was squatting down, a bucket by his side, grubbing happily in the border of the big vegetable bed, while Dennis Megson, stripped to his shirtsleeves although the wind was keen, dug a trench. Someone else was working in the far corner, huddled down over the earth, but as it was getting dark, Chloe couldn't make out who it was.

'Ach, do I have to go up?' Duncan whined when his sister arrived. 'I'm helping Dennis.' He shook the battered pail at her. 'I'm weeding.'

'And making a good job of it.' Dennis drove the spade effortlessly into the earth and straightened, wiping the back of an arm over his forehead. 'But it's time for us all to call it a day, son. It's getting too dark to see what we're supposed to be doing. We don't want the carrots and potatoes to be growing down the way by mistake because we couldnae see which way up to plant them.'

'You're not planting, you're weeding and digging,' Chloe pointed out.

'Le ... Mrs Fulton's putting in onions.' Dennis indicated the far corner, where the third gardener still worked, apparently oblivious to the conversation, then raised his voice slightly, 'We're going in now, Mrs Fulton, it's getting too dark to work on.'

As the woman rose and turned, Chloe saw that she had been sitting on a low stool. Dennis hurried over to lift it in one hand, offering his free arm to Lena to help her over the uneven earth and on to the flagged path. Once there, she released her hold on him and scurried into the tenement, with a murmured 'Good evening,' as she passed the others.

'I didn't know she was interested in gardening,' Chloe said as they turned to follow her.

'She's doing her bit, same as young Duncan here.' He fetched his jacket from the top of one of the coal bins as they passed, and slung it over his shoulder.

'Can I help you next time?' the lad asked eagerly.

'Any time. We can always use a good strong set of muscles. Good night, then,' Dennis said when they reached the first landing.

'Go on in, Duncan,' Chloe ordered her brother, and then, to Dennis, 'Are you working tonight?'

'Not at the station, but I'm fire watching.' He had volunteered to become part of the street team. 'My mother's on duty at the hospital so I'm keeping an eye on the rest of them as well,' he added.

She glanced round to see if Duncan had gone indoors, and was irritated to find him breathing on the brass letterbox then writing on it with one finger. 'Duncan McCosh, will you stop that at once and get indoors when I tell you? Now I'll have to fetch a cloth and polish it up again.'

'I'll do it,' he said, and disappeared into the flat. Chloe turned to Dennis, pinning a tolerant, older-sister smile on her mouth, only to find that he was already halfway up the flight leading to his own home.

There was nobody at home when Dennis returned on Thursday after working an early shift. He took the trumpet from its box beneath his bed and carried it downstairs.

'I brought it,' he said when Lena Fulton opened the door. Then, as she looked blankly from his face to the instrument he was holding out in his two hands, as though it was an offering, 'My trumpet. You said that you'd like to see it, but if you're busy I can come back another time.' He should have thought, he told himself, sick with embarrassment; he should have realised that she was just being polite when she said she wanted to hear him play.

Then, just as his heart was hurtling down towards his sturdy boots, she blinked the blankness out of her eyes and said, 'Oh, your trumpet! Of course I want to hear it. Come on in.'

In the kitchen, he looked at the open sewing machine and the materials strewn about the table. 'You're busy.'

'Not too busy, though.' Already, she was gathering up the cloth with those swift, neat feminine movements that fascinated him. 'I'm lucky, I'm getting plenty of work from folk these days; now that things are hard to get, they're all wanting their clothes made over. But I can make time for myself when I want. And for you.'

She listened solemnly as he explained the trumpet's functions, then asked hesitantly, 'Do you mind if I ... can I hold it?'

'Of course.' He put it into her outstretched hands and watched as she ran her fingers over it. A slow smile broke over her face.

'It feels ... comforting.'

Dennis grinned in return. 'That's what I think too. Try playing it. Don't push it against your lips,' he cautioned as she lifted the instrument to her mouth. 'Just lay them gently against the mouthpiece, as though you were giving it a kiss, then breathe into it.'

She made several tries at it, but had to give up and return the trumpet to him. 'You play it for me,' she said, and he put the mouthpiece to his lips and played the opening bars of 'The Way You Look Tonight', softly, so that nobody outside or upstairs would hear it. Lena listened, entranced, and when he stopped, after a long, hushed pause she said, 'That was lovely.'

'It's not too difficult when you know how.'

'It sounds as though you're part of the trumpet when you're playing, and it's part of you.'

He beamed at her. Nobody else had put it quite so well. 'That's exactly what it feels like.'

'What happens if you hurt your mouth?'

'Then I can't play. I mind once when I was supposed to play the cornet for a Boys' Brigade parade, and I got the toothache. I couldnae bear the touch of the mouthpiece and I'd tae miss the parade.' He grinned. 'My mother says the good thing about it is that I'd never let myself get mixed up in a fight, for fear of hurting my mouth. And she's right. Would you like tae hear something else?'

She nodded, then as the final notes of 'The Talk of the Town' died away, said, 'That's lovely.'

'You can hear more tomorrow night. We've got another practice. You could open your door and listen to it, everyone else does that. Sometimes folk from outside come in and sit on the stairs to listen.'

'Mebbe I will,' she said.

Somewhat against her husband's wishes, Julia had invited Charlie Hepburn to sit in on the band practice.

'There's little enough room for the four of us as it is, and you know what a practice is like ... all stops and starts. We have to be free to concentrate on getting it right.'

'That's exactly what Charlie wants ... to see musicians working at getting things right. And he'll not take up all that much space,' she coaxed.

'I suppose you've already told the lad he can come.'

'I might have mentioned it.'

'Oh, all right,' said Frank McCosh, realising that he had already lost the battle. 'But just this once, mind.'

'We'll not be playing the way you've heard us play in the dance hall,' he cautioned Charlie when the boy arrived. 'This is a practice so we'll be stopping and starting and stopping again to get things right. You'll soon get fed up listening to the same bits over and over again.'

'I'll be interested in seeing how you all work at things to get them just right.'

'Well, as right as we can,' Frank was saying drily as a knock came to the outer door. Chloe rushed to open it.

'Charlie's come to watch the practice,' she told Dennis as he came into the hall.

'Your boyfriend?'

'He's a friend, not a boyfriend!'

'He's a friend, and he's a boy, so does that not make him a boyfriend?' Dennis said maddeningly, and then turned as slow heavy footsteps began to trudge up the stairs from below. 'Hello, Bert. Grand evening.'

'It is if ye only have tae come down the stairs tae get here,' Bert grumbled as he appeared. 'Some of us have tae walk further than that, and it's bloody cold out. Oh sorry, hen.' He whipped his cap off as he reached the landing and saw Chloe in the doorway. 'Never noticed you there.'

'Think yourself lucky that you didnae have to carry your drums and all,' Dennis said cheerfully. The drums shared the McCosh's big hall cupboard with Frank's Home Guard uniform and kit. 'We've got a visitor tonight. He's a friend of young Chloe's and he's a boy, but he's not a boyfriend.'

'Eh?'

'Oh, for goodness' sake,' Chloe snapped, exasperated. 'Are you coming in or are you not?'

'What are the two of you on about?' Bert asked,

bewildered, as she flounced back into the flat.

'Don't let it bother you, I was just enjoying a bit of a tease. After you, sir!' As he stepped back to let the elderly man precede him into the flat, Dennis glanced across the landing and smiled as he saw that Lena Fulton's door was very slightly ajar.

Lena had pulled a chair from the kitchen into the hall, where she sat in the dark, waiting. She heard someone running down the stairs from one of the flats above, then the sound of knocking followed by the murmur of voices. She recognised Dennis Megson's laugh, and then there were more footsteps, this time coming up the stairs, and a deeper voice joined in the conversation. Then the door closed, and about five minutes later the music began.

She rose very quietly and opened her own door a little wider, peering through the crack to make sure that the landing was empty. Satisfied that it was, and that anyone passing was unlikely to notice her door ajar, she was about to return to her seat when the small band began to play 'The Way You Look Tonight'.

Lena paused, listening, unaware that she had begun to lean slightly towards the source of the music, her good leg going on tiptoe. Her thin body began to sway gently in time to the rhythm.

In his front room, Frank McCosh lowered his saxophone and tossed a brief nod at Dennis, who took a half-step forward, raising the trumpet to his lips. 'This,' he thought to himself, 'is for Lena.'

And across the landing, safe within the darkness of her narrow hall, Lena Fulton danced to the trumpet's golden, rounded notes, her body dipping each time her weight transferred to her shorter leg. The music stole in through the narrow space at the door to wrap itself about her like a soft, warm shawl. For the first time in months, perhaps years, she was happy, and at peace.

'They're holding another band practice downstairs,' Cecelia wrote, 'and I can't stop thinking about the last time, when we danced out on the landing. Oh, Fergus, I can't bear being so far away from you...'

The writing paper suddenly blurred, and she knuckled her eyes with a fist, then tutted with irritation when she realised that she had succeeded only in releasing the tears to splash on to the letter. She tried blotting them with her sleeve, but that only smeared the ink. Sighing, she crumpled up the page and threw it into the meagre little fire she had allowed herself, and then fumbled in her pocket for a handkerchief.

Once her eyes were properly dried and her nose blown hard she pulled the writing pad over and dipped the pen into the bottle of ink. Fergus had enough on his mind without her moaning and weeping all over his letter.

'They're holding another band practice downstairs,' she began again, 'which meant that I got a nice bit of dumpling, which I enjoyed for my tea. Not that they need to bribe me on practice nights, I love listening to the music. The people in the tenement are all friendly, and I am getting to know them and to feel at home.

'You'll never guess what happened the other day at work. We always have to check the buses after each shift and hand in anything that has been left behind. And I found a whole, unopened bottle of whisky, in a paper bag under the seat! When I showed it to him, Harry said that I didn't have to hand it in, I could keep it and nobody would know. He was desperate to get his hands on it. Well, *I* would know for one, and so would the poor soul that had left it behind by accident, so I took it into the office when we got back to the depot. The inspector was impressed, I think. He said that not every clippie would have done that. Harry isn't speaking to me at the moment, and some of the other drivers are being very offhand with me, but that can't be...'

'Oh, blast and bother!' she suddenly said aloud, staring down at the page she had almost covered with her neat writing. She had completely forgotten her decision to wait until Fergus's next leave before telling him the truth about her job, and now she had almost given the game away in a letter!

'Stupid woman!' she muttered as the second page flared up in the fireplace. At this rate, she would run out of writing paper, and it was hard enough to find these days.

Sighing, she started afresh on a new page. 'They're holding another band practice downstairs...'

14

'Here, let me help.'

Lena Fulton flinched as a hand came out of nowhere and took hold of the handle of her shopping basket. Then, peering up at the man who had stopped her on her way along the pavement, she said in relief, 'Oh, it's you.'

'Only me, on my way home like yourself. Did you think you were being robbed?' Dennis asked with a grin.

'No, it was just... I can manage,' she said. 'There's not much in it.'

'You're right there.' He glanced down at the two small parcels in the basket. 'But I'd like to carry it for you anyway.'

He had turned to walk alongside her, the basket already in his hand, and so she had no option but to let him accompany her. It was a moment before she realised that he had, indeed, turned before falling into step with her.

'You weren't on your way home, you were walking in the other direction.'

'Was I? I must have been going somewhere else then, but for the life of me I can't think where, so it can't have been important. So I might as well walk back to the tenement with you. Did you hear the music the other night?' he asked, before she could argue.

'Aye. It was good to hear music again.'

'Again?'

'My brother used to play the violin. Are you sure you can't remember where you were going when you saw me?' Walking along the street like this, in broad daylight where anyone might see them together, worried her. What if Aunt Cathy decided to call in and saw her with Dennis Megson? What if she mentioned it to George when he was next home on leave?

'I'm quite sure,' he said, and she quickened her step and kept as far away from him as she could, so that nobody could mistake them for a couple.

Dennis sensed her nervousness; he couldn't do otherwise because it radiated from her like spokes from the axle of a wheel. He fell silent until they were nearing Number 42, then as Lena reached out and almost snatched the basket from him, he asked, 'D'you ever go walking in the Fountain Gardens?'

'I've been there, but not often.'

'I go quite a lot. I wouldnae mind going there now, for it's a nice day. D'you fancy a wee stroll?'

'No, I couldn't! I'm far too busy!'

'Oh well. I'm going anyway,' he said, 'so if you change your mind, we'll mebbe meet up.'

Lena scurried up the stairs, head down as usual, and rushed into her flat. In the kitchen she put the basket down on the table and stood gripping the handles tightly until her breathing slowed. Then she started to unfasten her coat, looking round the four walls of the kitchen. They might as well be the walls of a cell, she thought, suddenly sickened by the limitations of her daily life. At least when George was home there was shopping for two and not just for herself. And on those days when he was in a good mood, they sometimes went out for a walk together. When he was gone, it never occurred to her to go anywhere other than to the shops for essential supplies, or to return work she had completed or, occasionally, on a visit to her aunt's flat in William Street, in Paisley's West End. She stopped unbuttoning her coat and went to the single window. Dennis was right, it was a nice day. The April sky was blue, with little white puffs of cloud floating across it.

Lena drew a deep breath, but only stale air filled her lungs. She bit her lip and turned to stare round the kitchen and then, making up her mind, she hastily buttoned her coat again and hurried from the flat and down the stairs, anxious to return to the fresh breezy day before she lost her nerve.

The large stretch of land bordered by Glen Street, Caledonia Street and Love Street had originally been the Hope Temple Gardens, created in the eighteenth century by Paisley manufacturer and florist John Love 'for the pleasure of the people of the town'. Over a hundred years later the area was bought by Thomas Coats, a member of a large family that had sprung from humble beginnings to become a local employer and benefactor. The Coats family had built the huge Ferguslie Thread Mill complex in Paisley's West End, and had then spun its web world-wide, with Paisley as its centre.

After creating a splendid park fit to grace the largest and most sophisticated city in the realm,

Thomas Coats had in May 1868 handed it over to the townsfolk to enjoy as their own, a haven of peace and greenery within the busy industrial town.

Still in a hurry, afraid that if she slowed down she would lose her nerve and bolt for home, Lena went through the gates and along one of the wide walkways that radiated from the centre. Dennis was sitting on a bench beside the magnificent fountain; hesitating, she turned to look at the gate, with some idea of scuttling back home to safety, then she dug her fists into her coat pockets and made herself walk on.

'I was thinking...' he said without turning his head when she sat down beside him, 'that it must be a grand feeling to be able to make a place like this and just give it away for folk to enjoy.' Then, turning to bathe her in one of his wide grins, 'On the other hand, the man that did it lived in a fine big house with a garden mebbe twice this size, all to himself.'

'It was still a good thing to do.'

'Aye, you're right.' He nodded at the nearest of the four huge sea lions in the bottom pool. 'I wonder what that fellow thinks of all the changes he's seen in the past seventy years.'

Lena, her racing heart beginning to slow at last, studied the beast's raised head. 'Whatever he thinks, he's keeping it to himself,' she said, and Dennis gave a bark of laughter.

'You're right. I wish, though, that that man over there had written something about it all.' He glanced over at the statue of Rabbie Burns close by.

‘It’s nice here, isn’t it?’ Lena drew in a deep breath, and sat back, looking round at the broad stretches of grass, the flowerbeds, the lush trees stirring in the breeze. ‘I should come more often.’

‘I come in quite a lot. It’s a great place if you just want to sit and think about things. You’d scarce know you were in the town.’

For a long time they sat in comfortable silence, content to study the fountain and the statue. Lena finally broke it. ‘I enjoyed the band practice very much,’ she said. ‘You’re all very clever.’

‘You should come to a dance some time and hear us properly. Lots of folk come just for the music,’ he hurried on as he saw her beginning to shake her head. ‘You don’t have to dance, you could just sit at the side and listen.’

‘George wouldn’t like it, not while he’s away.’

Dennis almost asked if George was opposed to his wife having any sort of life at all, but he stopped himself just in time. It was none of his business. Instead, he asked casually, ‘That brother of yours who’s musical; does he live in Paisley too?’

‘He did, until the war started. Then he went into the navy and his ship was torpedoed almost at once.’

‘I’m sorry.’

‘So am I,’ Lena said. ‘But these things happen when there’s a war.’ Then, while he was still wondering what to say next, ‘Alfie. He was christened Alfred, after my grandfather, but we always called him Alfie. It suited him better. Alfred always sounds like a middle-aged name to me.’

'I suppose that was because it was your grandfather's name.'

'You're right,' she said, surprised. 'D'you know, I never thought of that before. Alfie liked to play the sort of music you'd hear at concerts. He used to take me to concerts. I liked that.'

The fresh air had coaxed some colour into her face, and memories had softened and curved her mouth and given her blue eyes a soft, dewy look. The breath caught in Dennis's throat as he realised that he was probably seeing the young Lena that George Fulton had fallen in love with.

'Is it your mother that sometimes visits you?' he asked, and then, wondering if she would think that he had been spying on her, 'I've seen her at your door once or twice when I was going up and down the stairs.'

'That's my aunt. She looked after me and Alfie after our parents died of the consumption. Though I was working by then. We could have managed fine between us, but I think my aunt still saw us as bairns.'

'Folk do that; my mother for one. To hear the way she speaks sometimes, you'd think that I was still a child and she had to look out for me, when she's got more than enough on her plate.'

All at once Dennis began to pour out his worries about his mother, who never seemed to get enough rest. 'She works hard at the infirmary, and now she's taken to doing extra work at one of the First Aid Posts as well. And she tries too hard to take my father's place on top of everything else.'

'She's a fine woman. She was very kind to me

when I had my accident.'

'My dad used to say that she'd a heart the size of Glasgow.' Dennis laughed at the memory. 'But it's true, for she cares about everyone. She'd look after the whole world if she could, but she needs someone to look after her, the way my father did. The girls are good, though. Bessie's become a right wee housewife; she doesn't even seem to mind standing in queues after school to get the messages, and she knows everything there is to know about coupons and money. Amy's a great help too, and at least I'm bringing in some money now. I wish I earned enough to support all of us.'

'You will, one day,' Lena said, and then got to her feet. 'I have to go now. I've got work to do.'

'I'll walk back with you.'

'No!' she said sharply. 'Best not.'

He watched her walk away from him, head down, and was glad that she had stopped him before he mentioned Ralph. Speaking of his growing suspicions about his brother to anyone, even Lena or Tom McIntosh at the fire station, would have been a betrayal.

Ralph was without doubt the most intelligent member of the family; unlike Dennis, a steady plodder who enjoyed learning for its own sake, the younger boy had a quicksilver mind that learned quickly, then grew bored just as swiftly. To Ralph, school was a prison and he couldn't wait to be free of it. He thirsted continuously after adventure, and his main hope these days was that the war would continue until he was old enough to become involved. He had already made one attempt to enlist in the army, and had been furious when the recruitment officer told him kindly to go back to his mammy and give it a year or two yet.

It was Ralph's hunger for the material things of life, and for the money to buy them, that concerned Dennis the most.

There were ways to satisfy such a hunger, and for folk like the Megsons, folk who had very little to begin with, most of these ways were illegal.

Lena had disappeared from sight now. Dennis began to walk towards the gate nearest home, deep in thought.

Chloe, standing at the other side of the gardens and almost hidden from Dennis by the fountain, watched him walk away. She was fond of strolling through the gardens, and did it frequently, but this was the first time she had ever seen Dennis there with Mrs Fulton.

The two of them had looked so cosy, with their heads close together as though discussing something very important. But what could Dennis and Mrs Fulton possibly want to discuss? Chloe wondered, confusion, unease and a stab of jealousy mingling within her.

The children were shabbily dressed and not as clean as they might have been, and the woman's eyes were red and swollen in an ashen face. When they boarded the bus at Paisley's West End the older girl steered the woman to a seat, sitting beside her and patting her shoulder now and again, while the younger children, a girl and a boy, claimed the seat in front and immediately knelt up on it so that they could look at the other two over its back. Their small faces were tight with worry, their eyes solemn.

Going to collect their fares, Cecelia wondered if they had received that most dreaded of visitations, a telegram. These days, all telegrams meant bad news; a husband, father, son, brother or fiancé lost in action, taken prisoner, killed. Every time she herself saw a telegraph boy in the street her heart retreated into such a knot of fear that it almost stopped.

'Are you all right?' she asked as the woman fumbled in a purse that looked as worn as herself, bringing the money out coin by coin. 'D'you need help?'

'Nothin' you can help with, hen, though it's kind of you tae ask. It's my sister in Glasgow that's been taken ill and I've been sent for. Her man's in the forces and she's...' she glanced at the children, then leaned forward slightly to mouth the words, 'havin' a baby.' Then, aloud, 'And she's on her own so I'll have to go on the train.' The words rattled out as though once started, they refused to stop. 'She's had a lot of trouble that way before, poor soul. And my own man's away too, and when I took the weans to his mother's she was out so I'll have to take them with me and the wee ones are both under five so I don't pay for them,' she ended in a rush, indicating the two smallest children.

The girl was certainly less than five years old, but as for the boy... Cecelia opened her mouth and then closed it again. One missed fare wouldn't hurt, she told herself as she stamped the ticket, and the poor woman had more than enough to cope with as it was. In any case, the clippies had to use their own discretion where youngsters were concerned, for it was a company rule that no child should be put off a bus, even if he or she did not have the money to pay the fare. In this case, Celia decided, she was using her discretion.

When she had handed over the tickets she dug into her pocket and brought out a small bag of sweets. The children's eyes lit up and the smaller ones each dipped an eager fist into the paper bag then crammed the sweets into their mouths.

'What d'ye say tae the kind lady?' the woman prompted them, and they murmured a dribbly 'Thank you' round their sweets. The older girl shook her head shyly, and then as her mother nudged her, she took a sweet and thanked Cecelia before popping it into her mouth.

'Have one yourself.' She held the bag out towards the woman.

'It's very kind of you, but no thanks. They're chewy sweeties, and my teeth are nae too good. I don't want the toothache on top of my other worries, hen.'

The bus filled at the next stop, and Cecelia noticed on her rounds that the woman had gathered her brood together, squeezing the four of them into the one seat so that other people could sit down. At least she was more considerate than some.

'Move right into the bus, sir, please,' Cecelia said to a man who had remained on the platform. The Kilbarchan to Abbotsinch run ended at the

Fleet Arm installation, and so she was used to dealing with airmen and navy men of all nationalities ... Australians, Free French and Poles as well as British. This particular passenger was in a uniform unknown to her.

He stayed where he was. 'One ticket to Abbotsinch, please,' he said in careful English.

She told him the fare, and he searched through a handful of change then proffered a few coins.

'You need more than that, sir.'

'Not on the platform, madam.'

'You shouldn't be on the platform, sir, you should be inside the bus.' She pointed, trying to speak as clearly and slowly as he had. 'There are empty seats inside.'

'Madam, in Poland is only half the price to stand on the platform.'

'In Scotland, you have to go into the bus and pay the full price.'

He was a dapper little man, a good two inches shorter than she was. Now he pouted up at her and said, 'Madam, I prefer to stand here, so that I may enjoy your company.'

'In Scotland, sir, that is not allowed.' They were being so formal with each other that at any minute, Cecelia thought, the two of them might break into a minuet, or an old-fashioned waltz. But dancing was the last thing on the man's mind.

'You go out with me tonight?' he asked hopefully. 'You go to the pictures with me?'

'I beg your pardon, sir?'

He beamed up into her face, revealing several gold fillings in his teeth. 'You go out with me?' he repeated, and then, with a hopeful lift of the eyebrows, 'You be naughty with me?'

She felt the colour rush up into her face from beneath the collar of her crisp white blouse, and realised that she must look like a tomato on the vine, ready for plucking.

'I ... I...' she stammered, looking over his head at the passengers seated on the long seats nearest the doorway. Thank goodness none of them seemed to have heard a word, but as the bus neared its next stop several people had begun to make their way down the aisle towards her.

'I'm sorry, sir, but fraternising with a Glasgow Corporation uniform is not permitted,' she gabbled, slamming a rigid forefinger on the bell push. 'Please clear the platform, passengers wish to alight.'

He went to a seat, shoulders drooping, and each time she caught his eye after that he looked at her sorrowfully with big dark eyes.

Most of the passengers got off at the next stop, Paisley Cross. The red-eyed woman was among them, but when she tried to shepherd her little flock from the bus, the children hung back, arguing. Cecelia sighed, and went to investigate.

'Is there something wrong? Only we've got a timetable to keep to, and I can't hold the bus back.'

'You've been very kind already,' the woman said, then bit her lip. 'They don't want to go to my sister's and I don't blame them, it's just a single room with nothing for them to do. And what with her being ... in a delicate condition, it's no' really fittin' for them to be there.'

'Well...' Cecelia looked at the little family helplessly. 'Is there nobody you can leave them with?'

'There's his mother when she comes home but I can't leave them outside in the street to wait for her, can I? She should be home by the time the bus gets back to Broomlands,' the woman said, struck by a sudden thought.

'You could put them off there, couldn't you, on your way back? Sadie here has the address, she'll keep an eye on them if you'd just let them stay on the bus till it gets back there.' Then, as Cecelia stared speechlessly, still trying to make sense out of the sudden flow of words, 'Oh thank you, you're a very nice person! Be good now, and do what the lady tells ye,' she warned the children. And before Cecelia knew what was happening, she had gone and the few people boarding the bus had already seated themselves.

'Go and sit down,' she told the children, and belled Harry. Then she gave her bag of sweets to the eldest girl. 'Divide them out fairly,' she said.

15

At the terminus, the Polish man paused on the platform on his way out. 'No?' he asked.

'No!' Cecelia told him firmly, and he sighed, and dismounted.

'What are they doing here?' Harry wanted to know when he came round for his break before the bus set off again. Cecelia explained in a rush, finishing with, 'So on the way back, could you stop in Broomlands Street near King Street, and give me a minute to take these three to their gran's?'

'We can manage,' Sadie said at once. 'I know where she lives.'

'I need to make sure that you've been handed over safely.'

'I don't know,' Harry grumbled. 'This is a public transport service, not a nursery for abandoned weans!'

'Ssshhh!' She shot a swift glance at the children, lowering her voice. 'Don't say such things in front of them, they'll start to worry.'

'They're not the only ones. I've got enough to do just drivin' the bus from one place tae the other without havin' tae stop here and there while my clippie nips out tae see if someone's granny's at home.'

'It's all right for you, sitting in your cab all the time,' Cecelia shot back at him, her nerves beginning to fray. 'Nobody can pester you there. I'd a wee Polish passenger trying to get half fare by travelling on the platform. Then he wanted me to go out with him.'

'You should have gone,' Harry told her. 'And told him that the three weans were part of the deal. And you'd better hope we don't get an inspector on the bus on the way back!'

'Won't be a minute,' Cecelia told the startled passengers on the lower deck as the bus drew in at its unscheduled stop. She hustled the children off and ran with them up the nearest close. Sadie flew ahead, and when they caught up with her she was fishing about inside the letterbox.

'She usually leaves the key on a string if she's at home,' she said, then straightened, dismay in her round blue eyes. 'It's not there.'

'What does that mean?' Cecelia asked, her heart sinking, but the girl had already darted across to knock on the door opposite.

'D'you know where my gran is?' she asked the old man who finally opened the door.

'Eh?' He bent down and peered into her face, then said, 'Oh, it's you, hen. Come tae see yer granny?'

'She's not in.'

'I know that, I met her goin' down the stair this mornin' when I was on my way out mysel'. She's gone tae see some friend that's awful no-weel. She'll be back in the mornin', though, because it's her turn tae wash the stairs.'

'In the morning?' Cecelia asked, aghast.

The old man looked at her, taking in her uniform and ticket bag, then asked wheezily, 'Lost yer bus, hen? It's no' here. I'd have seen it if it had come up thae stairs.'

'Is there anyone who could look after the children until their grandmother comes back tomorrow?' Cecelia asked desperately over his gasping laughter.

'Eh? No' that I can think of, hen,' he said, and shut his door.

Three pairs of eyes fixed on Cecelia.

'Back to the bus,' she said.

'What am I going to do?' she asked Harry as they sat in the bus at the Kilbarchan terminus.

'Don't ask me. You wouldnae share that whisky you found below one of the seats,' he said huffily, 'so why should you expect me tae share these three? Ye'll have tae hand them in tae the office.'

'I can't hand in children!'

'Why not? Their mammy did. Here,' he said, relenting a little in the face of her despair, 'have half of this sandwich.'

She chewed on the unappetising sandwich, made of slices of national bread thinly spread with some sort of paste. The children had eaten all her sandwiches and now the girls were playing peevers on the pavement, on beds marked out by a stub of chalk Sadie had produced from her pocket, while the boy, Tommy by name, was busy with a handful of marbles.

The three of them travelled back and forth on the bus for the rest of the shift, and caused a lot of interest when Cecelia led them into the depot. Some of the clippies found food for them, while Harry, to his fury, had to put up with a lot of joshing from the other drivers about his new family. Then the inspector arrived.

'What are those kids doing here?' he wanted to know.

'Cecelia here found them on her bus,' Nancy smirked. 'She's handing them in to the lost property department and if they're not claimed in six months she'll have 'em back.'

'Their mother had to go and look after her sister and their grandmother won't be home until tomorrow morning,' Cecelia explained, colour rushing to her face.

'Well, you can just take them out of here ... and don't come back until you're got rid of them.'

'I'm on late shift tomorrow, they'll be with their grandmother by then.'

'You make sure of that,' the inspector snarled. 'Come back with these kids in tow, lady, and you'll be gettin' your books.'

There was nothing else for it but to take the children back to Glen Street with her. As they trailed along the street Cecelia tried to work out how she would manage to feed and accommodate them, and came up with only one answer ... she must throw herself and her charges on Mrs Borland's mercy.

The woman was at home, and more than willing to take over. 'Och, the poor wee things,' she crooned, sweeping them and Cecelia into her flat. 'Come away in, now. Donnie, see what we've got here,' she added as she opened the kitchen door.

'Oh aye? Come in, come in,' Donnie Borland said charitably from his usual armchair. 'Put the kettle on, Ellen.'

'If I could just borrow some milk, and mebbe some bread...' Cecelia began.

'They need more than that. A wee bit of sausage, eh? And mebbe an egg? And none of that nasty powdered stuff,' Ellen added as the children's eyes brightened. 'Fried bread an' all. It's what we were going to have for our own tea. Plenty for everyone. And they can sleep in our wee room tonight, it's where my own grandweans stay when they're here.'

'It's very kind of you, Mrs Borland, but I don't want to be a nuisance...'

The woman patted Cecelia's arm. 'Don't you worry, hen, there's no nuisance about it. We're happy tae do this for you, aren't we, Donnie? And mebbe some day,' she added, beaming at Cecelia, 'you'll be able tae do somethin' for me. We should always look after our own, pet.'

'That's a nice lady,' Sadie said when Cecelia collected her and her siblings from the Borlands' flat the next morning, their faces so clean that they shone, and each head of hair well brushed.

'We had porridge,' Tommy boasted as they set off up the street, while wee Molly added in awe, 'With syrup on it!'

All three children, full of porridge, golden syrup and high spirits, scurried ahead of Cecelia, who was hard put to keep up with them as they made their way up Gilmour Street then along the High Street into Wellmeadow and then, beyond, to Broomlands Street. She was relieved, when she reached the top of the stairs, to see Sadie opening the door. The missing grandmother had come home, just in time to save Cecelia's job.

'Wait a minute,' she called as they rushed into the flat, 'what's your grandmother's name?'

'Gran,' Molly, the last of them, shouted back. 'Come on in!' Then she vanished, leaving Cecelia to look in vain for a nameplate.

'Gran ... Gran, we've come to stay!' she heard them shouting as she ventured in through the open door. The children were all leaping about the small kitchen, talking over each other and waving their arms at the elderly woman who stood blinking at them. The noise was terrible.

As Cecelia appeared in the doorway, the woman's eyes widened, and she gathered the excited children to her.

'Who are you? What are you doin' in my home? I never invited ye in here!'

'Mrs ... er ... I'm Cecelia Goudie, and your daughter-in-law asked me to look after the children...' Cecelia began, but the woman was having none of it. She pushed the children behind her then moved towards Cecelia, her face set in grim lines.

'If ye're from the Social ye can just get out! These are my grandweans and they're not goin' tae be taken away by you or anyone else!'

Cecelia took a step back, into the tiny hallway. 'I'm bringing them back, not taking them away,' she said frantically. 'Their mother had to go and help her sister in Glasgow so I took them for the night because you were out. A neighbour helped and they've been quite safe. We made sure they did their homework and...'

The children, ignoring their grandmother's attempts to stay between them and Cecelia, had followed her, and were still leaping about like a pack of excited puppies. Now Sadie calmed down and said in a grown-up, matter-of-fact way, 'She can't hear you because she's deaf.'

'Stone deaf,' Molly agreed, nodding vigorously.

'It's all right, she'll make you a cup of tea when I've explained it all to her,' Sadie urged as Cecelia hesitated on the verge of flight. 'She's just glaring at you because she doesn't know why you're here. You have to talk to her like this...'

She tapped her grandmother's arm to get her attention, and then deftly, her hands moving at speed, she started to use sign language.

'I've never seen anyone speaking with their hands before,' Cecelia said to Harry that afternoon during their stop at Kilbarchan. 'It was really interesting to watch. The woman was very pleasant once she realised what had happened. And there was me thinking she was just ignorant because she kept waving at me to get out of her flat.'

He took a bite of his sandwich, then said, spraying crumbs, 'So the bairns are all right now? She's lookin' after them?'

'They'll be fine with her until their mother gets back.' Cecelia brushed crumbs from her skirt as unobtrusively as she could. 'You don't need to worry about them.'

'Worry about them? Me? If I was worried at all, it was that you'd bring them back with you today. Damned wee pests!'

'So you were just forcing yourself to play marbles with Tommy yesterday, then?'

'I wasnae doin' it for pleasure,' Harry said loftily. 'I used tae be the bools champion in our street, and I was just showin' the bairn how tae play properly. He was goin' about it all the wrong way.' Then, with a note of satisfaction in his voice, 'But now he'll be able tae give his wee pals a right trouncin' the next time he plays them at bools!'

'Chloe. Chloe!'

She had been dreaming about work, and about Dennis coming into the shop. He wanted to buy something and he was angry with her because she couldn't find what he wanted. As Chloe searched the shop someone kept getting in her way; a woman who kept her face averted, but seemed to be wherever Chloe turned. She had only just realised that it was Mrs Fulton from across the landing when Dennis started shouting at her so loudly that the shop began to tremble with the force of his voice.

'Chloe! Wake up, we have to go downstairs!'

She shot upright in bed as Dennis's angry voice was replaced by the wail of the air-raid siren and the ominous rumble of approaching planes. 'Wha'?'

'Can you not hear the planes? We have to go downstairs! Are you awake now? I have to get the boys.'

'I'm wakened, Mum.' Chloe threw the bed-clothes aside and reached for the chair by the bed, where warm clothes were set out every night in case of a raid. Because of the blackout the bedroom was so dark between dusk and daylight that she had to put her clothes out in the proper order so that she could dress without having to look.

The sirens were still wailing, and people were shouting in the street outside. The thunder of the enemy bombers, wave upon wave of them, was frighteningly loud now. There must be hundreds, coming fast.

She tied a scarf over her hair, which had been wound round rags, and felt for her bag and the torch she kept beside it, then snatched up her quilt and pillow and made her way out into the hall. The boys were already there, their eyes bright with excitement in the light from her torch.

Every evening before going to bed Julia made up some sandwiches, which, if they were not needed in the shelter, were used for packed lunches the next day. Now, each of the boys carried a big message bag holding the food and some books and games to keep them occupied, while Julia rummaged in the big hall cupboard for the canvas bag that held the spare blankets.

'Are we all ready?' she asked as she closed the door. 'Come on, then, fast as we can.'

'What about Dad?' Leslie quavered.

'He's gone to the Home Guard.' Julia opened the door.

'But...'

'He'll be fine,' Duncan told his little brother gruffly. 'He's got his rifle with him.'

Voices and hurried footsteps echoed up and down the stairwell as their neighbours all made for the room at the rear of the drysalter's shop on the ground floor. As the McCosh family emerged from their flat Chloe heard Mrs Borland's voice as she shepherded her husband and old Mrs Bell down to the ground floor. Dennis was coming down from the landing above with his brother and sisters, and at the sight of him, Chloe began to pray that her headscarf completely covered her shameful rag curlers.

But Dennis had other things on his mind. 'D'you think you could look after the weans, Mrs McCosh? I'm supposed to be firewatching, and my mother's workin' at the hospital tonight.'

'Of course, son.' Julia smiled at the two girls. 'We'll all look out for each other, eh?'

'I'm not a wean!' Ralph grumbled, half under his breath.

'If you're that grown up, why couldn't you get the girls up and ready instead of leaving it to me?' Dennis snapped, then asked, 'What about Mrs Fulton? D'you know if she's gone downstairs yet?'

'I've not seen her,' Julia said, and he lunged across the landing, almost knocking Ralph out of the way, and began rapping on the door.

'Mrs Fulton? Are you wakened? You have to go down to the shelter!'

'She's down there already,' Cecelia Goudie said from halfway up the last flight of stairs, 'and so are the Borlands and Mrs Bell. I came back up to see if I could help anyone.'

'That's everyone, then,' Dennis said with relief. He shepherded them all down to the close entrance and saw them into the shelter before going off to join the group of firewatchers set up from Glen Street residents.

There were two rooms behind the drysalter's; the smaller room was used during the day by the owners, and held a tiny gas cooker, some chairs and a table, as well as shelves packed with goods. The larger room at the rear of the building had been used solely as a storeroom before the war, but now the boxes and cartons and sacks were piled against the four walls so that there was an open area in the centre. At first, the residents had donated what they could spare – stools, boxes, sagging and collapsing chairs that they had finally managed to replace in their homes – but after one particularly long and uncomfortable night in the shelter Ellen Borland had taken charge, and now there were three sets of metal bunk beds and several deckchairs in residence. Where she obtained them nobody knew, and nobody asked. They were just grateful for the modicum of comfort.

When Julia McCosh ushered in her charges, Donnie Borland, wrapped so tightly in warm blankets that he resembled a Swiss roll with a head at one end, was stretched out on a lower bunk while Jessie Bell occupied one of the two comfortable armchairs, knitting so fast that her veined, almost skeletal hands were little more than a blur.

Ellen's knitting bag and the old leather bag containing family photographs and papers were on the other chair, while the lady herself was talking quietly to Lena Fulton. As the others came in Ellen moved to her armchair while Lena stayed where she was, in an upright chair on the edge of the group, her head bent over some sewing.

'Here we go again, eh?' Ellen said cheerily. 'Your man out with the Home Guard tonight, Mrs McCosh?'

'That's right, and Mrs Megson's working too.' Julia immediately began making up beds with help from Cecelia and Chloe. 'Come on now, you've got school tomorrow,' she told the children, 'so into bed with you. Amy and Bessie can share one bunk and Duncan and Leslie can share another, and that leaves one for you, Ralph.'

'I'm not goin' to any bed,' the boy announced. 'I'm no' a bairn.'

'You'll be tired in the morning,' Cecelia told him, and he shrugged his broad shoulders and said, 'I can handle that!'

'Fancy a game of Snakes and Ladders?' Chloe suggested, pulling the box from the bag her mother had brought with her. Ralph sneered, then said dismally, 'might as well, there's nothing else to do.'

The hours dragged by. The Megson and McCosh children finally managed to get to sleep despite Donnie Borland's snoring, while his wife dozed in her armchair, her head twisted to one side and her mouth falling open. Lena Fulton stitched busily at the work she had brought down with her, replying to anything Julia and Cecelia said with a brief 'yes' or 'no' . Julia and Cecelia both knitted, and talked a little as they waited for the All Clear to sound.

Chloe and Ralph played game after game of Snakes and Ladders, and more than once the boy had to be talked out of going into the backyard to see what was happening.

'It's not fair,' he grumbled. 'Why can't I be a firewatcher like our Dennis? He has all the fun!'

'I'd hardly call it fun,' Cecelia said dryly. 'What if an incendiary bomb comes down and sets fire to the place?'

Ralph's eyes glowed. 'Puttin' it out would be a lot better than sharing this damn...'

'I beg your pardon?' Mrs Borland boomed from her chair. They all jumped. 'What did you say, my lad?'

'Dice,' Ralph muttered, his ears going red. 'I said that putting out fires would be better than shakin' this dice.'

'That's just as well, for I'll not abide bad language in my shelter,' Ellen said grandly. 'I'll not abide it anywhere, as you well know. And you can just stop complaining and get back to your game, for your mother would never forgive us if we let anything happen to you while she was away ministering to the sick and the dying.' And she settled down again, closing her eyes, while Ralph scowled across the rickety card table at Chloe and shook the dice as though he held it by the throat.

Gradually, Julia and Cecelia talked less and less. Their fingers stilled and their eyelids began to close. Chloe left the card table and started flicking through a magazine, holding it close to her eyes in the poor light. Ralph moodily threw the dice over and over again, while Lena Fulton stitched away at her work, to the muffled drone of plane engines and the thud of anti-aircraft guns.

16

They had been in the shelter for over three hours when Julia jerked awake, then said, 'Listen ... I think the planes have gone.'

Cecelia and Chloe strained their ears. It was difficult to be sure above Donnie Borland's snoring, but it seemed to the three women that the drone of engines had all but ceased. Then they jumped when the door opened and a tall, burly figure strode in. His face was in shadow, the features hidden between the brim of his tin hat and the upturned collar of his khaki greatcoat. Ellen Borland, startled awake by the gust of cold night air that billowed in through the open doorway, shot upright in her chair and yelped, 'Oh my heavens, it's the Germans come tae get us all!'

Chloe, Cecelia and Julia stared transfixed while Ralph jumped to his feet and picked up the wooden kitchen chair he had been sitting on, holding it before him as a weapon.

Then the figure in the doorway said, 'Aye, that'll be right, Mrs Borland. Hitler asked me tae drop by when I was passing on my parachute and invite you all back tae Germany for your tea.'

'Frank!' Julia jumped up. 'Oh, Frank, you gave us the fright of our lives! What are you doing here? Has something happened?'

'Aye, it has, but not in this area. They're sayin'

that the First Aid Post at Woodside's been hit. I came to make sure you were all right, and to tell you that I don't know when I'll be back, Julia. We've got to go up there now.'

'I'll come too,' she said at once. 'The WVS'll mebbe be needed.'

'You'll stay where you are, woman. You're not on duty and the All Clear's not been sounded. Now do as you're told, for once,' he added sternly as she began to protest. 'The bairns need you tonight, and those livin' nearer the West End will be the ones tae help out. I'll be back as soon as I can.'

Then he went, as quickly as he had come, leaving them staring at each other.

'A First Aid Post?' Ellen said, stunned. 'God help the poor souls that were in it if it's true.'

'Mebbe there's been a mistake,' Cecelia suggested.

'I certainly hope so,' Julia agreed, as the All Clear sounded.

'Well, that's another raid gone by ... for us, at any rate.' Ellen struggled to her feet and started shaking her husband, who had slept through the panic caused by Frank's sudden arrival. 'Come on, Donnie son, let's get you to your bed, then you can have a proper sleep.'

'I thought that was what he was having already,' Cecelia commented when the Borlands had left; Donnie, still half asleep, had been leaning on his wife, who carried the big bag containing their belongings. 'Should we waken the children now?'

'I suppose so. Poor wee things, this is no life for them,' Julia said as they set about the task while

Lena folded her sewing.

The young Megsons and McCoshs were stumbling about, rubbing their eyes, when Dennis arrived.

'Any fires?' Ralph wanted to know.

'Just the one, from an incendiary. But we caught it early, and got it out before any damage was done.'

'You were in the wrong place,' the younger boy said excitedly. 'Mr McCosh was just in and he says that the First Aid Post at Woodside's been hit!'

Dennis stared, and then grabbed his brother's arm. 'Don't make jokes like that!'

'It's true! Ask them, they all heard it the same as me!' Ralph wrenched his arm free.

'Is it? Is it true?

'We don't know for sure, but the Home Guard's been sent up there,' Julia began, and was cut short.

'My mother,' Dennis said frantically. 'I think my mother was there tonight!'

'Surely she's working at the infirmary?'

'She was due to finish at midnight. Sometimes when there's a raid on and she's not needed at the infirmary, she goes to help out at one of the First Aid Posts. She's not come back here, has she?'

'No, but–'

'Ralph, get the girls upstairs and into their beds.' Dennis swung round on his brother, barking, 'Just do it!' when Ralph began to object.

'Where are you going?' Julia asked as he made for the door.

'To the West End, to see if it's true!'

'But if it is, there's folk there that know what to do for the best. Stay here until the morning at least–'

'It's my mother!' Dennis shouted at her, and ran.

Paisley's West End was seething with people and vehicles, and as Dennis Megson neared the site of the First Aid Post a soldier blocked his path.

'Can't go along there, sonny. No civilians allowed.'

'Is it true?' The words wheezed out of Dennis's tortured lungs. 'Was the post hit?'

'Look, lad,' the man said. 'I'm here to keep folk away. I cannae tell ye what's happening, even if I knew it myself.'

'But my mother...' Dennis crouched against a wall, hands on knees, trying to catch his breath. 'She's a nurse. She might have been working there tonight.'

'I'm sorry, son.' There was rough kindness in the voice now. 'You cannae go past, and they're all too busy up there tae answer any questions. Best go home and wait for word.'

'Go home? How can I just go home and wait when I don't know what's happened to her? If you won't help me, I'll go to the infirmary and find out from them.'

'They've got enough tae do tonight without you...' the man began, but Dennis was off again, his heart hammering and his lungs labouring.

Paisley's Royal Alexandra Infirmary was near the Cross, which meant that he had to go all the way back through the town, moving against the tide of people beginning to hurry to the West End as word of the bombing spread. Dawn was lightening the sky as he reached the infirmary, an imposing Victorian building. The entrance was seething with ambulances and people, and he had to fight his way through them.

The interior was just as busy as the exterior. Dennis tried to catch someone's attention, asking any porters, nurses or doctors that hurried by, 'Nurse Megson ... Nan Megson. D'you know if she's here?' But each time, they just looked at him blankly, as though he was speaking a foreign language, and then hurried on, too busy to think of anything other than the work to hand.

He finally managed to struggle as far as an inner door, where a porter stopped him. 'What are you doin' here, lad? What's your business?'

At last someone was willing to listen to him. 'I'm looking for my mother, she's a nurse here and she might have been working in the First Aid Post,' Dennis gabbled. 'Nurse Megson.'

'Don't know anythin' about her, son.'

'Can you not go and ask someone?'

'I've got more tae do than that. Anyway, I can't go roamin' about the infirmary and botherin' busy folk at your biddin'.'

'Then I'll go and look for her myself.'

'You won't!' The man put a big hand on Dennis's chest as he tried to push past through the doorway.

'I need to find out if my mother's all right!'

'What ye need tae do is, you need tae sit down over there and wait until someone's got the time tae find out for ye!'

'For pity's sake...!' Dennis made another bid for the door, and this time the man grabbed his shoulders, his fingers biting painfully into the muscles.

'You'll do as ye're told, sonny boy, or ye'll be thrown out and not allowed back in,' he was saying when the door behind him opened and Nan Megson hurried through, almost colliding with the two struggling figures.

'What's going ... Dennis?' Her face, already pale with fatigue, turned grey. 'It's not the girls, is it? Or Ralph?'

'No, it's you. I thought...' he began, then gulped as the words tangled themselves in his throat. To his horror, he felt hot and heavy tears pressing against the backs of his eyes.

'Get him out of here,' the porter growled at Nan, 'before I call the polis and have him escorted off the premises for gettin' in the way of folk with work tae dae.'

'It's all right, he's my son. I'll see to him.' She took Dennis by the arm and hurried him into a corner. 'What's wrong?' Her voice was frantic.

'We heard about the First Aid Post. I thought that...' he gulped again, and blinked rapidly. 'When you didn't come home, I thought you might have been working there.'

'No, I had to stay on here because...' she began, and then understanding dawned. 'You thought that I ... oh, Dennis! I'm fine, just very busy. What about the younger ones?'

'Mrs McCosh is seeing to them. I'll get back to them now.' All at once he felt slightly foolish, and in awe of her. She always changed for work when she got to the infirmary and so he had never before seen her in her uniform. Exhausted though she looked, the starched white cap and apron, the stiff white collar and the watch pinned to her bib gave her an air of authority and turned her into a stranger.

'You do that. Get to your bed and stop worrying about me. I'll be home as soon as I can.' She patted his face and managed to find a faint smile for him before vanishing into the milling crowd.

As Dennis left the hospital he passed an elderly couple on their way in, the man supporting his weeping wife. 'Mebbe it'll be all right,' he was saying. 'Mebbe he wasn't there at the time...'

As he forced his aching legs to carry him back to Glen Street, Dennis was almost overwhelmed by a thick black cloud of despair. He had thought until then that he was managing to deal with the triple burden of taking responsibility for his family, learning to be a fire-fighter and coping with his engineering classes. But the sudden shock of believing, for one terrified hour, that he had lost his mother had brought it all to a head. She had escaped death or injury this time, but it could so easily happen ... a bomb landing on the hospital when she was on duty, or a sudden raid when she was out in the night streets, making her way to and from work. The blackout had hurt and even killed folk who had fallen down unlit stairs or walked into the concrete baffle walls built in front of the town's tenement closes to protect them from shock waves. Death seemed to lurk around every corner, watching and waiting, and ready to pounce.

If anything happened to his mother, he doubted if he could manage to work and look after Ralph and the girls at the same time. Visions sprang to mind of Amy and Bessie pining in an orphanage, and Ralph going to the bad because his older brother did not have the time to watch out for him.

Dennis had thought that at eighteen years of age he was a man, but as he walked through the night, the years fell from him, and tears of fear and loneliness poured down his face.

The tenement was quiet when he got back, its residents snatching what sleep they could before morning took them off to work or school. In the close, he used his cap to scrub the tears from his eyes and his cheeks before taking a deep breath and ascending the stairs, pulling himself up by the handrail, moving like an old man instead of taking two steps at a time as he usually did.

Hesitating on the first landing, he glanced at Lena Fulton's door. He would have given anything to see her at that moment, to talk to her and find comfort in just being with her. But she would be in her bed by now, and fast asleep. Dennis started climbing the next flight of stairs, one by one.

Within her flat, Lena was sitting at the kitchen table, fingers curled around a cup of tea that had gone cold long since.

Mrs Borland had drawn her to one side as soon as she had gone into the room used as a bomb shelter.

'Nice tae see you, dear. Listen, I've got some work for you. A lassie at the mill's gettin' married, and she needs a dress for herself and one for her bridesmaid. I said you'd do them for her.'

'I don't know,' Lena faltered. 'I've got an awful lot of work just now, Mrs Borland, and...'

The woman's smile hardened a little. 'She's no' gettin' wed for three months yet, you've got plenty of time.'

'There's the material, and the time ... I'd need to charge for that as well.'

Ellen Borland's mouth thinned out and her voice took on an ominous undertone. 'I'll supply the material, same as I usually do, and as for cost, the lassie's a workmate of mine, and an awful nice girl too. You'd surely not expect her to pay you? After all...' she added with meaning, 'if she pays you, you'll only have tae give the money tae me, won't you, tae cover what ye owe me already? And that wouldn't help you at all, hen, would it? Best to stay with the nice wee agreement we've already got between us.'

Then, as the door opened to admit the McCosh family and the Megson children, the woman ended the conversation with, 'So I'll let ye know when she can come tae be measured, all right?' and turned away abruptly.

Lena put down the cup then got up from the table and went to fetch the large bag that held scraps left over from work already done. Sometimes, when life began to overpower her, it helped her to sort through the bits and pieces of cloth.

She shook the remnants over the table and began to put them into piles according to size, her mind still circling desperately round and round, seeking an answer to her problems. It would have made such a difference to her if only George had behaved like most servicemen and arranged for his Army pay to go to his wife. Instead, deciding that Lena was not capable of handling money without guidance, he had opted to have it paid to his father. The arrangement between the two men was that old Mr Fulton would put some of the money into the bank each month, and give the rest to his daughter-in-law, who was to augment it with the small sums she earned as a seamstress.

The scheme should have worked, and at first, it did. Mr Fulton senior stumped into the close at 42 Glen Street at the beginning of every month, climbed the stairs, and pushed the envelope through the letterbox without knocking on the door; but after the first six months the payments became sporadic, and the man had not once made the journey to Glen Street since his son's last leave.

Lena could not summon the courage to complain to George in her weekly letters; instead, in desperation, she had been forced to borrow from Mrs Borland, not realising that she was backing herself into a corner. In return for the occasional small payment, Ellen Borland expected Lena to do work for her family and friends at half the price she could charge others, and when Ellen supplied the material and threads, as she usually did, Lena had to do the work for nothing. Her timid attempts to reason with the woman had met with a sneering smile and a reminder that if she chose to, Ellen could go to George's father and demand full repayment of his daughter-in-law's debts.

'And I doubt if that would go down with your man, hen. After all, he's havin' a difficult enough time fightin' the Jerries without the shame of knowin' that his wife's spendin' money that's not hers by rights. We'll just keep it between ourselves, eh?' she always urged, taking Lena's roughened hand in her own and slipping two half-crowns or a ten-shilling note into it. 'Between friends. That's the way tae do it.'

The remnants had been sorted into neat piles according to size; now Lena began to divide each pile according to type and colour. She could remember where every scrap came from, and what she had made from that particular material. Now she picked up a piece of cream linen, rubbing it between her fingers. Her aunt had chosen the sleeveless cream dress for Lena to wear at her wedding to George. He had approved, though Lena herself would have preferred something softer and more romantic for what she had thought would be the most important day of her life. The dress had been taken apart to make a skirt for another girl's trousseau.

She reached out and picked up a soft brown patch that had come from a skirt a young mother had had cut down for her little daughter. Lena put the two fragments together, admiring the way they contrasted with each other.

Then she threaded a needle, reached for her scissors, and, oblivious to the dawn chorus outside the window, began to cut and stitch.

In the kitchen of his own flat, Dennis stopped short, staring. 'What are you doing here?'

Chloe, already flushed from the heat of the ironing she was doing, felt her face grow even warmer. 'I was just keeping them company till you got back.' She nodded at Amy and Bessie, huddled together on one of the two sagging armchairs flanking the range. 'They wouldn't go to bed until they knew about their...'

The girls, roused from sleep by their voices, struggled from the chair and ran to Dennis, their eyes dark with fear, while Chloe rested the iron on its base.

'What are you two doing up at this hour?'

'Is Mam all right?' Bessie asked anxiously as he knelt to put his arms about them. 'You don't need us to be brave, do you?' It was a term that children with fathers fighting in the war had become used to, a term that always preceded bad news.

'No, I don't need you to be brave. She's all right,' he assured them. They seemed so young and vulnerable, in their long nightdresses and with their hair carefully rolled up in rag curlers by Chloe.

'She'd to stay on at the infirmary, that's all, because of the raid.' He could feel the warm bodies within his embrace suddenly slump as the tension left them.

'Good,' Amy said, then, after a massive yawn,

'Does that mean we can go to bed now?'

Dennis looked at the two small faces, almost grey with fatigue, and with shadows under their eyes. 'You should have gone to bed ages ago.'

'They wouldn't, not until they heard that their mummy was safe and well. But now that we know, let's get you two settled down.' Chloe shepherded them out while Dennis sat down on the chair and began to take off his boots.

'Ralph?' he asked when Chloe returned.

'He went to his bed as soon as we came in. Would you like some tea?' She picked up the kettle and moved over to the sink, but he shook his head.

'I'm fine. You should be in your bed.'

'My mother was worn out, so I said that I'd stay with the girls until you got home.' She glanced at the clock. 'There's still time for an hour or two's sleep.' She added then, 'Are you sure you don't want some tea? You look awful tired.'

'I'd just as soon get to my bed. You didn't need to do this.' He gestured towards the small pile of neatly ironed clothes at one corner of the table.

'I had to have something to keep me occupied.' She began to fold the old blanket and sheet that turned the table into an ironing board. 'Was it the First Aid Post right enough?'

'I think so. Something's happened, but nob'dy would tell me anything. There were soldiers and police all over the West End, and the infirmary was busy too.'

'I hope there's not been too many folk hurt,' Chloe said soberly; then, putting the basket of ironed clothes in a corner, 'I suppose I'd best get off home now ... if you're sure there's nothing else you need.'

'No, you've done more than enough already. Thanks for your help.'

'Och, it was nothing,' she said. 'I'll let myself out.'

When she had gone he looked in on the girls, both sound asleep already, then went quietly into the small room he shared with Ralph, who didn't move or speak. Dennis thought he was asleep until, just as he was sliding into bed, his brother said from the darkness. 'Is Mam all right?'

'She's fine. She'd just had to stay on at the infirmary.'

'You saw her?'

'Aye. And I spoke to her. She's fine,' Dennis said again, and heard his brother's breath being released in a faint sigh. Less than a minute later, he could tell by the slow and even breathing that Ralph was asleep.

17

The whole town was abuzz with the news of the night's disasters. A mine dropped by parachute had made a direct hit on the First Aid Post at Woodside, killing ninety-two people ... doctors, nurses, pharmacists, first-aid workers, clerks and clerkesses, ambulance drivers and messengers. Had the wind carried the parachute and its deadly load a little to one side it would have landed and exploded in Woodside Cemetery, just over the wall from the post.

Another mine had exploded in a yard in Newton Street, close by the Woodside site, setting fire to an Auxiliary Fire Service vehicle, and killing two more men, both Fire Service personnel. Rescue workers had had to work through the night to release the dead and injured. More than twenty people had been seriously injured. Another bomb had fallen in the neighbouring town of Renfrew, killing two people and injuring half a dozen more.

The raid had then spread westwards from Paisley, culminating in the Clydeside shipbuilding towns of Port Glasgow and Greenock, which had been particularly damaged.

Almost everyone in the town had some story to tell in the next few days. Chloe's friend Marion's cousin had narrowly escaped death; a mill worker who had gained her certificate at the first-aid classes in Ferguslie Mills, she was among the personnel at Woodside, and should have been on duty that night, but another girl had agreed to change duties with her so that she could go to the pictures to see her hero, Clark Gable.

'My uncle and auntie near died of shock,' Marion told Chloe. 'When they heard about the bomb they thought they'd lost her ... then she walked in large as life and said, "Hello, I'm back." My uncle started giving her such a telling off for going to the pictures instead of being on duty before he realised that it had saved her life.'

'I can't be doing with this, Lena.' Cathy Blacklock stirred the spoon round and round in her teacup as though trying to grind the bottom of the cup away. 'My nerves won't take it.'

'It's war, Aunt Cathy,' Lena said from the sink, where she was doing some washing. 'None of us likes it, or wants it, but we have to put up with it.'

'Not me. I near died of fright last night when I heard the bang,' said Mrs Blacklock, who lived not far from the stricken First Aid Post. 'I said to Mrs Wilson that was under the stairs alongside me, I said, "It'll be us next time, you wait and see."'

'But it might not be.'

'There's plenty of next times to come, Lena. Look at me...' The woman lifted the cup from its saucer and held it up, 'I'm shakin'! I'm an old woman and I cannae be doin' with this. I'm going to write to my friend Effie Galbraith in Millport to say that I'm goin' over tae stay with her. She's asked me often enough.'

'There's warships in the Clyde, Aunt Cathy. It was the Clyde that the bombers were making for. They might come back while you're living on the island.'

'Mebbe, but Cumbrae's such a wee island that there's a fair chance of the bombs missin' it. And you'd best come with me.'

'Me?' Lena turned from the sink, soapy water dripping on to the linoleum from her hands. 'I'm not going to live in Millport.'

'Why not? You'll be safer there, and George would be easier in his mind, knowing that you were with me.'

'And what about when he comes home on

leave? He'll expect to find me here, looking after the place.'

'Surely if you write to him and explain what it's like living in a town, he'll see sense. Give me his address and I'll write to him myself.'

'No,' Lena said swiftly. 'I'll do it. You make your own arrangements to go to your friend in Millport, and if George agrees, I'll join you later.'

'I'm sure he will agree.' Cathy Blacklock drank down her tea then put the cup back on to its saucer and got to her feet. 'I'd best go, there's a lot to be done and the sooner I'm safe in Millport the happier I'll be.'

When the woman had gone, Lena scooped the wet and soapy clothes from the sink into a basin, washed the teacups, and then returned to her sewing. She would wait until her aunt was settled in Millport and then write to say that George preferred her to stay where she was, in their own home. She had no intention of asking him if she could accompany her aunt; it suited her fine to be here, within her own four walls, with her own things around her and without her Auntie Cathy buzzing around like a tiresome fly, asking if she was eating properly and going on about George.

The mood at the fire station was bleak. 'It makes ye realise how lucky this town has been up until now, compared tae some,' Tom McIntosh said to Dennis as they worked on an engine. 'Not that what happened the other night is anythin' like as bad as what these poor souls in London and places like that have had tae go through. Even so, when it hits close tae home, and it's folk that you know...' He stopped, shaking his head, then went on after a pause, 'And it makes ye wonder what else might be in store for us before this damned business is over and done with. But what's happened can't be changed, so we just have to get on with it the best we can. Pass me that spanner, lad.'

Getting on with things as best they could was what the people of Paisley did, once the funerals were over. There was still food to be queued for, ration books to be clipped, children to be educated and, always, work to be done.

Cecelia and Harry were moved from the Kilbarchan–Abbotsinch run to a Glasgow Clyde Street–Paisley Cross route, and this time Cecelia was experienced enough to deal efficiently with the task of memorising new stage fares and tickets. Most of the passengers were easy to get on with, and she had discovered that the occasional troublemaker or inebriate could usually be handled with a mixture of tact and firmness. Where drunk men were concerned, she discovered that a touch of firm motherliness went down well.

Her only problem, as the summer set in, was the heat. Her uniform was an asset in the winter, but on lovely summer days it could become unbearably hot. Some of the clippies found ways of subtly altering their uniforms to compensate, and as always, Nancy went a stage further. She tilted her cap to the back of her head and managed to push up her sleeves, as well as unfastening the top buttons of both jacket and blouse.

'I don't know how she gets away with it,' Cecelia said to one of the other conductresses. 'What if an inspector sees her like that?'

Inspectors were the bane of the conductresses' lives. Like birds, they seemed to travel in flocks; when they were spotted in an area the drivers flashed their lights at each other as a warning and each driver would then flash the bus's interior lights to put his conductress on her guard.

The woman shrugged. 'Les'll let her know if he sees an inspector waitin' at the next stop, and she'll be all smartened up and lookin' as if butter wouldnae melt in her mouth by the time the man sets foot on her bus.' She fanned herself with one hand. 'I wouldnae mind bein' on a run tae some nice seaside place like Largs in weather like this. I was on that run before the war when I worked for Youngs of Paisley; we used tae have a long turn-around there, so we'd time tae buy an ice-cream from Nardinis and take a wander round the town lookin' at the shops afore we had tae get back on the bus. Sometimes there was even time tae sit on the promenade an' watch the steamers comin' in and out. It was like havin' a wee holiday, the Largs run. There arenae any bus stops once you get right intae the country, so the folk just wait by the roadside and wave the bus down. And they sometimes brought a few eggs or some turnips or potatoes from their farms for the conductress and the driver. See this damned war? It's got a lot tae answer for.'

The Glasgow to Paisley run was a busy route, which suited Cecelia because keeping busy made the time pass faster. Under local regulations, buses running between Glasgow and Paisley and therefore crossing the city boundary could not drop passengers before the halfway stage at Crookston, and on the return trip they could not pick up passengers after Crookston.

On one particularly hot day the bus filled up rapidly and by the time Cecelia came downstairs after collecting fares it had reached the last stop before the boundary, where a considerable number of passengers waited.

She sped down the stairs and took command of her platform. 'Still seats upstairs,' she shouted. 'Upstairs if you can manage it, please. Give these to me, madam...' She relieved a harassed young woman who was carrying a small baby and trying to cope with a toddler as well as her heavy shopping bag. A heftily built man who was sitting on one of the long side seats by the door glanced up from his newspaper as Cecelia stared fixedly at him, and then got up hurriedly and offered the woman his seat.

'Thank you, sir, very kind of you. Move up to the front of the bus, please,' Cecelia called out as people continued to cram on to the platform. Then the line came to an abrupt stop. Craning her neck, Cecelia saw that one woman had paused halfway up the bus instead of moving as far up as she could. Irritation swept over her.

'Move up the bus, please!' she yelled, then as the woman, chatting to someone in one of the seats, paid no heed, she threw all the strength she could find into her voice. 'Would the lady in the red hat please move right up the bus NOW!'

A man in an officer's uniform had started up towards the top deck. Now he paused and said, 'Good God, woman, with a voice like that you should be a sergeant major in the army!'

'Thank you, sir, but I prefer my own command,' Cecelia shot back at him while the guilty passenger, her face turning as red as her jaunty hat, rocketed up to the very top of the passageway, thus making just enough room to accommodate everyone who wanted to get on.

Cecelia slapped the bell push twice and then, as Harry drew away from the kerb, set about the difficult task of squeezing by the standing passengers to collect fares. They had passed the halfway stage, which meant that some passengers alighted at the next few stops, easing the pressure for those remaining. There were still a few strap-hanging, one of them a man in army uniform.

'Fares please, sir,' Cecelia said briskly, and he started to manoeuvre round to face her.

'How much is it from Cessnock to... Cecelia?' Fergus Goudie said. 'What the blazes are you doing here?'

She gaped at him guiltily, then, remembering her mother's adage that attack was the best form of defence, said, 'Never mind me ... what are *you* doing here?'

'I asked first!'

'And this is my bus!' Cecelia rapped back at him and his eyes widened.

'I'm on leave...' he began, then altered the explanation to, 'Never mind that just now, what the dickens are doing in this bus, wearing that uniform and carrying that ticket machine?'

'What d'you think I'm doing? I'm working. I told you that I'd got a job with Glasgow Corporation Transport.' She was hugging the ticket machine close, as though ready to use it to defend herself.

'In the office, you said.'

'I didn't say that exactly, I just…'

'You just let me think you were. D'you mean to tell me that that was you, yelling at that woman just now?'

'I'm allowed to yell, it's my bus.'

'But I've never heard you raise your voice like that,' Fergus said, stunned.

'That's because I've never had to move you further up the bus,' she said stupidly, still unable to believe that he was really there, pressed tightly against her in the narrow aisle. 'On leave, did you say? You never wrote to tell me.'

'They didn't give us much warning.'

'Excuse me,' the woman in the red hat said from behind him. 'This is my stop and you've not collected my fare yet.' She glared. 'I'd not like to get off without paying, because that would break your rules, wouldn't it?'

'Look here...' Fergus said heatedly, and then winced as one of Cecelia's strong practical shoes kicked him in the ankle.

'That's very conscientious of you, madam. Did you see the look she gave me?' Cecelia said to Fergus after she had rung up a ticket, given the woman change, and belled Harry to stop and then start again. 'You can sit down now, there are empty seats.'

'I think I need to.' Fergus sank into a seat, and

then fumbled in his pocket. 'How much is the fare?'

'Don't be daft, you don't need to pay a fare on my bus.'

'Cecelia, what possessed you to become a bus conductress?'

'It was Mrs Borland's idea. She lives up the stairs from us. So I applied and I sat the exam and they took me on.'

'But your office experience...'

'It was the buses or munitions or mebbe the Forces or the Land Army. As Mrs Borland said, better to choose them before they chose me.'

'It seems such a waste!'

'You being in the army is much more of a waste. Anyway, I like it.' Glancing ahead she saw a knot of people waiting at the next bus stop. 'I'll have to go,' she said as she stabbed at the bell. 'I've got work to do.'

She collected fares from the latest passengers then had to return to the platform to usher some people off at the next stop. One of them was the young woman with the two small children and the bag of messages. Again, Cecelia took charge of the bag, and offered her free hand to the toddler. 'Oh thanks, that's kind of you,' the young woman said gratefully as they all arrived on the pavement.

'That's all right,' Cecelia said, then glanced up to see a uniformed figure hurrying along the pavement towards her. She leapt back on to the platform and scurried along the lower deck to where Fergus sat. 'Give me twopence ha'penny!'

'What?'

'For your fare!'

'But you said...'

'Just give me twopence ha'penny,' Cecelia ordered, low-voiced, as the inspector jumped on to the platform and belled Harry. She stamped the ticket with trembling fingers and stowed the proffered fare in her bag. 'You got on at the last stop, right? And you don't know me,' she hissed as the inspector began to patrol the aisle, intoning, 'Tickets, please!'

'That's me finished my shift now, but I have to go back to the depot at Ibrox,' Cecelia explained to Fergus as most of the passengers, including the inspector, got off at Paisley Cross. 'Then I'll come back to Paisley on one of the other buses. You go on home now and I'll see you later.'

'Can you not come home with me now?'

'I have to cash up and put in the takings,' she was saying when Harry came round from his cab.

'Havin' a problem, hen?' He eyed Fergus, who glared back at him.

'Harry, this is my husband Fergus.'

'Oh aye? Home on leave, are ye? That's nice. Ye never said he was comin' home, hen.'

'I didn't know till I saw him on the bus.'

'Ye've got a canny wee wife there,' Harry grunted, sticking out his hand. 'She's a quick learner and she's fairly taken tae the work.'

'Has she indeed?' Fergus took the older man's hand, looking from him to Cecelia, then said awkwardly, 'Well, I suppose I'd best get off now. I'll see you back home, then?'

'I'll not be long. Oh...' she fished in her pocket, 'here's the key.'

'He doesnae seem tae be very happy,' Harry observed as they watched Fergus walk away. 'Ye've never had a quarrel already, have ye?'

'It's just ... he didn't know that I was working on the buses,' she explained, and his brows shot up.

'Ye never told yer man what ye were doin'? Ashamed of the job, are ye?'

'No, it's nothing like that! It's just that I used to work in an office, and he thought that I was going to get the same sort of job again.'

'Someone should tell him that there's a war on,' Harry said, with just the glimmer of a smile tickling at the corners of his mouth.

On the way back to Ibrox Cecelia practised all the arguments she could think of in favour of her choice of work. If only Fergus had written to let her know that he was getting leave, she could have worked out a way of telling him the truth in a letter, instead of letting him find out as he had.

If only she had been honest with him from the start, she thought miserably as she alighted at Ibrox and began the task of directing Harry as he reversed the bus into its slot. In hindsight, that would have been the best thing to do. She held up a hand and Harry, watching her in his mirror, braked and then turned the steering wheel in answer to her next signal.

If she had only had the sense to write, he could have got used to the idea while he was far away, with his regiment. As it was, the two of them would probably spend what precious time they had together arguing and...

'Look out!' someone yelled, but it was too late. Cecelia snapped out of her reverie and watched in horror as the back of the bus caught a corner of the terminal building with a nasty scraping sound. A crowd gathered as Harry almost threw himself out of the cab and came running round to inspect the damage.

'Ye daft wee bitch, what the blazes were ye thinkin' about?' he yelled at her.

'I'm sorry ... I'm so sorry...!' Cecelia bleated, staring at the dent in one corner of the bus, and the scraped paintwork. 'I didn't realise...'

'Are youse two tryin' tae knock down the whole terminus?' One of the inspectors bulldozed his way through the crowd. 'Look at that! That's going to cost good money to repair!' Then, glaring at Harry and Cecelia, 'Intae the office ... right now!'

'I cannae leave the bus like this,' Harry protested.

'I don't see why not, since you're the one that got it like this! Les, Nancy, you take it in where it belongs.'

As Les climbed into the cab and Nancy, smirking, took up her position behind the bus, Cecelia and Harry were marched into the office, where they stood side by side before the desk like naughty children hauled up before the headmaster for talking in class. Only this was much more serious, Cecelia thought miserably. She had managed to damage a Glasgow Corporation bus that had cost goodness knows how much to buy. And she had got Harry, one of the best drivers in the depot, into trouble. Not to mention having to face Fergus when she got home.

'Well?' the inspector demanded, hurling himself into the chair behind the desk.

'I was–' Cecelia began, but Harry spoke over her.

'It was my fault. A damned great bumblebee flew intae the cab just as I was takin' the bus back. It hit against my face and I got such a fright that my foot skidded off the brake.'

'You expect me to believe that?'

'It's the truth. Have I ever damaged a bus before, in all the years I've worked for this corporation?' Harry asked heatedly.

'No, but–'

'Have I ever been late on a run, or not turned up for work apart from havin' tae get my appendix out fifteen years ago?'

'No, but–'

'Come on, Charlie, it's just a scratch, you know it is. And mebbe a wee dent too. But it can be sorted. And there's no harm done tae yer precious building.'

'Listen you to me,' the inspector began, glaring from one to the other. Then he sagged back in his chair. 'Oh, what the hell! You'll both have to fill in forms before you go off duty. And if you ever do a thing like this again you're in real trouble!'

'Aye, the next time a bumblebee comes intae my cab I'll swallow it whole and keep drivin',' Harry said sarcastically. 'Come on, Cecelia, let's get these forms filled in.'

As soon as they were out of earshot he rounded on her. 'Don't you ever let your mind wander when you're directin' my bus again!'

'I'm so sorry, Harry,' she said wretchedly. 'You should have let me tell him the truth instead of taking the blame. I'll go back in now and tell him if you like.'

'And make me out tae be a liar? Ye will not. Ach, the company owes me a wee slip, given the loyalty they've had from me. Let's get on with the forms and then you can go home and make a fuss of that man of yours.'

18

School was out by the time Cecelia reached Glen Street. Boys were kicking a football about the street while girls, the Megsons among them, played peevers and skipping ropes, or bounced a ball against any windowless wall they could find.

Reaching Number 42 she sucked in a deep breath and squared her shoulders. Fergus was waiting for her and now, for the second time that afternoon, she had to face the music.

'Excuse me,' someone said as she made her way along the close, and she turned to see a man hovering in the entrance.

'Yes?'

'I'm looking for a woman called Julia...' He hesitated, gave a rattly cough, then said, 'McCosh, I think her name is.'

'Mrs McCosh lives on the first floor. To the left.'

'Thank you.' The light was behind him and all she could make out was a tall, very thin figure with longish hair.

'I don't know if she's in…'

'Thank you,' he said again, dismissively this time, as though used to being obeyed. She shrugged and turned away. She had her own problems to deal with.

'Wait there,' Fergus ordered as soon as he opened the door.

'What do you ... Fergus!' she squeaked as he stepped outside and swept her up in to his arms. 'What are you doing?'

'Carrying my wife over the threshold.'

'You did that when we first came here!'

'And I'm doing it again. And again, if I want to, or if you want me to.' He turned as if to carry her out again, and she hastily reached over to shut the door.

'Just the once is enough. You can put me down now,' she said as he negotiated the small hallway.

'Not just yet. D'you know something?' he said when they arrived in the kitchen, where the table was set for two and the radio was tuned into a programme of dance music, 'I like the way you feel in that uniform.'

'Fergus, about the uniform, and the job–'

'It it's what you want, that's fine with me. Life's too precious and time's too short to argue. You look good in the uniform too.' He kissed her, then said, 'I made a sort of pie thing with mashed potatoes on top. It's in the oven. I just used what I could find.'

'It smells lovely.' He had probably used up all her rations for the week, but she didn't care. Fergus was back, and nothing else mattered. 'How long have you got?'

'Five days.'

'Five whole ... oh, Fergus,' she wailed, 'I'm working for the next four days!'

'We'll manage.'

'And I smashed the bus against a wall this afternoon.'

'What? Are you all right? Did anyone get hurt?'

'Nobody, it happened in the depot, when I was directing Harry while he took it in to its slot. I was so busy thinking about you ... about us ... that I forgot what I was doing and he scraped the bus against the side of the building.'

'And they let you keep your job?'

'Harry took the blame.'

'Harry,' said Fergus, 'is a gentleman.'

'And I'm on early shifts!'

'What does that mean?'

'It means that I have to catch the service bus at the Cross at ten past four in the morning.'

'Damn,' he said. Then, cheering, 'Early bed, then. That sounds fine to me. Come on, I'll help you to take your uniform off.'

'What about the pie in the oven?' she asked as he carried her in to the bedroom.

'It'll keep,' he said, and kicked the door shut with his heel.

Julia McCosh had spent the morning in the WVS shop, sorting out donations of clothing and furniture. Returning home via the shops, where she had to queue for food as always, she had snatched a ten-minute rest in an armchair with a hasty cup of tea and a slice of toast before starting on the housework. When Leslie and Duncan came home from school she was peeling potatoes for the family's dinner.

'I've put out a sandwich and a cup of milk for each of you,' she said as they came raging into the flat like two runaway trains. 'And mind and change your clothes before you go out to play. You can do your homework after dinner, since it's a nice day.'

Leslie, always in a hurry, crammed his 'piece' into his mouth, washing it down with gulps of milk, then tore off his school clothes and battled his way into his old jersey and patched trousers. Duncan, the elder and more serious of the two, took time to hover about his mother for ten minutes, fiddling with bits of potato peelings as he told her all about his day. Then he too got changed and headed for the street, where a football game was already in progress.

He came back almost at once. 'Mum, there's a man outside wants to speak to you.'

'Who is it?'

'I don't know.' His round face was frowning, uncertain. 'He just asked if Mrs Julia McCosh was in.'

Julia's stomach clenched, as it always did these days when anything unusual happened. Had there been an accident at the India Tyre factory? Was Frank hurt? She hurried to the door, Duncan at her heels.

'I'm Julia McCosh. You were looking for me?'

she began, and then the words died in her throat as the man on the landing pulled off his hat, revealing a balding head fringed with straggly, overlong hair.

'I was,' he said. 'And now I've found you.' Then, as she stared, speechless, 'D'you not know me, Julia?'

Duncan looked doubtfully from the stranger to his mother. 'Mum?' He tugged at her apron.

'Away you go and play, son.' Julia's dry tongue rasped against the roof of her mouth as she spoke.

'I'll stay here if you want.'

She wrenched her eyes away from the dark gaze holding them, and smiled down at the boy. He was Frank's child in every way; thoughtful and caring, and quick – sometimes too quick – to sense her moods.

'No need. On you go now, and get some fresh air.' She gave him a slight push towards the stairs, saying to her unexpected visitor, 'Come on in.'

He walked past her, and as she closed the door she saw Duncan, going down the stairs step by slow step, staring at her through the banisters. She smiled and flapped her hand at him, then closed the door. 'Through to the door at the end.'

'So this is where you're living,' he said, putting his hat on the kitchen table and looking around the small room with the piercing, taking-everything-in gaze she remembered so well.

'How did you find me?'

'I used to be a policeman, remember? I know how to find folk when I want to.' His gaze turned on her, raking her from head to foot and back again. 'You've changed, Julia. You're more confident than I remember.'

'I'm happier.' She put her hands on the back of the chair Frank usually sat in, curling her fingers tightly round the top spar.

'I suppose I should be glad about that, though I would have preferred it if you had found your happiness with me,' he said. 'After all, I am your husband.'

'Not any more. I've been with Frank for over sixteen years now.'

'Which makes you man and wife under Scottish common law, I'll grant you. But naturally, I prefer to follow the King's law.'

'Did you say that you *used* to be a policeman? You've left the force?' It was difficult for her to think of the police force and Thomas Gordon as two separate entities, for they had suited each other so well.

'A year past, when...' He began to cough, a deep, harsh sound that went on and on. One hand fumbled in his pocket for a handkerchief while the other reached out to clutch at the edge of the table. Alarmed, Julia hurried to take his arm and ease him into a chair.

'Sit here. I'll fetch a cup of water.'

The paroxysm was over by the time she brought the water. Her eye caught a splash of bright red as he stuffed the handkerchief back in to his pocket.

'What's the matter with you?' she asked sharply.

'Just leave me be for a minute.' He fumbled in another pocket and produced a small bottle. Opening it, he shook a few drops into the cup and then drank it down.

Julia seated herself opposite, watching him. His long narrow face, thinner than she remembered it, had been pale when he came in; now it was grey and he looked ill to the point of collapse. She wondered if Nan Megson was at home.

'Thank you,' he said after a long pause.

'Would you like some tea?'

'Isn't your ... isn't he due home soon?'

'There's time for a cup before you go back to Glasgow. Just sit quiet and get your breath back while I see to it.' Thank goodness, Julia thought as she filled the kettle and put cups and saucers out, Frank's working late. And thank goodness Chloe had been invited to the Hepburns' for her tea.

Setting the cup before him and resuming her own seat, she saw with relief that the frightening grey tinge had left his skin, though he still looked ill and drained. He had always been lean, with no fat on him, but now he was painfully thin.

'What's wrong with you, Thomas?'

'Oh, just some trouble with my chest.' His mouth twisted in a rueful smile. 'All those cold wet nights out on patrol have caught up with me.'

Julia remembered that smile; at one time it had charmed and attracted her, but that had been before she realised that behind it lay a cold man, incapable of giving any woman the warmth and love she needed.

Remembering the red stain she had seen on his handkerchief she asked, 'Is it bad?'

'Bad enough, apparently.' He took a sip of tea. 'Why else would I be here?'

'What do you mean?'

He leaned across the table, his deep-set eyes holding her.

'I mean that I'm dying, Julia. I've got the consumption and I've left Glasgow and the life I knew there. I've found lodgings here in Paisley because you're still my wife and it's up to you to look after me.'

'I have tae hand it tae our Charlie,' Joe Hepburn said, leaning back in his chair, 'for once he's brought an intelligent lass home to meet his old father.'

'Dad!' Charlie's open, honest face went red. 'You'll have Chloe thinking that I fill the place with girls. You know full well that she's the first!'

'I know it, son, and you know it.' His father gave Chloe a wink. 'But you don't want to have young Miss McCosh here thinking that no lassie's ever fancied you before.'

Chloe had been worried about meeting Charlie's father. Everything she had heard about him – a speaker for workers' rights, a demonstrator, a man who had been thrown into prison several times for his political beliefs and finally won through to become a respected Bailie – had, in her mind, built him up into a terrifying image. Instead, she had found a family man who, with his thin face, good bone structure, blue eyes and black hair, greying at the temples, looked like an older version of Charlie. Even the slight twist to the bridge of his nose made him look more distinguished than frightening.

'I'm not bothered about what the other girls

think of Charlie, Mr Hepburn,' she dared to say, 'though I'm sure that plenty have fancied him. It's not as if we own each other. I don't believe in men and women being possessive.'

Joe Hepburn raised his brows at her. 'Better and better, son, you've found yourself an independent thinker intae the bargain.'

'Behave yourself, Joe,' Mirren Hepburn said firmly, while Chloe felt herself turn red. 'What my husband is trying to say, Chloe, in his own wordy political way, is that he likes you.'

'That's very true, but as my wife would be the first to tell you, I've never been very good at making compliments. Am I being too hard on you, lassie?'

'Mebbe a wee bit. I don't like being made to blush,' she said, and he laughed.

'You're right as usual, Mirren. Here, Chloe, give me your cup.'

She watched in amazement as he poured tea and added milk and a spoonful of sugar before bringing the cup back to her, together with a plate of biscuits. Although her own father helped a little about the flat, it was always her mother who looked after visitors. And her father rarely poured his own tea, as Mr Hepburn was doing now.

'Oh, I've got him well trained.' Mirren Hepburn had been watching her guest's reaction. 'Chloe's more impressed by your housewifely skills than by your wit, Joe.'

'One day, lass, women like you will take it for granted that their menfolk should do more for themselves in the house.' He settled himself back in his chair. 'And the men will just have to accept it.'

'I should think so,' Grace said sharply. Bobby, the younger boy, was off on some ploy of his own, but Grace and Daisy were at home.

Now Joe smiled over at his daughter before going on, 'I looked after myself entirely before Mirren here took me under her wing, Chloe, and I still have it to do, when I'm travelling about and living in lodgings.'

'D'you like moving about all over the country?'

'I don't care for living out of a suitcase, but it's a job worth doing and it has to be done. And it's always grand tae come back to Paisley, and tae my own home.' As he said the final words, he gave his wife a smile that wiped the years from his face.

The door flew open and young Daisy rushed in. 'I'm going to practise,' she announced, and made for the piano.

'No you're not.' Grace, sitting near the piano, put her hand on the lid to hold it down.

'I am!' Daisy scowled at her, her face going pink as she tried in vain to open the lid.

'Mother, tell her!'

'Not while we've got a visitor, dear.'

Daisy turned and swept the room with clear blue eyes. 'That's not a visitor, that's Chloe,' she said, and whirled back to the piano.

'Chloe's been invited here for her tea, so today that makes her a special visitor. And she doesn't want to hear you playing the piano at the moment,' her father said. Then, ignoring Charlie's mutter of 'I'm sure she hears more than enough of your playing when you're at her flat,' he held out a hand to his youngest child.

'Come and sit on my knee and help me to eat this bit of cake,' he suggested, and Daisy eyed the cake and then the piano several times before opting for her father's lap, where she demolished most of the cake before kneeling up on his thighs and rubbing her face against his.

'Mr Bumpy Nose,' she said affectionately.

'Not my fault, Daisy. I just happened to get in the way of a policeman's stick during a peaceful law-abiding demonstration,' he said, and his wife rolled her eyes.

'It was probably peaceful enough before you started rousing them up with your speech.'

'You know, Chloe, my wife would have made a wonderful politician, probably better than me. But I could never get her to do anything about it.'

'I had more sense,' Mirren said drily. 'Anyway, if I'd gone on the march the way you did, who would have been around to bandage you up and visit you in the jail?'

'Aye, I suppose you're right. Were you shocked at the thought of meeting a man who'd been a lodger in His Majesty's Prisons, Chloe?' Mr Hepburn asked suddenly, catching her off-guard. She took a moment to think out her answer.

'Not shocked, but a wee bit worried, mebbe,' she said at last, and he laughed.

'There's nothing wrong with going tae prison, lass, if it's in a good cause.'

'It's still breaking the law,' Charlie pointed out.

'Aye, but sometimes when the laws are unfair they need tae be broken because that's the only way tae make folk realise how unfair they are.' Joe Hepburn settled his younger daughter against his shoulder and said over her head, 'This country of ours has always had wealth, Chloe, more wealth than you or me could ever imagine, but it's kept in the hands of just a few fortunate folk. They like it that way and they've always taken it for granted that, for them, life was going to keep on like that. Nice and cosy for them and to blazes with the rest of the folk. When I fought for them – the rich and the powerful – in the Great War, I fought because I thought that things would change afterwards; that they would appreciate what the ordinary folk had done for them, and make things fairer. But not a bit of it. We ended up with mass unemployment and misery. Now we're fighting again, and if you ask me, it could all go the same way once more after this war's been settled. The only difference is that this time my own lad's havin' tae go and fight for them.' His voice was suddenly serious, and Chloe, glancing over at Mrs Hepburn, saw the pain in her eyes.

'I'm not complaining, Dad,' Charlie said. 'I'm willing to do my bit. In fact, I'm looking forward to a bit of a change from the same old life.'

'I know you are, but this time we need to make sure that things really do get better for you and all the lads like you.'

'They will,' Charlie said confidently.

'We're off to a good start, I grant you that,' his father agreed. 'In the war I fought, the working classes were the foot soldiers and the gentry were the officers, with swords at their waists. You'd have thought at times that we were still in the

Middle Ages! But this new conflict's thrown all the classes together for the first time, like a big crucible. It's just a damned shame that it took a war to do it.'

'Language, Joe!'

'Sorry,' he said, and then, returning to his theme, 'And it's not just happening in the Forces, for civilians from different walks of life are gettin' together and learnin' new skills. Women are discoverin' that they can manage very well without having to lean on their menfolk…

'We always knew that,' Mrs Hepburn put in, and was ignored.

'…and the people of this country are showing that they can work together to get things done. And when it's over…'

'Dad, it's time Chloe was going home,' Charlie interrupted gently.

Once they were outside, he tucked Chloe's hand through his arm. 'He can go on a bit, but he's all right really.'

'I like him. I like him very much. He's like my own dad, only my dad doesn't talk as much.'

19

Chloe returned home to find her mother putting the final touches to the dinner. She set the table, talking all the time about her visit to the Hepburns, and it was a while before she noticed that her mother was very quiet.

'Mum, are you all right? You look pale.'

Julia summoned a smile. 'I've got a bit of a headache, that's all.'

'And here's me nattering away and making it worse!'

'No, it's all very interesting. I'm glad that you got on so well with Mr Hepburn.'

'I was surprised at how nice and ordinary he is. And he talks a lot of sense too. He says...' Chloe stopped, then said, 'Sit down, Mum, and I'll make you a cup of tea.'

'But your father'll be in at any minute, and there's the boys to fetch.'

'I can do that.' Chloe was already filling the kettle. 'And I can dish out the dinner.'

'This is supposed to be your afternoon off.'

'And I've had a very nice time. Imagine, Mum, Mr Hepburn actually gave me a second cup of tea ... poured it out with his own hands! And him a former Bailie, too!' Chloe put the kettle on the stove and fetched a clean dish-towel, which she folded and held under the running tap. 'There now, I'll just give this a good squeeze out, and then I'll put it on your forehead.'

'You're a good lassie, Chloe,' Julia said when she was resting in an armchair, her feet on a stool, the cold compress on her forehead and a cup of tea on a small table by her hand. 'A good lassie.'

And Chloe was startled and alarmed to see tears glistening in her mother's lovely green eyes.

Lena and Dennis were working on the vegetable garden when Fergus Goudie appeared and asked cheerfully, 'Need a hand?'

'We could always do with extra help.' Dennis straightened up and leaned on the handle of the fork he was using. 'You're Mrs Goudie's man, aren't you?'

'Fergus.' He held out his hand. 'I'm home on leave but my wife's had to go to work, so I'm at a loose end.'

'Dennis Megson.' They shook hands, and Dennis introduced Lena. She put her fingers into the newcomer's fist for a second or two then withdrew them and scuttled off to the furthest corner, where she sat down on the small wooden stool Dennis had found in the shed, and got on with some weeding.

'That corner looks as though it could do with a bit of digging.' Fergus nodded to a neglected patch.

'The soil's not so good there and we've not had time to tackle it yet.'

'Leave it to me.' Fergus spat on his hands and picked up a spade that was leaning against the wall. 'I'm in the mood for a bit of hard work.' He drove the spade deep into the hard earth and levered a compacted lump free, then moved a spade's width to the side and started again. 'Last time I was home on leave there was a right good band practice going on the night before I left. Are they still playing?'

'Aye.' Dennis forked the soil round a blackcurrant bush. 'That's Mr and Mrs McCosh's band. I play the trumpet in it.'

'Do you indeed? Where d'you play?'

'All over, wherever we're wanted. We're playing

at a dance in the Templar Halls on Saturday, so there'll be a practice on the Friday night.'

'A dance?' Fergus's eyes lit up. 'I think I'll take my missus to that. It beats travelling on the buses.'

'The buses?'

Fergus completed the row and started another. 'With Cecelia working and me on leave, the only way I can see more of her is by sitting on her bus all day, going back and forth and back and forth. It's not my idea of a proper leave.' He grinned over at Dennis. 'I got so fed up with it that I called off for today. I'd much rather be doing something like this.' He lifted another two spadefuls of earth then asked casually, 'Waiting to be called up, are you?'

It was a question Dennis was used to hearing. 'I'm training with the Fire Service. This is my day off.'

'Ah. You'll be kept busy.'

'Busy enough.'

By the time he had to leave to meet his wife coming from work, Fergus Goudie had turned over the entire corner, and broken up the solid clumps of soil.

'A good raking over and a bit of horse manure and it'll be as good a piece of ground as the rest,' he said, rubbing his hands together to remove the worst of the dirt. 'It was grand to get back to some diggin' again.'

'You're used to having a garden?'

'I was brought up on a croft. There was always digging of some sort to be done there. When this business is over I want to find a nice wee house for Cecelia and me with a nice wee garden that I can work in. Vegetables, mebbe a tree or two, some nice flowers for show and for the house ... that sort of thing. See you on Saturday, then.'

When Fergus had gone, Dennis put the fork and spade away. 'I think we've done enough for the day, too,' he said, then gave a low whistle as he inspected the corner Lena had been working on. 'You've got this bit looking like part of the gardens at Buckingham Palace.'

She gave her shy smile. 'It'll do. D'you want to come up for a cup of tea?'

When the two of them had washed their hands in her kitchen Lena nodded at the usual clutter of material on the table. 'Push that stuff out of the way while I make the tea.'

'Is there anything I can do for you while I'm here?' Dennis asked, and she shook her head. 'He's a nice man ... Mrs Goudie's husband,' he went on idly as he began to gather up the cloth strewn over the table. 'A grand worker too.'

'Yes.' Lena's voice was tense, just as she herself had tensed when Fergus appeared. Men made her nervous, Dennis thought, then his chest swelled with pride as he realised that she was different with him. She trusted and liked him, and that made him feel protective in a way he had never felt before, even towards his mother and sisters. He wanted to look after Lena, to banish the anxiety from her bluebell eyes and the worry lines from her mouth. He wanted...

'Ow!' he yelped as a sharp pain stabbed through one finger.

'What's wrong?'

'A needle, just.' He put the injured hand up to his mouth. 'I should have thought to look out for them!'

'Keep away from the sewing machine,' she said at once, 'I mustn't have blood on that material!'

'It's all right, it didn't drip on to anything.' He went to the sink and turned on the single cold tap so that the water could trickle over the bright bead welling from a tiny puncture mark. 'It's stopped bleeding already,' he said after a moment, fishing his handkerchief from his pocket and dabbing the finger dry.

He turned to smile at her, and saw that she was standing by the stove, clutching the battered tin teapot in both hands and staring at him, her eyes large in her stricken face.

'It's all right, no harm done.'

'You got hurt and all I could think to say was keep away from the work. You must think I'm a terrible person!'

'Of course I don't. You didn't want me spoiling that nice material.' He nodded in the direction of the sewing machine and the blue dress draped over it.

'Let me see.' Lena put down the teapot and came over to him, taking his hand in hers and turning it over in search of the wound.

'I told you, it's stopped bleeding. You can't even see where the needle went in.' Her hands were small and cold, the nails cut or bitten short, the skin rough. And yet there was something about her touch that made Dennis tingle from head to toe. Suddenly embarrassed, he cleared his throat and turned away from the sink so that their hands fell apart. Two steps took him to the sewing machine and the blue tulle dress lying across it.

'That's pretty.' He made sure to keep both hands well away from the delicate material.

'It's a bridesmaid's frock. A lassie that works with Mrs Borland's getting married and I'm doing the dresses.'

'That's a lot of work surely,' he asked, and when she shrugged in reply, 'I hope you're paid well for it.'

'Mrs Borland brought me all the materials, and bobbins of thread and things like that. They're difficult to get these days, and expensive too.'

'She can probably get them from the mill for nothing.'

Lena put cups on the table. 'That's something I don't ask about. Better not to know.'

'But even though she gets thread for nothing and supplies the cloth, she still pays you well for your time, doesn't she?'

'I think the tea's ready now. Sit in. Oh ... I got some biscuits,' Lena remembered, beaming at him. 'The kind you like.'

The flat was silent when he let himself in half an hour later. Time to do some studying in peace before the others got home, Dennis thought, stripping off his jacket as he went through the small hall.

He opened the bedroom door and halted in the act of tossing the jacket on to his bed. 'Where the hell did you spring from?'

Ralph, also taken by surprise, gaped up at him from where he sat on his bed, and then managed to pull himself together. 'I came in through the door, where else?'

'What are you doing here? School's not over yet.'

'Our teacher had the toothache, so we got sent home early while he went to the dentist.'

'I don't believe you. And what's that you've got?' Dennis pounced, and managed to grip his brother's wrist, dragging Ralph's hand out from beneath the pillow.

'Nothin'! Let go of me!'

'Open your hand.'

'No!' Ralph tried to lash out as Dennis threw himself on to the bed so that his body pinned the younger boy down.

'Open your hand!'

'No!'

'Do as you're told!' Dennis began to peel his brother's clenched fingers back one by one. Ralph, struggling hard, managed to pull one knee up so that it was wedged between them, then lunged it forward, breaking Dennis's grip and throwing him against his own bed, only some eighteen inches away. He rebounded and came straight back, reaching out for the boy's wrist again, but as Ralph squirmed round, trying to escape, Dennis's outspread hand slammed against his face, the tip of a finger prodding into his eye. As he uttered a howl of pain, both hands flying to his face, the money he had been guarding so jealously showered over the bed and the floor, coins jingling and notes fluttering.

'What the...'

'You've hurt my eye,' Ralph whimpered, then dragging himself upright as his brother bent to collect the money, 'You leave that alone, it's mine!'

'There's ... there must be five pounds or more here. Where did you get it, Ralph?' Then, as his brother glared at him in silence, one eye streaming tears, 'Have you been runnin' for some street bookie again?'

'No.'

'You must've got it from somewhere. Did you steal it?'

'No I didnae steal it. It's mine, I earned it.'

Dennis put the pile of notes and coins on his own bed, out of reach. 'If you earned it then you have to give it to Mam. All of it. And she'll want to know the same as me ... how could a schoolboy earn money like that?'

'I was goin' tae give her some of it, but I've got the right tae keep some for myself,' Ralph muttered, tears from his injured eye beginning to spill down his face.

Light was beginning to dawn. 'This has come from Mrs Borland, hasn't it? You've been goin' round doors, collectin' debts for her.'

'Mind your own business!'

'This is my business! The woman's a money lender and there's folk round here living in misery because of her.'

'She's good tae us. She's good tae all the folks that live in this buildin'.' Ralph knuckled his face, smearing the moisture from his eye all over.

'She's good to folk when it suits her, and if it

doesn't suit she can be a right old devil. If you keep on working for her you'll turn out to be just as bad as she is!'

'It'd be better than livin' the way we are now,' Ralph snarled back at him. 'What's wrong with havin' money and bein' able to do what you want?'

'Nothing, if you've earned it fair and square.'

'And I earned that, so give it back!'

'Not a penny of it.' Dennis used his old pay packets to save money – coppers in one, threepenny bits in another – and now he pulled open the drawer of the small locker standing at the head of his bed and drew out an empty packet. He poured the money into it and then folded the top over. 'I'm giving this back to old Ma Borland, and I'm going to tell her–'

Ralph kicked at his brother's hand, a vicious upswing that Dennis had not expected. As his arm jerked up with the force of the kick the packet flew from his grasp and landed on the floor. Before it could be retrieved, Ralph bunched his fists and went for his brother in earnest, his face twisted with rage.

Although Dennis was the older by five years and half a head taller, Ralph was sturdy and square built. He was also out of his mind with rage, and although they had often sparred before this was the first time they had fought seriously. Ralph's clear aim was to hurt his brother as quickly and as severely as possible, and Dennis was driven back on to his own bed, trying to defend himself from a barrage of hard, painful blows that landed on his head, shoulders and body.

Breathing heavily, grunting with effort, they struggled against each other, Dennis still in shock at the ferocity of the attack and Ralph, straddling his older brother's body, punching as hard and as fast as he could, pinning Dennis down on to the bed. He had gained the upper hand and Dennis could tell by the ferocious grin on the face above his that Ralph knew it, and was out to take full advantage of the situation.

'For God's sake, Ralph!' he gasped, and then gurgled as one of Ralph's hands clamped across his windpipe. The other hand was raised, slowly this time, the fingers clenched into a club of bone and muscle. Ralph's grin grew wider.

'Got ye, ye bastard,' he said softly. 'And now I'm goin' tae make sure that ye'll not play that precious trumpet of yours for a good long while. That should teach ye tae leave me alone!'

'No!' Dennis managed to wheeze the word out. His greatest fear, as Ralph well knew, was damage of any kind to his mouth. He thrashed his body about on the bed, desperate to dislodge the weight that pinned it down. Just as his brother's clubbed fist began to plunge towards him he managed to wrench his head to the side, despite the tight grip on his throat. Pain ripped through his neck and then exploded along his jawline and up into his skull as Ralph's fist came down hard, just below his ear.

Lights flashed before Dennis's eyes and for a moment he thought that he was going to black out; instead, as the grip on his neck eased slightly, he managed to find enough energy to heave his body upwards, throwing Ralph off balance.

They were so intent on their struggle that neither heard the door open, and it was not until Nan Megson's shocked voice asked, 'What in the name of heaven is going on here?' that they were aware of her arrival.

They immediately broke apart. Dennis, a hand to his bruised throat, fought to get his breath back, while Ralph whined, 'He nearly put my eye out!'

'For goodness' sake, have the two of you not got an ounce of common sense between you? Dennis, you're the man of this family now and you should know better. So should you, Ralph. You're thirteen years old and it's time you learned to act like it. Let me see.' Nan took the boy's head in her two hands and tilted his face up to catch what light there was from the narrow window. 'It's inflamed, but no harm done. Now put this place to rights, the two of you ... look at the mess you've made of your beds.'

Ralph scurried to obey, tossing a smirk at Dennis as he knelt to tuck in the bedclothes. 'Sorry, Mam,' he said as he got to his feet.

'So I should think. Now get into that kitchen and start peeling potatoes. As for you,' she said to her elder son as Ralph slunk out, 'there's to be no more of this fighting. I know that Ralph can be annoying at times but if you can't discipline him without having a fight you'd be best to leave it to me to deal with him if he misbehaves in future.' Then her voice changed as he pressed his finger-tips gently against the hinge of his jaw, wincing. 'What's the matter, son? Did he hurt you?'

He opened then closed his mouth gingerly. 'He

got in a lucky punch, just.'

'Away through to the kitchen and soak a bit of rag in vinegar and water, that'll help to keep you from getting too much of a bruise,' his mother ordered, unfastening her coat. She turned to go out of the room, then stopped as he said, 'Mam?'

'What is it, son?' She had put in a long shift at the hospital and then walked home; wisps of hair escaped from beneath her hat and she looked tired, as always. She had enough to worry about without him adding to it, Dennis thought guiltily.

'I'm sorry,' he said. 'I know that I shouldnae let Ralph anger me the way he does sometimes.'

She smiled, and put her hand lightly on his head. 'It's all right, Dennis. I've not been fair on you, expecting you to grow up so fast and be responsible for the younger ones. You've got your own life to lead.'

'I don't mind. I want to take my father's place. It's what he'd want too.'

'You're doing fine and he'd be as proud of you as I am. But no more fighting! Now, come through to the kitchen and I'll get the vinegar out.'

Before following her, Dennis looked down at the floor, then got on to his knees and felt about in the darkness below each of the narrow beds.

The packet of money was gone. Ralph must have taken it when he was tidying his bed.

20

Fergus was waiting when Cecelia arrived at Paisley Cross at the end of her shift. He kissed her, heedless of the people milling about, then tucked her hand into his arm as they turned to walk down Smithhills. 'Busy day?'

'Nothing special. I missed you.'

'I needed a day off. Travelling up and down between Glasgow and Paisley's not my idea of a perfect leave, sweetheart. Half the time you're too busy to speak to me.'

'I don't think Glasgow Corporation would like it if I refused to let passengers on to my bus just because they get in the way of us speaking to each other.'

'I know. The only excitement I get is when Harry spots an inspector waiting to board, and you've to rush up to me and demand my fare. Although I've learned something interesting about the woman I married.'

'What's that?'

'You can be surprisingly bossy when you're on that bus, and quite loud too. And yet when you're at home you're the same quiet, shy Cecelia I fell in love with and married.'

'I've noticed that too. It's got something to do with the uniform. Don't you feel different when you're wearing yours?'

'That's different,' he said. 'When I'm in uniform I'm just one part of a unit; if anything, I get quieter and more obedient. But you're in charge of your own bus, so you have to give the orders and see that the rules are obeyed. You love that job, don't you?'

'I do. I never thought I would, though. The war's taught me something about myself,' Cecelia said, surprised by the realisation. 'So what did you do with your day while I was bossing the passengers about?'

'Nothing much. A bit of reading, a bit of housework. And in the afternoon I saw that young fellow Megson working in the backcourt so I went down and gave him a hand. There was a woman doing a bit of weeding, a pretty little thing, very shy. She had a bit of a limp.'

'That's Lena Fulton; we met her and her husband on the stairs once, remember? He was on leave the same time as you. She was working in the vegetable garden?' Cecelia asked with surprise.

'Yes, but she kept herself to herself. There's going to be a band practice on Friday,' Fergus remembered, 'and young Megson said that they're playing at a dance in the Templar Halls on Saturday night. Fancy going?'

'I'd love it.'

'Good.' He withdrew her hand from the crook of his elbow so that he could put his arm about her. 'Come on, let's get you home and out of that bossy uniform.'

Cecelia knocked on the door, waited, and was wondering if she should knock again when she heard movement in the hall beyond. A moment later the door opened slightly and Lena Fulton peered out at her.

'Lena, I wondered if you had time to look at this skirt for me. The problem is, I need it in a bit of a hurry, for tomorrow evening.'

The other girl hesitated, and for a moment Cecelia thought that she was going to refuse. Then the door opened wider and Lena said, 'Come in and show me what you want done.'

'I've put on a bit of weight,' Cecelia explained in the kitchen, taking off her coat to show the skirt she wore underneath. 'I've managed to get the button in to the buttonhole, but it won't zip up, and Fergus is taking me dancing at the Templar Hall tomorrow. I wanted to wear this with a nice wee blouse I have, but when I tried it on ... it's all these slabs of bread and margarine I eat when we get to a terminus,' she babbled on as Lena examined the skirt, 'but I get so hungry, specially when I have to start early in the morning...'

'Take it off, will you?'

Cecelia slipped off the skirt and stood in her petticoat, watching as the seamstress examined the darts and the waistband.

'There's a bit of room left in the waistband, so I can let it out a little. And there are darts that could be opened.' She put it aside and took a tape measure from the table. 'Lift your arms away from your sides...'

While Lena fussed around with the tape measure Cecelia studied the work laid out on the table. 'What's that you're making?'

Lena cast a look over her shoulder. 'A patchwork quilt.'

'Are you making it for someone?'

'No, it's just something I'm trying for myself whenever I have a spare minute.'

'Can I have a closer look?' Cecelia asked when Lena finished taking her measurements and returned to study the skirt.

'If you like.'

The quilt was only the size of a large pillow as yet, but even so the combination of colours and textures gave Cecelia plenty to look at. 'Where did you get the material from?' she wanted to know, running her fingers over the beautifully stitched sections.

'All sorts of places,' Lena said vaguely. 'Clothes I altered for myself and bits left over from work I've done for other folk.'

'Would you do one for me when you've finished this one?' Cecelia dared to ask, adding hastily when Lena looked uncertain, 'I'd pay you whatever you wanted. I can see that there's a lot of work in something like this.'

'Mebbe ... yes, when I've got the time,' Lena said.

'I'd like that. It would be something to keep for ever, a memento of all the different frocks I had, and what they meant to me. Is that what you're doing yours for?'

'Yes, it is,' Lena said, after a brief pause, then held up the skirt. 'I think I can let it out just enough to fit you. Saturday, you said?'

'Fergus is going away on Sunday and he wants us to go to this dance on Saturday. Mr McCosh's band is playing ... you know, Mr and Mrs McCosh and Dennis Megson.'

'I know.'

'D'you want paying now, or when I fetch the skirt?'

'When you fetch it will be fine.'

'What about your own man?' Cecelia asked as she put on her coat, wrapping it about her and pulling the belt tight in case she met anyone on the stairs on her way back to her own flat. 'When's he going to get some leave?'

'I don't know. He's overseas just now, so not for a while.'

Cecelia hesitated, then said, 'Why don't you come to the dance with me and Fergus?'

'I couldn't! I'm ... I'm not very good at dancing.'

'You don't have to dance at all, you can just sit and enjoy listening to the music. We could have a nice night out.'

'No,' Lena said, her voice almost panic-stricken. 'I've got too much work to do.' She opened the door and waited for her visitor to precede her into the hall.

'Well, if you change your mind you know where we live,' Cecelia said at the front door.

'Aye, I do. Thank you for thinking of me.'

'It's a pity about your husband,' Cecelia said, stepping on to the landing. 'You must miss him.'

'Aye,' said Lena. 'I do.'

When her visitor had gone, she lifted the quilt and then laid it back down on the table, running her hand over it and letting her fingers rest on each of the patches. When she first started work on it she had used whatever material she picked up, but as the work began to gain importance to her, she had become more selective.

The centrepiece was the large patch from her wedding dress, the day she had given herself to George, not fully realising at the time just what 'giving herself' entailed. A silky turquoise patch came from a blouse she had been particularly fond of. She had been wearing it on the day she and her aunt got the telegram telling them of her brother's death in France, and she had never worn it again. Here was a piece from the scarf George had given her when she agreed to marry him, and there was a section from the blouse her aunt had worn when she attended their wedding.

A small bag of specially selected pieces lay beside the quilt; Lena chose one and sat down, drawing the quilt towards her and picking up a needle. She would stay up late tonight, working on Cecelia Goudie's skirt. For the moment, the quilt took precedence.

Frank McCosh had had a difficult day at work, and for once, he did not feel up to a band practice.

'It had better be a good rehearsal,' he told Julia as they got the front room ready, 'for I'm not in the mood for stops and starts all night.' Then he paused and eyed her closely. 'Are you all right?'

'Why wouldn't I be all right?'

'You look pale. Is it a headache?'

'I'm fine. Just a bit tired.' Her tone was dismissive as she began to lay out the sheet music she had laboriously copied.

'D'you want me to cancel the practice? I will, if you don't feel up to it.'

'For goodness' sake, Frank, don't go sympathising with me or you'll only make me feel even more sorry for myself! Everyone's tired just now, with interrupted nights and rationing and this constant worry about what's going to happen to us...'

He took the papers from her hands and put his arms about her. 'It'll be all right, love, I promise you. We'll not let that Hitler get the better of us.'

She drew away, biting her lip, and then said, 'I suppose I'm feeling down because Mirren came round to tell me that Charlie's call-up papers have arrived.'

'Already? They must be keen to get recruits in the Air Force.'

'I think they're getting desperate for new recruits in all the Forces. At least we're still a few years away from that worry as yet, and with any luck it might never happen to us. Now then, let's get on with it or Bert and Dennis will be here and nothing ready for them.'

Bert arrived just as they got everything setup, but Dennis Megson kept them waiting, and incurred Frank's displeasure when he finally arrived.

'It's not as if you've got a distance to travel,' Frank pointed out coldly as the young man stammered out apologies. 'Two floors away, that's all. Bert lives over in Orchard Street and he's been cooling his heels along with the rest of us for the past half-hour, waiting for you.'

'I'm sorry, I'd things to do and I didnae realise

the time was passing,' Dennis stuttered, his face bright red apart from a slight shadowing along his jawline, just below the ear. Frank's hand shot out to catch the lad's chin and turn his face to the light.

'And what's this? Have you been fighting?'

'Just a wee scrap with our Ralph...'

'I hope it doesnae interfere with your playing.'

'It won't, Mr McCosh, honest!'

'For goodness' sake, Frank, the lad's here now,' Julia interrupted, 'so can we not just get on with the practice instead of spending more time talking about why he was late?'

Her tone was unusually sharp, and when they all looked at her, surprised by her unexpected anger, she swallowed hard and added in a more reasonable voice, 'Let's just start work, shall we?'

Unfortunately, everything that could go wrong that night did go wrong. Time and again Frank lowered his saxophone and ordered them to stop. They had to go over small sections again and again before they got them right, and to make matters worse the air-raid siren started to wail just when they were into the final hour of the rehearsal.

'Damn and blast!' Frank exploded as feet clattered on the stairs outside and Chloe and her mother ran to waken the two boys, long since in their beds. As they got the youngsters up and were helping them to get dressed the two women heard the door of the flat open and then close. They stared at each other.

'Surely that's not your father going to the Home Guard?' Julia asked. 'He's not on duty tonight, and neither's Bert.'

'Mebbe it's Dennis gone to see to his own family,' Chloe suggested, but as they led Duncan and Leslie, blinking sleepily in the light and clutching their 'shelter bags', into the front room Dennis and Bert were still there.

'Where's Frank gone?'

'Just away to find out what's happening,' Bert said. 'He told us tae stay here and the mood he's in tonight, I'd not want tae cross him. Anyway, I'm not wantin' tae walk home in the middle of a raid.'

'Dennis?'

'My mother's home tonight and she knows where I am if she needs me,' the young man said as Frank returned.

'Right, I got hold of a warden and it looks like just the one fighter plane that's mebbe got separated from his squadron. They're tracking him now.' From a distance, as he spoke, they could hear the dull thumping of anti-aircraft guns. 'He doesnae think the raid'll be a long one unless it turns out that this chap's mates are behind him. So here's what we'll do ... you take the boys down to the shelter, Chloe, and the rest of us'll keep on with the practice.' He glared at the members of his band. 'Any objections?'

There were none, and so Chloe was sent off in charge of her brothers while the others picked up their instruments and Julia returned to the piano stool.

As the rest of the tenement folk settled into the drysalter's the faint strains of 'Marie' filtered down from above to make a pleasant background to Donnie Borland's snores.

Ellen, Jessie Bell and Nan Megson talked quietly together while Lena Fulton, on the edge of the group as usual, worked at some sewing. Fergus Goudie had dreamed up a variation on Ludo to keep the McCosh and Megson children occupied, and even Ralph joined in.

'Come and have a game, Chloe,' Cecelia Goudie suggested, and when Chloe squeezed in at the small card table, she whispered, 'your parents will be safe, I'm sure. If your father thinks there's any danger he'll bring them all down here.'

Chloe smiled wanly, and tried without success to concentrate on the game. Cecelia was right, her father wouldn't let any harm come to her mother, or to any member of his beloved band. But she was fretting about her mother, who had not been her usual self for the past few days, and she was still trying to take in the news that Charlie had been called up. Somehow, she had not thought that it would really happen, and she was still confused about her own reaction.

The music changed; she had learned to recognise a tune from just a few notes, and now she realised that on the floor above they were playing 'All I Do Is Dream of You.' Her father would start it off, she knew, and then give Dennis a nod so that the trumpet could come in for a verse.

Thinking of Dennis reminded her of the dark smudge of a bruise on his jawline, faint but definite, as though a sooty finger had been run lightly along the length of the bone. He, like her mother, had something on his mind, and it surely wasn't the fight he had had with his brother. Brothers fought all the time, she knew that well enough.

She glanced over at Lena Fulton. Had his preoccupation anything to do with Lena? Something was going on there; Chloe had seen them working in the garden companionably, and sitting together in the Fountain Gardens. And once, on her way out, she had even seen Dennis coming out of Lena's flat, looking pleased with himself. She had stepped back into her own hallway unnoticed, and waited until he was gone before venturing out again.

Were he and Mrs Fulton...? Surely not! Mrs Fulton was a lot older than him, and besides, she was a married woman. It must be something else, something innocent. But what?

Now she could just make out Dennis playing the solo section. She closed her eyes and dreamed that she was stroking the tips of her fingers over his face, and smoothing away the faint bruise that had shadowed the line of his jaw.

'I'm going to miss dancing with you, and listening to your parents playing,' Charlie Hepburn said as he steered Chloe round the Templar Halls dance floor. Saturday night dances were popular in Paisley, and the place was crowded. As well as the local folk there were foreign servicemen based at the Fleet Air Arm station at Abbotsinch and even some seamen from the Clyde base at Gourock, who had become friendly with

Paisley girls.

'You'll be coming home on leave. We can go dancing then.' Chloe knew that she should be trying to make the evening enjoyable for him, but her mind was on other matters. The band was playing well enough, but not as well as it usually did; although she wasn't as musical as her parents, Chloe had heard enough practices to know how it was doing.

'...a drink of juice?' Charlie asked from above her head.

'What?' Chloe started from a daydream and realised that she and Charlie were now at the side of the dance floor, which was clear except for people standing in small groups, talking. The band members were laying down their instruments. It must be the interval already.

'For the third time of asking, d'you want a drink? It's flattering,' Charlie said with mock annoyance, 'to know that my presence is so riveting that you don't even hear a word I'm saying.'

'Sorry, I was thinking about something that happened at work.'

'See what I mean? Even work is more interesting than being with me.'

'Don't be daft, and yes please, I would like a drink of juice.'

'Won't be long,' he said, and pushed his way into the crowd gathered around the counter, where women were serving tea and cold drinks to the thirsty dancers.

Chloe waited, perched on the edge of a seat, her hands clasped in her lap, missing Marion. Usually they had a good gossip during the interval, but tonight was Robert's grandmother's birthday, and Marion, now 'going with' Robert in a serious way, had been invited to the family celebrations.

On the stage, her father was talking earnestly, both hands gesturing and the tea someone had brought for the band in danger of flying from the cup he held. Chloe could tell by his face that he wasn't pleased with the night's performance.

'Here you are.' Charlie thrust a tumbler into her hand and took a seat by her side. 'The music's good, isn't it?'

'Not as good as usual. My mother hit a couple of wrong notes.'

'Did she? I didn't notice,' he was saying as Cecelia Goudie and her husband came towards them.

'Hello, mind if we join you?' Cecelia asked.

'No, that would be nice.' Chloe introduced them to Charlie, who leapt to his feet to offer his chair to Cecelia. Almost at once he and Fergus were talking about Charlie's call-up.

'I sometimes think,' Cecelia said into Chloe's ear, 'that men still treat the war as a game.'

'Mebbe it's as well they do, otherwise they might not be able to keep going.'

'I hadn't thought about it like that. You're probably right.' Cecelia eyed the younger woman with a new respect, then said, low-voiced, 'But it's nothing like a game for us, is it? If you ever feel that you want to talk to someone once your boyfriend's gone, you're welcome to come to my flat anytime.'

'Thanks, Mrs Goudie.'

'Call me Cecelia ... "Mrs Goudie" makes me feel old!'

'Cecelia.' Chloe smiled, still young enough to be thrilled by the thought of having a mature, married woman as a friend. Then she added hurriedly, 'Not that Charlie's my boyfriend, really. Just a friend.'

'Quite right, you're both young to get too serious. Or is there someone else on your mind?'

'Nobody,' Chloe lied, only just stopping herself from glancing up at the small stage, where the band was taking its place in readiness for the second half of the evening.

Fergus Goudie had noticed them and now he held out his hand to his wife. 'Come on, Cecelia, we don't get the chance to dance together often, so I want us to dance every dance tonight.'

21

'What happened to you?' Lena's hand fluttered towards Dennis's bruised face, and then she drew her fingers back, trapping them in her other hand. 'Have you been in a fight?'

'Aye ... with Ralph.' He wished that she had not pulled back, for he ached for her soothing touch. He needed it; he needed her, he suddenly realised.

'You fought with your brother? Why?'

'He's up to his tricks again.' Dennis gave her a brief description of the scene with Ralph and the money he had found in the boy's possession, ending with, 'I told him already that he had to keep well away from her, but he's disobeyed me. When I tried to take the money away from him, he went for me.'

'He might not have got it from her.' She sat down at the kitchen table and reached for the patchwork quilt, which she had been working on when he came to the door.

'He did. Who else would pay so much money to a lad of his age? The woman's a money lender.' Dennis sat down opposite. 'The whole street knows about it, and it's her business, not mine. But it's another matter altogether when she brings our Ralph into it. Ralph likes money and he likes to feel important, but he's only thirteen. She's paying him for the errands he runs, mebbe even to collect debts for her, and that's a bad thing.'

She glanced up at him, a swift flick of the eyes from beneath her tumble of fair hair. It was a glance that made him shiver in a pleasant way; he wondered if she realised what an attractive woman she was, or if that husband of hers had ever told her. Probably not.

'Why tell me about it?' she asked.

'I have to speak tae someone, and you were the only one I could think of.'

Lena made a few more tiny stitches before raising the work to her face and biting off the thread. Then she selected another needle to be threaded with a different colour. 'What about your mother?'

'That's the last thing I want to do! She's

working long hours at that hospital and she worries enough about the four of us as it is. Are we happy, are we getting enough to eat, what's going to happen to us if this war goes the wrong way ... she tries to cover it up, but I know fine that she worries, day and night,' Dennis said helplessly. 'And if she knew what Ralph was up to she'd only worry even more. I have to sort it out for myself. Mebbe I should go and have it out with old Ma Borland.'

Lena had been trying to introduce the end of the thread through the needle's minute eye. Now, she paused for a moment and looked across the table at him, her face suddenly tense. 'Best to leave things as they are for a wee while. You don't want to cause trouble with neighbours. That might be worse for your mother.'

'D'you think so?'

'You say you've told your brother to stop whatever it is he was doing. Give him the chance to do it.' She blinked and then rubbed at her eyes as though they were sore. 'Don't do anything that'll cause trouble for anyone.'

'Mebbe you're right. Here, let me try...' He took needle and thread from her, and after a few tries managed to ease the end of the thread through the needle's tiny eye.

'There!' he handed it back, and watched as she began to stitch. It was a relief to talk to someone, and to make the decision to just let things go for the time being. Dennis reached out and touched the quilt, which now spilled over most of the table. 'That's growing fast.'

She smiled at him. 'I like working on it. It

soothes me.'

To his eye it appeared sombre, with few of the bright patches he would have expected, but it seemed to satisfy Lena. 'D'you have to buy the bits of cloth specially?'

'I just cut down scraps left over from work I've done ... mostly from clothes I used to wear.'

For the next few minutes they enjoyed one of the companionable, comfortable silences that they had grown into, with Lena sewing and Dennis studying the quilt. Finally, he stirred and said reluctantly, 'I'd better go. Is there anything I can do for you before I go? Wash the cups, mebbe?'

'I can't have you washing my dishes. That's not a man's work.'

'Aye it is. My father washed dishes and he was a man. I wash them and I'm a man. Look...' He thrust his arms towards her, hands outspread. 'I've got two hands the same as you. That's all that's needed for dish-washing.'

'It's kind of you to offer, but I can see to the cups.'

When he had gone, Lena finished working on the patch she had cut from a pretty handkerchief George had bought her, and sifted through the bag of pieces.

Finding nothing there to suit her, she walked about the flat restlessly, opening drawers and cupboards, fingering clothes, bedding, everything she could find.

One of the drawers in the large bedroom dresser held nothing but a baby's pale lemon romper suit and a little bib. 'For my son,' George had said with pride on his last leave, as he unwrapped them and held them up for her inspection.

'You went into a shop and bought clothes for a baby?' she had asked in disbelief.

'Not just for a baby, ye daft woman ... for my son! I told the woman in the shop that. I said to her, I only want the best you have because it's for my son. We'll get more things the next time I'm on leave, so save up your clothing coupons,' he had ordered.

She had tried to do as he said, but as her debt to Mrs Borland mounted, and no more money arrived from old Mr Fulton, the coupons had gone to Ellen Borland in part payment of her debt.

Now, she took the bib out of the drawer, hesitated, put it back, and lifted the romper suit instead. The material was silky soft against her rough-skinned fingers and she caressed it as she carried it back to the kitchen.

Sitting back down at the table, she picked up her scissors and carefully cut a large piece of cloth from the front of the rompers. There was still enough left, she noticed happily as she rethreaded the needle, for another patch. They would help to brighten her precious quilt.

A fragile sense of contentment stole over Lena as she tied a knot on the end of the thread and began to stitch at the silky yellow patch.

It didn't get any better, Cecelia thought drearily as she tapped the bell twice and the bus drew away from the stop. The missing and the longing only seemed to get worse with each parting.

Twenty-four hours had passed since Fergus's leave had ended, and she had scarcely slept on the previous night. Once or twice she had dozed, then reached out in her sleep to touch the warm solid body that should have been in the bed with her, only to be awakened by the realisation that he was not there any more.

As she collected fares from the two housewives who had just boarded, one of them said encouragingly, 'Cheer up, hen. Worse things happen at sea.'

'What?'

'Ye look as if ye'd hung yer best knickers out on the washing line and gone back tae find a pair of flannel drawers. Cheer up, you're too young to look so worried!'

'I'm fine.' Cecelia summoned up a smile.

'Here...' The other woman delved into her pocket and produced a small crumpled paper bag. 'Have a sooky sweetie,'

'I can't take your sweet ration.'

'Aye ye can,' the first woman told her, jerking her head sideways at her companion. 'She made me wave the last bus by just so's she could get on yours and give you a sweetie. So you take it, hen.'

'Thanks.' With some difficulty Cecelia prised a round black-and-white striped sweet free of its companions and put it into her mouth.

'That's for bein' such a nice wee clippie,' her benefactor said, as Harry, spotting an inspector at the stop ahead, flashed the interior lights in warning and slowed down.

The sweet helped Cecelia to cheer up a bit, but

the inspector, unsmiling and officious, did not do her spirits any good at all. He trudged up and down the aisle checking tickets, then came back to the platform to go over the day's takings with Cecelia.

'Seems in order,' he admitted at last, sounding faintly put out. Then he lifted his head, sniffing the air. 'What's that?'

'What?' Cecelia, who had been doing her best to conceal the fact that she was sucking a sweet while on duty, tucked it hurriedly into her cheek and prayed that she wouldn't swallow it or inhale it by mistake.

'That!' He sniffed again. 'For pity's sake, lassie, you're not goin' tae tell me that ye can't smell anythin'!'

Cecelia suddenly noticed that the passengers sitting on the long side seats nearest the door were screwing up their noses and eyeing each other furtively. She stepped up into the main section of the bus, sniffed, and then recoiled at the stench that hit her.

'I don't know ... it didn't smell like this a wee while ago when I was taking the fares,' she told the inspector, who turned red.

'Are you saying that that ... stink ... came on to the bus with me?'

'No, of course not. I just meant...'

More passengers were beginning to notice that something was amiss. Up and down the length of the bus heads were turning, noses lifting and sniffing, people doing their best to edge away from each other.

'Open a window, for pity's sake,' the inspector

muttered, and as Cecelia hurried to obey she heard the first ominous murmurings from the passengers.

A woman who had brought a small baby on board glared at those nearest to her and then whipped the infant out of the shawl that had been wrapped about her own body to act as a carrier. Turning the child about, she sniffed noisily and energetically at its little rump.

'Whatever it is, it's no' her,' she announced to all and sundry, and then, shoving the baby at the man sitting next to her, invited, 'Here you, have a good sniff, why don't ye?'

When he declined, choosing instead to leap to his feet and head for the exit, she went on loudly, 'An' it's not me neither, so it must be one of youse!'

As Cecelia paused in her window-opening and reached for the bell to signal Harry to stop the bus, the woman who had given her the sweetie turned round in her seat at the front of the bus and shouted cheerfully, 'Keep your hair on, everyone, it's just me.' She dipped into her bag and brought out a small glass jar, which she flourished in the air. 'I got a bad egg from the grocer yesterday and I'm takin' it back and gettin' a fresh one. With eggs on the ration I cannae afford tae throw out a bad yin.'

The entire bus seemed to heave a collective sigh of relief. 'I'd one just last week, hen,' a respectable-looking woman in the seat across the aisle said. 'I took it back an' all. It's a disgrace, so it is. It's bad enough, being expected to manage with just one fresh egg each a week, but it's a right insult when you get one that's not even fit to eat. And nobody can tell me that that powdered stuff can replace a real egg from a real hen.'

As the entire lower deck settled down to a cosy discussion about the merits of shelled and powdered egg, and another woman began to impart the secret of how to make two cakes from one 'proper' egg, the bus began to slow for the next stop.

'D'you really want to get off here, sir, or would you prefer to stay on until you reach the right stop?' Cecelia heard the inspector murmur to the man who had previously decided to alight.

'I think I'll stay on.' The man scurried gratefully back to his seat as the first of the new passengers put one foot into the main section then hesitated, sniffing.

'Bad egg,' Cecelia heard the inspector say as she finished opening the windows. 'Going back to the grocer's. There'll be another bus along in five minutes if you'd prefer to wait.'

He belled the bus back into motion, and then beckoned her down to join him on the platform.

'I was just going to collect the new fares,' she protested as she reached him.

'You can do that when I get off the bus at Paisley Cross,' he said. 'For now, lassie, you can just stand here beside me, for I prefer the smell of the sweetie you're sucking to the stink from that addled egg.'

22

'I kept hoping that the war would suddenly turn our way,' Mirren Hepburn said wistfully, 'and that my Charlie wouldn't have to go. But I suppose every poor soul who's had to watch a son or a brother or a husband go off to war has prayed for the same thing without success.'

'I suppose they have,' Julia agreed, 'but that doesn't make your worry any the less. Are you sure you don't just want to go home again? I could see to this work on my own.'

'It's kind of you, Julia, but I'm better to be occupied. Would you look at this?' The two women were sorting out clothing that had been donated to the Women's Voluntary Service, and now Mirren held up a strapped evening blouse consisting of layers of glittering beads. 'I can just imagine some poor woman bombed out of her home and left with nothing but the clothes on her back wanting something like this! On the other hand, it might cheer someone up, who knows?' She put it to one side, shaking her head. 'I wish the better off folk would give a bit of thought to what they donate.'

'Perhaps they don't have much that's useful for ordinary people,' Julia offered.

'They must have warm coats and skirts ... good woollens and tweeds that would keep the women we're trying to help warm and decently covered.

And proper underclothes. It makes a difference to a woman, doesn't it,' Mirren said, 'having decent underclothes?' Then, with the ghost of a smile, 'I meant to tell you, when I was giving out clothing last week one woman who came looking for help was telling me that her husband sent her a beautiful pair of silk drawers from Singapore with a note saying "Please fill and return." Isn't that a lovely, romantic gesture? It fairly cheered her up, and the dear Lord only knows she needed it, because she'd just heard that she'd lost two brothers in France.' She shivered, and Julia knew by the darkness of her eyes that she was thinking of Charlie again.

'He'll be all right, Mirren. I'm sure he will.'

'Of course he will.' They worked in silence for a while, then Mirren said, 'One of my brothers was killed in the Great War. The older one. He was married, with a wee boy. My mother's health was never the same after she heard that our Crawford was gone. It's a hard thing, losing a child. You expect them to live on after you.' She sighed, and then held up a skirt with a frayed hem. 'This is past mending.'

'Give it to me and I'll put it in the sack for the ragman. What happened to your brother's wife?' Julia asked as the garment changed hands.

'Agnes? She married a good man that cared for wee Thomas as much as for the bairns that came later to him and Agnes. Not that Thomas is wee now; of course. He's married with two children of his own. And he's in the navy, but so far he's survived and please God he'll come home safely.'

Mirren paused, then added with a sidelong

look, 'You're awful quiet, Julia. Are you not feeling well?'

'I'm fine.'

'You don't look fine,' Mirren said bluntly. 'In fact, you look right poorly. Is there something wrong with your man, or the children?'

'No, not a thing.'

'It's not ... another bairn on the way?'

'What? Of course not!' Julia was startled in to an abrupt laugh.

'It's not all that impossible. You're young yet, and you seem to be happy enough with your man.'

'Oh, I am,' Julia said from the heart.

'There you are, then, you still enjoy a wee cuddle together in bed at night. So what's wrong?'

'You're beginning to sound like a gossipy schoolgirl instead of a respectable married woman, Mirren Hepburn!'

'Those were the days, eh?' Mirren heaved a nostalgic sigh. 'I mind the chats me and my pal Ella had when we worked in the mill together, about clothes and the dancing ... and about lads, and what we were going to be when we were properly grown up.'

'Did your dreams come true?'

'Not the way we expected at the time. In those days, right after the Great War, I was all set to go to America to join my sweetheart Donald. He'd gone out there with his family to build a new life for us. And Ella ... well, she was never going to tie herself down to marriage. But I'd my mother to look after, and then Donald found someone else.'

'He jilted you?'

'He did that. It was terrible at the time. Then after a while he decided that it was me he wanted after all and not this other lassie. But by that time I'd met Joe, so the upshot of it is that I'm still here in Paisley. And the same Ella that wasn't ever going to get married changed her mind too. She wed my brother Robbie, and now she's the one living in America. They're doing very well for themselves; it's them we get the food parcels from. My cousin Grace sends them too; she left Paisley not long after the war and now she's married to an American. It's funny how things turn out, isn't it?' Mirren folded a pair of trousers neatly and put them on top of the growing pile of acceptable clothing.

'Not so funny, sometimes.'

'Look, Julia, you're going to have to tell someone what's bothering you or the misery of it will make you ill. And surely we're friends enough for you to tell me. You know it won't go any further.'

'I've no doubt of that, but...' Julia hesitated, then said in a rush of words, 'Oh Mirren, I've done such a terrible thing and I know we're good friends but, if I tell you, you'll not want to be my friend any more and–'

'I doubt if that could happen, for I know the sort of woman you are, Julia McCosh, and I like you; and unless you've committed some terrible murder my liking won't change. If you can't tell me, then at least tell your husband.'

'Frank? He's the last person I'd want to tell ... though he might have to know, and perhaps it should come from me first and not from... Oh,

Mirren, what am I going to do?'

Mirren took the blouse that Julia was fumbling through her agitated fingers and put it to one side, then said slowly and firmly, 'You're going to tell me what this is all about before you destroy yourself completely with the worry. Two heads are better than one and mebbe I can help you.'

'It's my husband.'

'Frank? Is he ill?'

'No, not him. Frank and me ... we're not married,' Julia said in a shamed whisper. 'We couldn't marry because when we met each other I already had a husband.'

'Oh, my dear. And the two of you have kept your secret all these years? I think that's very brave of you,' Mirren added when Julia nodded.

'Brave?'

'It must have taken courage to leave your legal husband for someone else. I presume that he deserved to be left, for you don't strike me as the sort of woman who would just go off with another man on a whim.'

Mirren's matter-of-fact acceptance made it easier for Julia to tell her friend about her marriage to Thomas Gordon, and the realisation within months that she had made a mistake.

'He was a hard man to live with ... or perhaps I was just the wrong woman for him, I don't know. Thomas had been a military man and when he left the army he went into the police force. He was good at it, firm but fair, someone once told me, and he was made up to sergeant not long after we married. But he was the same in the house as he was in the police office ... everything had to be just so, and he'd no time for what he called slacking.'

'In other words,' Mirren said crisply, 'he was a bully.'

'Oh no! Well, he never hit me, if that's what you mean; he didn't have to because he had other ways of showing his disapproval when I did something wrong. And he didn't like me to be out of the house unless I was at the shops or with him. He used to make out a list of housekeeping duties ... a rota, he called it,' Julia recalled with an inward shudder. 'He worked out the exact time it should take me to do each task, and he wrote down when I should start it and when it should be completed. That way, when he was on duty he knew exactly where I was and what I was doing.'

'He sounds a bit like my Joe's family. From what I've heard, they were strict, humourless folk. I'd a hard struggle teaching him how to be a proper father, I can tell you, once the bairns came along. I wasn't going to let him raise them the way he had been raised. Or the way I had been raised, if it comes to that.'

'To be fair to Thomas, he didn't just show his annoyance when I got things wrong, he also had ways of rewarding me when I pleased him,' Julia hastened to explain.

'A lot of men follow that line, but it's usually with their dogs or their horses, not their wives,' Mirren said drily. 'So, where does Frank McCosh come into the picture?'

'Through music, what else?' The shadow of a smile tugged at Julia's strained mouth. 'I had taught piano lessons from home before we married, and since it brought in some money, Thomas allowed me to go on with that. Then about a year after we married, the mother of one of my pupils asked if I would play the piano for a fundraising concert. And Frank was there, playing the saxophone. After that I was asked to play at other events, and Thomas agreed to let me do it. He was quite proud of me, poor man,' Julia went on, too involved in her story to notice Mirren's sharp, angry intake of breath at the thought of Thomas Gordon 'agreeing' to allow his wife to play at concerts. 'And each time I was asked to play at some function I found myself hoping that Frank would be there too, that I would see him again. Then a few months later...' The shadows came back into Julia's striking green eyes. 'Thomas was away for a few days on a course and I agreed to stand in for a pianist who had taken ill. And Frank was there in the audience, because he had heard that I was playing that night. He walked home with me, and...' her voice faltered.

'Julia, my dear, we're two grown women, no need to be coy with me. In any case, it all happened many years ago.'

'You're right. We started meeting whenever we could ... with Thomas working some nights it made it easier for me to see Frank. I knew it was wrong, but I couldn't help myself. Frank was so kind, so easy to talk to. I just lived for the times I would see him again. Then someone told Thomas. They must have seen me and Frank together, though we tried to be careful.'

'What happened?'

Even after all those years Julia flinched at the memory. 'He was very angry, of course, but he said that he forgave me, and we would say no more about it. I wished that he would put me out of the house, disown me, for then I could have gone to Frank, but mebbe he knew that that was what I wanted, so he wouldn't do it. He stopped my piano lessons, of course, and he made me watch while he burned all my music in the fireplace then smashed up the piano. He had to bring in a man to take the pieces away and he was angry with me because the man had to be paid.'

'It must have broken your heart,' Mirren said quietly.

'My spirit more than my heart, because I knew what Thomas was like, and all the time I was seeing Frank I knew what might happen if I was found out. But I went ahead anyway because once I met Frank, I couldn't help myself.'

'He ... Thomas ... didn't hit you, then?'

'Oh no, he wouldn't hit a woman. Anyway, he knew that destroying the piano and the music would hurt me more than any blows could. Bruises fade faster than memories. It was Frank that he hurt,' Julia's voice trembled and tears glittered on her lashes. 'He came in one night and told me that my "friend" had got himself hurt on his way home from work the night before. An unfortunate incident, he called it. He was smiling when he said it. Thomas had been on duty that night, and he had been patrolling the area near where Frank lived.' Julia's hands twisted tightly together in her lap. 'He said that I'd best stay well away from Frank in future, because he must be prone to accidents and it could easily happen again. The next day when he'd left for work I went to Frank's lodgings and got his landlady to tell me what hospital he was in. I went there out of visiting hours and they didn't want to let me into the ward, but I made such a fuss that they had to give in. I scarce recognised him, Mirren, he was in such a bad way. But they said it looked worse than it was ... he said that too, bless the man. And it turned out to be true.'

'What did you do then?'

'I told him about the baby I was carrying ... that was Chloe ... and oh, Mirren, I've never seen such joy in a man's face! Then I went back home and bided my time for a whole month while Frank got out of hospital and found a new job here in Paisley, and a room where the two of us could be together.'

'Could the baby not have been your husband's?'

Julia shook her head. 'Thomas had an illness in his early twenties, before we even met, and he was told afterwards that he could never father children. I didn't know about that until his sister told me, not long after we were married.'

'That means that if Frank had turned his back on you, you couldn't have stayed with Thomas and pretended the child was his. What would you have done?'

'Found work as a servant, mebbe, somewhere where I could have kept the wee one. But Frank did want her, and he wanted me too, and one day when Thomas was at work I packed my things, wrote him a note and left. It was a cowardly way to do it.'

'But wise as well, given the man's temper. He never tried to find you?'

'I didn't expect him to. He was a very proud man; I knew that once he found out that I'd ... betrayed him with another man, he wouldn't have taken me back if I had begged him on my bended knees. Chloe was born several months later, and she's always been special in Frank's eyes, because he says that she was the one that brought us together in the end.'

'But now something's happened, or else why would you be telling me this?'

'Last week,' Julia said quietly, 'Thomas came to see me.'

'What?' Mirren sat bolt upright in her chair. 'But you said that he would never want you back!'

'He's ill, Mirren, very ill. And he's got nobody to look after him.'

'He surely doesn't expect you to do it after all these years?'

'He says that I owe it to him. He's taken a room in Clarence Street and he wants me to go there and stay with him until he ... until he dies.' Julia looked up, her eyes haunted. 'I don't know what to do!'

'You must have no more to do with him!'

'Julia, the man's ill, and he's still my legal husband. He's got the right to expect me to care for him.'

'That's what he told you, I suppose? He's got a damned cheek on him,' said Mirren Hepburn emphatically. 'So what's supposed to happen next?'

‘He gave me a week to get myself ready, and it’s almost up. I’m supposed to go to his lodgings the day after tomorrow, to stay there for as long as I’m needed.’

‘Let me go to see him. Just to talk to the man and get the measure of him,’ Mirren added as panic flared in Julia’s eyes. ‘Then you and me can decide between us what’s best for him, and for you. And no arguing, for I’m used to sorting things out for folk, and thanks to Joe having been on the Council I’ve got to know some very useful people. I’ll visit this husband of yours, and there’s no more to be said on the matter.’

‘Need some help?’

Dennis turned to see Chloe McCosh hovering on the path, eyeing him hopefully.

‘Not at work today?’

‘It’s Tuesday. Half-day.’

‘Oh. You could earth up these potatoes if you want.’

Her smile faltered slightly. ‘How do I do that?’

He rammed the blade of his spade in to the earth and made his way over to where the gardening tools leaned against the wall. ‘You use the hoe ... this is the hoe ... to scoop the earth up against the plants on both sides. Like this, see? Now you try it.’

She plied the hoe vigorously. ‘Like this?’

‘Aye, that’s fine, but you don’t have to work so hard at it. Just draw it up nice and easy, then you won’t tire yourself out.’

He went back to his own digging, and for a while they worked in silence. Then Chloe asked,

'Why am I doing this?'

'Because the potatoes grow in the ground. When you earth the plants up, the main stem starts to throw out more roots, then you have layers of potatoes. And it's a good way of keeping the weeds away too.' He straightened and eyed the section of ground he had been working on, then dragged a heavy sack over and opened it. Chloe wrinkled her nose.

'Phew! What's that?'

'Horse manure. This ground's getting starved and it has to be built up for the winter vegetable crop.'

'You're going to grow things to eat,' Chloe asked, horrified, 'in horse dung?'

'It's the best thing there is if you want to enrich the soil.'

'You mean that I've eaten food that was grown in dung?' Her face paled, and he laughed.

'Not pure dung ... it changes once it's dug in. And the vegetables are washed and cooked.'

Chloe said nothing, though as she went back to work she was thinking of the time when she and Marion had filched a young carrot each from the vegetable plot, rubbing the soil off and eating the sweet flesh with relish. Never again!

'How d'you know so much about gardening?' she asked after another pause.

'Your dad taught me some of it, and Tom MacIntosh – he's one of the firemen – told me a lot. He's got an allotment, and he's given us a lot of cuttings and seeds and stuff for this place.'

'Are you still enjoying working at the fire station?'

'Aye.' Dennis forked manure from the bag.

'Have you been to many fires?'

'Some, though I'm still learning. Most of the fires I've seen are wee things,' he admitted, 'like chimneys going on fire, and folk being careless in the house. Fire doesnae start on its own, you know, it's always someone's fault. Being careless with matches and cigarettes and pipes, and inflammable stuff like paraffin.' As he spoke, he made a mental note to remind Lena that the tins and containers her husband had used in his peace-time job as a painter were still waiting to be brought out to the shed.

'Have you ever been in danger?' Chloe was asking now.

'No. We're taught to do the job properly. Putting ourselves in danger doesn't help to put out fires, does it?'

'That's good,' she said in a small voice. 'I'd not like to think of you getting hurt.'

'That's nice of you, Chloe, but don't worry. I'll be all right.'

Another silence fell, then she said, 'That's the first row finished. Did I get it right?'

Dennis straightened and looked over at the potatoes. 'You did a grand job.'

Chloe felt a self-righteous glow sweep over her. 'Would it be all right,' she asked as she started earthing up the next row, 'if I helped you in the garden some other time?'

'Of course. You know what they say, many hands make light work. And your father would no doubt be pleased at getting some help when he's out here as well.'

'I'd not be in the way? Only,' she hurried on as he shook his head, 'I've seen Mrs Fulton helping you and I wondered if you...' her voice almost gave out on her, and she had to clear her throat before continuing, 'if you'd rather have her working with you than me.'

Dennis shot her a swift glance, but she had anticipated it, and she was apparently concentrating on the work in hand, her auburn hair falling forward to hide her face.

'We all eat the vegetables,' he said, 'so what difference does it make who works with them?'

'Who you work beside might make a difference to you.' She took the plunge. 'You like Mrs Fulton, don't you?'

'I like everyone. I even like you, when you're not pestering me with daft questions.'

'You know what I mean.' Chloe stopped work and leaned on the hoe, using her free hand to tuck a strand of hair out of the way, behind her ear. 'I've seen you, Dennis,' she said. 'I've seen you going in and out of her flat, and talking to her in the Fountain Gardens.'

'You've seen me going in and out of your flat as well,' he said shortly.

'That's for band practice, and there's plenty of folk in our flat when there's a practice on. But it's just Mrs Fulton and you in her flat, and she's a married woman, Dennis...'

'I know she's a married woman. Her husband's away fighting for his country and she needs someone to see to things for her now and again.'

'What sort of things?'

'Clearing drains and mending things, and...' He

threw the spade down and turned to glare at her. 'What sort of things did you think?'

'Dennis, it's mebbe not wise to get too friendly with a married woman...'

His face flamed with anger. 'And it's mebbe not wise to push your neb into other folks' business.' He picked up his jacket and slung it over his shoulder. 'I'll go where I want, Chloe McCosh, and I'll see who I please. And you'd best mind your tongue in future!'

She was watching him march away from her and back to the tenement when tears suddenly flooded her eyes. As Dennis's figure seemed to shimmer and then dissolve she blinked hard, but it was no use; the tears overflowed and began to trickle down her face. She spun round just in case he happened to turn and see her weeping, and gulped back a sob as she picked up the hoe and got on with her work. She had tried to help him, to warn him that folk might notice as she had, and might begin to talk. Instead, she had turned him against her.

23

As Dennis stormed up the stairs and gained the first landing he saw Ellen Borland standing in her open doorway talking quietly to a woman who stood humbly before her on the landing, her head nodding and bobbing as though it was on a spring.

'You mind now,' Dennis heard Ellen say as he reached the top of the stairs.

'Aye, I promise, missus,' the woman said in reply, then turned, her eyes widening at the sight of Dennis. Hurriedly, she buried her hand, fisted round something, deep into her pocket.

'Hold on there, Mrs Borland,' Dennis said as the door began to close. 'I want a word with you.' He couldn't bring himself to take out his anger on Chloe McCosh, but Mrs Borland was fair game.

The other woman, a stranger to him, ducked round him with her head well down, and went scudding down the stairs, her shoes clattering and flopping as though they were too big for her feet, or the soles were parting company with the uppers. Either could be possible in these days of wartime shortage when shoes were hard to find and folk had to make do with what they could get.

'Aye, what is it, son?' Ellen Borland folded her arms. She was dressed in her usual wrap-around pinny and her greying hair, which was always pulled into a bun at the back of her head, was escaping in wisps.

'It's about our Ralph and the way you've got him working for you.'

The woman's gaze didn't flicker. 'Don't know what you're talkin' about, son.'

'Aye you do. He's only thirteen, still at the school, and if he's going to make anything of his life he'll have to work harder at his lessons instead of running around the town collecting debts for you.'

'Debts?' Ellen's voice rose slightly. 'I don't know anythin' about debts. I pay my way and if other folk won't do the same, it's got nothin' tae do with me.'

'You lend them money, Mrs Borland,' Dennis said levelly. 'You charge them interest on the loans and because they're desperate they agree. Then when it's time for them to pay, you send someone round to collect the money. Ralph's big for his age, and strong too. Folk wouldn't want to deny him when he's at their door with his hand out, saying Mrs Borland sent him.'

'Ye're haverin'!' the woman snapped. 'And I've got more to do than stand here listenin' tae ye!'

Dennis moved swiftly as she began to shut the door, slapping one hand on the panels while a booted foot landed on the threshold.

'Tell Ralph that you've no more need of his services, Mrs Borland.'

'Listen you tae me, son,' the woman said, her voice low and sharp. 'Your mammy's a decent widow woman that works herself half tae death for her family. I respect that, because I've had tae work my way up from nothin'. I've seen folk lookin' at me as if I'm no more than the dirt under their shoes and I've toiled all my life tae prove them wrong. I've no quarrel with your mother and I've no quarrel with you, and if yer brother wants tae earn a bit of money so's he can help his poor mammy out, it's none of my concern.'

'It is your concern, and I'm telling you that I don't want him being part of whatever you're doing!'

'Then speak tae him about it, or tae yer mammy.' The woman's face was ugly now, her tone menacing. 'Just don't tangle with me, son, or you'll be sorry!'

Dennis was seeing a side to Ellen Borland he had never seen before. Possibly the only people to witness it were those poor souls who found themselves in her debt and unable to pay what they owed. He swallowed hard, then said, 'It's not me that'll be sorry, Mrs Borland. I'm sure the factors would be interested to hear what sort of business is being carried on in their tenement.'

'Threatenin' me, are ye? Well mebbe ye should just remember, sonny, that two can play at that game.'

'If you do any harm to my brother, I'll–'

'Don't be daft, I'm not talkin' about your Ralph. I like Ralph, he's a civil lad with a good brain in his skull. He could go far. No, I'm thinkin' about someone closer to you than he is.' The woman gave Dennis a cold-eyed smile. 'Before you come accusin' decent folk of breaking the law, you should think about your own secrets. A young laddie messin' about with a married woman whose man's away fightin' for his country ... it's not seemly,' she reproved, her mouth turning down at the corners in distaste.

Colour flooded into Dennis's face as he caught her meaning. First Chloe and now old Ma Borland. 'There's nothing goin' on between me and her!'

'I'm sure there's no', son, but other folk might not be as decent-minded as me. I thought you were a fine upstandin' young man but now I'm beginnin' tae wonder if ye're such a fine example to that wee brother you're so concerned about. I've been wonderin',' Ellen Borland said, gazing at a spot just past Dennis's left ear, 'if someone shouldnae let that poor Mr Fulton know what's goin' on behind his back.'

'You mind your own business. And when it comes to Mrs Fulton,' Dennis said, recovering, 'I know that you don't pay her for the work she does for you. That's as good as theft!'

'Did she not tell you about our wee agreement? It suits her, and it suits me, and that's all that matters. Now, if you're quite finished...'

One minute she was standing there, arms folded, and the next, a large hand was on Dennis's chest, pushing him away from the door. Taken by surprise, he stumbled back, and by the time he had recovered himself the door was closed.

As he turned, shaken by the encounter, he heard a low cackle, and looked across the landing to see that Jessie Bell's door was ajar. Something stirred in the darkness beyond the open space; a tangle of white hair, a glittering eye, a sharp chin. Then the door closed and he was left wondering how much the old woman had seen and heard. How much, indeed, she had already known?

'Good afternoon,' Mirren Hepburn said pleasantly, 'I believe you have a Mr Thomas Gordon lodging here?'

The woman who had opened the door gave her a suspicious stare. 'Aye, mebbe. Who wants him?'

'He won't know my name, but I think he'll

want to see me all the same. Is he in?'

'Aye, he is, but he's sleepin'. He's not well.'

'I know that, it's why I came to see him.'

'Are you a nurse?'

'No,' Mirren said, 'just a friend of a friend. Someone who might be able to help him.'

'Ye'd better come in, then.' At last the woman stepped back, and Mirren followed her into an untidy kitchen that smelled strongly of boiled cabbage and urine. A baby slept in a pram pushed into one corner, and a toddler playing before the range scrambled up and snatched at his mother's skirt, hiding his face when Mirren smiled at him.

'Give it five minutes, he'll probably be awake by then. He gets intae a right temper if he gets wakened before he's ready. I've had a terrible time tryin' tae keep the weans quiet enough tae please him. Ye'd think he owned the flat instead of just bein' the lodger.' The woman indicated one of the chairs at the table. 'Just push the stuff off it. D'ye want some tea, then?'

'No thank you.' Mirren picked up the jumble of bits and pieces and put them on the table before sitting down. The baby woke and began to cry, and her hostess took the infant from the pram, sat down in a sagging fireside chair and unbuttoned her blouse. The toddler, brushed away from her skirt, settled on the shabby rug at her feet.

'Has Mr Gordon been here long?' Mirren asked.

The woman produced a breast from within the unbuttoned blouse and pushed it in to the baby's face. Tiny hands shot out of the bundle of wool, the squalling mouth fastened on a nipple, and the room became blessedly silent.

'Not long. About two weeks. And if I'd known how ill he was I'd never have said he could have the room. But I need the money, see, with my man bein' away in the army.' She indicated the small head buried in the softness of her breast. 'He's never even seen her yet and I'm just wond'rin' if he ever will. My sister's man was torpedoed on the way back from Dunkirk ... left her with three weans tae feed and house. But nobody ever thinks about the wives and bairns when there's a war, do they?'

'No, they don't. If Mr Gordon's ill, shouldn't he be in hospital?'

'I wish he was, but he says there's someone comin' soon tae take him away and look after him. It that you?' the woman asked hopefully.

'I know who he means, and perhaps I can do something for him instead.'

'I'd be right pleased if ye could, missus! I thought it'd be nice tae have the wee bit of money comin' in, but it's no' worth it. Sometimes he's so bad that I worry in case he dies on me. I'd not know what tae dae if he did.' The woman raised her head, then plucked the child from her breast and struggled to her feet. 'I think I heard him, so he's mebbe wakened now. Here...' She thrust the baby at Mirren, 'you hold her while I go and see.'

The baby's milky mouth was moving, seeking the food source it had suddenly lost. Blue eyes gazed up at Mirren, puzzled, then as she rocked the little bundle and crooned to it, the eyes began to glaze with sleep and the lids lowered.

The wee thing's clothing was damp, and the sharp smell of ammonia brought tears to Mirren's eyes. The pram mattress was probably soaked through. She longed to strip the little creature and bathe her, then dress her in dry clothing, but, knowing that even if there had been fresh clothing readily to hand, such behaviour by a mere visitor would mortally offend the young mother, she had to content herself with rocking the baby in her arms.

Her lap and her sleeves were beginning to feel distinctly damp by the time the woman returned, the toddler in tow.

'He says tae go in.' She took the baby and returned her to the pram.

'I think she needs changing,' Mirren ventured.

'She always needs changin'. It goes in at one end and out the other all the time. I'll see tae her later. Ye'd best go on through now; he wants his dinner so ye'll have tae be quick. He doesnae like tae be kept waitin'.'

The most that could be said for the small bedroom where Thomas Gordon lay was that it was not covered with clothing and it did not smell of permanently wet baby. It did, however, smell of ill health.

'Who are you?' The hoarse voice was unfriendly, as were the piercing dark eyes set in the hollows and caverns of a gaunt face.

'Mrs Mirren Hepburn.'

'Never heard of ye.'

'I'm a friend of Julia's.'

'She sent ye here? I told her tae come herself!'

'She couldn't do that. She has a family to care for.'

'And a husband that she swore before God tae love and honour and obey for the rest of her life!'

'A husband who also swore before God to love and cherish *her*, Mr Gordon. Marriage isn't worth much unless both parties keep to their vows. Once one breaks them, the other has to work twice as hard to keep them.'

'What's she been tellin' you?' Mirren could tell by the wrists and the big hands protruding from his pyjama jacket that this man was probably tall, and had once, when the bones were overlaid by muscle and fat, been burly, but now face and body were wasted, the flesh all but gone. His eyes were the strongest part of him, and they burned his dislike and resentment at her.

'Enough,' she said calmly. 'She had to talk to someone, and she knew that she could trust me to keep her secret ... and your secret as well, if it comes to it.'

'She couldnae tell that man of hers about me, could she?' There was a sneer in his voice, and the tell-tale patches of red on the sharp ridges of his cheekbones flared momentarily.

'She's feared about what he might do if he knew you were here, in Paisley.'

'Get his revenge, you mean? He's welcome tae it now. I'm past carin'.'

'From what I know of Frank McCosh, I doubt if he'd stoop to harming a defenceless invalid,' Mirren said levelly, and got some satisfaction in seeing him wince, though whether it was her reference to Frank or her description of him that caused it, she had no way of knowing.

'Julia should be here, lookin' after me!' he said harshly. 'It's her duty tae care for me in my last days.'

'Julia owes you nothing, man, and even if she did, she couldn't possibly care for you now. You're sick, very sick...' Her eyes flickered to the shabby, slightly lopsided table by the bed, and the crumpled blood-smeared cloth on it, 'and you need proper nursing.'

'Goin' tae fetch a private nurse in for me, are ye?' he jeered.

'The care you need can only be got in hospital and we have a very good institution here in Paisley ... the Royal Alexandra Infirmary.'

'I'm not goin' tae any infirmary!'

'Don't be a fool, man, you can't stay here. Your landlady has more than enough to do with caring for her children, and you're probably a threat to their health into the bargain. You'd be more comfortable in hospital, being properly looked after.'

'Aye ... by strangers! I'll not die among strangers!' He began to cough, and almost at once he was doubled over, what little breath he could catch whistling through his diseased lungs.

Mirren caught up the bloodied cloth and pushed it into his hands before hurrying through to the kitchen. 'D'you have a wee bowl of cold water?' she asked. 'And a clean cloth?'

'Is that him away again?' The young woman's eyes were bright with fear. 'Honest, missus, when he starts on like that I'm that scared he's goin' tae die right there in my spare room!'

'He won't die. Give it to me.' Mirren snatched at the basin the woman had picked up from beneath the table; moving to the sink she turned on the leaky tap and half filled the basin. 'A cloth, if you have one.'

'Er...' The woman grabbed something from a pile and handed it over, and Mirren hurried back to the bedroom, where Thomas Gordon lay exhausted, the pillow he lay against as grey as his face. Fresh spots and streaks of red glistened on his chin.

'Here.' Mirren put down the basin and picked up a cup from the table. It was half full of water, and it looked reasonably clean. She held it to his lips and he took a few sips before waving it away. His eyes, the only part of him with any life in them, closed, and she thought that without their strong, angry gaze, he did indeed look as though it would take very little to push him over the fragile line between life and death.

The cloth she had been given was a dish-towel, smelly and stiff with dirt; she put it aside and used her own clean handkerchief instead, dipping it into the water and wringing it out before wiping his face and neck and hands.

'There now,' she found herself soothing them both as she worked. 'There, that's better, isn't it?'

She dried his face as best she could with the edge of the tattered quilt that covered him, then sat down and waited. When his eyes finally opened, she said, gently but firmly, 'You'll surely agree with me now, Mr Gordon, when I say that you cannot stay here. You must get proper care.

Somewhere where you will be much more comfortable. And you'll not be among strangers. I'll visit you, and so will Julia.'

'You'll get me in there and you'll leave me tae rot.'

'We'll do nothing of the sort; you have my word on that. I think I can speak for Julia as well as for myself; she's worried about you and she wouldn't just leave you.'

'She did before.'

'That was because she couldn't stay. For one thing, you made it impossible for her to go on living with you, and for another, she loved Frank McCosh. She still does and she always will,' Mirren said with brutal honesty, 'but as you say, she made vows on the day she married you, and I know that she'll want to keep them as best she can.'

'Mebbe ye won't be able tae get me intae this infirmary of yours just as easy as that. Not the way things are these days.' His voice was very weak and the intensity had gone from his eyes; the bout of coughing had drained him.

'I think I'll manage. Just leave it to me.' No sense in telling him that she had a certain influence, and knew which strings she could pull. She got to her feet. 'I'll be back tomorrow to let you know what's happening.'

And she would be bringing some decent food with her, and clothes for the children. It wasn't just those who had been bombed out of their homes that needed help; the woman in the kitchen, probably a good ten years younger than she looked, had donated her most precious possession – her husband, the father of her children, the bread-winner of the house – to this war that had been set in motion by men with wealth and power, men who often cared for the warriors they sent to the trenches as little as young boys did for their lead and tin soldiers.

Joe was right, she thought as she left the flat and returned to the street outside. War was the ultimate obscenity, and it should never be part of a decent society. And soon it would swallow her own precious firstborn up in its hungry maw.

Forcing thoughts of Charlie from her head for fear that she might end up weeping, she found herself thinking instead of the man she had just left. Tyrant and bully though he had been in his prime, there was something pathetic about Thomas Gordon's fear of dying alone among strangers; he appeared so vulnerable, perhaps for the first time in his life, that Mirren could not let it happen to him.

24

'Goin' somewhere nice?' one of the other clippies asked Cecelia when she arranged her first week's holiday.

'Nothing special. There's no chance of my husband getting home, so I'll just catch up on my sleep and get the flat put to rights,' she said vaguely. It would arouse altogether too much interest if she were to reveal to anyone, even

Harry, that she had arranged the time off in order to attend her father's wedding.

His letter had come as a complete surprise; not the news that he and his lady friend, a widow named Elspeth McFadden, were going to be married, but the fact that after such a long silence between them, broken only by the occasional single-page formal letter, he wanted Cecelia to be there.

Clothing coupons had just been introduced, and Cecelia used up most of her first allowance in Cochran's, where she bought a dark green two-piece costume, to be worn over a cream blouse she already owned.

'And I'll need a hat...' she said to the shop assistant, who immediately disappeared and came back with a tiny pillbox creation, the same colour as the suit.

'This would finish off the ensemble perfectly, madam.'

Cecelia, who was given to wearing sensible hats with nice brims, eyed it with misgivings. 'I don't know ... it's not really my sort of hat.'

'Try it on. No, madam, like this...' The woman took it from her, and pinned it into place with a few deft movements. 'There now. Have a look in the mirror.'

The hat, a velvet creation, was perched on Cecelia's fair hair, inclining rakishly over one eye. It made her look completely different. 'Oh,' she said, half in surprise, half in horror, then, 'I don't know. Have you got something in straw, with a nice brim?'

'This goes very well with the costume, madam,

and you did say that it was a wedding.' The woman reached up and tweaked at the hat, and when she stood back, Cecelia discovered that her vision had gone slightly misty, with dots. 'It has a very pretty little half-veil,' the woman was chirruping, 'which can be worn up or down.'

Cecelia edged closer to the mirror and peered at her own reflection. Whether the mistiness deceived her or the hat really did suit her she didn't know, but she was beginning to like it.

She gasped a little when she heard what it cost, but told herself that it was after all to be worn at a wedding, and she could afford it, thanks to the good money that bus conductresses earned. And she would have something nice to wear the next time Fergus came home, she pondered as she carried her new clothes home. She would think of somewhere nice for them to go, some outing in keeping with the smart costume and hat.

Still trying to justify the outlay, she scuttled upstairs to her flat, flushing guiltily as she encountered Dennis Megson coming down the second flight.

'Hello,' she said breathlessly, and kept on climbing. As she went, she heard him tap at a door below. Going to see Mrs McCosh about something to do with the band, she thought, then forgot Dennis as she gained her own landing and rushed to open her door before anyone else saw her and asked about the parcels she carried.

Instead of standing back to let Dennis in, Lena hesitated when she saw him on the doorstep. 'I'm busy.'

'I need to talk to you,' he said urgently. 'It'll not take long. Please,' he said as she began to shake her head, 'it's important.'

She stepped away from the door to let him pass, and when he moved into the hallway and glanced back, he saw that, as usual, she was peering out of the door to make sure nobody had seen him. With good reason, he thought bitterly, since they seemed to live in some kind of an ants' nest where everything that happened was spied on and immediately passed from door to door.

In the kitchen, he gestured to the sewing machine on the kitchen table, and the floral material lying on it. 'Is that something else for Mrs Borland?'

'Why should you ask that?'

'Most of the work you do these days seems to be for her.'

'She knows a lot of people. She brings in work for me.'

'Work that doesnae pay.'

'Sometimes it does.' She sat down at the machine, fidgeting with the cloth. 'What did you want to talk about?'

'I've just been telling Ma Borland to stop giving work to our Ralph.'

Lena paled, and one hand – she seemed incapable of sitting still these days, he realised – went to her throat. 'You've had a row with her?'

'I'd no choice. We all know that she's into black market coupons and money lendin' and goodness knows what else. As far as I'm concerned that's up tae her, but I'll not have her draggin' my brother into her web.'

'But now she knows that you know what she's up to.' Lena's eyes were frightened. 'She might find a way to make things difficult for you and Ralph, and your mother.'

'Is that what she does when folk try to defy her?'

'How would I know?' She plucked at the material in the sewing machine. 'I have to get on with this, Dennis.'

'Lena, are you in debt to Ma Borland?'

Her already pale face went bone white. 'Me? She mentioned me?'

'Not in so many words.' It was a lie, but he couldn't tell her the truth. 'It was just the way she was rantin', that's all, about how she helped folk. Bartering, and that. And I remembered you saying that you don't charge her for the work you do for her because she gives you thread and cloth.'

'Yes, she does, and it's good of her. It would be difficult to do my sewing if she didn't help out.' She was breathless now, as though she had been running.

'So I'm asking ... is it just sewing stuff, or has she loaned you money as well?'

'That's got nothing to do with you!'

'It has. I care about you, Lena. I ... I care for you, and I don't want to see you caught up in that woman's trap.'

'You've no right to come in here, questioning me.' Two bright spots burned in her cheeks, and her eyes were glittering sapphires. 'My life is none of your business!'

'I thought we were friends. If you need help,

Lena, I'm earning, and I could mebbe...'

'I can manage fine, and anyway, you've got enough to do with your own family.' She clasped her head in both hands. 'I've got a headache coming on; it's the heat, I think. I'll need to go and lie down.'

'Lena...'

'I need to lie down,' she repeated. 'You can let yourself out, can't you?'

When he had gone and she had the flat to herself, Lena walked from room to room and up and down the narrow hallway, rubbing her hands up and down the sides of her skirt and trying to control her shaky breathing. 'Pity,' she said aloud several times, her voice harsh. 'I can't be doing with pity!'

The sewing for Mrs Borland's niece was waiting in the machine, but when she returned to the kitchen Lena ignored it, going instead to the cupboard where the patchwork quilt lay waiting for her. She shook it out with trembling fingers. It was time for a new patch.

She went in to the bedroom and looked at the bed, her marriage bed, made up just the way George liked it, with not a crease or a wrinkle, then she began to work her way through the drawers. There was nothing there to catch her eye. She opened the wardrobe, which was half empty now; George's best suit was in a pawn-shop, and every Monday Lena paid a small deposit to ensure that instead of being sold, it would stay where it was, to be redeemed, some-how, as soon as she got word that he was coming home on leave. Her own clothes took up little space, for most of them had already been cut up for the quilt.

She hesitated, then took down George's favourite shirt and carried it into the kitchen, where she reached for her big scissors and got to work.

'It was a good film,' Chloe said when she and Charlie finally reached her close. 'That Will Hay's very funny.'

Even though it was summer, the day had been overcast and the night was dark.

'I enjoyed it, but I thought you'd have chosen to see *Mark of Zorro*,' Charlie said, 'with it being Tyrone Power. Girls think he's handsome, don't they?'

'That would have been a good picture, but I like the Regal ... it's more comfortable than the Astoria. And me and Marion might–' She stopped suddenly, wishing that she could bite her tongue out.

'If you and Marion do go to the Astoria later in the week,' he said, 'you can write to me and tell me all about Tyrone Power and Linda Darnell.'

Chloe's right hand fingered the silver bracelet on her left wrist. Charlie had given it to her a few days earlier, for her sixteenth birthday, and before tonight's film he had treated her to her tea at Cochran's handsome restaurant before they walked along to the Regal.

'Mum said I should ask you up for your supper.'

'D'you think they would mind if I didn't?' he asked. 'I hate goodbyes. I've had to go through all that at work, and I'll have to go through it tomorrow at home.'

'It'll be all right. She said, if you felt like it, just.'

'Your mother's very understanding. Come here...' He seized her hand and drew her into the close.

'I thought you didn't want to go up to my house.'

'We're not. I'm just looking for somewhere more private than the street. Will the washhouse be open?' he wanted to know as they emerged into the backyard.

'It's kept locked and our key's in the kitchen.'

'Let's try the wee shed, then.'

She pulled back as he tried to draw her across the backcourt. 'It's probably locked, and in any case, it'll be dirty and full of stuff to fall over. I'm not going in there wearing my good cloth–' The words were cut short as he eased her against the house wall and kissed her.

Chloe had not had much experience of boys, but from what she had heard in the school playground, and from Marion, she was quite sure that Charlie Hepburn was a good kisser. She enjoyed being kissed by him, and responded with enthusiasm, but when his lips moved from her mouth to her neck and his hands began to rove she pushed him away.

'That's enough, Charlie!'

'Chloe, this is our last time together till goodness knows when!'

'I don't care, I'm not going to let you do that!'

'Other girls probably do, when their boyfriends are called up.'

'I'm not other girls, I'm me, and you should be

ashamed of yourself, expecting me to ... to do whatever you want, just because it's your last night in Paisley!'

'But I really like you, Chloe!'

'And I like you, you know that.'

'How much do you like me?'

She drew him back towards her. 'This much,' she said, and kissed him on the mouth. 'And this much.' This time the kiss was longer, warmer.

'Enough to be my proper official girlfriend?' he asked hopefully when he could speak again.

'I've told you, I'm too young to make promises like that.'

'You're sixteen now, old enough to get married.'

'Old enough to make up my own mind about whether or not I want to be tied down. Charlie, your whole life's going to be changed; you could easily meet someone else while you're away.'

'I won't, because I don't want to.'

'I could meet someone else!'

'There isn't anyone now, is there?' he asked sharply.

'No, of course not.' Dennis Megson popped into her mind, and was pushed away. 'I only said that I might. We never know what's ahead.'

'All the more reason for us to have an understanding, then.'

'An understanding won't make any difference if one of us meets someone else, can you not see that? Can we not just stay best friends?'

'But you'll write to me, won't you? Every week?'

'Of course I will. Not that I'll have much to tell

you. Nothing ever happens round here.'

'Write about the ordinary things,' he said, 'like what you're doing, and thinking, and what's happening with the band, and your family. I want to go on being part of your lives even though I'm away.'

'I wish you weren't going away, Charlie.'

'I'll be back on leave, lots of times. You're sure you just want us to be best friends and nothing more?' Then, when she nodded, her head bumping gently against his shoulder, 'You're a tease, Chloe McCosh.'

'I am not! A tease is someone who lets a man think he's going to get more but he doesn't.'

His breath was warm on her cheek as he laughed. 'How do you know that?'

'I read the women's magazines.'

'Oh, Chloe,' he said, against her lips. 'I'm going to miss you!'

'And I'm going to miss you,' she said from the heart.

They lingered for another ten minutes before the coolness of the night signalled the end of the evening.

A few minutes after they went inside, hand in hand, to enjoy a final, chaste kiss outside the McCosh's door, Dennis Megson stepped cautiously out of the little tool shed, where he had been smoking a cigarette.

For a moment he stood in the backcourt, looking up at the darkness of the building. It was too dark to make out Lena's windows, but he knew exactly where they were anyway. She would be in her bed by now.

He sighed, and went into the close, almost bumping into a youth on his way down the first flight of stairs. As the lad brushed past, muttering a greeting, Dennis gave an answering mutter and continued to climb, slowly, still thinking about Lena.

'Charlie?' a voice said from the landing above. 'Is that you coming back?'

'Chloe?'

There was a little gasp, then she said, 'It's you, Dennis! I thought it was...'

'The lad I met in the close?' He had gained the landing now.

'We were at the Regal to see the Will Hay picture.' She looked at him warily; it was the first time they had spoken since he had stormed off and left her weeping in the backcourt. 'Is this you just coming home from your work?' she asked, desperate to find a way to apologise for what she had said about him and Mrs Fulton.

'No, I've been having a smoke out the back.'

'The backcourt?' They had been speaking in whispers, mindful of the people already asleep in the flats, but now her voice rose. 'You've been in the backcourt?'

'Aye, the tool shed. I sometimes go there when I want some peace to think.' He grinned down at her. 'Some courtin' couple came through from the street for a bit of privacy and I was stuck in there waitin' until they went away.'

'Courting couple?' Chloe said faintly. 'Who was it, d'you know?'

'How would I know, in the dark, and with them over by the doorway. It happens sometimes, but usually they don't come in further than the bottom of the stairs…'

'Oh!' she said, then, 'Oh!' And she turned and ran through the partly opened door of her flat, leaving him alone and puzzled on the landing.

The Royal Alexandra Infirmary was a honeycomb of large high-ceilinged wards and long, tiled corridors housed in an imposing Victorian building on Neilston Road, on the south side of the town.

By the time he had been wheeled along corridors and around corners and along more corridors and, once, into a large and clanking lift, Thomas Gordon, who had only just managed to glimpse the exterior of the large building while being taken from the ambulance, had no idea whether he was at the rear or the front of the place, or perhaps in a side wing. All he had been able to make out on his long journey was high ceilings, rushing towards, over and then past him like a moving ribbon.

Finally the porter stopped the trolley and a woman in a starched white apron and cap bent over Thomas. 'Mr Gordon? We'll get you into bed now, and get you comfortable.'

'I can manage it mysel'.' He tried to sit up, but the effort made his head swim and it was almost a relief when she pushed him down gently and said, 'I'm sure you can, but why don't you just lie still and leave it to us?'

When he had been manhandled on to the bed, albeit gently, the porter trundled the trolley away without as much as a glance at him; for all the world, Thomas thought with feeble anger, as though in his illness he had become no more than a parcel that required delivering. He lay still, staring up at the ceiling, avoiding eye contact with the nurses who efficiently stripped him and then washed him before dressing him again, this time in pyjamas. Finally they went away; all except one, who drew up the bedclothes around him and tucked them in.

'There now. Are you comfortable, Mr Gordon?'

'As comfortable as I can be under the circumstances.'

'Would you like a drink?' When he nodded, she raised him up and held the spout of an invalid drinking cup to his lips, then eased him back down again and wiped his mouth. 'The doctor will be coming round in about an hour, and there'll be a cup of tea for you before that. I don't know if they told you already, but you're in Ward–'

'In prison, that's all I have tae know. The number of the cell makes no difference tae me.'

'This is a hospital, Mr Gordon, not a prison.'

'So when can I expect tae get out of your ... hospital?' For the first time since the ambulance men had tramped into the little bedroom in Clarence Street to collect him, he allowed himself eye contact with another human being. Rather than being some young thing on the threshold of life, this nurse was much his own age, which was something of a comfort. Her face was pleasantly homely, and lined, reflecting that she had had good experience of the ups and downs of life, and her hazel eyes were serious as she said quietly, 'I think you already know the answer to that one, Mr Gordon.'

'Aye, I do. I've been handed a death sentence ... and you're tryin' tae tell me that I'm not in a prison?'

'It's only a death sentence if you give up hope, surely. I tell you what...' To his surprise, she leaned forward, her breath tickling his ear as she whispered, 'on my next day off, I'll bake you a cake with a file in it.'

For a moment Thomas was taken aback, then he rallied. 'Put a map of the place in it an' all,' he grunted, 'for I've got no idea where tae go once I get out of this room.'

She laughed, her eyes lighting the whole of her face. 'You'll do,' she said. 'Do you need anything before I go?'

'My health back again?'

'If I could do that for you, Mr Gordon, I would, with pleasure,' she said as she swept the screens away, revealing the row of beds opposite, some of the occupants reading, some sleeping, some talking to their neighbours.

'I have to go and torment some other poor patient now. I'd appreciate it if you could behave yourself till I come back. No rioting allowed in my cell.'

He watched her go off down the ward, shoulders back and head up despite the exhaustion that cast shadows beneath her eyes, then he took stock of his surroundings, wondering if that bossy friend of Julia's would tell her where he was, and wondering, too, if Julia would visit him, or decide to let him rot on his own.

25

'I've got a job for you.' Dennis closed the bedroom door and leaned back against it.

Ralph, sprawling on the bed, looked up from the latest copy of the *Beano* comic. 'What is it?'

'A real job, I'm talking about, for an hour after school and on Saturday mornings, and through the holidays. When I was passing Coghill the ironmonger's today I saw a notice in their window, advertising for a message boy, so I went in and had a word with the manager. There's shelves to stack too, and a bit of sweeping, and mebbe the chance of helping behind the counter when they're busy. You could work your way up the ladder.

'What?'

'They were looking for someone a bit older, but I managed to persuade the manager to give you a chance. You start tomorrow, right after school. Five shillings a week, so we'll make it four to Mum, and one for yourself. I think that's fair enough.'

'I'm already workin' for the Co-op.'

'I had a word with them and all,' Dennis said blandly. 'Told them you'd found something better. They didn't seem to mind. It seems that you weren't all that reliable, but you'd better smarten up for the new place because I'll be keeping a check on you.'

'I'll not do it!' Ralph squirmed off the bed, his face red with anger.

'Aye you will. You wanted to be kept busy and you wanted to earn money, and you'll be doing both ... and keeping out of old Ma Borland's clutches as well.'

'Five shillin's? You think I'd be satisfied with that after–' Ralph started, and then suddenly shut his mouth.

'Five shillings made legally is better than fifty for workin' against the law. I've not said to Mum because I thought you might like to pretend that it was your own doing. She'll be pleased.'

'I'll not do it,' Ralph said. 'You can't make me!'

'I can, because until you're old enough to leave school, you have to do what you're told. If you don't take that job, Ralph, I'm going to tell on you, and on Ma Borland. And if that happened it would mean that you wouldn't be able to go on working for her anyway. And there's another thing...'

Before Ralph knew what was happening his brother had swooped down and slid one hand under his pillow. It emerged with the newspaper Dennis had seen the boy push out of sight when he came into the room.

'I thought so ... the horse racing. Well...' He crushed the flimsy sheets into a ball and stuffed them into his jacket pocket. 'You'll not be needing that any more, will you?'

Ralph sat upright, his face burning and his eyes damp with childish frustration. 'Just you wait, Dennis Megson. Just you wait until I leave the school and get tae be my own boss!'

'I'll be waiting, and I'll be ready. But until then, you'll do as you're told. And now I'm going down to do some work in the backyard. I could do with a hand, when you've finished your homework. I'm sure you've still got some to do.'

'Go tae hell!'

'And that's another thing ... you mind your language in future. Don't forget to let Mum know about your new job,' Dennis said, opening the door. 'She'll be right proud of you.'

Julia, who had been blessed with a healthy family, had had to venture within the Royal Alexandra Infirmary only once before, when Duncan, an adventurous three-year-old at the time, had managed to get a large seed jammed in one ear on a family picnic, and had to have it syringed out.

There was something about infirmaries, she thought as she walked down the long corridor leading to one of the men's wards, that struck fear, or at the very least nervous anticipation into the hearts of those who entered. It might be to do with the smell of disinfectants, or the silent-but-echoing size of the rooms and passageways, or perhaps the very title, suggesting as it did that it was a place only for the infirm. Whatever it was, she glanced longingly at the high windows as she passed, envying those outside on the street, going on with their everyday lives.

The visiting hour had already started by the time she reached the ward.

'Mr Gordon. Third bed on the left,' the uniformed nurse at the desk said in a voice as cool and starched as her crisp cap and apron.

'Thank you.' Julia hesitated and then laid a small parcel on the desk, well clear of the large ledger the nurse was studying. 'I didn't know what to bring... I thought an egg for his tea...'

'Oh.' The nurse looked at the package for a moment, then picked it up gingerly. 'I'll have it sent to the kitchens. They will prepare it for Mr Gordon,' she said.

Most of the beds already had men and women seated by them; all were perched on the edge of their chairs, craning uncomfortably towards the men lying in the high narrow cots so that they could converse in low murmurs. The various colours of the visitors' outdoor clothing seemed incongruous, intrusive almost, when set against the muted white, blue and grey shades of the ward and Julia wondered, as she began to traverse the great expanse of polished floor, if the nurses secretly resented the general disharmony that visiting hours must cause to their ordered, disciplined hospital routine.

The first bed on the left from the door had two people by it, an elderly woman and a young man. A young woman murmured at the second bed, but there was nobody at the third. Julia hesitated, swallowed hard in an attempt to subdue the butterflies swarming around in her stomach, and then moved forward.

She had not seen Thomas for two weeks, because after her own first visit to the flat in Clarence Street, Mirren had persuaded Julia to stay away until he was settled in the infirmary. 'It's worrying you sick, seeing him in that state, and in that place,' she had said.

'But when all's said and done, we used to be married, him and me. In the eyes of the law we still are. I can't just abandon him for a second time.'

'You'll not be abandoning him, because I'll be visiting in your place, and letting you know how he is. And I doubt if he'll thank you for your concern in any case. We've got the measure of each other, Thomas Gordon and me, I can see for myself that he's not an easy man to get on with. He's the sort that would think nothing of using your guilt and your sense of responsibility to keep you by him until he draws his final breath. He needs to be properly looked after, and I've half convinced him of that. It's best for you to stay away until I get him out of that wee flat.'

'You've got enough to do without taking on my worries.'

'What's a visit here and there, to help out a friend?' Mirren had asked. 'Lassie, if you only knew what's already been in my life ... and I'm not just talking about years of marriage to a man who'll always put others before himself and his entire family ... you'd know that my shoulders are broad enough for anything. If they hadn't been, I'd have given up the fight long since.'

As she approached Thomas's bed Julia saw that he was asleep, his head lolling to one side on the immaculate pillow, and the sheets drawn up and tucked neatly in just below his shoulders. The illness had progressed rapidly since she had last seen him; there seemed to be no muscle or tissue beneath the skin of his face, only bone, and when he opened his eyes, sensing her presence, they were dull and listless.

'So.' His voice was a shadow of the deep, hectoring tones she had known so well. 'You decided to visit after all.'

'Did you think I wouldn't?'

'I didnae know if ye'd the courage.'

'I've got courage all right, Thomas. I'm older and I'm wiser, and I know who I am.'

His eyebrows rose, laboriously, as though they had had to be cranked up from behind the skin of his forehead. 'So who are ye, then?'

'I'm Julia McCosh.'

'Julia Gordon.' A spark of anger lit his face, but it was only a spark, and although she sensed an echo of the fear his anger had once roused in her, she was able to suppress it almost at once.

'Not for years, Thomas. You said it yourself ... I'm Frank McCosh's common law wife now, with the right to bear his name. Me and my children. And if you're going to start on at me about Frank, I might just as well get back to them now.'

'Sit down, woman. I don't get many visitors and I suppose I cannae afford to chase away those I do get.' Feebly, but with determination, he began to fight his arms free of the sheets. 'These damned nurses, they never seem tae be done tuckin' folk in. Ye'd think we were parcels instead of human beings.'

'Here, I'll do it.' Julia cast a swift glance at the stern nurse on duty, and seeing that the woman was writing busily, she stooped over the bed and loosened the sheet, then helped him to free his arms. She could feel the bones and sinews and loose skin through his pyjama jacket, and although he smelled of carbolic soap it was underlain by another aroma ... one, she thought, of sickness and impending death.

'Is that better?'

Aye,' he said, exhausted by his struggle. Then, almost forcing the word out, 'Thanks.'

Julia drew up the chair that stood at the bottom of the bed, and sat down. 'How are you?'

'You can see that for yerself.'

'You're surely better here, being looked after, than where you were.'

'I suppose so. Though it's hard tae think that this is where I'll be for the rest of my days. Dyin' in Paisley instead of Glasgow.'

'You didn't need to come to Paisley.'

'I came because I'd nob'dy else tae turn to but you.'

'What about your sister?' Thomas's sister Kate had been just like him; sturdily built, strong and totally convinced of her own righteousness.

His pale mouth twisted in something that might have been a smile, and might have been a grimace. 'She moved tae Clydebank last year after her man died, tae be near her daughter and her grandweans.'

'But Clydebank's not far from Glas–' Julia began, and then stopped short, remembering the terrible raids on the shipbuilding town in March. Scarcely a house left undamaged, Frank had told her. 'The blitz?'

'Aye, the blitz. Kate and the rest of them went quick, I was told. Never knew what hit them, and that's the way she'd have wanted it. She was luckier than me, I'll tell ye that.' Then, his mouth giving that brief twist again, 'And I'll tell her that when I see her.'

Julia put a hand on his. The skin was icy cold beneath her warm palm. 'Thomas, I...' She hesitated, not knowing what to say, then ended lamely, 'I brought you an egg for your tea. The nurse said she'd see that it was cooked for you.'

'What'll your man have tae say about his rations goin' tae the likes of me?'

'It's my rations, and anyway, he'd not object.'

'Does he know that I'm here, in Paisley? That you're visitin' me?'

'Not yet.'

'Scared tae tell him, are ye?'

'I've never had to be afraid of Frank,' she said clearly and deliberately.

He looked away from her gaze, while his hand eased itself out from beneath hers. 'You never needed tae be afraid of me.'

'Oh, I did. And I was. That's all you knew, Thomas, frightening folk into doing as you wanted and behaving as you expected. I'm not blaming you; it was the way you were taught in the army, and then in the police force. It just became part of you. You should have married someone stronger than me, someone able to stand up to you.'

He ran his tongue over his chapped lips, then said, 'I married you because you were the one I wanted.'

'And I thought it was what I wanted too. I would never have said yes otherwise. I meant it to be for the rest of my life.' This was the first chance she had had to explain things to him. 'But things turned out differently.'

'That woman you sent, the one that got me put in here.'

'Mirren Hepburn. She's a friend of mine.'

'She's a strong one.'

'She's had to be.' Mirren had told Julia something of the way she had had to combine her job as a twiner in Ferguslie Mills with caring for her invalid mother and working in a chip shop in the evenings in order to save up towards the day when she had expected to join her fiancé in America.

'She visits me.

'And I'll visit too, whenever I can, if that's what you want.'

'It passes the time,' he said, then turned his head on the pillow so that his eyes were on the locker by his bed. 'There's an envelope in there.'

She opened the locker, drawing out the long brown envelope within. It was quite bulky, and the flap was sealed. 'D'you want me to post it? It's not addressed to anyone.'

'That's because it's arrived where it was goin'. You take it and keep it safe. It's got all my papers and all the instructions ye'll need.' He raised himself up slightly and said emphatically, 'I want tae be buried in Glasgow.'

'Time enough to talk about that sort of thing when you're a bit stronger...'

'I'm not a bairn, Julia, and I'm not a weakling either. This is where I am and this is where I'll stay for as long as it takes. I want you tae see tae my ... tae things afterwards. It's not much tae ask of my own wife, is it?' His eyes had found a new intensity, and now they were burning into hers.

'No, it's not much to ask.' She put the envelope into her bag and then said as he fell back, suddenly exhausted, 'Mebbe I should go. You're tired out.'

But his gaze was now on a spot just beyond her arm, and a slight smile was lifting the corners of his pale mouth. 'Here's my nice nurse comin' tae chase ye away.'

'You've been overdoing it, Mr Gordon, I can tell.' The nurse swept past Julia and bent over the bed, one hand going to his wrist to take his pulse. 'Now lie quiet for a minute.'

Julia wanted to leave, but as she hadn't said her goodbyes properly she felt that she had no option but to wait until the woman was finished with her patient.

'As I thought, a bit over-excited. A wee sleep, I think.'

'Aye, I'm ready for a sleep. Nurse, this is my wife.'

'So she came to see you right enough. That's good.' The woman straightened from the bed and turned towards Julia, who was horrified to discover that she was face to face with her neighbour, Nan Megson.

'He's been waiting for you, Mrs...' Nan was saying, and then she faltered, but only for a moment. 'Mrs Gordon,' she went on smoothly. 'I'm so glad you were able to visit, but I think your husband needs to rest now.'

'I was just going.'

'You'll come back?' Thomas asked.

'I will, I promise,' Julia said, and almost ran from the ward.

‘There’s a girl at work,’ Chloe said later that afternoon, her voice subdued, ‘who had to be fetched home by a policeman today because her brother got killed. Blown up in the trenches, they said.’

‘Are you all right, pet?’ Julia, summoned from a piano lesson in the front room by a concerned Duncan, was alarmed by her daughter’s pallor.

‘I’m fine. I just ... it’s the first time I’ve known someone that’s been killed like that, in the war. I didn’t know him, of course,’ Chloe gabbled on, ‘but I know his sister well and she’s talked about him. So I felt as if I knew him, and I suddenly thought, what if it happened to Ch-Charlie...’

‘Sit down, Chloe.’ Julia took the girl by the shoulders and eased her into her father’s chair, the most comfortable chair in the flat. Then she knelt on the fireside rug, taking the girl’s cold hands between her own. ‘Duncan, put the kettle on, there’s a good lad. Your sister and I could both do with a nice cup of tea.’

She certainly could, she thought as she massaged Chloe’s hands. Her head had been aching ever since she came back from the hospital. Somehow, she had to see Nan Megson on her own, tell her the truth, and persuade her not to say a word to anyone. And that, Julia thought miserably, would be yet one more person to share the secret that she and Frank had kept so well for so many years.

‘What about your piano lesson?’ Chloe asked, recollecting the tune that had been thudding rather than dancing from behind the closed door when she arrived home.

'I'm not bothered,' Daisy Hepburn's clear little voice said from the doorway, where she stood surveying the scene. 'If you want me out of the way, I could always go down to the backcourt and play with your Leslie,' she went on hopefully.

'It's not what your mother's paying me for, but just this once, off you go,' Julia agreed, and the little girl skipped off, her face wreathed in smiles.

'She drives Leslie mad, you know she does, Mum,' Duncan said from the stove, where he had just lit the gas.

'You go as well, then, and keep the peace between them. Just until I come to fetch Daisy. I'm taking her home today. Chloe,' Julia said gently to the figure huddled in Frank's big chair when Duncan had gone, 'you must know that folk get hurt and killed in a war. Not just the soldiers and the sailors and the airmen either; there's all these poor souls that were killed in Greenock and Clydebank and other places. And here in Paisley too.'

'I know that, but it's all too much to take in!' Chloe's tone was almost irritable, and she glared at her mother with eyes bright with unshed tears. 'Up to now it's been lists in the newspaper, and folk saying things, and I always knew that it was real, but I didn't know any of the people. And now I do! Well, almost.'

'We've been lucky so far.' Julia got up to make the tea, spooning in more of her precious stock of tea-leaves than she would have used normally. 'This whole tenement's been lucky, though there's been telegrams delivered to quite a few of the other families in Glen Street.'

She set the teapot back on a low gas to mash, then after a moment's hesitation she went to a corner cupboard and took out the small bottle of brandy kept for emergencies and slipped it into the pocket of her cardigan.

She poured out the tea and added a double spoonful of sugar, then just before carrying it over to Chloe, she tipped some brandy into both cups. 'Drink this up, it'll make you feel better.'

Chloe clutched the cup in both hands. 'It's not right, is it, Mum? That boy had just finished serving his apprenticeship at Fleming and Ferguson's shipyard. Young men like him shouldn't have to go and fight wars they didn't start!'

'It's the way life is, pet.'

'Can they not just use the men that are soldiers anyway, instead of making lads like Pearl's brother join up, just to get killed?' Chloe's voice began to wobble on the last few words, and she dipped her face into the warmth of the steam coming up from her cup. Julia stroked her pale auburn hair.

'They *have* used those soldiers, Chloe, but when they get killed, they need to find more men.'

'It's not fair!'

'I know, but life isn't always fair. We have to make what we can out of it.'

'Mr Hepburn fought in the Great War, and he doesn't believe in lads like Charlie and Pearl's poor brother having to fight for their country all over again.'

'I can understand his way of thinking.'

Chloe took a drink of tea and then, without

looking at her mother, said, 'Before he went away, Charlie asked me to be his girlfriend and I said no.'

'Well, you're both young yet, and mebbe it's not a good thing to get tied down like that. You don't know how you'll feel in two years' time, or even in two months.'

'That's what I said. We're friends, but that's all.' Chloe took another drink. 'This tastes different.'

'I made it strong and put extra sugar in.'

'Is that what it is?' The girl took a deeper drink, and then gave her mother a faint smile. 'It's nice.' A little colour had come back into her cheeks and her eyes were clear again.

'Take your time with it,' Julia said over her shoulder as she took her own cup to the sink. 'I'd better take Daisy home. I have to get back in time to get the dinner ready.'

'I'll start it while you're away. Mum?' Chloe said as her mother went to the door.

"What is it, pet?'

'I wish I had told Charlie that I would be his girlfriend. Mebbe I should say it in my next letter.'

'Would you have meant it?'

'No. Yes. I don't know!' Chloe said frantically. 'I don't even know what it feels like to love someone, so how can I know if I really love Charlie or just like him?'

'It's not something you recognise,' Julia said. 'It's just ... a feeling. It happens when it's ready, and when it does, you'll know. And that's all I can tell you.'

'Then I don't think I do love him.' Chloe's

voice was forlorn. 'I wish I did, Mum, it would make things much easier.'

'Better to be a good friend than a fickle sweetheart.' Julia hesitated, then said tentatively, 'Chloe, pet, is there someone you like better than Charlie Hepburn?'

The girl opened her mouth, closed it, and opened it again to say, 'No.' Then she buried her face in the teacup.

'I'll not be long,' Julia said, and went to fetch her coat.

26

As Julia and Daisy reached the Hepburns' close they met Mirren on her way home. Daisy gave her mother's thighs a warm hug before racing into the close and up the stairs, leaving the two women to talk on the pavement.

'It's understandable,' Mirren said when she heard about Chloe. 'I was a bit younger than her when the Great War started and now that I think of it, it wasn't until my own brother was lost that I realised just what war can do to ordinary folk. She'll be all right.'

'She's got no choice, has she? It's hard, seeing our children getting caught up in something as terrible as a war ... something that has nothing to do with them.'

'I know, but there's nothing we can do but thole it and hope for the best, and make up our minds,'

Mirren said grimly, 'that we're never going to let it happen again.'

'I'm sorry about Daisy's lesson being spoiled.'

'Och, a break now and again does no harm.'

'I'll not charge for this time.'

'Whether you charge or not you'll be paid for it, and don't argue. She's enjoying her lessons, so you must be a good teacher. It's the first time in her life that our Daisy has kept on with anything. And she practises every day, no matter how much Grace and Bobby and their daddy go on at her to stop.' Mirren looked closely at her friend. 'Is there something wrong, Julia? Something other than Chloe? You look shell-shocked.'

'I went to visit Thomas this afternoon, in the infirmary.'

'Is he still managing to upset you? Mebbe you should just leave the visiting to me.'

'It wasn't that. One of the nurses came over just as I was leaving. Mirren, it was Mrs Megson who lives on the top floor of our tenement.'

'Did she say anything?'

Julia shook her head. 'Thomas introduced me as his wife, and she called me Mrs Gordon and behaved as if she'd never seen me before.'

'That's a blessing.'

'But now I'll have to go and see her. I'll have to ask her not to say anything to the other folk in the building. Her son plays in our band ... what if Frank found out about Thomas from him, or someone else?'

'All the more reason to make sure he hears it from you first,' Mirren pointed out gently.

'He's working so hard just now, and as often as

not he has to go out again at night to the Home Guard. I never seem to find the right time to break it to him. Thomas looks a lot worse than the last time I saw him,' she hurried on, 'for all that he's more comfortable, and well cared for.'

'Aye, poor man. I doubt he'll last much longer,' Mirren said.

'I just want to pop up to see Mrs Megson for a minute,' Julia said after she and Chloe and the boys had finished their evening meal. 'If I go now, I'll be back before your dad comes home. Could you make sure that the boys do their homework? They can go out for a wee while once they've finished.'

'All right.' The girl was still listless.

At the Megsons' door, Julia knocked and then waited, rubbing her hands down the sides of her skirt. When the door opened she shied back, her heart hammering.

'Yes?' the younger Megson boy said, sticking his chin forward aggressively.

'Is your mother in?'

'Aye.'

'Could I have a wee word with her?'

He stared at her suspiciously, as though wondering if the wee word was about him, then turned and went along the hall to the kitchen, leaving her on the doormat. 'It's for you,' she heard him say. 'That woman from down the stairs.'

'What woman? And for goodness' sake, laddie, why didn't you invite her in?' Nan Megson's voice came nearer and then she appeared, no longer crisp and cool in her nurse's uniform, but flushed and wrapped in a large apron, with her hair wisping out from the loose bun at the back of her head.

'Mrs ... McCosh, I'm so sorry you were kept standing. Come on in.'

Julia shook her head. 'I've only got a minute. I wondered ... could I speak to you out here?'

Nan cast a swift glance back into the hall before stepping on to the landing and drawing the door to behind her. 'Of course.' She led Julia to the top of the stairs, well away from both doors on the landing.

'I wanted to explain about what happened this afternoon.'

'My dear,' Nan said swiftly, 'there's no need for you to explain anything to me. It's none of my business.'

'It is, now that you're nursing him. And I'd like to tell you, for if I don't, he probably will.'

'Patients tell us all manner of things,' Nan said, 'but we know how to keep their confidences.'

'Even so, I want to explain.' Julia took a deep breath and then, realising that her carefully prepared and rehearsed story had vanished, she told the other woman the truth as swiftly as she could, finishing with, 'and now that he's ill and has nobody to care for him he's come to Paisley, looking for me to help him. But I couldn't care for him by myself; apart from having Frank and the children to think of, I wouldn't know how to nurse him properly.'

'Of course you couldn't,' Nan agreed. 'The man's in the final stages of his illness, as you've probably realised, and there's no doubt that he needs constant nursing.'

'D'you think there's a chance he can ever be well enough to leave the infirmary?'

'No, my dear, no chance. But you can be sure that he'll get the best possible care for the time left to–' She stopped short as heavy footsteps were heard from below, then went on, 'I would suggest a cold compress, Mrs McCosh. That's the best thing for bringing down a lump on the head. And if the laddie seems to be all right otherwise, no need to trouble the doctor.' Then, as Ellen Borland peered up at them from the lower landing, 'Good evening, Mrs Borland.'

'I thought I could hear voices.' The woman, dressed in her working clothes, clutched at the newel post. 'Thae stairs are goin' tae be the death of me. The sky's awful clear out there, I hope it doesnae mean another air raid the night for I'm fair desperate for my own bed. I don't know when I last had a decent night's sleep. If we're no' havin' tae go down tae the shelter, we're lyin' awake waitin' for the sirens tae start.'

She paused, then, as the two woman above said nothing, she added, 'This war's goin' tae be the death of me,' and disappeared in the direction of her own door.

'As I was saying, lumps on the head usually look worse than they are,' Nan said. 'And if the skin's not broken the compress should do the trick. And if you feel that you want a second opinion, you know that I'll come and have a look at the wee chap.'

'I think he'll be fine,' Julia said, and then, as a

door on the landing below opened and closed, 'Thank you.'

'Best not to spread things around, eh? And kind though Mrs Borland is to the rest of us, I sometimes feel that she takes too much interest in what goes on in our lives.' Nan put a cool, firm hand on Julia's. 'Don't worry, my dear, if there's anything you should know, I'll make sure to tell you.'

Frank was coming up the stairs just as Julia reached her own door. His face lit up at the sight of her, as it always did. 'Where have you been?'

'Just having a word with Nan Megson.' She went into the flat ahead of him.

'I'm going to my bed,' Chloe said as soon as they went in.

'Already? Are you sickening for something?' her father asked anxiously.

'No, I just had a busy day.'

'Are you sure she's not ill?' Frank asked his wife as he took off his jacket and began to roll up his shirt sleeves. 'She doesn't look right to me.'

'One of the other girls at work was fetched home because her brother's just been killed. It gave Chloe a bit of a turn, with Charlie going away recently.'

'I can see that it would. Charlie Hepburn's a decent young fellow, but I hope Chloe doesnae start moping and worryin' about him. Not at her age. Where are the lads?' he asked, pouring water from the kettle in to a basin and getting down to the business of washing away the day's grime.

'If you didn't see them playing in the street, they'll probably be down in the backcourt. We've all had our dinner.' Julia fetched his plate from the oven, where it had been keeping hot. 'It's shepherd's pie but it's been in too long,' she said, vexed. 'It's dried up, Frank.'

'I quite like it that way, with the gravy well soaked into the potatoes.' He soaped his face vigorously and then tossed a double handful of water over it, sending drops showering the surrounding area. 'It's been a bugger of a day. Thank God I'm not on Home Guard duty tonight. With any luck there won't be a raid.' He scrubbed water from his eyes with one hand, fumbling about with the other, and showering more water about the place. 'Where the dickens has that towel got to now?'

'It's right there, beside you.' Julia handed it to him and as he dried himself he glanced out of the window to the yard below.

'Young Dennis is working out the back, and the boys are down there pestering him. I'll mebbe give him a wee hand after,' he said as he sat down to his meal.

'I thought you were tired. Can you not just take an evening to yourself, for once?'

'Working out in the fresh air will be just as good as a rest. And Dennis could probably do with a hand. He's a good lad, and a fine musician too.' Frank forked up a load of meat and vegetables and mashed potato and then grinned at his wife. 'But don't tell him I said so. I'd not want him to get too big headed.'

'I don't think he's the type to get big headed. That young brother of his, though ... he's completely different from Dennis. I still think that it's

Dennis that Chloe really fancies.'

'Ach away! I've said before that he's too old for her.'

'He's only about two and a half years older than her, Frank. That's not a big difference.' Thomas Gordon was five years older than Julia herself, but Frank was her senior by only six months.

Frank pushed away his empty plate with a sigh of contentment. 'That was good. What's for after?'

'I managed to get some stewing apples, and there's custard to go with them.' Julia set the bowl on the table, together with a small jug of custard. 'The tea might be too strong, I'll make fresh.'

'Never bother, what's in the pot will do me fine. Sit down for a minute,' he urged, 'you look worn out.'

'I spent most of the day queuing, and there was WVS work to do as well.'

Frank spooned up apple and custard. 'What was it you were speaking to Mrs Megson about when I got home?'

'It was nothing special.'

'The two of you aren't usually pally, are you?'

'We get on fine, her and me; it's just that we don't live in each other's pockets. We're both busy people.'

'She's a nurse, isn't she?'

'Yes, at the RAI.'

He reached across the table and took her hand in his. 'Are ye ill, Julia?'

'Me ... ill? What put that notion into your head?'

His eyes were suddenly dark with fear. 'You've not been looking well these past few weeks. I should have made you go to the doctor's, but I've been that busy at work ... and now you're having wee talks with the nurse that lives up the stair. What's wrong, Julia?'

'Nothing's wrong. We're all tired these days because we're worked off our feet, and life's not exactly easy, is it? And as for Nan Megson, I was asking her advice for a woman who works alongside me in the WVS. She's got a bit of trouble,' Julie said carefully, knowing that he would construe that as some female problem, and probe no further, 'and she's too scared of the outcome to go to see her own doctor. Mrs Megson was very helpful.'

'Are you certain that was all?' His fingers tightened on hers and his voice deepened as he said, 'Julia, if anything happened to you I don't think I could bear it.'

'Don't be daft!'

'I'm not being daft, woman. You're my whole life, you know you are, and all I want is for you to be well, and happy.'

'Oh, Frank...' For a moment she was tempted to tell him about the dying man in the infirmary, to let him share her burden. Then, telling herself that he had enough to deal with, she went on briskly, 'You're a good man, and if there was anything to tell you, I would. Now, can we drink our tea before it goes cold?'

On the day of her father's second marriage Cecelia Goudie went into Glasgow by train rather than by bus, just in case she met a driver or conductress she knew.

Two men were standing outside the registry office when she arrived; they turned as she paused on the pavement, and with a sudden stab of panic, she realised that the smaller man was her father, almost unrecognisable in a suit.

'Cecelia?' he asked tentatively, peering down at her.

'Father. I'm not late, am I?'

'No, not at all. We're just waiting for ... for the others.' He began to hold out both hands towards her as she climbed the few steps, then hesitated and made as though to shake her hand formally. Then he changed his mind again, his face reddening. To her astonishment, Cecelia realised that he was just as nervous about their meeting as she was. 'This is Jack Liddell,' he said, putting his hands behind his back. 'He's agreed to be one of the witnesses. Jack used to work alongside me in the engineering works. You'll mind me mentioning him, I'm sure.'

'Yes, of course I remember,' she said, although she didn't. Her mother had had a great memory for names, but Cecelia needed to be able to link them to faces. She shook hands with Mr Liddell, and then her father took her arm, the first contact between them in a year.

'D'you mind watchin' out for the others, Jack, while I take my daughter inside?'

In the foyer, he said hurriedly, 'I just wanted the chance to thank you for comin' Cecelia. I know you're not too pleased about me marryin' again.'

'You weren't pleased about my marriage either, Father, but even so, you gave me away, so I felt that I owed it to you to attend your marriage.'

'Aye, well, I appreciate it.' His eyes, the same shade of grey as her own, travelled to the smart hat perched on her head. She had pushed the veil back because the tiny velvet dots stitched all over it kept making her feel as though she was turning faint. 'You look very nice,' he said. 'Very grown up.'

'I am grown up, Father,' she was saying when the outer door opened and Mr Liddell ushered two women into the foyer. Turning towards them, Cecelia was taken aback as she saw that the motherly woman in a grey silk dress and matching coat, being introduced to her now as the bride, bore a striking resemblance to her own mother.

The other woman, who, like Jack Liddell, was standing as a witness to the ceremony, was Elspeth McFadden's cousin. It seemed that the five of them made up the entire wedding party.

'I was an only child,' Elspeth said to Cecelia, 'like your father. And since my two boys are in the navy, and neither of us has close family apart from our children and my cousin Netta here, we decided to make it just the five of us. After all, at our age, we don't need to make a fuss about it.' Then, as they were summoned through the inner door, she clutched the small bunch of roses she had brought with her, and smoothed her hair – pepper and salt hair, just like Cecelia's mother's – with fingers that were suddenly nervous.

The ceremony was over almost as soon as it

began, and afterwards, they went back to the large, high-ceilinged second-floor flat that had been Cecelia's home all her life until she left it to marry Fergus. Her stomach began to flutter as she climbed the stairs and waited on the landing for her father to put his key in the lock. At least the registry office had been neutral ground, but this was different.

The others were joking about the groom carrying the bride over the threshold. 'Only if I was willing to let the poor man wrench his back,' Elspeth said, and then, briskly, 'Come on now, let's get inside and get something to eat.'

For some reason Cecelia had got it into her head that her father, egged on by the new woman in his life, would have replaced everything that he and her mother had bought, but it was all still there ... the upright chairs, the big polished parlour table, now set out for the wedding breakfast, the big comfortable sofa that had doubled as a house, a boat, a shop or whatever Cecelia wanted it to be when she was small, the dresser with the ornaments on its shelves ... even the curtains and carpet were familiar.

'Mebbe you'd give me a hand with the tea, Cecelia,' her stepmother suggested and then, to the others, 'The rest of you can just sit down and have a glass of sherry. We'll not be long.'

In the kitchen, which was also just as Cecelia remembered it, the woman pulled off her hat and scratched her head vigorously. 'Oh, that's better. D'you mind if I get rid of these shoes, dear? My feet are killing me!' She sat down on a chair and eased off the smart, square-heeled shoes, then stretched out her plump legs and wriggled her toes. 'I only bought them this morning,' she confided, 'so I'd no time to get my feet used to them. Could you put the kettle on? The cups and plates are all laid out and there are trays of sandwiches in the pantry. Netta helped me to get them ready before we got dressed for the registry office.'

She sat watching as Cecelia moved about the kitchen. 'You look very smart, dear, and so slim! I bet you don't have to wear corsets.'

'No, I don't.' Cecelia found the tea caddy in its usual place, and measured tea-leaves in to the pot. 'There's another teapot in this cupboard; I'd best use it as well.'

'I think so. Corsets are so uncomfortable,' Elspeth confided. 'I never wear them if I can help it, but I couldn't have got into this dress without one.' She looked ruefully at her shoes. 'D'you know, I don't believe that I could bear to put them on again. It'll have to be my slippers.' Then, as she eased her feet in to a pair of shabby slippers, 'Daniel tells me that you're a clippie.'

'That's right. He wasn't very pleased when I wrote to tell him about it. Just like Fergus ... my husband. He wanted me to find the sort of job I'd done before, in an office.'

'Not nearly so interesting, though. It's great, isn't it, being a clippie? Did your father not tell you that that's what I did myself, before my boys came along?' the woman asked as Cecelia turned to stare at her.

'He did not.'

Elspeth gave a warm, full-bodied roar of

laughter. 'That's men for you. I was on the trains myself. That's where I met my husband ... my first husband, I should say.'

'He was a driver?'

'An inspector,' Elspeth said, with a grin. 'My cousin'll tell you that I always did have ideas above my station. Come on through to the parlour, I'm sure we're both ready for a glass of sherry.'

'Is everything all right with you?' Daniel asked his daughter an hour or so later.

'Everything's fine. The only thing I need is for this war to be over and Fergus to come back home.'

'So the marriage is working out, then?'

'Didn't I tell you that it would? You shouldn't have doubted me, Father.'

'That's because I couldnae believe what I was hearin'. A wee shy lassie like you, always afraid of her own shadow, wantin' tae get married tae a farm laddie from the back of beyond? What father in his right mind would agree tae that?'

'Plenty, surely, but there's no sense in arguing over that now, for it's all water under the bridge and we've both made our own decisions.'

She glanced across the room at her new stepmother, sitting on the big sofa with her stockinged feet planted on the familiar carpet. She had thought all along that, by courting another woman, her father was supplanting her mother. But Elspeth, though more relaxed and easy-going than Cecelia's mother, was so like her in looks that it had suddenly became clear that far from forgetting his first wife, Daniel had sought to bring her, or at least a strong reminder of her, back into his life.

'You and Elspeth must visit me in Paisley,' she said.

'Paisley?' Her father, a Glasgow man born and bred, considered Paisley to be beneath his notice. Fergus's decision to work there, and take her to live there, had been yet another bone of contention between them.

'Yes, Father, Paisley. It's not a bad place at all, as you'll see for yourself if you come to visit me.'

Daniel gave his daughter a long, probing look, then nodded.

'Mebbe we will, at that,' he said.

27

Cecelia, returning to work after her week off, heard the latest gossip as soon as she got on to the service bus taking her into work her first shift.

'That Nancy's moved in with her driver,' the conductress she sat beside breathed into her ear.

It was just after four o'clock in the morning, and despite the walk from Glen Street to the Cross, Cecelia was still half asleep, but astonishment stopped her in mid-yawn. 'With Les? But he's married, isn't he?'

'Oh aye, well married. But his wife's had tae go off tae nurse her mother, and she was no sooner on the train that Nancy was in there. One of the clippies got it from a cousin who's a friend of one of Les's neighbours. Not that it was a secret anyway; the bold Nancy comes in with him at the start of their shifts, arm in arm, and they go off together when they've finished work, as cosy as if it was all legal.'

'But what'll happen when his wife comes back?'

'Nancy says that she'll move out when they get word that the woman's comin' home.'

'But a neighbour could easily tell his wife what's been going on.'

'Exactly. If you ask me – and I'm not the only one that thinks this – Nancy wouldnae mind if the woman did find out. Then she'd get Les tae herself for good.'

'Are you sure that that's what Les wants?'

'He's that daft about her that he's not even thinkin' straight. And it must be a temptation for a man, havin' a bonny young lassie like Nancy after him. You mark my words, hen,' Cecelia's informant said with relish, 'there's goin' tae be sparks flyin' before this is over!'

At the depot, she was warmly welcomed by Harry.

'I'm right glad tae see ye, lassie. They gave me this clippie, then that clippie ... whoever they could spare, and not one of them comfortable tae work with.'

Cecelia glowed. It was good to know that she was appreciated. 'Never mind, Harry, I'm back.'

'Aye, ye are, and it'll be like puttin' on a nice old pair of slippers that have shaped themselves tae fit a man's bunions instead of all thae tackety boots I've had tae work with,' he said. Then, as

Nancy entered the canteen, hanging on to Les's arm, 'There's been fun and games while you've been away, hen.'

'So I heard, on the service bus. It's true, then?'

'Oh, it's true, right enough. The man's taken leave of his senses, that's all I can say.'

Cecelia looked at Les. The man's face was glowing with embarrassed pride, while Nancy smirked to left and right, well pleased with herself. 'He's in love, Harry.'

'If that's love then you can keep it.'

'You're married, aren't you? You must have been in love once.'

'I'd a boil on the back of my neck once, tae,' Harry said, 'and I still mind that well, but for the life of me I cannae mind anythin' that could be cried love. I just got married because the wife wanted it that way and it was easier tae give in than tae argue. That's the secret of a successful marriage.'

It was the school summer holiday, and the streets were filled with youngsters; boys playing football or testing their skill with marbles, girls deftly spinning their skipping ropes, or bouncing balls against tenement walls or sitting on the steps at the close entrance with their dolls. Pavements blossomed with chalked peever beds, tops spun, hoops rattled, and parents' wardrobes were raided for costumes for backcourt concert parties.

With the technical college closed for the session, Dennis threw himself into his work and also spent long hours in the vegetable garden, stopping every now and again to look up at Lena Fulton's kitchen window and wonder if she was watching him. She no longer came down to help when she saw him digging, and on the few occasions he had tapped on her door, there had been no sound from within.

Ralph, even more sullen and withdrawn than usual, worked at his new job as messenger boy, hating it but afraid to skive off in case his brother caused trouble. 'Keep yer head down, son,' Mrs Borland had advised him when he complained to her. 'I cannae afford trouble and neither can you. Ye'll be out of the school by the end of the year and able tae go yer own way. And then you and me can do business together, eh?'

Cecelia wrote long letters to Fergus and suffered the misery of wearing her sturdy uniform on hot days. She became involved in the lives of her regular passengers, sharing their sorrows when the news from the front was bad, and their joy on the occasions when word came that a son or brother or husband who had been reported missing was still alive. Some were in hospital, some in prison camps, but always the women said, their tired faces glowing, 'At least he's still breathin', hen, and where there's life there's hope.'

And the war dragged on.

'What's it like outside?' Thomas Gordon asked his favourite nurse.

'Nice. A wee bit of a breeze, just enough to keep me cool as I was walking to my work.' Nan Megson wiped his face and neck gently, so as not to hurt the paper-thin skin, then dipped the face-cloth into the basin and squeezed out the surplus water before wiping away the soap.

Thomas, who had been staring out of the ward's high windows at the blue sky and fluffy clouds, all he could see from where he lay, transferred his gaze to the strong hands twisting the cloth and coaxing every last drop from it. 'I missed you yesterday. The other nurses are all right, but they don't have your gentleness.'

'I'm sure they do, Mr Gordon.'

'Thomas.'

'Mr Gordon.'

The glimmer of a smile touched his mouth, and she smiled faintly in return. This gentle argument over whether or not it was seemly for a nurse to call a patient by his first name had become something of a game between them.

'So what did ye do on yer day away from this place?'

'I cooked and I cleaned the flat and I went along the street to watch my daughters singing and dancing in a backcourt concert. Then at night I washed their hair and then my own, and did some darning and went to my bed. Nothing very exciting, but it suited me well enough.'

'Was it a good concert?'

'The bairns put a lot of work into it. They're trying to raise funds to buy a battleship.'

'Is your man in the navy, Nurse?'

Nan put the basin of water aside and began to dry his face with gentle dabs of the towel. 'He died a few years ago,' she said levelly. 'He was an officer in the Fire Service and he got trapped in a fire.'

'I'm sorry tae hear that. It must be hard for ye, raisin' a family on yer own.'

'There's plenty other women in the same boat, Mr Gordon, especially these days, but fortunately, most of us have got broad shoulders.' She raised him slightly, one arm firm behind his back while with her free hand she plumped up his pillows. Soon, she would leave him, and go to minister to some other patient. His mind beat about in search of something, anything, to keep her by his side for a few minutes longer.

'Can I have a sip of water?'

She raised him again, holding the spout of the cup to his lips, then lowering him and wiping his mouth when he had finished.

'I was in the Great War myself,' he said. 'I mind once in France, early on, going through a deserted village in search of wood so's we could make a bit of a fire, and comin' face tae face with a German soldier. A lad in his teens, like myself. I hadnae thought that there would be any of the Boche still there, and he was as surprised as I was.'

'What happened?'

'We just looked at each other for a minute, not knowin' what tae dae. It was my first sight of the enemy close up, and probably his, too. Then I minded what I'd been telt time and again when we were in trainin' ... kill him afore he kills you. So I lifted my rifle, and he lifted his, but I fired first.'

'You killed him.'

'The bloo ... the thing had jammed,' Thomas managed a wry smile. 'So I couldnae do anythin' but stand there and wait for him tae kill me. But he didnae. He just lowered his gun and gave a sort of a shrug as if tae say, what's the sense? And then he turned away.' He was silent for a moment, then said bitterly, 'I wish tae God he'd put an end tae me there and then.'

'You can't wish away your whole life like that!'

'Aye I can, and I do.' His eyes were suddenly angry. 'If that lad had done his duty like a proper soldier should, he'd have killed me there and then. But he didnae, and so I'm lyin' here like a bairn, dyin' inch by inch and gettin' in everyone's way. If I was a dog I'd have been put down, but because I'm a man I have tae suffer!'

'You mustn't talk like that,' Nan Megson said firmly. 'You talk about your training ... well, don't forget that I'm trained too ... trained to look after you and make you comfortable, and show you that there's always someone who cares. So no more of that wishing, d'you hear me?'

Then she patted his hand as someone further along the ward called for her. 'I'll look in on you in a wee while, Mr Gordon. Try to get some sleep now.'

Left on his own, Thomas Gordon, the all-pervasive stink of hospital disinfectant in his nostrils, stared up at the patch of blue sky showing in the window opposite his bed and wondered if his wife, the wife he had lost to another man, would visit him later.

His eyelids began to close, and as he drifted off into a restless sleep he saw the young German soldier shrugging, half smiling at him, and then turning his back. Dereliction of duty, that was.

'Remember, lads, if you don't kill them, they'll kill you,' the sergeant had told them time and time again; and 'It's your duty to wipe out the enemy.'

Duty had been the backbone of Thomas Gordon's life, all his life. It had helped him to serve with honour in the army and then in the police force. Duty. The word still had a good strong ring to it. That German boy deserved to be punished for his negligence in lowering his own rifle when he had had the enemy in its sights. And punished he was, by having his brains dashed in by the butt of Private Thomas Gordon's jammed rifle.

'What do you want?' Lena Fulton asked through the narrow space between door and frame.

'I thought you might like some carrots.' Dennis held out his cupped hands. 'I've just dug them up.'

'I don't know...'

'Carrots are good for your eyes, and with your job that's important. I'll wash them for you,' he offered, and at last the door swung open wide enough to let him through.'

'They've done well,' he said as he followed her through the hall. 'You'll enjoy them.'

'I'm not fond of vegetables.'

It had been a while since he was last in her flat; as usual, there was material spread over the table, and Lena immediately went back to work while he washed the carrots in the sink, asking over his shoulder, 'What are you going to have for your dinner tonight?'

'I don't know yet.'

'Tell you what, my mum used to grate carrots and let us eat them from a saucer, with a spoon. Why not try that? D'you have a grater?' he forged on, as she said nothing.

'I think there's one in that cupboard.'

He found it, and dried the vegetables before starting to grate them. 'Still got lots of work, have you?'

'Yes.'

'Me too. We're kept going at the fire station.' He chattered on about work until the few small carrots had been grated on to a plate, then found a spoon and sat down opposite her. 'Here you are, try that.'

The golden-red carrot glowed in the dim room. With a slightly impatient air, Lena put a spoonful into her mouth and chewed slowly.

'Nice and fresh, isn't it?'

'Yes.' She took another spoonful, then another.

'I've knocked on the door a few times but there was no answer.'

'I might have been out, or sleeping. Or just busy with the quilt...' She gestured towards the alcove that had originally been used for a set-in bed. In the Fulton flat, where only one bedroom was required, the recess held a chest of drawers, and when she was not working on the patchwork quilt, Lena draped it over the big piece of furniture. Dennis glanced at it, and then gave a low, surprised whistle.

'It's fairly come on. You must have put in hours of work. If you ask me,' he said, turning back to study her, 'you're overdoing it. You don't look well.'

'I'm fine, and I like my work.'

'There's more to life than work. I've got tomorrow morning off, so why don't the two of us go out for a walk? We could meet at the West End,' he added swiftly as she opened her mouth to object. 'The top of Maxwellton Street at ten o'clock, say, then we could go to the braes, where nobody from round here would see us.'

'There's too much to do. I have to get ready. I'm thinking of going away.'

'Away where?'

'To Cumbrae, on the Clyde. My aunt's staying in Millport with a friend and they want me to go too.'

His heart sank. 'When would that be?'

'Any day now.'

'When will you be back?'

'After the war finishes, mebbe.'

'But that might not be for years yet!'

She got up and took the empty saucer and spoon to the sink. 'I'll be back some day, when George comes home for good.'

'But then he'll...' Dennis got to his feet and took her shoulders to turn her about from the sink. She felt fragile beneath his big hands. 'Lena, I don't want you to go. I ... I care about you and I need to know that you're not far away.'

She had been glancing everywhere but at his face, but now she looked full at him, her blue eyes narrowed and bisected by a frown. 'That's one of the reasons why I have tae go away, d'you not see?'

'No, I don't see! I know you belong to ... to him, and there's nothing I can do about that, but where's the harm in us seeing each other sometimes, having a wee talk...'

'No.' She twisted away from him. 'I've got enough to think about, I don't want the responsibility. Go home, Dennis. Leave me be.'

'But ...' he began, and she rounded on him.

'Leave me! If you care for me at all you'll do what I ask,' she said sharply, and he had no option but to turn away from her and walk out of the flat.

Julia knew as soon as she opened the door to Nan Megson why the other woman had called. She turned without speaking and led the way into the kitchen, relieved that the boys were playing out in the street.

'Sit down. You'll have a cup of tea?'

Nan nodded, lowering herself slowly and carefully into the chair as though her bones ached. Then she sat quietly, watching Julia busy herself about the cooker, waiting until the other woman was ready to hear more.

'When?' Julia asked as she put the teapot down on the table between them.

'Early this morning, during the air raid. He haemorrhaged, very suddenly, and then ... it was over. I'm sorry.' There were tears in Nan's eyes.

'God rest his soul, he's at peace now.' Julia lifted the teapot and then put it down suddenly. 'Would you mind...?' She looked at her hands, which had started to shake.

'Of course.' Nan poured tea for them both and spooned sugar into Julia's. 'I told the Matron that I'd break the news to you. I'm sorry to have to bring it up so soon, but there's the question of the funeral...'

'Oh ... yes, of course. He left instructions; an envelope. I'll start seeing to things today.'

When the other woman had gone, Julia fetched the brown envelope from its hiding place and sat down to open it. Thomas Gordon had organised the last few months of his life with his usual efficiency; there were details of the family lair in a Glasgow cemetery, where he would be laid to rest beside his parents, and a fat envelope which proved to be stuffed with bank notes held together by a piece of twine. A piece of paper included with the notes turned out to be Thomas Gordon's last will and testament, a brief statement declaring that all debts had been met in full, and that the balance of any money left after his funeral expenses were paid to go to, 'Julia Alice Gordon, née Wallace, my wife.'

Their wedding certificate was the only other document in the envelope. Julia smoothed it to flatten the deep folds, and studied Thomas's bold signature, then her own, small and tidy. The witnesses had been his brother-in-law and her best friend of that time, a young woman whom Thomas had effectively removed from her life once they were married.

'I can't feel anything,' she told Mirren an hour later. 'I wish I did, because everyone deserves to be mourned. Nan Megson had tears in her eyes when she told me that he'd gone. She said that she had come to like Thomas in the short time she nursed him. Everyone should have someone to mourn them, and yet I can't feel a thing.'

'I know we're not expected to speak ill of the dead, but for myself, I think that they need to earn that right while they're still with us. Be grateful that Mrs Megson thought kindly of him. You'll have to tell your man now, surely.'

'Tonight. I'll tell him tonight. In the meantime...' Julia looked at the envelope she had brought round to Mirren's flat.

'In the meantime there's a funeral to arrange. D' you want me to help?'

'Would you? I've never had to do anything like this on my own before.'

'I have,' Mirren said briskly. 'Come on, sooner started, sooner done.'

28

For once, Frank McCosh was home from work at a reasonable time that evening, and as luck would have it he was not on Home Guard duties. One of Chloe's workmates at Cochran's was getting married, and her friends were celebrating the occasion with a night at the La Scala Cinema, where a Robert Taylor film was showing. Duncan and Leslie were playing football in the street with their pals, and Julia and Frank were alone in the flat.

'Let's leave the dishes for a wee while,' she said when he began to run water into the sink.

'We always do them straight off, between us.'

'Tonight I'd like to have a talk. I could make

more tea, if you want.'

'What I want is to know what's going on.' His brows were drawn together in a frown.

'Nothing you need to worry about.'

'I do worry. You've not been yourself for weeks. Sit down.' He took her shoulders and pushed her down into one of the fireside chairs, then seated himself opposite, leaning forward intently. 'You've not been eating properly, you're tense all the time, and you're not sleeping much at nights.'

'Nobody sleeps very well these nights. Mrs Borland was just saying a while back that if we're not wakened by the sirens we're lying awake listening for them to start that terrible wailing–'

'What's wrong, Julia? For God's sake tell me, before the lads come charging in and interrupt us.' He took her hands in his. 'Whatever it is, we'll see it through together.'

His grip was strong and warm and reassuring. Julia drew a deep breath and then said, 'It's about Thomas Gordon. He died this morning.'

There was a short silence, then Frank let his breath out in a long sigh. 'So that's it, then. He's finally out of our lives once and for all. How did you know? Did you get a letter from Glasgow?'

'He didn't die in Glasgow, Frank. He was in the Royal Alexandra.'

His eyebrows shot up towards his hairline. 'Here in Paisley? What the blazes was he doing in Paisley?'

'He moved here a few weeks ago, when he discovered that he was dying of the consumption. It was Mirren Hepburn who got him into the infirmary.'

A tremor ran through Frank, and from his hands into hers. 'I still don't see why he was here!'

'Because he didn't have anyone else to turn to. His sister was killed in the Clydebank blitz and there–'

She stopped as he pulled his hands free of hers and got up, pacing to the window to look down at the backcourt, then turning to lean back against the wooden surround that framed the small sink. With the light behind him, his face was in shadow.

'How long had he been in this town?'

'About five or six weeks.'

'Did you arrange it?'

'No, of course not! The first I knew of it was when he came here.'

'Thomas Gordon came to Glen Street ... to this flat ... this room?'

She nodded. 'I had to ask him in. The man was clearly ill, and–'

'Did any of the children see him? Did he see them?' Frank's voice had gone flat and expressionless, as hard to read as his shadowy features. Julia shivered; it was like being interrogated by a stranger. She cast her mind back to Thomas's one and only visit, trying to recall the details.

'Duncan was just going out to play. He met Thomas at the door and came to tell me I'd a visitor. Then he went out. That was all.'

'So, how did the man know where to find you?'

'He was trained to find folk, Frank. We always knew that he could track us down if he really wanted to.'

'After all these years, I thought we were safe from him.'

'But we're safe now, that's what I'm telling you! He died in the infirmary this morning and I've spent the whole day seeing to his funeral. It's over, Frank!'

'What do you mean, you've been seeing to his funeral?'

'I was still married to him. That's why he came to Paisley when he realised that he wasn't going to get better. He took a wee room in Clarence Street ... he wanted me to look after him because there wasn't anyone else. I was at my wits' end, Frank, and I didn't know what to do. So I told Mirren Hepburn, and she was such a help. She got him into the infirmary, and–'

'Who else knew about him, besides Mrs Hepburn?' the flat voice probed.

'Just Nan Megson from upstairs; and that was only because she happened to be on duty in his ward and she saw me during visiting hours. But when I told her the truth of it, she promised not to say a word to a soul. She's a good woman, she–'

'You visited him while he was in the infirmary.'

'I couldnae desert the man, not in the last days of his life. You'd surely not have wanted me to do that?'

He gave a short laugh. 'I doubt if what I might or might not want ever came intae it.'

'Frank!'

'Weeks, you say. Five or six weeks he's been here, in our town, and you've been seeing him and talking about him to Mrs Hepburn and Mrs Megson. And you never said a word to me?'

'I didn't want to upset you.'

'Upset me?' His voice began to rise. 'For God's sake, woman, I've been out of my mind with worry about you. I thought you were ill, and I was convinced that if you couldnae talk tae me about it, then it must be something serious. I was so afraid in case you were going tae die...'

His voice broke on the last word, and Julia got up and went to him, only to be fended off.

'No, leave me be, I don't want tae...' He raked a hand through his brown hair. 'I don't want you tae touch me, not just now. I didnae have anyone tae talk to about my fears, Julia. No Mirren Hepburn, no Nan Megson. I just had the worry, gnawin' away at me. And all the time you were seeing that man, talkin' tae him, helpin' him. Keepin' him a secret from me.'

'I wanted to tell you, but you'd enough to do, what with your work and the Home Guard. And anyway...' She tried to swallow, but her mouth was too dry. 'I didn't know what you might do.'

'You surely didn't think I'd beat a sick man the way he thrashed me, did you? After all these years, d'ye not know me better than that?'

'Of course I didn't think you'd hurt him, I just felt that it was best that I kept quiet about him. And I'm sorry about that, Frank, I can see now that I was wrong.'

'That makes everything all right, does it?' He pushed past her and snatched his jacket from the hook on the back of the door.

'Where are you going?'

'Out. I need some fresh air ... a drink, mebbe.'

'Frank!' She followed him out into the tiny hall. 'Can we not sit down and talk about it?'

He paused, his hand on the door handle. 'We went through a lot just so's we could be together, you and me. As far as the world's concerned we've been man and wife for ... how long? Over sixteen years now. We've had three bairns together. I thought we'd no secrets from each other, Julia, and it sticks in my craw tae find out that for all these weeks you've not said a word ... not once asked for my help or my advice. You've managed fine on your lone, with the help of your friends. You don't need me, Julia. And that's what angers me most of all!'

The boys and Chloe were all in their beds when he finally arrived home, surly and with the smell of drink on his breath. He turned his back on her as soon as they got into bed, and when the sirens went in the early hours of the morning and they had to hurry down to join the others in the shelter, he sat apart, scarcely talking to anyone.

'Is Daddy not well?' Chloe asked anxiously after he had gone to the India Tyre Company the next morning. 'He's not like himself at all.'

'He's fine, but he's just got a lot of work on. Best to leave him in peace for the time being,' Julia said calmly, while inside her heart was breaking. Only now was she beginning to realise what a terrible error she had made in keeping the news of Thomas's arrival in Paisley from Frank.

She and Mirren Hepburn were the only mourners at the funeral. Dry-eyed and numb, Julia watched the coffin containing her lawful wedded husband being lowered into the ground. If this was the end, if Frank refused to forgive her for what she had done, then it would mean that after all those years, Thomas had won. She could not bear the thought.

She said nothing to Mirren about Frank's reaction to the news, and Mirren did not ask any questions. On the way home in the train, Julia opened her bag and brought out the envelope containing the money left over once the funeral expenses had been paid.

'Here.' She put it into Mirren's hand. 'This is what Thomas left, to be disposed of as I see fit. I want it to be put to good use. You'll know best where it should go.'

The other woman opened the envelope, glanced inside, and looked up again, startled. 'My dear, this is a considerable sum. Even if you don't want it for yourself, it could come in very handy for your children.'

She held out the envelope, but Julia shrank back in her seat, shaking her head. 'I'll not touch a penny of his money,' she insisted, and Mirren had no choice but to put it away, and promise that it would be used wisely.

In the middle of August George Fulton wrote to tell his wife that he was coming home on leave at the beginning of September. 'With any luck,' he wrote, 'I'll be there when the bairn arrives.'

It was the letter that Lena had been dreading. She scanned the single sheet, crumpled it up, smoothed it out again, read it for the second time and glanced over at the quilt, spread over a chair.

It was a considerable size now, and she had become so involved in its creation that she had almost forgotten that George did not yet know about the miscarriage.

Panic formed itself into a lump in her throat and she snatched up her dressmaking shears and hurried into the bedroom. Opening the door of the big mahogany wardrobe, she searched through the clothes hanging there. There was scarcely anything left of hers, and now every one of George's shirts had had patches cut from them. She was running out of materials.

She surveyed the bed, covered as always by a beautiful damask quilt, which had been made by her mother-in-law. On the occasion of her marriage the woman had presented it to her, carefully wrapped in tissue paper. 'I made two of them when my two lads were just wee,' she had said. 'One for William's wife, and one for George's wife, that was what I intended them for all along.'

It had been like receiving a sacred trust and on the few occasions they had had visitors, George had made a point of taking them into the bedroom to show off the quilt, made with his mother's own hand.

Now Lena gathered it up and took it into the kitchen, where she spread it over the table and began to cut out the patches she needed. Her quilt had to be completed before George arrived. There was a lot of work still to do.

Over the next two weeks she concentrated solely on the patchwork quilt, ignoring the other work she had undertaken. Occasionally, someone knocked on the door – a customer, or perhaps Dennis – but she was too busy to pay any heed, and after a while, the knocking always stopped.

In the larder, milk turned sour, bread grew mould and her cheese ration dried and hardened. She raided the store of tins that George had started to amass when talk of war first started, and when she ran out of tea-leaves she drank water. She dozed occasionally in a chair, but most of her time, day and night, was devoted to the completion of the quilt.

'All the way tae the depot,' the woman in the unbecoming black velvet hat snapped when Cecelia went to collect her fare. She stamped the ticket, and then returned to her place on the platform, glad of the breeze generated by the bus's movement. It was a hot August day, and the lower deck in particular was so stuffy that she had had to open all the windows. She and Harry had one more run to do before the shift ended, and she was looking forward to getting home, and changing out of her uniform.

When the remaining passengers left the bus at the final stop the woman with the black hat stayed where she was, and Cecelia had to make her way up to the front of the bus to tell her, 'This is the final stop before the depot.'

'I know that.' Beneath the hat, which resembled a pudding basin with a small brim, the woman's face was flushed with heat, and her eyes sparked fire. 'I said I was goin' all the way, and that means intae the depot.'

'But passengers have to–'

'I've got business there, so the sooner ye get a move on the better for you and me ... and him.' The passenger nodded at Harry, who was beginning to twist round in his seat, wondering about the delay. Deciding that it would be better to give in and let someone else deal with the matter once they reached the end of their journey, Cecelia belled her driver, and returned to the platform.

As soon as Harry turned the bus into the depot the woman got up and stumped down the aisle, her large leather handbag swinging from her arm.

'Right, hen,' she said as Harry brought the bus to a standstill and Cecelia prepared to jump off and start directing him into his parking slot, 'where are they?'

'Who?'

'My man and that floozie o' ... never mind,' the woman said as a group of drivers and clippies emerged from the canteen. 'I've found them for mysel'. Here, hold that.' She thrust the handbag at Cecelia, and then, showing a surprising turn of speed, given the heat, she leapt off the platform and went charging across the yard, yelling, 'Right, Les Nisbet...!'

The group by the canteen door stopped and stared. From her vantage point on the platform Cecelia saw the colour drain from Les's face as he saw the woman bearing down on him. Hurriedly, he disentangled himself from Nancy, who had been hanging on to his arm as usual, while the others began to drift aside, out of the way.

'Didnae expect tae see me back so soon, did

ye?' The woman's voice soared through the air, every word as sharp as a knife. 'Didnae think I'd hear about yer shenanigans, eh?' She came to a halt in front of him, arms akimbo.

'What the blazes is goin' on?' Harry wanted to know, arriving on the platform. 'And who's that?'

'I think it must be Les's wife. She came in on our bus.'

'Jeeze oh,' Harry said gleefully, 'this should be interestin'.'

'Mary...' Les was protesting shrilly, 'ye cannae come in here. This is Glasgow Corporation property!'

'I can go wherever I want!' She glared about the yard. 'Unless anyone wants tae try tae stop me?' she invited, and it seemed to Cecelia that everyone present took a step back, while Harry muttered into her ear, 'Speakin' for mysel', I'd as soon try tae stop a Nazi Panzer division.'

'So...' The woman turned and looked Nancy up and down. 'This is yer tart, is it?'

'Les...' Nancy shrilled. 'Are you goin' tae let her talk tae me like that?' Then, facing her rival, chin up and bosom thrust forward. 'If ye must know, Mrs Nisbet, me and Les–'

'Oh, I know all about you and my Les, hen. I've heard all about it. Ye stupid lummock,' Mary Nisbet turned on her husband again, 'bringin' that ... that creature intae my house, where all the neighbours could see what was goin' on. Makin' a fool out of me when I was away on an errand of mercy!'

'Mary, come intae the canteen and we'll talk about it, eh?' He stepped in front of Nancy and then yelped as his wife knocked him to one side with a well-placed blow from her fist. He staggered back, arms flailing in an attempt to keep his balance, as she lunged towards Nancy.

'C'mere, you!' she snarled, and began to drive the girl back under a barrage of open-handed slaps.

'Harry, someone should stop them before Nancy gets hurt!'

'You do it then.' The driver folded his arms. 'Nancy got herself intae this mess and as far as I'm concerned she can get herself out of it.'

Even as he spoke, the clippie, recovering from her initial astonishment, ripped the hat from Mrs Nisbet's head and sank her red-tipped fingers into the woman's dark springy hair, holding on tightly while at the same time swinging around like an athlete tossing the caber. Mary Nisbet, screeching at the top of her voice, crashed into the wall of the canteen with one shoulder before managing to clamp both hands about Nancy's wrists. She broke the younger woman's grip, and immediately fastened her own fingers into Nancy's hair, ripping off the uniform cap and tearing apart the sleek chignon that the girl spent hours perfecting in the women's toilets at the start of each shift.

By now, word of the fight was spreading. All work had stopped and a crowd was gathering in the yard. People pouring from the canteen to see the fun were forced to skip aside as the two women, clawing and slapping and punching at each other, reeled about the yard. Les, keeping well out of the way, gnawed at the knuckles of one fist as he watched his wife and his girlfriend fighting for his favours.

'What's going on here?' The inspector on duty burst out of his office. 'Stop that at once,' he ordered the two women. 'This is a bus depot, no' a boxin' ring!' Then, as they paid no heed, 'For pity's sake, someone stop them!'

There was a general shaking of heads. 'I'm paid tae drive buses, no' tae risk my life,' Harry said as the man's eye alighted on him. Just then, Mary Nisbet managed to trip Nancy up and the two of them crashed to the ground, screaming like banshees, with Les's wife on top.

'Right!' The inspector pounced, gripping the woman round the waist and hauling her back inch by inch from her prey. As soon as she was freed, Nancy scrambled to her feet and would have continued the attack on her rival, who now had one arm pinioned by her side, if a burly older driver had not stepped between them.

'Fair's fair, Nancy lass,' Cecelia heard him say, 'the woman cannae hit back now.'

'Fair?' Mary Nisbet screeched, struggling as the inspector managed to pinion her other wrist. 'Fair, did ye say? What's fair about stealin' another man's wife? Tell me that!'

Nancy's attack had left her thick hair standing on end all about her red face. A scratch down one cheek oozed blood, and most of the buttons had been ripped from her coat, which was half off and skewed awkwardly round her shoulders.

Nancy had not fared much better; her long black hair was hanging in rat's tails and the makeup she applied so skilfully had been smeared and streaked, so that her face resembled an artist's palette. Her uniform, too, was dishevelled and missing buttons.

'Whose wife? Who's stealin' who?' the bewildered inspector asked, and then, as a dozen voices began to explain and a dozen hands to point, his eyes landed on Les, cowering among a group of drivers.

'You're the cause of this business, are you? Right, you three intae my office! And the rest of you, get on with your work. There's passengers waitin'!'

'What d'you think will happen now?' Cecelia asked Harry when they stopped at the terminus for a break after their first run.

'I reckon Les and Nancy'll be lookin' for new jobs by now, and it serves them right for no' bein' a bit more careful. As to which of them he'll end up with, that's his problem. If it was me, though, I'd not touch either of them with a bargepole.'

'I've never seen women fighting before.' Cecelia gave an involuntary shiver. 'I never knew they could be so vicious.'

'Oh aye, there's nothin' like a good catfight,' the driver said with relish. 'See, lass, men use their heads as well as their fists when they fight. They think ahead and plan things out. But women ... they get the blood lust and they just go for the kill. That's why a catfight's much more interestin'.'

The depot was still buzzing with excitement when they returned from their final run. As Harry had predicted, both Les and Nancy had been dismissed on the spot.

'He went off lookin' right sorry for himsel',

with Nancy and his wife still tryin' tae snatch him from each other,' one of the other drivers said gleefully. 'And if that's what it means tae have two women after ye, I'll be happy just tae keep tae the one I've already got.'

'It's my belief that he'll stay with his wife,' a clippie predicted sagely. 'He's got a home with her, and he'd have tae start all over again with Nancy. Anyway, she'd leave him soon enough. With Nancy, it's more likely tae be the pleasure of nabbin' someone else's man than keepin' him. You're wanted in the office, Cecelia, by the way.'

'Me? What's it about?' she asked nervously, then when the woman shrugged, 'I've not been doing anything wrong, have I, Harry?'

'No, hen, ye've not bashed any of the buses intae the wall since the last time. And I've got no complaints about ye. Unless...' He paused, then said, 'Mebbe it's because it was you that brought Les's wife intae the depot on our bus.'

'I couldn't help that, she wouldn't get off!'

'Whatever it is, ye'd best no' keep the man waitin',' the clippie advised. 'He's been in a right mood ever since this morning's trouble.'

'There ye are at last,' the inspector greeted Cecelia sourly when she trembled her way into the small office.

'Is it ... did I do somethin' wrong?'

'If ye did, ye'd best keep it tae yersel', for I've had quite enough for one day. That bottle of whisky ye found on yer bus six months back...' He reached into a cupboard and brought it out. 'It's no' been claimed, so it's yours.'

'Here,' Cecelia thrust the bottle at Harry when

she emerged from the office on rubbery legs. 'Have it.'

He took it reverently, the tip of his tongue moistening his lips as she stared at the rich golden liquid sloshing about behind the glass. 'I thought ye wanted tae keep it for yer man...?'

'After what's been happening today,' Cecelia said, 'I'm not bothered any more. Share it with the other drivers.'

29

Dennis Megson was hovering by Lena's door when Chloe and her mother came back from doing the Saturday shopping. 'You've not seen Mrs Fulton about, have you?' he asked.

'Not for a day or two, but she's never out and about much. We could easily miss each other.'

'I chapped her door a minute ago to see if she wanted to come down and do a bit of weeding, but there was no answer.'

'I'll help with the weeding,' Chloe said at once. 'I'll just go and get changed.'

'Oh ... right,' he said, after just the slightest hesitation, then as the girl scurried into the flat he went on, 'She ... Mrs Fulton, that is ... was talking about going to Millport to join her aunt. I just wondered if she'd gone already. Did she mention it to you?'

'No, but she might have gone there, or she might just be doing a bit of shopping, this being

Saturday. I'll listen out for her,' Julia offered. 'If I see her, will I say that you want to speak to her about something?'

'No, it's not that important. I expect you're right ... she's up the town getting her messages in,' he said, and went on down the stairs. She heard him going through the back close as she went into her own flat.

Chloe had already changed into casual clothes, her face alight at the prospect of spending time in Dennis's company. 'Bring Dennis up for a cup of tea later,' Julia suggested, and the girl beamed at her.

'Thanks, Mum,' she said, and then the outer door slammed and Julia was on her own. The boys were out playing as usual, and as for Frank, there was no knowing where he might be these days. He could be working overtime, even though it was a Saturday afternoon, or perhaps having a drink with his workmates somewhere. Up until ten days ago Julia had known where he was every minute of the day, but nowadays he went his own way in silence.

She began to unpack the shopping, her heart heavy. The children had sensed that something was wrong; they went about the flat quietly, watching their parents with anxious eyes.

How long, Julia wondered, before she was forgiven? Or would that never happen? Had she and Frank reached the end of the road? She finished putting away the food and fetched the ironing board, so wrapped up in her own worries that she forgot about her promise to listen out for Lena Fulton.

Lena spread the completed quilt over the bed and smoothed it out carefully, the tips of her fingers brushing over the neatly stitched patches. It was a perfect fit, and a complete history of her life. Her childhood, the happiest time, took up a small space in the middle, with pieces from a party frock, the blouse she wore on an outing with her parents and her brother, a favourite scarf, and her mother's favourite dress. Then the other patches, radiating outwards and taking up most of the quilt, marking George's courtship, their engagement and wedding and married life.

She gave a sigh of contentment, and straightened, both hands pressing into the small of her back to ease her stiffness. She was very tired, and now it was time to rest.

Back in the kitchen, she tidied up quickly and took one last glance out of the window. Dennis Megson was working in the vegetable garden, and the McCosh girl was helping him. Lena smiled, pleased to see that he had found someone to replace her. It put her mind at rest.

She took off her apron and folded it neatly before hanging it over the back of a kitchen chair, then went to the hall cupboard, where George had stored all his brushes and paints.

Taking the bottle of Ligroin, the stuff that Dennis had wanted to put safely into the garden shed, she returned to the bedroom. He had fastened the stopper so tightly after using the Ligroin several weeks earlier to clean his hands that for a few panic-stricken moments Lena thought that she was not going to be able to loosen it. But she succeeded, with some difficulty, and proceeded to scatter its contents evenly over the quilt.

When the bottle was empty she returned to the kitchen to fetch the big box of matches she always kept beside the stove. And finally, when she was sure that nothing had been forgotten, she took off her slippers and climbed into bed, fully clothed, to settle herself comfortably below her lovely new quilt. The matchbox was still clutched in one hand ... the hand that bore George Fulton's wedding ring.

She gave a deep, contented sigh. The quilt had taken a lot of work, but it was done now, and she could finally allow herself a good long rest. She was ready for a rest, Lena thought as she took a match from the box. She was wearying for peace and quiet, and an end to worry.

She nestled her head on the pillow, untroubled by the reek of Ligroin, and struck the match.

It was like talking to a brick wall, Chloe thought, glancing over at Dennis, who had replied to everything she said with a grunt, or a brief 'yes' or 'no'. She took a deep breath and tried again.

'You're digging there as if you're trying to get to China.'

'Eh?' He stopped and straightened his back for a moment. 'Australia, isn't it?'

'What is?'

'Where you'd get to if you dug all the way from here.'

'Mebbe it is. I was never much good at geography at school.'

'Nor me.'

At least he was talking now. Emboldened, she said, 'It's nice, being grown up and out of school, isn't it?'

'It's all right. You missed a dandelion over there.' He returned to his work, and Chloe, feeling a little more cheerful, launched a vicious attack on the dandelion.

Ellen Borland yawned and settled herself more comfortably in her chair. She and Donnie and Jessie had had a nice midday dinner, after which the old woman had gone back to her own flat for a lie-down while Ellen started work on a pile of darning.

By the time she had finished a pair of Donnie's socks and started on a second pair, the soothing rhythm of her husband's snores had begun to have an affect on her. Her eyelids drooped, opened, began to droop again, and the sock she had been darning gently drifted down to her lap. Her jaw sagged open and a slight snore escaped ... and then she frowned and stirred, opening her eyes and sniffing the air. There seemed to be something ... but mebbe it was just her imagination. The pleasant aroma of the chops and onions they had recently eaten still hung around the kitchen. That must be what she smelled, she thought, then sniffed again.

'Donnie?' When her only answer was another snore, she raised her voice. 'Donnie!'

He jerked suddenly in his chair. 'Eh? Wha...?'

'D'you smell somethin'?'

'God, Ellen,' he mumbled. 'Ye're no' goin' tae

start fussin' about me takin' my slippers off, are ye? A man's entitled tae wear his stockin' soles in his own house.'

'It's not yer feet I'm talkin' about! It's...' She heaved herself to her feet. 'Can you smell smoke?'

'How can there be smoke when there's no fire in the grate?' he asked, settling back into his chair and closing his eyes. Throwing a half-exasperated, half-affectionate glance at him, she got up and went into the hall, sniffing as she went. There was definitely a trace of something in the air, she thought. Then she opened the door of the bedroom she shared with Donnie, and her face went blank with shock as she realised that she could scarcely see across the room for smoke.

'Donnie!' She slammed the door and raced back into the kitchen. 'Get up, man!' she yelled, shaking his shoulder. 'There's a fire somewhere. We have tae get out of here!'

'Eh? He sniffed the air. 'By God, ye're right,' he said, then leapt to his feet, showing surprising agility in a man who had not moved at more than a snail's pace for years.

'Get Jessie!' his wife ordered, snatching the canary's cage from its stand. 'Bang on her door and tell her tae...' Then she screeched as one of Donnie's stockinged feet skidded on the polished linoleum surround, and he smacked into the doorframe and then collapsed backwards on to the floor. 'Donnie! Oh my God! Get up, Donnie.'

'I cannae!' He writhed at her feet, clutching an ankle. 'I've busted my leg. Ye'll have tae get help!'

'There's no time for that, we have tae fetch

Jessie and get her downstairs.' She grabbed his arm, trying to pull him to his feet, and he howled in pain.

'It's no use, I cannae get up.'

For a few moments Ellen ran about like a squirrel in a trap, going from Donnie to the door, then back to Donnie, the birdcage swinging wildly from her hand, and its occupant hanging on to its perch for dear life. Then she ran to the window, from where she had earlier seen Ralph's interfering brother working in the backcourt. To her relief, he was still there, and the McCosh lassie with him.

Ellen tried to open the window for the first time in years, but it refused to budge, even when she used her strength, honed by years of manual labour.

The smell of smoke was stronger now; whimpering in panic, she banged on the windowpane, shouting, and when the young people below worked on, oblivious, she slammed the birdcage on her polished table, heedless for once of the danger of scratches, and then snatched up one of the upright chairs by the table and pushed it, legs foremost, at the glass.

It finally shattered, but the anti-blast tape held it in place, and she had to swipe at it several times with the chair legs before she managed to create a space. She leaned across the sink, heedless of the danger from jagged glass, and bellowed at the top of her voice, 'Fire, there's a fire and my man's hurt! Ye've got tae come and help him!'

'It's Mrs Borland, she's broken her kitchen

window.' Chloe pointed up at the woman, who was gesticulating frantically. 'There's something wro...' Then as the spade fell from Dennis's hands and he sprinted for the back close, she followed hard on his heels.

She smelled smoke as she chased up the stairs after him, and when she gained the first floor she could see pale grey tendrils twisting lazily in the air.

Dennis was hammering on Mrs Fulton's door, screaming her name.

'It's coming from in there,' he said frantically as she reached him. He pointed at the ground, and she saw the smoke oozing out from below the door. 'And I don't know if she's in the flat!' He thudded his fist against the door. 'Lena! For God's sake, Lena, if you're in there, open the door!'

'Help me!' Mrs Borland roared over the stair railings. 'My man's hurt and I have tae get Jessie out.'

'What's going on?' Julia asked from her own doorway, and then began to cough as the smoke caught at the back of her throat.

'There's a fire. Go down to Mr Binnie's shop and tell him to telephone for the Fire Brigade, then stay out in the street,' Dennis ordered. 'Go with her, Chloe.'

'I'd better help Mrs Borland, and I can knock on the other doors and warn folk.' She was already scrambling up the next flight of stairs.

'No! Chloe, come back!' Julia shouted, while at the same time Dennis bellowed, 'Damn it, lassie, get out of here when you're told!'

'You can't do it all on your own,' she shouted back at him. 'I'll be out in a minute, Mum. You do as Dennis says.'

Dennis gave up on her. 'Someone's got to fetch the Fire Brigade,' he told Julia. 'Go on now. I'll see that Chloe's safe.' Then he turned away from Lena's door and began to follow Chloe.

As soon as he reached the next landing Ellen Borland grabbed him. 'Thank God ye're here, son! It's my man, he's fallen. He's on the kitchen floor and I cannae get him ontae his feet. Ye have tae get him out of there!'

Dennis looked after Chloe, already halfway up the next flight and out of his reach. 'Where's Mrs Bell?'

'In her own place.' The woman's face was distorted by fear.

'Get yourself and her downstairs and outside as fast as you can!'

'Donnie...'

'Leave him tae me, and just do as you're told!' he shouted at her, and then plunged in through the open door of the Borlands' flat.

Feeling his way through the smoky hall, he touched each of the doors as he passed. None was hot to the touch, which indicated that although the flat was filling rapidly with smoke, the seat of the fire was elsewhere. He knew already that it was located in the flat directly below ... Lena's flat.

In the kitchen, he almost fell over Donnie Borland, who immediately clutched at his legs.

'It's my ankle, son, I think it's broke,' he wheezed as Dennis tried to untangle himself.

'It's all right, Mr Borland, I'll get you out, but you'll have to get on to your feet.' Using the techniques learned at the fire station, Dennis almost got the man upright, before Donnie let out a scream and slumped down again, almost pulling his rescuer down with him.

'Ye're hurtin' me!'

'You'll get more than hurt if ye don't get off that floor and out of here!' They were both coughing now, and their eyes were streaming. 'Here...' Dennis grabbed at a kitchen chair and swung it away from the table. 'Try to get on to this.'

Donnie Borland was large, well-fed and almost twice Dennis's weight, but finally Dennis succeeded in getting him on to the chair. 'Now ... stand up on the foot that's not hurt, and put your arm about my shoulders.' Then when Donnie, whimpering with pain and fear, managed to do as he was told, 'That's grand, well done. Now we're goin' to get out of here. Just keep thinking of moving forward, and let me take most of your weight.'

As the two of them inched along the hall, smoke curled up through the floorboards to twine itself about their ankles like a horde of friendly cats. Dennis's stomach lurched as he remembered the tins of paint and bottles of thinners, relics of George Fulton's civilian work, crammed into the cupboard of the hall in Lena's flat ... tins and bottles he had meant to store safely in the garden shed, and had forgotten. Please God, he prayed behind clenched teeth as he and Donnie Borland lurched towards the open door, let Lena be at the shops, or safe with her aunt in Millport!

From outside the open door, he could hear voices calling out and feet pattering down the stairs as the tenement evacuated. Just as he and Donnie gained the landing, Ellen Borland, the canary cage still clutched in one hand, came out of the door opposite, with her free arm about Jessie Bell. The old woman, wrapped in a quilt, was blinking and confused, still half asleep.

'My insurance books,' she said suddenly, turning to go back into her flat, and then, 'my teef, Ellen, I cannae go anywhere without puttin' my good teef in.'

'We'll get them later, Jessie. Best get down to the street just now, just till the smoke's gone, eh?' Ellen coaxed, and then gave a piercing scream as two figures appeared through the smoke. 'Donnie, ye're safe!'

'My leg ... I'll never be able tae manage the stairs...'

'Dammit man, stop moanin' about your leg and get moving!' Dennis snapped.

'Don't you speak tae my Donnie like that!'

'I'll speak tae him any way I like, and tae you too.'

'Leave me here,' Donnie wailed. 'I've had my life!'

'No! If he stays, I stay with him. Jessie...' Ellen tried to push the birdcage into the old woman's hand. 'Take wee Tommy down the stairs.'

'Nobody's staying!' Dennis's voice was beginning to rasp painfully. 'We're all going down, even if I have tae throw you. Now get on with it, woman, and we'll follow.'

'Dennis?' Chloe called from halfway up the flight below. 'D'you need help?'

'Take Mrs Borland and Mrs Bell down. My mother and the girls and...'

'They're all down in the street...' She clutched at the banister as a fit of coughing bent her double, and then continued when it was over, 'and the fire engine's been sent for.' Then she struggled up the rest of the stairs to take Mrs Bell's free arm.

'Lena?'

'I don't know. Nobody knows where she is. Are you all right?'

'We're fine, we'll be right behind you.'

As the three women descended the stairs, linked together and shuffling sideways like crabs, Dennis followed with Donnie, who was now coughing uncontrollably as the smoke penetrated his lungs. They had just gained the next landing when three men sped up towards them. One stopped to help the women while the other two squeezed past and continued up.

'Anyone else in the building?' one of them shouted.

'Just the one woman, mebbe, but I don't know for sure if she's there. Here, take him.' Dennis relinquished his heavy burden and as the men began to ease Donnie Borland down the final flight of stairs he threw himself across the landing towards Lena's door. The paintwork was blistering now and the panels, when he beat at them with his fists, were burning hot. Then they suddenly quivered beneath his hands, and to his horror, he heard a series of explosions within the flat as the fire found George Fulton's tins and bottles.

'Lena!' Her name tore itself from his throat over and over again. He took a few steps back and ran at the door, but it was solid enough to resist his shoulder. He tried again and again, even though he knew that, if she really was inside, it was almost certainly too late.

He was still trying to force the door in, still screaming her name, when the first fireman came racing up the stairs.

30

The McCosh and Megson children had been playing in the street when the alarm was first raised, and now the smaller children were huddled close to their mothers. Even Ralph, white and shaken and looking more like the child he still was, stayed close to Nan.

'Look, Mammy!' Amy pointed up at one of the windows. Following her gaze, the two women saw flames dancing behind the taped glass. Smoke was already curling out of the cracks.

'It's Mrs Fulton's flat,' Nan said; and then, swiftly, 'She's not in it, is she?'

'I don't know. I hope not.' Even though it was a mild day, Julia found herself shivering. She drew the boys closer.

'Mrs Goudie's at work, I saw her going out,'

Ralph offered.

'Dennis ... where's my Dennis? He was in the backcourt...'

'The last I saw of him he was on his way up to help the Borlands,' Julia said. 'Chloe was with him. She said she'd knock on all the doors...'

'It was Chloe that told us what was happening,' Nan said.

'Where is she?' Julia asked in sudden panic. 'Did she come out with you?'

'She started down the stairs after us, but I don't see her now.'

'Chloe...?' Julia looked wildly around at the people now pressing in all sides, but could see no sign of her daughter. She should have stayed with Chloe, should have insisted on dragging her outside instead of letting her run off to warn the rest of the tenants. How could she ever face Frank again if anything happened to Chloe?

'I want my daddy.' Leslie's voice quivered, and he looked up at his mother, tears glittering in his eyes. 'Where's my daddy?'

'He'll be here soon, pet.' Her own voice shook, while her eyes kept flickering from face to face in search of Chloe.

'Come on intae my place,' a neighbour from across the street offered. 'There's nothin' you can dae here, and the brigade'll arrive any minute now.'

'My daughter... I have to make sure my daughter's safe.'

'She will be,' Nan told her firmly. 'Dennis won't let any harm come to her. Or to any of them if he can ... look!'

She pointed across to the street to where Chloe was emerging from the close, together with Ellen Borland and Jessie Bell. The three of them were coughing and choking.

'Chloe!' Julia started to cross the street and then drew back as the fire engine, bell clanging, screeched to a halt outside the close. As the firemen began to disappear into the building, Frank McCosh shouldered his way through the crowd and made straight for his daughter.

'Chloe, are you all right?'

'Oh, Daddy,' the girl choked, while Ellen, anxious about her husband, argued with a man who was trying to lead her away from the close. 'Daddy, I'm so glad to see you!'

'Here...' Frank put one arm about her and the other about Jessie Bell, leading them across the street to where his wife and sons waited.

'You're safe now, Mrs Bell,' Nan soothed the old woman. 'It's all over.'

'I've no' got my good teef wi' me,' Jessie whimpered.

'Never mind that, pet, at least you've still got your gums,' said the woman who had offered hospitality earlier. 'Come and have a sit down. All of ye,' she added over her shoulder as she swept Jessie and the Megsons into her close.

'On ye go, pet.' Frank gave Chloe a gentle push. 'And take the boys with you.'

She hung back, her reddened eyes searching the front of the tenement. 'Dennis is still in there...'

'The firemen'll see that he's safe,' he said, and she went, with one last anxious look at the building opposite. Just then, two men came out of the close, half carrying Donnie Borland. Ellen pushed the birdcage at one of the men, and gathered her husband into her arms.

'Our home, Frank...' Julia wailed, almost at the end of her tether. 'What are we going to do if it's burned down? Where are we going to go?'

'It'll be all right, pet.' He put an arm about her shoulders and began to lead her into the nearby close. 'Everything's all right now. I'm here.'

Lena Fulton's flat had been more or less destroyed by fire, and the flooring in the Borland's flat, immediately above Lena's, had been badly damaged, and would have to be replaced. Mrs Clark's sweetie shop on the ground floor had suffered some ceiling damage, but the other flats were still habitable, though reeking of smoke.

Ellen and Donnie Borland went to stay with their daughter Chrissie, taking Jessie Bell with them. A few days after the fire, the entire street watched open-mouthed as an apparently endless procession of Borland relatives trooped in and out of the building, carrying away furniture, ornaments, and carpeting.

'Stuff that looked more like what ye'd have found in a palace instead of a tenement flat,' the women who had watched from windows and close entrances gossiped. 'That Ellen Borland must have been ontae a good thing with her money lendin' and all the other bits and pieces she was intae.'

Nobody knew if the Borlands or old Mrs Bell

would ever be back. There were those, Dennis Megson among them, who had reason to hope that they would settle elsewhere.

George Fulton, who had been due to come home on furlough in any case, was given compassionate leave and arrived in time for his wife's funeral.

'I'm told that you tried tae get my wife out,' he said to Dennis who, along with his mother, Chloe, Julia and Frank, had attended. 'Thank you for that.' He held out his big hand, and after a moment's hesitation, Dennis shook it.

'I'm grateful tae ye all for comin',' George told the others in the little group, then turned on his heel and rejoined his family. Chloe, who missed nothing where Dennis was concerned, saw the muscles stand out along the line of his jaw, and the hand that had clasped George Fulton's being scrubbed along his jacket as he followed his mother from the cemetery.

She had arranged to go out with Marion that evening. Making some excuse, she went home early, slipping through the close and out the back to tap on the shed door.

'Dennis?' she said softly against the rough slats of wood. 'Are you in there? It's me, Chloe.'

'What d'you want?' His voice was gruff and unwelcoming.

'I have to talk to you.'

'Not now!'

'Yes, now. I'm coming in,' she said.

He was sitting on an upturned crate, his face in shadow, and as she went in, he scrubbed his hand over it from forehead to mouth. 'Well?'

'Are you all right?'

'Why wouldn't I be?' He fumbled in his pocket for his cigarettes, then after taking one he hesitated before holding the packet out to her. 'Want one?'

Chloe had tried smoking at school, and then with Marion, but had never cared for it. Now, she nodded. 'Yes please.'

As he lit her cigarette and then his own, the flare of the match showed that his eyes were reddened.

'So ... say what you have to say and then leave me in peace.'

'I'm...' she began, and then choked on the tobacco smoke. It was just like being in the fire again, with her lungs stinging and tears gushing into her eyes. A few minutes passed before she was able to speak. 'I'm sorry about what I said that time we were working in the garden.'

'What time?'

'When I said that you and Mrs Fulton were getting to be too friendly. It was none of my business and I should never have said it and I'm very sorry,' she said in a rush of words, then waited nervously for his reaction.

For a long time he said nothing, and then, just as Chloe was beginning to wonder if she should go, and leave him on his own, he said, 'Lena ... she was special.'

He dropped his cigarette on the floor, grinding it out under his boot as he went on, his voice rising, 'I know that she didnae care for me as much as I cared about her, but that brute of a man didnae deserve her. It fair sickened me today, havin' tae shake his hand and hear him thankin' me for trying to save her. What the hell's the sense in thankin' anyone for that? The point is that I didnae manage it!'

'Nob'dy could have got her out alive, son,' Tom MacIntosh had told him. 'I probably shouldnae be tellin' ye this, but for some reason of her own the woman must have soaked the beddin' with somethin' inflammable, then set it alight.'

'She'd not do a thing like that!'

'We can never know what's goin' through other folks' heads, Dennis. Whatever caused that lassie's death, it was her decision and she'd made no effort tae escape. The shock of what was happenin' would have stopped her from feelin' any pain, though, and it would've been over quick. Believe me, son, I know what I'm talkin' about.'

'Dennis...' Chloe's voice brought him back to the present, and to the small shed. She reached over and put her hand on his, tentatively, half expecting him to fling it off. Instead, he burst into tears.

Chloe sat motionless, paralysed with shock and not knowing what to do for the best, then after a moment, Dennis's hand turned beneath hers, his fingers twisting about hers and clinging so tightly that it hurt.

The deep, wrenching sobs were finally beginning to quieten when a sudden sharp pain in her free hand made her jump. At first she thought that she had been bitten by a rat, and then she realised that the forgotten cigarette had smouldered down until the lit end was against the delicate skin on the inside of her index finger.

'Dennis?' she said cautiously through gritted teeth. 'Dennis, my cigarette's burning my fingers...'

'What? For goodness' sake!' He snatched at her hand, stamping out the cigarette end when it fell on to the floor and then blowing on the scorched skin. 'Are you daft? You should have put it out if you werenae going to smoke it!'

'I forgot I had it!' Tears of pain and humiliation made her voice shake.

'Go home and run your hand under the cold tap,' he ordered, his own tears gone, though his voice sounded thick. 'And tell your mother to–'

'I'm not going to tell my mother anything! She'll give me what for if she thinks I've been smoking.'

'You'll have to pretend that you're washing your hands, then. Rub soap over the burns and leave it on. Bicarbonate of soda's good too, and if it blisters, you'll need to prick them with a needle and then use more bicarbonate. And put a clean cloth round them before you go to bed.' The words whirled round her head as he bundled her to the door. 'Go on now,' he ordered, and she scurried through the backcourt, nursing her stinging fingers in her other hand.

'D'you want me to find somewhere else for you to live?' Fergus Goudie asked his wife as they walked along Glen Street. He was on a four-day leave, and she had managed to get two whole days off work. Earlier in the day they had survived a visit from Cecelia's father and his new wife, and after seeing the older couple off on the Glasgow train they had gone to see a film.

'Why should I want to move away from Glen Street?'

'After all that's happened ... the fire, and that poor woman being killed ... I thought you might want to go back to Glasgow, now that you've made it up with your father.'

'I'd not dream of it. I like my neighbours and I like my job.' She twined her fingers through his. 'This is home and I'm staying, at least until this war's over and we can look for that nice wee house with the garden that you keep talking about.'

They turned in at the close, meeting up with Chloe McCosh, who was hurrying in from the back of the building.

'Hello,' Cecelia called, and then, as Chloe swung round guiltily, 'What's happened to your hand?'

'It's just a wee burn ... a cigarette burn.'

'I didn't know you smoked.'

'I don't,' Chloe confessed. 'That's why I got the burn. I was just trying it out.'

'We all do that. Let me see...' Fergus took the damaged hand in his and peered at the fingers in the dim stair light. 'It looks sore.'

'I was just going to put some soap on it. I don't want my mother and father to find out. My dad'll say that I'm too young to smoke.'

'Come to our flat,' Cecelia said at once. 'Then you can get it seen to without them knowing. At least it hasn't blistered,' she said five minutes later, inspecting the burn under the kitchen light.

'Hold it under the tap for a wee while. Soap, did you say?'

'Or bicarbonate of soda.'

'You seem to know quite a lot about treating burns,' Fergus remarked, and Chloe blushed.

'We got it at school once ... first aid.'

'Fergus, put the kettle on, will you? I think there's enough water in the kettle. There's some bread in the bin that would be better for toasting, too. Now then ... soap, and bicarbonate of soda...'

'I don't know when I'll ever get the stink of smoke out of the flat, or out of our clothes,' Julia said from where she stood at the ironing board.

'At least we've still got solid walls, and a roof over our heads. There's a lot of folk much worse off than us,' Frank said, and then, putting the paper aside, 'Julia, I've been thinkin', there's nothin' tae stop us getting' wed now.'

The iron slowed and stopped, then she set it aside. 'There's nothing to stop us just going on as we have been all these years, either.'

'Does that mean that you don't want tae marry me?'

'No, I'm saying that you don't have to feel obliged to make an honest woman of me. I'm content to go on as I am.'

'Well, I'm not. I'm a right fool, Julia, gettin' so jealous of Thomas Gordon even though I was the one you chose over him. And I'd like us tae resolve the matter once and for all. So ... will ye marry me?'

She paused in the middle of ironing the collar

of Duncan's shirt. 'You know I will, you daft man.'

'I'll see to the arrangements, then. Just a quiet affair, so's nob'dy knows about it. We'll need witnesses ... d'you think your friend Mirren Hepburn would do that for us?'

'I'm sure she will. And mebbe her man'll be willing to stand as a witness too.'

Frank grinned. 'I never thought I'd have a former Paisley Bailie as a witness at my weddin',' he said, and then buried himself in his paper as the landing door opened and shut.

'You're late,' Julia said as her daughter came into the kitchen.

'I met the Goudies on my way in and they asked me into their flat for some supper.' Chloe had taken off her coat; she still carried it over one arm, draped so that it covered her entire hand. 'So I'm not hungry now. I think I'll just get to my bed.'

Workmen moved in to repair the fire-damaged flats and the ground-floor shop. The building rang to the sound of hammering and sawing, the stairs were liberally sprinkled with sawdust, and the smoky smell began to give way to the more pleasing aroma of fresh timber and paint.

Dennis kept his eyes averted each time he went past the flat that had been Lena's. Despite what Tom had told him, he still felt that he could, and should, have saved her.

The sight of George Fulton at the funeral, staring down without any apparent emotion at the coffin that held his wife's remains, had almost made him sick. He had even made up his mind to forget about the Fire Brigade and enlist so that he could get as far away from Paisley as possible. He had gone as far as visiting a recruitment centre, but at the last minute he had turned away and caught the next bus home, realising that he would be punishing his mother rather than himself. So he chose the harder path, and stayed where he was, in the building where Lena had died.

Charlie had changed; Chloe could tell as soon as she saw him on his first leave. He was more confident than before, and full of talk about the people he had met, the rigorous training he had been through, and life in the big RAF camp.

To his delight, he had been selected to take a training course for aircrew in London.

'You're enjoying yourself,' his father accused, and Charlie grinned at him.

'Tae tell the truth, I am.'

'And long may that last, since you're enlisted and it's better to enjoy it than hate it,' Mirren put in swiftly, shooting her husband a warning look as he opened his mouth. He closed it again, shrugged, and said, 'Well, everyone tae their own choice, I suppose.'

'Exactly,' Mirren said crisply. 'So read your paper, Joe.'

Charlie had had his photograph taken while he was away, and brought several copies home ... two to be sent to his relatives in America, one for his mother, and one for Chloe. 'Will you put it beside your bed?' he asked hopefully as she stared down at his likeness. He looked handsome in his uniform, the cap set at a jaunty angle on his dark head.

'Of course I will, and I'll give it a big kiss every night.'

'Now you're just being sarcastic.'

'Well, mebbe about the kiss,' she admitted. 'But I'll keep it on the cupboard by my bed.'

'I keep yours on my locker.' He had taken a framed snapshot of her with him – a photograph that Marion's boyfriend Robert had taken with his box Brownie camera in the Fountain Gardens, with the main fountain as a background. In the picture she was laughing as she put a hand up to push back a strand of hair that had blown across her face, and she was wearing her favourite dress, v-necked and in pale blue cotton sprigged with pink and white flowers.

'What ... on your locker for everyone to see?'

'We all have pictures on our lockers,' he said defensively. 'The other lads think you're pretty.'

'Do they?' Despite herself, she was flattered.

Charlie had changed in another way; as Chloe had anticipated, the new lifestyle was broadening his horizons, and although they enjoyed the time they spent together during his leave, it seemed clear to her that they really had become just friends.

31

The first booking in a while, the chance to play at a dance in the Co-operative Halls, came along in October, and the band gathered in the McCosh's front room for a practice.

It was a pleasant October evening, and neighbours gathered in the street, the close and on the stairs to listen as Frank ran his small group through its paces. Despite the fact that they had not played for a while; everything fell into place and there was scarcely any need to stop and replay sections time and time again.

Frank and Julia had chosen all the favourites ... 'Talk of the Town', 'String of Pearls', 'Stardust', 'Music Maestro, Please', 'Chattanooga Choo Choo', 'Who?', and the rehearsal ended with a trumpet solo rendition of 'I've Got the World on a String'.

Chloe sat in her usual corner, knees drawn up to her chin and arms wrapped about them, her eyes, as usual, on Dennis as he stepped forward on her father's nod to take a solo. Raising the trumpet's mouthpiece to his lips, he breathed into it, coaxing the notes into life, using sound to create pictures.

Chloe was careful to keep her face still and her mouth soft and relaxed, but inside her head she was singing the words, her voice as true and beautiful as Vera Lynn's.

She wondered if trumpet players were better kissers than most. As yet, she had not been able to find out, but she would, in time. She had known that since the night she had burned her fingers in the old shed, the night Dennis had cried. On her way to the back close afterwards, her hand stinging as though it had landed in a bed of nettles, she had suddenly remembered her mother saying, 'It's not really in your body or your head or even your heart. It's something that happens, and when it does happen, you'll know.'

It had happened that night, in the shed, and she knew it. Dennis would know it too, one day. Not yet; perhaps not for a long time, but suddenly he would know, the way she had. And when he did, she would be waiting.

She sang on behind still lips, each note in perfect harmony with Dennis's playing.

'Our turn'll come, if the war keeps going,' Marion prattled on. 'You could go into the Woman's Auxiliary Air Force, then you might meet up with Charlie somewhere. You never know. I'm going into the ATS myself, because of Robert being in the army.'

'I might be a land girl.'

'Why?'

'So that I can learn about gardening.'

'They don't garden on farms, they work in fields and drive tractors and they have to tramp about in horrible smelly mud in all weathers.'

'Some of them do horticulture. I'd like to try that,' Chloe said. She had been reading about the Land Army. 'Anyway, the war'll probably be over by the time we're old enough. D'you remember how that new dance goes? The one that couple danced last night at the Templar Halls?'

'Ballin' the Jack? It's a daft name!'

'But it's a good dance.' Chloe jumped up and began to dance in the paved section before the fountain, humming the tune and waving her arms, bouncing and dipping, swaying and side-stepping while Rabbie Burns, leaning on his stone ploughshare, watched with solemn approval from atop his plinth.

'You look daft,' Marion criticised from where she sat on the bench.

'That's because I'm on my own. Come on, Marion.'

'Why should I look daft too?'

'Och, come on!' Chloe held out a hand and Marion glanced nervously around.

'Folk'll see us.'

'There's scarcely a soul about, and anyway, who cares? There's no law against dancin', is there? C'mon!' Chloe wiggled her fingers impatiently and then, as Marion hesitated, she darted forward to haul her friend off the bench. 'We'll start off facing each other and holding both hands, all right? Now, you just need to do what the song says – stand with your two knees together.' She started to sing.

They both had a good sense of rhythm and a good ear for music, and it was not long before Marion relaxed, and they began to get into the dance. Throwing caution to the winds, they whirled around the fountain, singing to the four sea lions as well as to Rabbie. A few children gathered to jeer, and Chloe stuck her tongue out at them and kept on dancing, snatching at Marion's hand when she would have stopped, and dragging her back into the dance.

Two footsore housewives, wearied from queuing and taking a short cut through the gardens with their message bags full of small, hard-gained parcels, stared as they went by.

'Daft lassies,' said one.

'Ach, it's only a bit of fun,' said the other, wistfully. 'Leave them be, they'll grow up soon enough.'

They trudged on through the park, oblivious to the beauty of the trees and the flowers, absorbed instead with talk about the coming winter and the miseries of the recently imposed coal rationing, while Chloe and Marion danced on, bouncing, dipping, swaying and twirling and side-stepping.

The sun was shining and they were still young, and for the moment, at least, life was still sweet and brimming over with promise.

Bibliography

Images of Fire – 150 Years of Fire Fighting by Neil Wallington, published by David and Charles, London, 1989

What Did You Do In The War, Mummy? – Women in World War Two by Mavis Nicholson, published by Chatto & Windus, London, 1995.

The publishers hope that this book has given you enjoyable reading. Large Print Books are especially designed to be as easy to see and hold as possible. If you wish a complete list of our books please ask at your local library or write directly to:

Magna Large Print Books
Magna House, Long Preston,
Skipton, North Yorkshire.
BD23 4ND